ARE YOU LISTENING
RABBI LÖW

ARE YOU LISTENING RABBI LÖW

J. P. DONLEAVY

THE ATLANTIC MONTHLY PRESS

NEW YORK

•

First published in Great Britain in 1987 by Viking
First published in the United States of America in 1988

Printed in the United States of America

Library of Congress Cataloging-in-Publication Data

Donleavy, J. P. (James Patrick), 1926–
    Are you listening Rabbi Löw / J. P. Donleavy.
    ISBN 0-87113-237-0
    I. Title.
PS3507.0686A89   1988   823'.914—dc19   88-10321

The Atlantic Monthly Press
19 Union Square West
New York, NY 10003

FIRST PRINTING

To
Rabbi
Jehuda Löw ben Bezalel
1523–1609

Who
Out of faux pas
Can make
Mitzvah

ARE YOU LISTENING RABBI LÖW

The London sky darkening over the western reaches of Knightsbridge and the falling snow thickening as it began to whiten the streets and sidewalks. Schultz's limousine comes around the corner skidding on an icy patch as a taxi swerved out of the way. The chauffeur manoeuvring the long vehicle to park, backing into a space in front of Lord Nectarine's tall austerely elegant townhouse. Schultz jumping out.

1

'Holy canine shit. I've just stepped in it. In my brand new loafers.'

Schultz scraping the bottom of his shoe on the edge of the kerb and wiping it off in the snow. Turning to cross the pavement and hopping up the steps two at a time to the grey stone framed entrance. Pushing the ebony button of the door bell. Snowflakes settling on his black curly locks as he waited chewing a fingernail and turned to look back out into the street. Twin clouds of white exhaust smoke puffing into the air from the rear of this long black limousine. The sound of an aircraft passing in the sky above. A light going on in the dining room window of the house across the roadway and the curtains drawing closed. On the top step of a stoop a black cat creeping towards a wary fat pigeon that takes off to disappear up into the pearly grey snowy sky.

'Come on your Lordship what's taking you so fucking long in there.'

Schultz slamming the golden hued brass dolphin knocker against the gleamingly white door. The black cat disappearing as a curvaceous legged, moss green tweed suited lady hurries out of the house next door. Brown hair severely drawn flat back on her head and parted in the middle, a black scarf flying from her neck. With her sleeve she brushes the snow off the windscreen of a low slung bright red sports car. Her knees and thighs showing as she crouches in on the seat. The engine exploding into life, rattling window panes. Attesting to his Lordship having at least one elegantly beautiful fuckable neighbour.

'Hey come on in there, open up.'

An elderly grey suited butler with a shock of wavy white hair holding the door slightly ajar, and inclining his ear out towards the waiting figure.

'Yes.'

'Lord Nectarine.'

'May I enquire as to the nature of your business sir.'

'Personal.'

'Who shall I say is calling sir and I'll see if he's in.'

'He's in don't worry.'

'It is possible he may not be sir.'

'I spoke to him just five minutes ago on his private line from the

1

telephone in my private car. And it's Sigmund Franz Isadore Schultz calling. For a private visit.'

'Just a moment sir, if you wouldn't mind privately waiting.'

'I do mind. I'm coming inside. It's publicly snowing out here for christ's sake. And I ain't got no overcoat on.'

Closing the door behind Schultz the butler turning on the hall light. A crystal chandelier sparkling its rainbow hues down across the black and white tiled hall. The butler picking up a salver with several envelopes, his heels clicking on the floor as he disappeared through a door beneath the balcony of the staircase landing. Schultz lifting a copy of a glossy fine art auction catalogue and turning through the paintings, drawings and sculptures.

'His Lordship will receive you sir if you'll come this way. I had thought that he might have already left for the House of Lords for a committee meeting.'

In a sombre oak panelled room a wall lined with books. A log fire blazing. Two large desks stacked with papers either side of a high white marble chimney piece facing a leather sofa and two chairs. The tall blond figure of Lord Nectarine, a magnifying glass in hand, standing at drawings laid out on the inclined surface of an architect's desk.

'Jesus christ no wonder nobody ever sees you anywhere. Look at all this solitary peace and tranquillity you got going here. And who is this new butler who doesn't know me you've got all of a sudden.'

'He's not new, Schultz. While my housekeeper and secretary are on a skiing holiday, he's temporarily come out of retirement to assist and keep at arm's length various and sundry individuals such as yourself who elect to descend upon one suddenly out of snowstorms. You did indeed get here in an awful hurry.'

'You bet your fucking ass I did, all the way from Maida Vale and circling about six times around Marble Arch. This is an emergency. I need confidential advice and I need it fast. Look at both my eyes. She rushed me on my own private doorstep yesterday on my own butler's afternoon out shopping. And at my age and recent income I don't need this.'

'Good god both your peepers appear to be turning rapidly black.'

'She did it for the last fucking time I can tell you. And jesus christ almighty. Do you know what I suddenly discovered. I married a whore. Her fucking mother was procuring for her. Charging innocent guys a god damn fortune for maybe twenty god damn minutes in a penthouse suite they had rented in the afternoons. I mean half the guys didn't get

2

fucking well even to touch her, walking in with their pricks out, can you imagine what a disgusting scene.'

'Well dear me I can quite, but this is all awfully mournful Schultz.'

'Some guy having an orgasm right there and then on the floor. The whole god damn thing is giving me a moral breakdown.'

'Well we mustn't have that Schultz, must we. But I'm sure you'll find when you look more deeply into matters that there is an entirely innocent explanation.'

'Don't worry I looked. And there's nothing innocent about that bitch. Just imagine out of the whole wide world someone can come into your life you've never met before and fucking well stay there, getting on your nerves, spending your money, opening your mail, tearing up previous girlfriends' pictures. Some of whom I worshipped. And just when I'm able to keep my life in a style to which I adore being accustomed, I get a writ. This. Handed to me right in the theatre at today's standing room only matinée. She's suing me for divorce.'

'I'm about to have a spot of tea Schultz, will you join me.'

'Hey I think my appetite even has even been ruined. In one of her lawyer's letters I'm even accused of glaring at her. Imagine.'

'Did you.'

'Of course I did. Who wouldn't glare at that bitch for christ's sake.'

'And will Schultz have tea.'

'Yeah I'll have tea.'

'Ah but Schultz you have the pleasant distraction of having the top grossing show in London.'

'And that's what's caused all this trouble I know it. Pure insane greed. But when they thought the show looked a flop, her and her behemoth mother were nowhere to be seen. Let me tell you boy, friends were scarce including some others I could mention. You were the only single guy who didn't let me down. Hey don't turn it off. What's that soothing music.'

'Choral evensong. For Epiphany. Choir of Trinity College Cambridge. But I can see by this conversation that such a background could be more than a little inappropriate.'

'Jesus this is how I always dreamed of living. In calmness and peace with a fire on the hearth glowing like that.'

'And ah if you do look out there Schultz, across the gardens in the evening light through which the snow is falling and the ground turning white. You will see the lights going on in the house directly opposite where one of your female star performers has just taken up residence.'

'Jesus I know who you mean. Jesus what legs on such a body, in which there is hardly any brain. Which makes her body even more beautiful. And I'd like to get my hands on her but meanwhile evidence is being collected against me. Two fucking private detectives were trying to follow us here in a taxi. We lost them first at a red light up Edgware Road but then it took us in and out all over Marylebone to finally give them the slip. And I'll get the bill for the taxi. I mean if you saw what she was claiming I did to her. No human being would have the time to do it all. She wants half the profits of my share of the show. Plus capital to purchase residences for her to live in in the manner to which she thinks she has become accustomed. Plus meanwhile to evict me from the matrimonial home out of which I am never never getting. Holy christ what do I do your Lordship. Can she get away with it. Come on you must know. I mean this is an onslaught upon me without an end in sight. Right in the middle of while I'm deeply and madly in love with somebody I deeply and madly love.'

'Well dear me Schultz I don't suppose I can be of a fat lot of help to you as you know I don't approve of divorce. I do of course approve of your being deeply in love for a change.'

'Well all I'm asking is could she really get me out of my own house and get her hands on half my share of the show. She and her fucking fat mother.'

'Depends perhaps Schultz on where she is presently living and what other halves or three quarters of other assets you give her.'

'Holy shit three quarters. Nobody but nobody is ever going to get three quarters off me. For anything. That's gospel. Hey what about when I stood embattled and alone with nobody, I mean nobody giving me even the fucking time of day. Now just as I'm poised to make it big and able to pay off a mortgage with the first time money pouring out of my ears and slapping a fat cheque into the vaults of the bank every week and with a chance to move in on the movie industry, this has to happen to me. Her god damn lawyers the fuckers want further and better particulars of my fucking assets and income all over the world. The world. I mean the whole world. Like coast to coast from Los Angeles to New York.'

'It also Schultz could include the touring rights in the jungles of Ethiopia not to mention amateur rights deep in the backs and beyonds of Manchuria. Plus the merchandising rights from one end of the Kalahari desert to the other.'

'Holy shit. Don't mention any more. All I know is I've got a battering ram of tremendous proportions slamming at the foundations of my life. I had a nightmare last night I was in some sleazy Paris hotel unable to pay the bill because I lost all my charge cards and cheque book. This could do permanent psychological damage to me.'

'Schultz you'll be lucky if that's all it does.'

'This conversation is setting off pains in my stomach. I got two children I adore for christ's sake. She's a mother. I mean you can't fight a mother. But shit she's trying to destroy me. I mean she even shakes her fist at my butler when he's chauffeuring me.'

Tea set on the table before the fire. His Lordship's houseman wheeling in a silver tea service on a trolley covered with cakes and a stack of wholewheat bread prawn sandwiches. A bottle of whisky and two glasses. Hot scones stacked under a napkin. Bowl of Devon clotted cream and strawberry jam. A blaze of sparks up the chimney as Noble struggling with a pair of brass tongs places two more logs on the fire and pulls the crimson drapes closed across two tall leaded mullioned windows and the French door to the garden. The chimney piece clock chiming four with a light tinkle.

'Thank you Noble. That will be all this evening.'

'Very good milord. But shall I wait up.'

'No thank you Noble. I'm liable to be quite late.'

'Goodbye Mr Schultz.'

'Goodbye.'

Noble withdrawing. The door clicking quietly shut. Schultz quaffing back gulps of tea in which he plunked several slices of lemon. Then digging out a dollop of clotted cream to drop down on a scone and slathering a knife full of strawberry jam in the soft whiteness.

'Jesus wait up. Do you have to pay him overtime for that. Hey who you screwing these days that keeps you out late.'

'I fear that to both of your questions Schultz one must reply that it is really none of your bloody business.'

'Jesus I really knew what I was doing all those sensible years of free unhindered bachelor life, before I was stupid enough to let myself get trapped in marriage. But jesus the way you live. I'm going to do this every afternoon like you do. Keep up a routine under the pressure, that's the secret to my survival.'

'Well I don't Schultz do it every afternoon. But those afternoons upon which I do, one likes to make a proper occasion of it.'

'Hey what's the whisky for.'

'A tipple.'

'A tipple. What do you mean a tipple. Hey you're not becoming an alki are you.'

'Dear me Schultz, if you intend introducing this custom into your life you must become aware that a spot of pure single malt whisky is quite a sensibly enjoyable indulgence following a spot of tea.'

'Boy, you tell me. I'm listening. Because I'm going to start enjoying life after what I've been through.'

'By the sound of things Schultz you haven't been through it quite yet.'

'Holy shit, you're right. This could be the beginning of a reenactment of the holocaust. But nobody and I mean nobody is going to shove me in a fucking gas chamber and then get the gold fillings out of my teeth. She and her lawyers are going to learn that unrelenting tenacity is my double barrelled middle name.'

'Sit down. For god's sake Schultz. You're going to knock over your tea. I must say you do sometimes dance about like a man who thinks he is being attacked by the wind.'

'That's because it's a female whirlwind out of a female fucking hurricane. Jesus you know you could be just about the only last person left I got who I can turn to in a crisis.'

'Well Schultz, you'd be advised not to depend upon me in a crisis either.'

'O K sure. Who doesn't accept that. But then if you were out to fuck me up at least you'd be polite about it. And if it weren't for that fucker Al Duke holding incarcerated the woman I love, there'd be one certain somebody I could really trust in my life. It's been like an empty lifetime since I saw her last. She was naked, steam coming out of the bathroom behind her. Like she was the most beautiful apparition. Gorgeous fucking body. Beautiful gentle mind. And that fucking old dried up geriatric celebrity collector pretending he's some kind of king of the cultural universe, has got her up there behind locked doors in tax dodgers' towers. When he should be perverting himself on some hag his own age.'

'Talking of taxes Schultz. And dodging. And especially of depending upon me in a crisis. As recently as two days ago the company of Sperm Productions has been the subject of some more than superficial scrutiny relating to you on that particular subject.'

'Fuck them boy. Nobody is going to get taxes out of me. I've out-witted those fuckers for years and I'm going to outwit them for more years. Schultz don't pay taxes. That's gospel. I'll fucking well chisel those accounts and dump suitcases of receipts on top of them till they can't tell one number from another.'

'Aside from the indiscretion of your words making one wince Schultz, I may say that as someone who is enjoying the benefits of life here as

6

we know it in the United Kingdom, that is simply not cricket. Nor awfully wise.'

'Hey why should I pay full taxes. I don't deserve to pay after all the worries struggles and treachery I've had to suffer. Who has struggled like me. You and Binky silver spooned from babyhood have had fortunes heaped on you. I had two parents making peanuts squeezing a bargain basement living out of the fashion fickle lingerie trade up a side street in Woonsocket Rhode Island. Do you know how hysterical it is in the garment business.'

'Well Schultz perhaps not. But I do have an eye for a well made shoe.'

'Hey you like these new loafers.'

'As complementing the style in which you dress Schultz they are perfectly acceptable. However what is not acceptable is seeing the bill for them and a few other costuming items charged against the production account.'

'Hey come on when is a few paltry miscellaneous items like a pair of shoes such a big sin on a big production budget.'

'Handmade to measure footwear obtained in the vicinity of St James, is not paltry, Schultz. And taken together such items listed under miscellaneous expenses are staggeringly considerable. And rather, I should think, be thought of as defrauding the production budget.'

'O god. You really are persnickety sometimes.'

'I hope you're not going to say it's persnickety Schultz if I continue to object to my office private phone being used by you. Apparently you have been giving my number to charge against when making your long distance calls to New York, Sydney. And Tokyo. Not to mention one call to Valparaiso, Chile during which you spoke for nearly an hour.'

'For christ's sake do you want to stifle the potential west coast South American Spanish rights to the show.'

'You were speaking in an amorous manner to a young lady in an hotel there Schultz and whom you had once fucked here in London and were begging her to return to recommence such fucking.'

'So now I have spies betraying me. For christ's sake an afternoon that's suddenly being blissful. Now I'm a tax dodger committing fraud. Cheating on someone else's phone bill. Hey come on. How much do you want. I'll give you a cheque right now.'

'I want nothing Schultz except for you to discontinue the practice.'

'Jesus do you mind if I help myself to another cup of tea. And put it on my bill. No. Instead. Pour me a big glass of whisky. And put that on

7

my bill. And come on your Lordship can't you turn off that accountant's mind of yours for a few minutes. Forget money. And think of love and beauty and some of the finer things in the world for a few seconds.'

'Schultz while we're on this subject and it will be the very last I'll say about it, you've also, when not charging a call to me, been consistently giving the operator a false number from which you pretend to be calling thereby not only cheating the telephone company but also possibly charging to someone else.'

'So come on. A big fucking company like that can afford it. Tell me how they're going to miss just a few hundred quid here and there. I got no scruples cheating them. Besides I had to survive.'

'That may be Schultz but they think it's me who's been doing the cheating.'

'Hey stop. O K if they come to arrest you I'll admit I did it. Does that satisfy you. I've got big emotional problems to attend to. Without worrying now about a few free phone calls. I mean I'm ending up in my life now lonely for christ's sake. Because all the fucking people who ratted and turned their backs so blatantly on me haven't yet worked up their nerve to come crawling back on hands and knees to start kissing my ass again now that my balls are hanging jingling in happy unison with the cash register on top of the biggest smash hit grosser of them all. They were all little scaredy cats when the chips were down. Present company excepted of course. So why don't we just both relax, forget the horrors we went through, and sure, why not, let's throw a big sumptuous dinner party. Like I mean big. And make those other fuckers feel how small they are.'

'Well Schultz you're the very last person I ever thought I'd hear say he was lonely.'

'Sure I am. Soon as I've checked the accounts at the box office I sometimes have to escape back to the Dorchester at night, bereft, all by myself. O K you don't have to tell me, I know, I'm charging it to the production. But that fucking detective in some bloody disguise is always outside around my house somewhere waiting for me to show up to get evidence I'm an unfit father fucking women not my wife. So I don't show up. And here I am when I should be utterly hysterically happy in my favourite suite at the Dorchester Hotel, and I am, since I am at last making money. Nevertheless too, I am utterly hysterically sad and fucking depressed in misery. I have some shish kebab on room service, I turn on the television, then order an Armagnac and coffee and then I can think of nothing but those windows up there in tax dodgers' towers, and when the lights up there go off. And the idea of that crawling creep Al at that moment with his soft big belly pressed all over her young voluptuously beautiful body. It destroys me. I can't stand it anymore. I got to do something.'

'Rumour has it Schultz that you are in fact already doing something and are there down in the street watching the windows in tax dodgers' towers.'

'Jesus. Who told you that. It's my wife's fucking detective isn't it, spreading that rumour to the box office staff where the fucker tried to get a pair of free tickets the other night. Maybe it's also known I also have a stiff god damn neck from looking upwards. Plus I'm paying on top of a chauffeur and limousine for a cold freezing rented car to sit in.'

'Why don't you sit to watch in the heated comfort of your own softly upholstered motorcar with your telephone available to call Tokyo when you have to.'

'The fucking thing is one and a half inches longer than the second largest Rolls Royce in London and it's too conspicuous that's why. People looking at you in a car that big expect you to be going somewhere not just sitting there. And hey jesus please stop talking about my long distance telephoning will you.'

'And of course Schultz peering out of a pair of binoculars in such a precipitously upwards direction at that hour of the night doesn't help your inconspicuousness either. Indeed you were parked in front of a well known fish shop.'

'Hey you know that too. Binky told you that didn't he. Betrayed my confidence as to where I buy fish. Jesus is nothing sacred anymore.'

'Well Schultz you did have the nerve to telephone my legal counsel to explain your little routine when you got arrested for suspicious behaviour and you haven't paid his bill either.'

'Shit every one of those lawyers' names are in the phone book. Plus he sent me an outrageously enormous bill.'

'Schultz he happens to be one of the most distinguished lawyers in England and his time is valuable.'

'Hey why don't you just say outright your Lordship that you don't like me anymore. I didn't want to look a fool to my own legal counsel. That's why I got yours.'

'So that I, Schultz, could look as though I had a peeping tom fool for an associate.'

'Hey who's peeping. I go wait there just to make sure the girl's not suffering at that geriatric's hands.'

'Ah Schultz. To use your parlance, you do take the fucking cake sometimes. And may I ask you a personal question.'

'Sure shoot.'

'Why must you want to fuck every woman you see.'

'Jesus that's exactly what Al that creep was always asking. But qualify that your Lordship by saying every fuckable woman and I'll answer it.'

'Consider such qualification made.'

'Because how else can I find if the girl has a beautiful mind that's why. It takes the embroilment of uninhibited intimacy to discover that. And that's what I'm looking for. Not exactly the embroilment but the uninhibited intimacy. And by trying to fuck them that's how I find out and that's how, one totally unpredictable night I found the present girl I love. And now on principle I don't want any woman near me who doesn't sincerely love me.'

'Schultz, if I may respectfully suggest, you have a long way to go in learning about women. A while back you were trying to get rid of every woman who claimed she loved you. However I'm delighted to know you now seem totally and utterly obsessed by this present signorina. You who have left desolate dozens of ladies in the wake of your sexual appetite having been temporarily satisfied.'

'Hey what's this morality about sex suddenly. You guys have already tried to frighten the sexual wits out of me with fatally incurable disease stories. Every girl I have ever been with has cost me emotionally plenty and always financially a fortune. While this girl hasn't cost me one fucking penny yet. Which I would pay gladly even if it was a fortune. In fact she gave me the most delicious meal followed by the most fantastic fuck of my life.'

'You make me sigh Schultz.'

'Why because I'm straightforward honest about my emotions. Hey shit I know I ain't no saint, but jesus your Lordship don't drive me out of this room with virtuousness. Please. This is such bliss. Hey and you're right. This whisky. Wonderful. Here let me pour you some more too. Change the subject. Before we end up establishing the world museum dedicated to morality and ethics. Let's talk about the Australian rights we got an offer for. Where this show's vulgarity will be a virtue and could clean up from Wagga Wagga to Walla Walla.'

'Your spouse's lawyers will be pleased to hear that.'

'Your lordship, I love you very much. I know that you occasionally take my interests at heart. But please don't make this wonderful occasion into a parody of my problems. What I got to know is can a wife really do this to me. Take me to the cleaners.'

'In a nutshell, Schultz, yes. But I suspect from the sound of things you may find yourself taken to the laundry where you are to be dipped and boiled in bleach in various vats. Then taken out, dried thoroughly and then pressed into finely sharpened pleats.'

'Jesus don't say things like that. Can't you say something as if there's hope. I mean she's got her gorgeous looks.'

'That could only mean the price being higher still for your using them in marriage as long as you have.'

'Hey I mean after we got an amicable divorce she could still marry guys in this town who make me look like a pauper. And take them to the cleaners. Or fucking laundry.'

'Of course Schultz that's precisely what she may do as soon as she secures from you as much of your assets as her lawyers can get.'

'Hey that would be fucking unfair for christ's sake. Jesus here you are in all this wonderful peace and tranquillity, I mean how did you escape.'

'By making adequate provisions Schultz, under a legal separation.'

'Adequate. How big the fuck is that.'

'The normal requisites Schultz. House in London. House in the country. Skiing flat in Switzerland. And a cottage in the Bahamas with a small sailing yacht for her boyfriend to amuse himself with. And the principle is to at all times always give to a woman slightly more than she ever asks for.'

'I won't do it. Never. Right for a start you can take that misguided English gentleman's principle and let me shove it right up her lawyer's ass. Jesus put on some beautiful music like Ave Maria, will you. O god don't say anymore. I can't take it. Plus I know what you're going to say. That you provide her with an income to keep her and her boyfriend in the manner in which they both got accustomed in each other's fucking company.'

'You are quickly getting the idea Schultz. Of course too, this gentleman of my wife's has an expensive hobby, he fancies himself as an inventor. And when he's not inventing something, he fancies himself as a chef. And you might find too there is the odd occasion when the boyfriend with too much to drink of an evening is ringing you up at midnight suggesting an added amount of emolument.'

'What. Asking more.'

'Yes. More. Because his latest invention that he's spent ten thousand pounds on of money I'd placed recently in my wife's account, has failed.'

'Holy shit you didn't give new money, did you.'

'Well Schultz, one preferred he continue his inventing. Because he was in fact contemplating opening up a restaurant called the Lady Nectarine, named after my wife and therefore me.'

'Holy jeeze. Your Lordship. So you do have a few troubles after all and here I am shouting my mouth off and unloading mine. Jesus I'm sorry. But you see I never ever heard you talk of troubles before.'

'Well I repeat them Schultz only to illustrate what you might find yourself encountering.'

'But hey what did the guy invent.'

'It was in fact an alarm which goes off when the toilet flush is leaking.'

'Holy shit that's fucking brilliant. World water shortage is a fucking serious thing. Think of the number of toilet bowls there are already and the water that could be saved, especially in Los Angeles. Hey this guy sounds like something. I mean once you started teaching backward countries to shit in toilet bowls you got a massive global market on your hands. Think of Africa, the Sahara desert, India, China. Flush. Flush. Leak. Leak.'

'And think too Schultz of a fucking alarm going off day and night all over the world shrill, shrill, when someone was peacefully trying to defecate. Leading to world wide constipation.'

'Well then you could sell ear muffs to deaden the sound which was driving people crazy. Then we buy stock in the laxative market. It all adds up to a profitable special situation. Jesus I got to have another whisky. My own bowels are moving but my emotional life is at a fucking bereft standstill. Previously I was able to obsess myself worrying about money. Now with money it makes me feel even worse. Without the woman I love. Hey by the way, jesus who is that next door. That's my idea of a real soignée female.'

'Schultz don't think for one second I'm going to have you next going philandering in my proximity. She happens to be, as far as I can perceive, happily married. Of course they do have late night parties. And one can on Sundays after lunch hear strange sounds reaching through the walls.'

'Holy shit he whips her. Jesus you know that's what I really want to do. I did once on this sylph of a girl with the neatest little ass you ever saw who asked me to but the buckle of the belt landed first and she screamed ouch and she jumped up and started fighting me.'

'Dear me Schultz sometimes I do believe you do think women are nothing but fuck objects to be abused in your spare time.'

'Hey your Lordship, you can afford to romanticize women. Jesus

12

because every one of them is fawning all over you. I mean christ for a start if they marry you they end up with a list of titles as long as your arm, with butlers, maids, chauffeurs and palaces. It makes you think women are all saints. Well let me tell you what I heard over the tannoy.'

'Schultz so it is true.'

'What's true.'

'That you are eavesdropping on the cast now.'

'I was trying out an electronic device. Plus it's my fucking cast in the theatres I rent. I got to know what's the mood back stage and who's plotting to fuck up.'

'Well if you continue to spy on their members like that Equity will fuck you up by closing us up if you're not careful.'

'I'm not spying. Hey all I did was to have a bug put in certain dressing rooms so I could hear if anyone was unhappy and then I could run to the rescue.'

'Pure pish and pother. I think you're becoming a strange type of auditory voyeur Schultz.'

'Hey do you want to hear what the women said or don't you.'

'Well I suppose in the interests of the personal privacy of the cast I don't. But clearly your eagerness is such to tell me Schultz that I feel you might perhaps explode if you don't.'

'I'm not going to explode don't worry, but those girls were. With their enthusiasm. They were talking, three of them, about sucking pricks.'

'I'm reluctantly listening.'

'Yeah now you are.'

'Must I remind you Schultz that I have money in this show, and a vested interest in the cast. But I most heartily disapprove of eavesdropping.'

'OK, you may hate what I heard even worse. One didn't like to suck pricks. The other two loved to. So the two who like sucking pricks were graphically and I mean graphically describing to the one, trying to convince her, who didn't like sucking pricks what was so wonderful about sucking pricks.'

'Won't you have another spot of tea Schultz. You sound quite outraged.'

'Yeah I am. Holy fuck I mean they were talking as if all guys are to women are just anonymous pricks good only for sucking. Especially ones they thought would spurt a lot of semen. One had three sixteen year old boys lined up like wonderful flavours at a soda fountain or something. And how the different taste could be relished. And I mean relish. Like accomplished wine tasters talking about vintages.'

'This sounds like more of your pish and pother Schultz. But surely you Schultz should be the last to suggest that women be denied a little of what they fancy.'

'Hey come on there's no more liberal mind in the world than me. So O K they're just actresses. But it's the cold blooded attitude. Accompanied I may add by belly laughter. And you wouldn't believe what else they said. Even I, with my low moral profile, was offended. Let me tell you I learned things I never knew. Plus I felt god damned demeaned as a man.'

'I suggest Schultz that you remove those bugs immediately before you are more demeaned. And I would adore to go on with our little discussion but I fear it's time for me to dress as I've got to dine before going to the theatre.'

'Hey you're not going to see an enemy show.'

'Well as a matter of fact it's Shakespeare. Hardly on the level of Kiss It Don't Hold It It's Too Hot.'

'Hey now don't go demeaning the show. You're nearly making as much money out of it as I am. But boy I'm glad of one thing. That fucker Binky sold his share of the show to Gayboy when he thought it was a flop. Then bought it back, then sold it again.'

The chimney piece clock chiming five. A distant rumble of thunder. His Lordship putting down his tea cup and distinctly clearing his throat.

'I'm afraid I have bad news for you Schultz. Binky did sell his share of the show to Gayboy but Gayboy was so shaken and demoralized that Binky bought it back at less than half the price. Then Gayboy thought it had a chance. Bought it at a third more than he first paid for it, lost his nerve again and Binky bought it back again for a fifth of the original price.'

'Jesus that shrewd son of a bitch, Binky. Like he's always there waiting to sink in his fangs. What a partner to have. One day I'm going to give him a demonstration of his own urbane back stabbing.'

'Well Schultz, why don't you take that whisky with you. Just peeking out through the curtains here there must now be a couple of inches of snow.'

'Hey come on, I don't mind waiting a few minutes, my car's outside your Lordship. I'll give you a lift wherever you're going.'

14

And let
Me tell you
That was some fucking
Gorgeous tea
Thanks

2 'Good morning Schultz. You're looking elegantly tall dark and quite attractively semitic this morning. Adding complement to this fine old show biz firm of Sperm Productions.'

'Good morning Binky.'

'And dear me, what brings you Schultz rushing, as one assumes you did, by the beads of perspiration on your forehead, to the dead centre of town at the ungodly hour of twelve p.m., a foot of snow all over London. Ah, what two lovely black eyes.'

'I'm taking over those two rooms down the hall. Once those useless guys you keep saying are brilliant intellectuals assisting you, leave.'

'Those two gentlemen, let me remind you Schultz, were double firsts in Mental and Moral Science at Oxford and Cambridge respectively.'

'Yeah well I don't have time for that crap.'

'And dear me, then, is it any wonder, that I, with so many of these heartlessly ruthless show biz deals raging about one, try to keep a mind to the scholarly world in which one contemplates the more perplexing moral questions of the day, involving as they do a search for any serene sweet reason which may lie locked hidden in the spiritual minefields of polemics, logic, bibble babble and your general chaotic fuckology. Ah but does one sniff the smell of the sudden emergence of the Schultz global empire along with an air of invincibility, this morning.'

'You fucking well do Binky. The first free second I get I'm flying to New York.'

'Ah I say do tell.'

'Yeah you say and I do fucking well tell.'

'You know Schultz before this great raging hit of ours dawned, one did tend to see you more in the light of being somewhat of a hanger on. But I dare say times have appreciably changed. And now here you are brash, boastful and full of profitable smash hit business intentions. Which is not to suggest you are not still possessed of a naïve charm.'

'You better bet the fuck that things have changed. The only time I've had to be a hanger on is to my self preservation with you guys around. But right now I'm going to auction the American rights to this show for the biggest price ever paid in history. Joe Jewels who nearly could have had this show for practically nothing if he paid my price a while ago, is now with his tongue hanging out.'

'O dear, we're all going to be unconscionably richer. O well, we'll face it with fortitude and courage. Buy bullion. Open up new Swiss bank accounts if necessary. But O dear, whatever shall we do when all the vaults are stuffed and crammed. Doesn't bear thinking about does

16

it Schultz. With these Swiss chappies telling us no room is left at the bank and to please take our money and stuff it elsewhere.'

'You son of a bitch. You think this is all so fucking funny now, don't you. You sold us out twice. I heard what happened with Gayboy.'

'Ah Schultz. Yes. All true. I sold and resold my part of the show making a not immodest profit, in the background, as it were. And upon my final repurchase at a considerable doubled discount, ah let me see. Yes I do own a very substantial holding. And on, as it appears now, a very minimum investment.'

'And you were the first to try to close the show down, weren't you.'

'Yes I was Schultz. Yes I was. Awful of me wasn't it. Ah but before you jump on the plane to New York Schultz and speaking of occupying the two rooms you intend commandeering and kicking out my in house intellectuals with whom I enjoy to chat, there is just a little item here under production salaries that has perplexed me for some weeks.'

'Yeah. What.'

'Ah one particular, and very adequate little salary, I must say. Yes it says here in the smaller print. Directorial assistant, following which there appears a name a Mr Jorricks. I do believe that name rings a bell. Doesn't someone of that appellation work for you, Schultz.'

'Yes they do.'

'But surely not as your personal butler in your private household, Schultz.'

'What is this. Am I being investigated.'

'Not in the very least Schultz. Just drawing attention to a tiny coincidence that's all. Butlers you know, don't come cheap these days. If indeed they come at all.'

'Come on Binky cut out the shit will you. Since when is this salary going to hurt out of dozens and dozens of salaries. Plus he's also my chauffeur.'

'Ah Schultz. Yes. Persnickety is how I believe you put it to his Lordship. Ah I shall not be that. No not this morning. It is simply too nice to see you. How are you. Leeches you know are very good for black eyes. And dear me. There seems I hear, an indecent amount of cocksucking going on backstage. And O yes. And by the way, there was what seemed like an urgent phone call for you. Just a few minutes ago.'

'Who. That's why I rushed in here early. I'm waiting for one. I knew those fuckers in New York would blow their cool. All up at seven in the morning to be first to get in their bids.'

'Well Rebecca said it sounded like a name Rubella, Louella or maybe even Vyella or something akin. Left a number I do believe. Ah now, top of all these contracts, here we are. Have it right here. And I will put it to my intellectual Oxbridge team to see what they suggest might be helpful in stamping out these childish practices backstage among the cast.'

'Jesus give me that fucking telephone number.'

'Good god Schultz, please don't grab and snatch. One likes to keep a semblance of an air of calm and relaxed behaviour about, especially at this early hour of the day.'

'This could be my life's blood on this paper. With every numeral adding up to the sum of my destiny.'

'Ah. Perchance it is then a call to do with the sale of the rights behind the Iron Curtain. I hear the Russians if not the Czechs are mad keen to get our little saucy musical to lighten up the lives of party notables.'

'Cut out the foolishness, Binky. I'm talking about my emotional future. Hey his Lordship's not around is he.'

'Ah you'd like to use his private line Schultz.'

'I got to I'm being followed. My telephone tapped. Come on don't kid with that tone of voice Binky. Is he in yet.'

'No he's not Schultz.'

Schultz turning, staring at the slip of paper as he moves towards the door, tripping over a curled up edge of the rug and crashing hands outstretched onto the floor. Binky pushing the button on his intercom.

'Rebecca, will you come in here please. I do believe we've had a little accident. Bring the first aid kit. Don't open up the door too quickly as Mr Schultz I think is slightly unconscious, just inside. He does as you know tend to rush headlong into things.'

'I am like fucking hell unconscious. Holy jeeze, the dust down here. I could sue for negligence, over this carpet, it's been like this for weeks.'

Schultz struggling to his feet. Digging in a pocket for a handkerchief as he puts a hand to a wall for support in a paroxysm of sneezing.

'Gesundheit Schultz. And you should have known to step over that little bump. You realize, don't you that we must keep that there as it is, in order that we can test the reflexes of those we audition. As you know one might be misled by those who read word perfect, particularly with the attractively large bosomed ladies who have been barging in here in a bevy recently. But when they trip over the carpet going out we know not to hire them. Especially if their heads hit the floor before their cushioning hands or bosoms do. As indeed your noggin just did.'

'I'm not only going to get my own suite of offices separate from you guys. But I'm also going to get my own building. My own theatre. No let me correct that. My own theatres. And my own dozen private telephone lines. And tell you guys to go fuck yourselves once and for all time.'

'Dear me we are being purposeful this morning. But have you Schultz given thought to how you might miss us. Think of what we've all been through here together.'

'What I've been through here you mean. And the joint I set up is going to have an army keeping guys like you away from me.'

'And ah so marvellous to hear this plan Schultz. May we take it then that you'll be getting your own telephone bill which you will pay all by yourself. That's it Schultz steady as you go now. Brush yourself off. Straighten your tie.'

'I ain't got no tie.'

'O of course. You're adopting that new, and I must say unpleasantly smooth, devil may care style of show business dress. O dear, well at least it lets one know at a glance and a little distance who the very deepest and most indelible arse holes are.'

'Jesus you know Binky something awful is going to happen to you one day and maybe I might be just around to gloat for a change. And then I'll be laughing when you finally fall fucking flat on your face.'

Rebecca opening the door. A first aid kit in one hand and carnation buttonholes in the other. Her stunning pocket Venus like figure under her loose brown sweater, her string of pearls and her brown tweed skirt. Schultz squeezing past. Taking in a whiff of perfume.

'O Mr Schultz are you all right.'

'Swell honey, swell. Hey what was the name that came with this number.'

'Louella. That's all she would say. Said you'd know who it was. She sounded a little upset Mr Schultz, wouldn't leave a message but said it was absolutely imperative you call as soon as possible.'

'Thank you honey. Thanks.'

'Would you like a buttonhole.'

'Hey jesus, yeah I would. Thanks.'

'Just a moment, put these down.'

Binky standing behind his desk, elevating himself up and down on his toes. Rebecca pushing through the stem of carnation in Schultz's buttonhole.

'Hey jesus, honey. Hey that's nice. Hey that's wonderful. Makes me feel like dancing suddenly. Or something. Here a little kiss for you on the cheek. Jesus why does a marvellous creature like you have to work for such a guy. I mean he doesn't deserve it.'

'I think you're quite right Schultz I most certainly don't deserve Rebecca.'

Schultz making his way hurriedly down the hall. Turning left into the small shadowy room of his Lordship's office. Schultz standing dialling the number. His finger sticking in the hole as he winds the dial back.

'Hello.'

'Hello, jesus Louella. It's me. Sigmund.'

'Yes of course I recognize your voice.'

'Hey where are you.'

'I'm at a girlfriend's house. I'm sorry to leave such a message for you. But I'm afraid something awful has happened.'

'What honey, what. Come on. Hey what is it. Jesus don't cry, tell me.'

'Al has had a heart attack.'

'Holy jeeze. When.'

'It happened Saturday night during the snowstorm. He fell to the floor. He's at the Celestial Pavilion Hospital, their private clinic. They don't think he will live.'

'O hey honey, jesus. Now calm down. I mean was he unconscious.'

'I don't know. He just lay on the floor turning blue, and I called an ambulance.'

'Honey stay right where you are. What's the address. I'm coming to see you.'

'O no no no, please I beg of you don't.'

'I got to for christ's sake. To see if you're all right.'

'I'm all right but I thought you might go and see Al and find out how he really is.'

'See how he is. Honey you're calling me up to ask me to do that. Are you crazy, honey. The sight of me could kill him for sure.'

'Please. You and he were nearly life long friends. I can't go to the hospital myself. With all his wives, lawyers and everyone there.'

'Jesus honey we're sworn mortal enemies. But if that's what you want me to do, I'll go and do it. But he's in the best place getting the best care. You're the one now who needs the attention.'

'I'm so worried. The phone never stopped ringing at Al's. And I don't know what to say to anyone. And I've got to go back there now. But I have, all these weeks and months been trying to get Al to be friends with you again.'

'Jesus honey, you're wasting your time. How could we be friends both wanting you. Al hates me with a vengeance. I tried calling him twice, and each time it's like a spitting cobra on the other end of the line. Plus for christ's sake I'm making him and the other investors rich. Even the profit he's getting out of me gives him resentment.'

'Well that's exactly what I'm saying. Even with his resentment he admits that you're a show business genius.'

'He said that. Jesus no wonder he got a heart attack.'

'Please don't try to be funny.'

'I'm not. I'm not honey. Believe me. And also believe me, nobody in show business is a genius. O K. You got a deal. I go see Al and of course I'm telling you, even if they let me see him, I can predict he'll blow the gaskets out of another two fucking ventricles. But I'll do it. But then you agree I come and see you. Come on. I love you for fuck's sake. Is it a deal.'

'All right. But ring me first. To make sure I'm there.'

'No problem. And I'm gone this second to the hospital. Take care honey till I see you.'

Schultz slamming down the phone. Smashing the cradle and sending plastic flying with the concussion. Jumping into the air, clicking his heels and falling over backwards on his arse on the floor.

'Holy jeeze I broke his Lordship's phone. I'm so seriously desperately horny, I can't control my explosive energy. And now I bust my fucking backside in joy. Even the grime on his Lordship's windows looks good. But hot diggety dog. My day if not my whole fucking entire life is made. That creep Al has at last got his just desserts. Jesus I'm sure he gave himself a heart attack trying to get an erection.'

'Mr Schultz, is everything all right in there.'

'Yeah Rebecca. No problem. Except somebody like me must have busted his Lordship's phone. Which I just did. For all time. But don't tell his Lordship it was me.'

'O dear. I'll call the company right away. I think Binky would like to have a word with you.'

'And honey would you do me a fast favour and call Jorricks in my car to come back.'

'Of course Mr Schultz.'

Mario, in his white coat, a menu tucked under his arm, leaving Binky's office and smilingly holding open the door for Schultz. Binky with his feet propped on the desk and puffing a long fat Havana cigar. The snow brightened sunlight streaming in the windows behind his head. His long blond locks of hair gleaming.

'Jesus Binky one thing always fucking well amazes me why you just didn't go and become a movie star. You've got such fucking matinée idol looks. Then you could have left me alone to produce shows in peace. I'm going to suggest your name around Hollywood when I'm there.'

'So kind of you to say that Schultz. But dear me something in my soul always screws up on my face at the merest attempt of mine to act. But my dear, you have suddenly cheered up. No frown. No scowl. Even your black eyes seem to have brightened up a bit. And one of our buttonholes does add just that little pleasant touch of piquancy to your appearance. But ah. I trust it was all good news. You seem like the Cheshire cat smiling inwardly ear to ear over some outwardly brimming bowl of cream.'

'Yeah I'm smiling. But what the fuck are you smiling so much about.'

'That name Louella, mentioned. Now let me see. Doesn't that remind of something. Ah yes. It's all coming back to me. Al Duke's little lady if I'm not mistaken. Al as you know was always one of our very most helpful visitors ever to come to this office. And with so many midgets, impersonators, contortionists and impostors about I always found his appearance particularly agreeable.'

'Now Binky, stop. Don't go on with one of your little suspense games I know by the look on your face you got up your sleeve and are about to spring.'

'No suspense Schultz. I do at times find it refreshing to see you in another perspective, especially when you're not wearing that brilliant business cap of yours. And ah yes, I do now recall. It was on the very eve of your triumph that you were crouching stark naked in the garage alley of the aptly referred to tax dodgers' towers, your clothes fluttering down twenty two or was it twenty three floors from above, shoe by shoe, button by button, following the incident of your being confronted in flagrante delicto with a certain lady of that pretty name just previously mentioned. And dear me. Yes. You crept half dressed across Hyde Park. And what early morn park pedestrian would have thought seeing you shuffling in your déshabillé over that large parade ground that you were in fact at that very moment the most celebrated producer in all of London's West End with its biggest ever hit. Tell me, did that considerable contrast occur to you.'

'Are you finished. Now let me tell you. Al Duke is at this moment dying of a heart attack not more than a few hundred yards from here.'

'O dear, O dear me. That has quite ruined my thought of lunch I've just ordered from Mario. Pray tell. Poor old Al. We must immediately attend upon him with suitable flowers and nourishing little groceries from one of London's better emporiums. But I hope Schultz such news isn't why you seem so pleased.'

'O K I'm not crying. He tried to kill me. But christ he was my closest most intimate friend.'

'Ah till you I believe were intimate with his little lady.'

'Come on Binky. Give me a break.'

'But Schultz, you did didn't you in fact try or in fact have, according to certain rumours, considerable carnal knowledge of and other divers diversions with the lady.'

'It was an unpremeditated one single fucking night stand. We didn't know it was going to happen. Two people. There suddenly in the same room. Happy in each other's companionship. It took us both by surprise. I may have fucked in lust but I fell in love first. Hey why should I explain to you for christ's sake. I'm leaving. Goodbye. And if it's any consolation to you Jorricks helps out as my chauffeur occasionally too. Plus more news for you. I'm auctioning the songs and music to the show on a step by step, territory by territory deal around the globe.'

'O dear Schultz, I believe I may have already sold more than a few of those rights.'

'You what.'

'For, if I do say so myself, some not immodest little prices.'

'You did this behind my fucking back.'

'I find it the best place to do things Schultz. People get so upset just as you're doing now when you do it in front of their faces.'

'My fucking signature of approval is required on any contract. I'll get even for this.'

'Goodbye Schultz. I'm sure you will. And Schultz perhaps we ought to put it up in lights. A big sign. For the whole world to see.'

> Schultz
> Is coming again
> This time as an
> Even greater
> Orgasm

3

'O K Jorricks let's hit the road. Celestial Pavilion Hospital.' In this narrow shadowy street Schultz's limousine skidding out from the kerb through the mounds of snow heaping the gutter. Turning left into Piccadilly. Ploughs ramming into the drifts to clear the roadway. Traffic crawling as the limousine turns to proceed slowly down Duke Street St James past Fortnum and Mason's windows illuminated full of ladies' fashions and gleaming displays of china.

'You are all right Mr Schultz. There's nothing wrong I hope.'

'No. Just visiting a sick friend.'

'Fortnum's order came this morning sir, shall I expect you for dinner.'

'No don't expect me. I got to stay loose. A few things have turned up unexpectedly.'

The fine art in all the windows of this street. And always some gorgeous creature sitting inside behind a desk. With that kind of ability to make you feel like a leper even before you've opened up your mouth to ask them out on a date. This is the part of the town for me. The peace and beauty around this square. And look at the grey looming edifices of these clubs along Pall Mall. Sit in there like Binky and his Lordship do, safe from all women and that bitch giganticus and calmly reading the newspapers. Jesus there's the National Gallery. O my god I had trouble in there. Only last week. Louella please. Don't force me to go back in there making more fucking embarrassing tries at picking up women. Jesus you'd think you'd have grabbed their leg the way some of them get so god damn touchy when all you did was just to come up to friendly pass the time of day. When instead it could be a fucking lot more interesting talking to me than looking at those dead pictures. When I've got a live cock between my legs. Louella please. Let me fuck you, at least while Al's dying. Then when he's dead I'll meet you in Positano, you could recover from the bereavement, while I'm fucking you some more. Christ what is the painful mystery of horniness anyway. Driving one into so much humiliating predicament. Jesus what is it Rabbi, you think you're cured after an orgasm and twenty minutes later like a disease it's back. Sigmund you're lucky, if you were nineteen years young the disease would be back in ten minutes. Touché Rabbi, touché. And now that I am reminded, the disease when I was sixteen, was back in four minutes and fifty seconds. And it makes you wonder who holds the world's record. It sure ain't his Lordship. Who said he required a prelude of dark complexioned dancing girls working up a sweat before he felt a tingle in his gonads.

Binky says his Lordship gets oiled up on the very best distillery products and merely refers to telephone numbers on slips of paper, and black ladies just appear in his Mayfair townhouse by the dozen. Maybe that's what I should start doing. And talking about his aristocratic Lordship, so many of these London streets are named after some king. And christ the fancy fucking some of them did down the centuries. O K you, you and you. Be in my bed at sundown. O K honey baby it's dawn, I just heard the cock crowing. Time for you to fuck off honey while the footmen bring me my breakfast.

'It looks like it's snowing again, Mr Schultz.'

'Yeah I see it.'

The limousine proceeding into the Strand past Charing Cross Station. People pouring in and out. Jesus the snows in the past when a snowflake descending would make me get hysterical. And I'd count each one as if it was a bomb landing on each seat in the theatre with a sign don't sit here you'll get blown up. God it's so fucking marvellous now in a blizzard knowing I don't have to panic. With every seat booked solid for seven weeks, not one empty, and the advance building like a skyrocket every day. To have money this week, next week and to just float along on these wheels in this cosy comfort with the cold snow heaped out there. People having to wear galoshes and getting their socks wet jumping over the drifts. But jesus sometimes I get so fucking sad that all this money didn't happen to me sooner. Christ look at that beautiful girl lifting up her skirt on what a marvellous pair of legs to step over the snow. O god Louella, Al's demise, much as I wouldn't really rejoice over the old fucker dying, now that he is dying, could bring us back together. And it will be like Mount Etna erupting when we fuck again. Lava is going to go flying over the moon. And christ I'd have somewhere at last sacredly into which I would love to put my prick for all time.

'I'll wait here sir, the police might require me to move along. If they do I'll circle the block sir.'

'O K Jorricks. I'm not going to be long. If the phone rings take a message and just say I'll ring back. It could be New York calling.'

'Yes sir, have my pad and pencil ready right here.'

Schultz mounting the steps of the hospital two at a time. Into the smells. Phones ringing. White coats flying by. Crossing the waxed floor of this hall to the reception desk. Run a hand through my black curly locks and see if I can drape a couple of curls over my two black eyes.

'I'm here to see Mr Al Duke.'

'Name sir.'

'I'm just a close friend.'

'I must have your name sir.'

'Yeah well I'm incognito so to speak. I want it to be a surprise.'

'I'm sorry sir. I would have to have your name. In any event Mr Duke is on the critical list and is not receiving visitors.'

'Well just so I can send flowers and a few vegetables. Sorry. I mean fruits. Exotic ones. What's his room.'

'I'm sorry I can't disclose that either sir.'

'Holy cow this place sounds like a prison.'

Schultz turning on his heel. Crossing back towards the entrance. A figure in a soiled white coat passing by. Schultz tapping him on the shoulder.

'Excuse me. Do you work here.'

'I do.'

'You're not a doctor.'

'No. I'm a porter.'

'Hey look. Step over here a second. Now listen I'm in a little difficulty. Do you want to make ten quid. Sorry I mean two quid.'

'I do indeed your honour. Two or ten will suit me.'

'Hey you're Irish.'

'I am without shadow or substance of a doubt your honour.'

'You're then just the man I'm looking for. Two quid is yours if you find out and tell me how to get to the room of Al Duke.'

'Sure no problem sir. Hand it over and as we poor mortals stand here, I'll issue you with the most accurate instructions that would get you to Palestine and back blindfolded and crippled.'

'Well I'd rather be getting directions to the south of France and I already got black eyes so I don't need to be blindfolded but how do you know the room just like that.'

'My humble sad and profound duty sir is to collect the deceased. And by the look of things I believe this gentleman is to be soon collected.'

'Holy shit. Here's the money.'

'Right your honour. Now if you just go back down that way. You'll see a sign, Casualty. Take no notice of it. Then you'll see a big sign on a door which says No Admittance. Take no notice of that either and go in. Climb the stairs up to the second floor. There'll be three corridors leading off the landing. Never mind the two to the side, take the one in the middle. It will be Room A, the last door you come to down on your left. Sure I'll be around up there any minute myself after I have a cup of tea.'

'You mean you're going to collect him.'

'No it's the man down the right side corridor I'll be measuring for his coffin and who's met his maker that I'll be fetching first.'

'Holy christ OK.'

The heels of Schultz's loafers clacking on the shiny hospital corridor. Groans and moans. On a stretcher, a woman with her face criss crossed with cuts, a blood soaked sheet on top of her. Holy shit. The Irishman says take no notice. I wish I had my sunglasses on, here I am hale hearty and healthy and I got to see all of this. Maim death and injury. The quicker I get up these stairs the better. That woman just prostrate with injuries with no one even noticing her. To find anyone these days who gives a shit about anyone else for five minutes is a miracle.

Bright light from snowy rooftops outside coming through tall windows at the top of a staircase landing. Schultz passing through swing doors into a brown tiled vestibule. Potted palms. This looks more like a hotel than a hospital in here. Go backwards through the alphabet on these doors. There it is at the end. By that table by the wall with vases of flowers. Holy god the Irishman's right, Al must be due to be collected, it looks like a funeral parlour already. Why do I need such things as this in my life right now. When I could be spending the afternoon at the final reductions they got for shirts in Jermyn Street. Having to screw up my fucking courage. Son of a bitch may be dying in there but I just know he'd be more dying to kill me. This is perfect. A nurse is coming out of the room. I got to barge in by her.

'Pardon me nurse.'

'Excuse me sir. Who are you.'

'It's just me. I'm going in here.'

'I'm sorry. This patient is not having visitors. How did you get up here.'

'I walked. Up the back stairs.'

'There is the strictest security in force on this floor sir. Who are you. Are you next of kin.'

'I'm a friend. And already I saw through the door he's got people in there.'

'Well you cannot be admitted. In any event the specialists and the priests are with him now.'

'Priests.'

'Yes.'

'Hey christ, you mean Catholic, those are Catholic priests in there. Hey what is this, have I got the wrong room. It is Al Duke in there. That's the letter A it says there on the door.'

'And I'm afraid the Press are especially not allowed sir if that's who you are.'

'Hey I'm not the Press I'm a life long friend. I told you. And what are priests doing in there.'

'If it's any of your business sir, Mr Duke is receiving the last rites.'

'He's Jewish for christ's sake. Made his bar mitzvah. He can't be getting the last rites. Someone should be reading Kaddish.'

'Would you mind awfully sir. I don't know who you are. But I'm not going to stand here and have an argument with you concerning Mr Duke's religious affiliations. This happens to be a hospital. And if you don't leave I will have to call someone to have you escorted away.'

'This is a circumcised Yiddish speaking life long friend, nurse, whose father was a rabbi.'

'Don't you raise your voice to me sir, I am in fact the head matron of this hospital.'

'O K matron. I get excited at anything anti semitic like Catholic priests. Sorry I shouted. Stay calm will you. Keep your cap on. I'm just giving you a couple of facts. Hey matron, has anyone invited you for a glass of champagne recently. Followed by dinner. What about it.'

'I would appreciate it if you would go that way out those doors and down the stairs.'

'But matron he must be really dying in there.'

'Well that's entirely understandable sir, if I may say so, if he has friends like you ranting in this fashion outside his hospital room. However you may enquire at the reception desk or call the appropriate number at the hospital who will give all the necessary details referring to Mr Duke's condition. And now if you would not mind. I do have better things to attend to, thank you. Now before I summon someone.'

'O K matron I'm going. Sigmund Schultz is the name. And I'll give you a call.'

'Please don't bother.'

'O K I apologize matron. I'm sorry. But if a close pal is dying you get excited. So long. Matron. Goodbye. You see I'm going. I'm blessing myself with the Catholic sign of the cross. But if I can't see where I'm going because not seeing my best buddy is giving me tears which if they blind me going down the stairs and I fall and break my ass because this little confrontation with you has caused me such grief, I'm going to sue the fucking shit out of this hospital. Goodbye.'

Schultz, heels loudly clacking on the corridor floor, pushing out through the swing doors onto the landing. The hospital porter backing in front of him pulling a trolley covered by a sheet with the outline of a figure underneath.

'Ah now your honour sir, didn't you find your Mr Duke.'

'Yeah I found him. Thanks.'

'Ah he was wasn't he passed away already. You're seeing here right now what I'm doing. Would you like to have a look. Here let me show you. Homo sapiens kaput.'

'Hey no, don't bother, how the fuck do I exit, is this the main stairs down.'

The porter with gap toothed smile lifting the sheet back from a grey balding head of a man with a chain and cross around his neck, his eyes still staring open as if he'd seen a ghost in death.

'Now you'd never know once we remove this little decorative item what he was when he was alive, by the frightened look of him dead.'

'Hey christ, put the sheet back will you.'

'A monsignor. A dignitary of the Catholic church. All five foot eleven of him. But I hate priests and only measured him five foot six for his coffin.'

Schultz swaying forwards raising a hand waving the porter and his trolley of death away. Heading down the stairs. Grabbing the bannister. O god. Death. The final ignominy. The Irishman's robbing a corpse in front of my eyes. And he's going to have one big fucking harvest ripping all the clanking gold chains off Al. Holy fuck. I've tripped. Now what have I done, broken or maimed. Every time I come into a hospital healthy I go out feeling I'm dying. And now shit I am, twisting my god damn ankle and nearly killing myself. I could be dead before Al is.

Schultz to the choral strains of Gounod's Ave Maria rubbing his ankle in the back of his limousine. Slowly making headway in and out through the streets of Mayfair. Up Park Lane. The snow starting to fall again. Through the tree branches, tax dodgers' towers looming in the distance against the grey patchy skies and its windows catching a red tint of a sinking western sun. Schultz dialling on the car phone.

'Hello.'

'Louella.'

'Who is this.'

'This is Sigmund. I'm on my way. Have you forgot already what my voice sounds like.'

'I'm sorry. All the other phones are ringing and I can hardly hear a thing.'

'Honey, they won't let me see Al. I tried.'

'I know I said come. But please. Ring me later. I've just had the most awful phone call.'

'Honey I got to see you. I hear it in your voice. You're utterly distraught. I'll only stay five seconds. Please. That was the deal.'

'All right. But don't please go by reception. Come in the garage entrance. Park in one of Al's reserved spaces, D twenty one, two or three. Take the lift and ring the door with two rings and do it twice.'

'Hey what is it honey. Don't cry. I'm coming to you. In only seconds. Goodbye.'

Schultz's limousine wheels crackling over the hardened ice and snow, heading up a street of terraced Georgian houses. Turning right into a street of shops. Jesus it's always reassuring to see my favourite fish shop outside of which I have faithfully sat so many fucking nights. With the smell of fish. Making me more than once remember I come from a hick town in Rhode Island. Where whaling was one of the state's first big industries.

'Take the right fork in the road, Jorricks just past the restaurant. Then turn left and go down the driveway there.'

The limousine descending a long curving ramp into an underground garage. In this shadowy labyrinth Schultz jumping out at an entrance and limping in the door. Everything connected with Al Duke seems to have a big capital letter now, even his parking space. Press the button at these elevator doors which last time they opened were casting me fucking naked out into the world. Step in. Smell of nice damn perfume. Which I got to go now ruin with one god awful fart. And here I go now upwards in some new drama. And the most dramatic one in my life was the last time I ascended in this elevator. Up to this twenty first floor. To both joy and disaster. And the most cliff hanging but wonderful time of my life. And found what I most wanted in this entire fucking world besides money, was a woman I could love. I got to steel myself. Like jesus it was like the shock I got when I was a kid, in a snowball fight. Making a dozen all stacked up like ammunition. After crouching in my bunker I stood up to throw one and just as I was taking aim I suddenly got slammed in the face with an ice hard snowball which knocked me out.

The elevator stopping at the ground floor. Door opening. A befurred bejewelled lady stepping in with two poodles in arm. Jesus she's sniffing her nose and giving me what a fucking dirty look and she's riding all the way up to the penthouse. O K madam there's a stink in here but the smell could be dog shit all over your poodles' paws or something. Although I'll admit I had bratwurst and hot dogs for breakfast. And christ I'm just about to blast another one worse than the last. Could distract her from the fume if I try to sell her a ticket to the show. Might put a smile on that face of hers that makes her grimness look like it's carved in granite.

'Have a good day madam. And go see Kiss It Don't Hold It It's Too Hot.'

Schultz limping out on the twenty first floor. Barks from the poodles and a distinct inhuman growl from the lady left behind. Schultz crossing the lobby into the enclosure of a small entrance hall. Pressing the bell twice. Christ you try to say something polite to people and they flatly ignore you. But I forgot how nice and quiet and private it was up here. A spy hole in the mahogany. As well as a bell, Al's got a knocker now in the shape of an anchor. Suitable enough since he's sinking into the deeps. The door coming ajar. Jesus Louella open it wider. Let this Schultz step in.

'Gee honey christ it's me. I'm a friend. Let me in. Hey you look even more beautiful. Even under these gruesome circumstances. I really am glad to just see you. But what the fuck have you done. You dyed and cut off your hair. Jesus honey it's blonde. With streaks no less. Hey what happened.'

'Please. Just come in. And please. I'm too nervous and distraught. Please sit down. I've just got to go and turn off my bath. How is he.'

'Hey jesus never mind Al. You've lost weight.'

'Please you must tell me.'

'Honey he was as well as could be expected.'

Louella turning away from the door of this room. Out the window the sky grey above and westwards, purple with pink slivers. Beams of warm light from a red edge of the sun peeking above the horizon. Another cloud unleashing another flurry of snow. Sit on this tweed covered sofa I remember so well. But what the fuck is this in here. Candles burning and incense and chanting music. That Russian stuff Al's so fond of listening to. The celebrity pictures are even thicker over Al's walls. Christ you can't get to be president of the United States unless you're seen photographed with Al's arm draped around your back. And there. Would you believe it. Al in top hat in the Royal Enclosure at Ascot, with Louella on his arm. He'd do anything to impress this lovely girl. But the fucker really knows how to live. Imagine he could find a girl like this to listen to him hocking and spitting all morning and watching him try out his toupee in front of the mirror. But I wish our friendship didn't have to break up like this. Al always set an example for me. But the principle I learned in my Coast Guard career always seems to come true. When you find a friend who is good and true fuck him before he fucks you. And right there through that serving hatch, the wine bottles. O jesus the wonderful gorgeous vintages that I got served right on this bloody table. That memorable night. The crisis night of my career. Can there be anything greater than savouring a wine and peeking across its bouquet rising out of the glass while you're gazing into the eyes of a woman whose every square inch of flesh you want to kiss and who you're going to fuck after you've had two more glassfuls of velvety burgundy. And maybe topped off with a half glass of chilled Château d'Yquem. Christ I sound like an alki. But jesus just touching her a second ago again set my prick and balls on fire. O honey don't for christ's sake let Al's demise ruin our relationship which could be gorgeous. Jesus that matron. She did something funny to me. She must have been all of thirty eight years old. But christ she had something. I don't know what it was. But the way she used her authority was impressive. Maybe I should call her up and talk to her about it.

'Can I get you something.'

Louella back standing in the doorway. Her once long brown soft curled locks of hair now short frizzy and blonde. Makes her look more vulnerable. That you want to grab her up in your arms so she'll feel protected. Her once ample breasts look thinned down but the shape is just as I remember. They always looked so soft, curvaceous and fucking kissable under a black sweater. The nipples just that perfect size. Two works of priceless art I'd like to smother under my mouth.

'Hey honey, the sounds, the smoke, you got it like it's a church in here.'

'Al so loves his Russian orthodox church music and the incense. That's the Grand Litany they're singing.'

'Honey it's a little sombre isn't it. But I'll tell you one thing. Which nearly gave me a heart attack. Two priests were in there with him. The matron said Al was taking the last rites of the Catholic church.'

'O is that true. O I'm so glad.'

'What do you mean you're glad honey. Al's indelibly Jewish.'

'Al is becoming a Catholic. He made a promise to me. He's in the process of being received into the Church.'

'You sent the priests.'

'Yes.'

'I can't believe it. No disrespect to you honey or your beliefs.'

'We go every Sunday to mass and vespers at Farm Street Church.'

'Holy yiddish cow. Boy that really takes the cake. Al, the biggest Jew this side of Jerusalem with a couple of specialists in black magic at his bedside.'

'It's not black magic.'

'OK honey. Sorry. I know it's not. I know you believe your beliefs. But this I can't believe. The Catholic Church honey. What the hell are you doing, that's the only pure unadulterated asset Al has got left in life is being Jewish.'

'That's not true. Al loves Catholicism. Just last week we attended Fauré's Requiem at mass and there were tears of joy streaming down Al's cheeks.'

'What. I mean I'm not knocking Fauré's Requiem honey. I mean what could be more appropriate in reference to Al at this moment. But I mean shit Al's already dedicating his life to behaving like a Christian what do you need all the hocus pocus for in addition.'

'I believe in my religion as a Catholic.'

'OK honey. But why do this to Al. Holy christ here I am trying to save Al's soul from a fate worse than death. Just like the times he tries to convince me to go back to the synagogue, he behaves sometimes like he was the only Jew in the world. Pretending being a Catholic is going to be like that toupee Al started wearing, which looks as phoney as a three dollar bill flying off his head.'

'How can you be so unsympathetic.'

'I swear honey I'm just trying to be honest. OK that's right, I am, I'm highly unsympathetic. What the fuck would you expect me to be. But I am also faithful and courageous. Hey did I just say what I said. Listen to me. Mr Megalomania. All due to you honey. Because I want to shine in your eyes. But you could have compromised. Both you and Al could become Russian Orthodox. Listen to that music. It's wonderful.'

'Please let's not go on talking like this. I love Al, dearly love him. Don't you understand that. I know I shouldn't have asked you to go to the hospital. But I don't have one single soul I can turn to.'

'Honey you know I'm always available. Even to send to the hospital again. Don't worry. I only slightly broke my ankle in there. Frightened out of my wits by the sight of a dead stiff.'

'His last wife, right in the middle of their divorce is making anonymous obscene phone calls to me and telling me to get out of this flat. And now just before you arrived someone is threatening to kill me.'

'Honey now calm down, those threats don't mean nothing. I'll break anybody's ass comes even near you. And remember I loved Al too, once. And even though I hate funerals I'm going to his funeral. Hey sorry. Didn't mean to say that. No kidding. Just talking practical, if the inevitable for all of us, happens. Like I got so many hot irons in the fire these days I'm going crazy. Even right now sitting here talking about Al I should be negotiating with New York. But sorry what I said. You know you wouldn't believe it but success has isolated me. Christ on some of these lonely afternoons I sometimes dream I'm on the deck of the Titanic sinking in the cold Arctic waves, in my dinner jacket singing Abide With Me, like a Protestant Baptist. Jesus maybe I'm the one should become Catholic.'

'Al said he thought you took a proprietary interest in being Jewish only when it suits you. And then you behave as if you were the only Jew in the world.'

'Honey that's exactly the feeling that every Jew in the world has for plenty of reasons.'

'Al said anti semitism was invented because of people like you.'

'Honey please don't. You're sounding just like Al. Anyway anti semitism runs off me like water off a duck's back. But jesus let's forget the Jews a second. Have your bath. I'll scrub your back. Just talking to you is like listening to a beautiful piece of music. And jesus just listen. This passage. This. It's fucking touchingly beautiful those voices. Christ I'm going to go to Moscow.'

'If you like I'll make tea.'

'Gee swell. I'd adore some. Just what the doctor ordered. Now we're being sensible.'

'How would you like it.'

'Honey I'd love it.'

'I mean the tea.'

'Honey I know you mean the tea but I would love nothing more than just, holy shit, us. Just us honey. Just us. Entwined together for all time. To me you really are like listening to the most magically beautiful piece of music.'

'Please not now. I don't really want to talk like this.'

'Honey sure OK. But Al would talk like this, wouldn't he.'

'He wrote poems for me.'

'Poems. You mean poems like in poetry.'

'Yes.'

'Holy cow, poems yet.'

'And he could recite them all from memory.'

'Jesus I should have known all along what was wrong with Al. He was a poet.'

'Is.'

'O K. Is.'

'And he had them privately printed and published. And they were beautiful.'

'Maybe I may as well have tea then the way Al has it. Jesus honey. Maybe we really should change the subject. Hey honey I forgot how high up this is. Let me hobble over a second and look out of the window.'

'O but you really are limping.'

'It's nothing. Just a few ligaments torn and ripped apart around the ankle honey, nothing that a few weeks in traction won't fix.'

'O poor you.'

'Don't worry about me honey. Please. I do fifty five sit ups a day. Hard as nails.'

Schultz standing at the large expanse of window of this familiar room. On top of the soft fitted green carpet, Persian, Afghan and Turkish rugs. The mahogany gleaming tables and crystalware. A slow, nose to tail procession of silver great birds of aircraft passing westwards in the sky floating down to land at the airport. The whitened squares and the great stretch of Hyde Park and Kensington Gardens. The rooftops of all these townhouses. You'd wonder how so many people could get all this money it takes to be down there in this expensive looking part of town. They can't all be in show business with a hit on their hands. Christ this really is a great place to live. Like being a soaring bird, you can look down on all the victims. A lonely tiny cemetery I never knew existed tucked in down there hidden behind the backs of houses. Holy shit, I wonder who they all are those lonely dead. Al whose motto always was. Is that bad that I don't want to hurt people. Then he went after me with a bread knife. To sink it twelve inches down in my guts. Now it's his turn on his deathbed. Just like it is for so many of those fuckers who ratted and ignored me, wouldn't answer my telephone calls and are now drowning like rats without leaving a ripple. While for last week's take I go to the bank with three thousand eight hundred and eighty six pounds and eighteen shillings. With not a trace of sarcasm left on that bank manager's face as the money pours in now. On top of that, what more bliss and beauty could you ask for in life except this girl. Jesus her clothes. What clothes. At least one can say that for Al. His money and her good taste makes for a fucking devastating combination. Patent leather black shoes, and these low high heels and the way her beautiful ankle under her blue stocking shows between the cuff of her trouser. Even the way she said she'd make tea sent a glow of appreciation exploding right through my gonads. Plus the soothing relief to hear just a word of sympathy for a change. Jesus I really could take up residence high up in a place like this and no one I didn't want to see would know where the fuck to find me. Where at the moment christ I have a whole fucking house with nearly fourteen windows including the basement facing right out on to a public street.

'Sigmund what happened to your eyes.'

Schultz turning around from the window. Louella in the ash white light. In this chamber. Where one of the most delicious meals both gustatory and fuckatory in one's entire life was had. And now tea. A ceremony which is becoming close to my heart and one of the most fucking enjoyable pastimes of my recent life. Which if I go on living, how can I endure to keep my hands off her.

'That's right honey. Black. A couple of accidents that's all. One in each eye.'

'And O dear, as well as your ankle.'

'Yeah. Which is swelling like a football I can feel.'

'O dear. Things haven't changed for you, have they.'

'No honey they haven't. It's battle battle all the time. Only now I can afford to pay the doctor's bills.'

'Well I'll put an extra slice of lemon in your tea and cut you an extra large piece of Sachertorte. You weren't in another fist fight were you.'

'Truth honey of the matter is, my wife came who I thought was a telegram being delivered and socked me a couple right on my front stoop. And then the same day someone goes berserk backstage in the cast and I got socked again. Right in the same eyes.'

'O Sigmund.'

'Yeah. Fucking actors, dancers and singers they're all like spoiled children. Success has really gone to their heads. The outfits you see them wearing coming out the stage door. The fucking poses they strike dispensing autographs and flaunting themselves going out the alley. Prima donnas right down to the most insignificant girl in the chorus line. But it's not the fights I mind so much. A rash of compulsive cocksucking has broken out backstage. Some women can't get enough of it. You know how it is.'

'I certainly don't think that I do.'

'Sorry honey I'm casting no aspersions on anybody. But you must remember this blonde bombshell the lead girl in the chorus line built like a brick shit house who does her solo song and dance tour de force in the second act. Terence Magillacurdy has a ten minute conference with her every night in his dressing room during intermission and when she exits with her eyes rotating like criss crossed planets and her knees wobbling like they have got suddenly triple jointed, she ruins the whole fucking opening of the second act by performing like she's a rag doll.'

'Can't you replace her.'

'What. Jesus no. Every night she's got the first ten rows of expensive seats full of guys in raincoats folded over their laps with their hands pumping away.'

'How revolting.'

'Sure honey it is. But business wise it ain't. What's revolting is that I got her agent calling me to double her salary otherwise she might suddenly be sick. When I also have fifty girls begging who want that showcase part. I swear the low moral behaviour of some of these people who need an honest kick right up the ass.'

'O dear Sigmund I am sorry.'

'Hey holy shit honey I'm not complaining. That's what a management fee is for. I get paid. Plus some of the cast are pure sweetie pies. And I accept all this other stuff with the equanimity of pure bliss. There are just some of the little points of perfection one likes to get straightened out. Like no night should you let go by on that stage without trying an improvement however small or insignificant.'

'That's what Al said. You never gave up on anything till it was perfect.'

'Christ honey, at least there's one point Al was absolutely perfectly right on.'

'But how awful. The first ten rows. Imagine men behaving like that. With all you have to contend with backstage as well.'

'Well it is kind of a shock to the system. But honey meanwhile remember christ, we're doing all right with none of the usual Chinese torture of the agonizing horror of grieving over the daily gross which has turned into a glorious gusher even bigger than we ever imagined. The show's paid back. My take doubles next week. So you just have to graciously accept a little bit of the rough with a lot of the smooth.'

'Last Wednesday I walked past the theatre and saw the sign saying full house for the matinée. I did think of you. I really was thrilled for you.'

'Hey honey for christ's sake why didn't you come in and see me. I was right there that day. I'm always there at matinée performances or in the box office or in my room backstage. Or conferring with

Magillacurdy in his dressing room when he isn't conferring with somebody. And jesus christ. I must have known. I swear that day that moment I was thinking of you too.'

'Yes and I thought of all your struggles and battles to get the show on.'

'And honey one thing now I am sure of is that I rose like the Phoenix from the ashes. And while I'm making sure those box office fuckers answer the phones, nobody now but nobody is going to fuck it up or fuck around with Sigmund Franz Isadore anymore. That's gospel according to Schultz. Hey but this my god, is the most fucking gorgeous chocolate cake I've ever tasted in my life, honey.'

'It's Al's favourite from Fortnum's. They even write Al Duke on the top.'

'Christ honey you just cut him in half then. Sorry honey I'm just trying desperately to be funny. But jesus eating this every day, no wonder Al had a heart attack. But it's delicious.'

'Well have another slice.'

'I've had two already.'

'You've had three Sigmund. But who's counting.'

'O christ honey you're smiling. Jesus, that's so beautiful to see suddenly a smile come on your face. What are we going to do with our lives.'

'What are our lives going to do with us.'

'Touché honey. Touché. Jesus, I'd like just to be able to kiss your feet. Even your gorgeous shoes if you take one off and throw it over here.'

'Be careful I might.'

'Honey go on, throw one.'

A shoe landing next to Schultz's foot on the floor. Schultz picking it up and placing a kiss on the shiny patent leather tip and sniffing inside and drawing in a deep breath and exhaling a long sigh.

'O jesus honey I'm no shoe fetishist yet but shit I swear this is so wonderful to kiss and smell your shoe that I am one now. Here, you want to try my moccasin.'

'No thanks. Not just now, with tea.'

'Gee honey I don't want to bring up old painful memories. But that night, the phone dropping out of my hand when I heard the gross. That memorable night right here in this room when I just squeezed by by a whisker. And I made love to you and my whole life was just beginning for the first time. After all the months of nail biting nightmare, waiting and struggle. And now honey they're descending in busloads from every nook and cranny. From John O'Groats to Land's End. There's nothing now in this world nearly that is impossible for me to give to somebody I love. Hey honey don't cry. What's the matter. Jesus, please. Don't cry. Eat your cake and drink your tea.'

'I can't. Al. He's in there in a lonely hospital bedroom. Dying.'

'I know honey. I know he is. Jesus I was there and there is nothing you can do. Anyway the place is jammed with Catholic priests hosing cold holy water or something all over him. That alone might jolt Al back to life. But maybe we should worry more about what's happening to his good Hebrew soul turning baptized into a Catholic and the pneumonia he could get from the head soaking.'

'Please don't.'

'I'm just trying to cheer you up a little bit honey.'

'Well you're not.'

'What good would it be, you there with tubes like an octopus all over him. With doctors needing to be all over the place as well.'

'Al always said that if he was ever to go he wanted me there beside him. And I'm not. He has such a fear of loneliness.'

'We all have honey. But christ the Press and everyone is trying to break down the door just to get in to take down in shorthand his last immortal words before they shake his hand goodbye. The matron even thought I was the Press.'

'So you do, you do think he's dying don't you.'

'Well honey to be honest it ain't as if I think old Al, much as I always did admire the way he could blow on a trumpet, is going to grab up his skis and ski poles and fly off to St Moritz as he usually does this time of year to break his ass as he always does on the slopes.'

'God you can be cruel.'

'Honey no. No I can't. I can be fucking realistic at a time like this, that's what I can be. Al smokes like a chimney honey. His lungs were wheezing. And all I know is that I'm still confused over why you should send the sight of somebody he now hates to his bedside to sing Auld Lang Syne with him.'

'Al loved you. He truly loved you like a son. Many a night he would shake his head back and forth over it.'

'Honey you were unfaithful to Al and I betrayed him. That would make anybody shake their head. And it happens all the time to more people than you think. But he would have never have known a thing about it if he hadn't been the fucking cunning scheming bastard that he is to fly back the whole way from New Orleans to waltz right in on us. But I love you and I did love Al and now I'm the one shaking my head back and forth over it.'

'It sounds so brutally dreadful the way you say that.'

'It's got to be said honey. It's got to. It's the truth.'

'But you simply don't know how much he did love you, Sigmund. He always said that when everyone thought you were down, he would say to me that Sigmund's going to show them. He'd say Sigmund will zing mit der dick dick. As if he were right there fighting your battles with you side by side.'

'Honey O K I believe you. And believe Al. And believe me. I was zinging mit der dick dick.'

'And now if he dies I have nowhere to go.'

'Well honey if you'll forgive me saying so, you're now talking sense for a change.'

'Well I don't, I have nowhere.'

'What are you kidding. Sure. They'll throw you out. All of Al's assets will be frozen. But you have everywhere. Where you can go on having this wonderful chocolate cake, tea and all the fucking groceries delivered you want from Fortnum's. I got an account there. And honey when this show's a smash on Broadway I'll go buy or build a palace for you so we can both chomp our ivories on what they unload from the van every morning. Anywhere you want in this town. You name it. How many bathrooms you want. Go on tell me. How many.'

'One is enough. O dear. It's all such a horrible mess. And what about your wife.'

'No problem. I'll find a good architect to build a perfect prison for her. With one beautiful toilet bowl for her to sit on.'

'I don't think that's funny.'

'Honey it may not be funny but it's fucking mandatory. Before she kills me. But shit. I'll go down talk to the estate agents right now, over there on the street corner. They're open till five. I'll even set you up right here in this building if you don't want to leave. We'll knock down walls and ceilings of two flats. Make it into a duplex, triplex penthouse, whatever you want. Right on the top of fucking tax dodgers' towers.'

'Don't please call it that awful name. Al pays his taxes. And no matter what you say you've still got a wife. And I don't want to be kept. I can look after myself. And it'll only be temporary that I have nowhere to go.'

'I know you can look after yourself honey. I know you can. And who said anything about keeping. Just maybe a little subsidy to help you along. To adjust if Al, and I'm sorry if I have to say this again in the realism of the moment, but if Al croaks. Jesus christ honey, look, me. I'll go with you to Farm Street Church. I'll get converted for you.'

'Would you throw me my shoe back please.'

'Sure honey. And would you mind maybe if you could get me some whisky, will you. His Lordship says that's what is customary taking tea these days. And if you've got some of that pure Highland scotch stuff. Because the energy I am using up in this conversation, I really need it.'

Out the window a curtain of grey white falling snow shrouding the sky. Louella slipping on her shoe. The smooth soft curving contours of her thighs. In her navy blue satin slacks. A chiffon scarf tied around her ultra slender waist. Her breasts under her black sweater like two blossoming night flowers as she stands up from the settee. Crossing to the sideboard covered in bottles. Pouring whisky into a heavy squat glass. And god what a good deceptively strong ass she has. The kind you get from climbing stairs. Maybe that's what she does instead of taking the elevator up here. The light fading in this blizzard outside. Holy cow it's really snowing hard again. Nothing but millions of flakes. No two alike. Just like tits and asses. My god even to look at hers right there. Makes me want to throw myself on them. Bury my face kissing all over those delicious mounds. Fucking hell I won't be able to stand it. If with the box office keeping my mind calm and my prick hard, I have to spend another minute of my life without her.

'I'll take it straight honey with just one lump of ice, just like it is. Thanks. Do you mind if I just ring down a second to Jorricks.'

'Do.'

'Thanks.'

Schultz dialling the phone. Watching Louella turn back to the sideboard and pour herself a drink. God, thinking about every other part of her I forgot she's tall. Comes right up to my eyebrows. She's stately. And her so beautifully fucking warm hearted soul pervades the whole room.

'Hi Jorricks, it's me. Could you mosey over to that good faithful fish shop across the other side of the street and get us a selection of fish for the deep freeze. I won't be long. Hey what's that I'm hearing.'

'I'm listening to Rigoletto sir.'

Schultz hanging up. Louella sitting down with her drink, leaning back on the cushions and crossing her legs. Jesus there are little hollows under the poor kid's eyes. Fuck it she really must love the old cunt. He's got to fucking die. One girl like this is only once in a lifetime.

'Gee honey, you know it's just nice to relax a minute.'

'You do, don't you, have your life pretty well organized.'

'Only a little honey. Not enough to call it bliss. Because one thing important is missing.'

'When did you get Jorricks.'

'It's how I got him honey which is a story worth telling. Besides being able to cook he's a genius who loves the theatre.'

'How nice for you.'

'Honey what would be nice for me and worth ten butlers is you. Jesus give me another slug of this marvellous whisky will you. Christ I never thought in all my fucking life I'd be taking a slug of whisky at three thirty in the fucking afternoon. I'm getting drunk.'

'Sigmund it's going on four.'

'Christ my watch stopped. And gee honey you got to face it. I don't want to be boringly philosophical, but we all got to die. Meanwhile we could even take a thatched cottage in the country. Miles from wives, threats of death, detectives. With roses round the door. Keep bees, grow fucking carrots and escape this turmoil. Come on what about it. Let me tell Jorricks downstairs to go home. God you look gorgeous. In spite of the hair change. You really do. Even with your eyes a little red. Christ honey I want to embrace you. Excuse me. I got such a hard on already. Let me take you away from all this trouble. After all these wasted months. And if you want I got a nice little suite at a reasonable rate from the manager just waiting reserved right over there in the Dorchester. Just an elevator ride down to the garage and in two seconds Jorricks will have us there. And who's to know.'

'No.'

'But jesus why. It's not as if I don't know you got in touch with me again using Al as an excuse to see me.'

'You can be insufferably conceited at times, can't you.'

'Honey of course I can. Everybody can.'

'Well, if you want to know the fact of the matter.'

'Is what honey. What. Come on, tell me. That's what I'm after, the truth. So now honey tell me what the fact of the matter is.'

'It was you who caused Al's heart attack.'

'Me.'

'Yes. Down there on the street the first night of the snowstorm.'

'Don't tell me Al was out of his nice cosy nest up here and was out down there shovelling snow or something.'

'Al saw right into your binoculars through his binoculars from the bedroom window. While you were parked in your car.'

'Parked in my car.'

'Yes. And he flew into such an uncontrollable rage that he went to the kitchen for the bread knife. He was on his way down to the street. And as I struggled to stop him. It happened. And it's why I want you never again ever to come near spying on Al and I again. Ever.'

'Honey I think you're a fucking liar about all of this. Sorry but I think you are. Al had his heart attack coming for years. It could have happened over an erection, I'm sure he's always had difficulty with.'

'I could slap your face for that.'

'O jesus honey, let's not get into all this. Not about the heart attack. It's ruining our relationship. I mean if the possibility is there any little thing could cause Al's gaskets to blow. Even a calm erotic dream in sleep. But why did you want me to see Al. Jesus pour me more of that stuff. No. Not even ice. I need this hot straight down into my gizzard. Jesus at this late stage I should become an alcoholic while I'm on the brink of my gold mine.'

'Your wife told Al you were spying on us.'

'Hey holy shit. Come on. She for a start invents fantasies around the clock.'

'Well she didn't invent Al going for the bread knife.'

'Yeah to try to cut off my balls again.'

'Yes he was if he hadn't collapsed.'

'Well thanks he collapsed. O K sorry. I didn't mean to say that. No kidding.'

'There are a lot of things you don't mean aren't there.'

'Hey come on it's a coincidence too. I buy fish from that shop down there. You heard me just now to Jorricks. It's the best fish shop in town. O christ now I'm going to have a fucking heart attack. Yeah and it's right. I was there.'

'And then the ambulance leaving had an accident going around the corner.'

'Holy shit. That was the ambulance. Christ I saw it. Hit right in the side. Then it came right by me. Jesus Al must have been in it. I can't believe all this. Wow. Fuck a duck. It's too incredible. But honey you know why I'm watching these windows up here. Trying to know where you are. That you're safe and O K. Yes and I even suffer the horror of thinking that geriatric Al is taxing his brain and strength to stimulate himself enough when the light goes off to attempt to make love to you.'

'For your conceited information and if I may put it so crudely as to make you understand, Al is stimulated by his merely looking at me and his cock stands up like a fence post and he has on more than one occasion even ejaculated before he's been able to touch me.'

'Jesus will wonders never cease. He should join a circus. OK honey. I'm finishing my drink. Goodbye.'

See you
At Al's funeral
When he's
Polevaulting on that
Prick of his
Into heaven

Schultz descending in the elevator. The floors light by light
going by. Stopping at the eleventh. Dark overcoated gent
steps in. He looks like my Uncle Werb who I hope I should
never have to look like if I ever had to become a diamond
merchant. Which I nearly did till this show hit. Jesus Al's
arteries maybe are still good enough to get his prick up to
assault her. O god how cruel women can be. To devastate you right in
the intestines. Jesus now I'm the cause of Al's heart attack when all
he's done all his life is smoke like a chimney and gobble down lox,
bagels, caviare and chocolate cake and then knock himself out watching
television. Exercise is reaching to relight his cigar while the ash falls
over his shirt. But who knows maybe he was going down to the tenth
floor by the fire stairs and climbing back up every evening adding
muscles to his prick. I should have known going up there was disaster
and now going down I really am on the deck of the Titanic but not
singing abide with me. But shouting out.

'Hey Lord call that creep Al up to heaven.'

'I beg your pardon.'

'Sorry sir I was just talking to myself.'

Schultz approaching his limousine. In this echoing cold underground
labyrinth. Jorricks closing the boot. Good place for murders down in
this garage. There's one of Al's cars. His sky blue convertible. Sitting
there waiting for spring, so Al can drive with the top lowered and the
wind whistling through his toupee which has to be screwed down on
his head. His other two cars must be confidently waiting for him
outside the hospital.

'Home Jorricks.'

'That was very good timing if I may say so sir. Fish is all packed up
in the boot. Got the evening papers for you too, sir. And there were
three phone calls from New York. The numbers and names are on the
pad.'

Limousine wheels skidding climbing up the incline. Third time
lucky as the furiously spinning tyres wore down through the snow to
grip and the vast long vehicle pulled forward. The snow falling thicker.
A blizzard again. Out of which I could have kept if I had played my
cards right. Three calls from Broadway. Eleven o'clock in New York.
Let them all call back. Start bidding you bastards. You Joe Jewels first.
And your bid better be big. And then I'm going to hit that town. In
the Stage Door Deli have a hot pastrami on rye mit pickles, mit
coleslaw, mit stage hands and stars. Who are all going to witness
Schultz blasting away on Broadway. And zinging mit der dick dick.

Then it's voom off to the coast. Where it's going to be voom, lights, action, camera, as Schultz hits Hollywood like a dose of salts. Voom. And all you nonentity fuckers are going to go on shitting in your drawers for your jobs as I show you how it's done. Holy shit power and money is going to my head. Hey that's dangerous with so many deals to do. And with so many fuckers after power and money waiting around to screw you.

In the stopped traffic, Schultz switching on the reading light and turning to look out the window. A lady walking by on the sidewalk, her dog wearing a jacket and red little boots. Hey that's real cute. Life's not that bad. Picking up the evening newspaper. Check the classified ads for the show. They always leave something out or get something wrong and I'll get a reduction. The papers folded right by my hand. Don't have to do more than bend a knuckle. No fucking doubt a butler's better than a wife. Hey what is it with the women in this world. What the fuck satisfies them. Maybe I should go bald on top and dye the rest of my hair grey. Get jowls, a belly, look like death warmed over. Then turn red white and blue throwing a heart attack. Jesus, maybe then the women will love you. Plus like Al, to intensify the love, there must be coming into his coffers a half a million dollars a year. And a beautiful idyllic apartment. But I'm not going to fucking well believe that story for one second. Al fastest gun in the west getting his rocks off like some infantile teenager. Jesus maybe it's premature ejaculation as a result of a mental aberration. Al's brains at his age must be missing a billion or two of neurons. Al once said he was a tit man. And jesus she has one of the most gorgeous sets of tits in Christendom. Of which maybe she gave him a teasingly premeditated flash. And he blew his load. And that girl. That magic wonderful creature. Watching that. O jesus the thought is too horrendously crucifying. The fucker maybe is taking monkey injections. It must be these desperate images are coming to mind because I so badly need to get laid. Badly. That's priority. And that's gospel. By Schultz. Take out my address and telephone numbers again. Been through this diary a dozen times. Tempted to call the numbers. Scraping the bottom of the barrel. Even calling girls up who are thirty years old. Then couldn't face it. O christ that fucking Louella has ruined me for all time. For all other women. Making it now that I can't fuck somebody I don't love. If it took me nearly my whole life to fall in love like this, that kind of thing could stop the whole world in its tracks. It would be paltry if you ever stopped to count up the number of people who are really in love. But jesus the fucking hasn't stopped in China yet. And in India by the latest popu-

46

lation figures someone is still grabbing the odd piece of ass. But the worst revelation of all is. She might really love Al.

'Hey I changed my mind Jorricks. Head back into town while I think a second.'

'Very good sir. Would you like music.'

'No thanks.'

'Are you still staying loose sir, or shall I expect you for dinner.'

'Yeah. Expect me. Drop me off at the theatre first. I'll take the taxi home.'

'Very good sir. But if there's any trouble with this snow let me know.'

'Sure.'

Schultz paging through his address book. Ragged, blotted and torn. Just like some of the names. Holy christ, that come up at you out of the deep dark past. Freddie Joy, a grade B starlet but one of the most dazzlingly fabulous females of them all. I once looked down as the two of us were standing on a staircase and the hard on I had was the biggest ever in my personal history. But jesus she was career crazy. Instead of more hopeless women, dial his Lordship. That's what I'll do. He always has the most amazingly good advice at his fingertips. Which is usually to take tea, take a whisky, and take a hot bath. And pull your own pudding. In that order. Jesus no answer at his private number. And don't like talking to his butler without my butler first from now on putting through the call. Now I can't get Louella off my mind. Christ I dumbly tried to act tough like it didn't matter and now my guts are squirming like a can of worms. It's like after getting turned down by the first girl I asked to the high school prom. Which sent me kicking my way through a pile of autumn leaves. That with a match put to them is going to burn a lonely hole in my brain. Leaving an awful smell of smoke in my life. I got to call her back. Jesus don't. Fucking well hold it. Stop your hand. Jesus fingers, don't go in the holes of that dial. Don't. Stop. Don't do it.

'Hello honey it's me. I want to apologize for what I said. I really am sorry. Hello. Hello.'

'I'm here.'

'Honey let's not break the last thread we got hanging us together and come asunder.'

'We were never together.'

'But we made love. Doesn't that mean something.'

'Why should it.'

'Why should it. Don't you know why. Hey christ. Look would it help if I told you Jorricks is taking me to Farm Street Church and I was putting fifty quid in the till and lit a couple of dozen of them Catholic candles for the memory of Al's soul. Sorry Jesus. I mean, I swear I mean Al's recovery honey. My words are mixed up. Three deals coming out of New York are bouncing around in my brain. Honey for christ's sake have mercy on me too, the way you do on Al.'

'Al is dying.'

'So am I honey.'

'You're not listening to me. He's not expected to survive the night. Your partner Binky just rang me.'

'That interfering bastard. How would he know.'

'He was at the hospital. And if you don't have the good manners not to start picking over Al's bones before he is even dead I don't want to hear of or even speak to you again.'

'O jesus. Let me call you later. This is all such a fucking misunderstanding honey. And look, you know my number home. And if I'm not there I'm at the Dorchester Hotel. To reach me all you do is ask to speak to Mr Jeremiah Kelly. It's the code. Tomorrow the code name is Mr Hans Arafat. And I swear. I really do. Right in this snowstorm. Where traffic's crawling at the moment, that I'm heading to Farm Street. Jorricks, Farm Street, please. Now you just heard me. We're on the bridge now crossing the Serpentine in the Park and we're taking the next turning left to go to the church.'

'Where you go is entirely your own business.'

'O jesus don't do this to me. Come on.'

'Please don't whine and beg.'

'I'm not begging. Whining a little maybe. O K. Ring you later. After I've been to the church. Which will give you an idea of how sincere I am. Goodbye.'

Through the churning snow the limousine cruising slowly eastwards past the whitening stretches of the Park. The shadowy tree branches bending their snow laden boughs. Up Park Lane and across in front of the tiny garden and fish pond in front of the Dorchester Hotel. Christ that building rising white and resolute like the prow of a ship has saved me many a time in a storm. Jesus, what happens to all the little goldfish in that pond this weather. Flick on the lamp. This is such a sudden relief to just sit and read the papers. Always good gossip stuff in this Londoner's Diary. Written with a certain flair. Holy jeeze. What the fucking hell is this.

MOST EXPENSIVE MUSICAL EVER

This awed reporter finally cornered the elusive heir to two of Britain's larger fortunes, Binky Sunningdale, the Eton and Oxford educated legendary figure of recent show biz fame and the only son of the fabled beauty Lady Ottoline. Finding him comfortably luxuriating in his elegant West End suite of offices, where lunch was lavishly served by Mr Sunningdale's private chef, Mario, I ventured to ask Mr Sunningdale, producer of London's biggest current smash hit 'Kiss It, Don't Hold It, It's Too Hot', which some critics advised to 'Miss It, Don't See It, It's Too Awful', how it was that he is now launching what is thought to be the most lavishly expensive and star-studded musical ever to be seen in London, dwarfing even his present show. The blondly handsome Mr Sunningdale, as he blew his cool cigar rings over one's head and commented upon my grandmother's real pearls, upon which it appears Mr Sunningdale's attention endlessly lingered, enlightened one immediately. 'Of course, my dear, with the public so much behind us and clamouring for seats to our present little effort, we are rather planning something new and entirely different, in financial if not aesthetic terms so to speak.'

Regaling this reporter for more than a pleasant hour on antique theatrical posters, and serving some of the most exquisite wines with pheasant and judging by the charming Mr Sunningdale's past performances as a producer, one was enchanted and assured that we can only sit now on the very edge of our seats with eager anticipation for the new delights this unapologetically upper-crust gentleman has in store for us. I for one will be there on opening night, wearing my real pearls and hoping again to catch sight of and have a further few amusing words with the elusive Mr Sunningdale.

'Holy jesus christ that fucking son of a bitch, who the fuck does he think he is giving himself credit for my fucking production he tried to close. And thinking he can now go and do this without a word to me.'

'Is everything all right back there Mr Schultz.'

'No everything is wrong. Let's just get to the church.'

The limousine pulling up to park in Farm Street. Past a pub and in front of this ecclesiastic building. Schultz limping up the steps. Pushing in through the two swing doors into the solemn candlelit darkness. Jesus this nice quiet little street here in the middle of Mayfair. And my stomach has to be churning in anger. I don't believe in this Catholic shit. But I need somewhere to pray. That that fucking Binky is put in his place. And Al goes burning up in ashes at the crematorium. But jesus holy mackerel, this place in here is beautiful. Peaceful. God. Christ. Voices singing. An organ playing. What the hell do these Catholics do. I guess go kneel down. These voices are fantastic. Listen to that tenor and that bass and the choir back up. Nobody must be paying them that much to be singing here in a church with nothing but a priest, a couple of kids on the altar and few old people hanging around in the place. I could put this on in the West End. Design a bigger altar. With a big back lit backdrop which could be heaven. Jazz the music up a little with a few risqué lyrics, put a little nudity around the edges, and shit, pack 'em in. Next time I get any shit from any singer in the cast they're going to get fired and replaced by these gems here.

In front of the votive display of candles Schultz taking out a roll of bills and counting off five ten pound notes. Reaching to stuff the folded bills in the slit of the brass receptacle. Suddenly stopping. Hey christ this is fifty quid. What am I doing, taking and putting in five tens. When I could put in five singles. Who's to know the difference. It's the gesture that counts. Plus how's God to know.

Schultz taking twelve candles and lighting each with a taper. Stick them here to burn. I guess five quid is a small token to pay to see the end of Al. Although jesus I'd stuff in a hundred as an offering if I really knew it would mean the last that I'd ever see of that old fart. O christ I guess it's too sad. All those flaming candles. Jesus and I guess if the truth were to be known I'm going to kind of miss the son of a bitch. All the fucking enjoyable conversations we used to have on the phone. And some not so fucking enjoyable. Goodbye Al. It was nice knowing you. But a fucking lot nicer fucking your girlfriend. O christ my mind keeps putting words into my mouth that I don't mean. Even though I mean them.

'Excuse me, Mr Schultz, New York is again on the line.'

In the last pew of the church on a side aisle Jorricks tapping the shoulder of a kneeling head bowed Schultz. Schultz turning to look up. Tears in his eyes.

'O Mr Schultz I am sorry to disturb you like this. But I thought you might want to take this call. A gentleman Mr Jewels on the line said he wasn't going to phone back again.'

'O K Jorricks I'm coming. In a second. Tell them to hang on.'

Schultz standing by the pew. Turning in the shadowy light. Sniffing the smoke of incense. A lady dipping her fingers in a font and blessing herself. Touches her forehead breast and shoulders in turn. Christ I'm doing the same. And see what this hocus pocus does for me. Now that I find I'm surrounded by a lot of fucking betraying enemies again in the form of one guy called Binky Sunningdale. Getting up and assuming all the credit. And my motto is. Don't let anyone go through the revolving doors of life in front of you. And if it's ever a matter of eating humble pie, I'll eat it if it's there but not if some fucking bastard is shoving it in front of me.

Schultz stepping down the church steps. Holding the car door open, Jorricks with an umbrella, the big snowflakes making white spots on the black silk. Schultz lowering himself on the soft upholstery and picking up the phone.

'Hello. Schultz here.'

'Joe Jewels here. Hi ya kid. Well well. Tracking you down is getting to be difficult. Someone said you were in a church. Must be a misunderstanding. Anyway I won't beat around the bush. One hundred and thirty five thousand. Half up front on signature. Half on the opening night. You listening.'

'Yeah I'm listening.'

'Well you heard me.'

'Yeah I heard you.'

'Well is it a deal.'

'I got two more bids to hear from.'

'I just withdrew mine kid.'

'OK goodbye.'

'Hey wait a minute kid. I've been at the top of this business twenty five years. What the hell's wrong with you. You know how much one hundred and thirty five thousand dollars is. Plus two and a half percent of the Broadway gross. Plus equal billing. Plus mutual artistic approval. Plus round trip first class expenses to New York.'

'I know. I just said I have two more bids to hear from. You could have bought this show when it opened for a tenth of the price. What are you bellyaching about now.'

'If you call these kind of terms I'm giving you bellyaching.'

'You're giving me. You're giving me a competing bid that's what you're giving me.'

'OK I tell you what I'll do kid. One five O. That's final.'

'Hey Mr Jewels keep your toupee on. Nothing's final.'

'Hey you ought to talk to Al. You tell him what you're doing. Turning down a record sum of money against a record cut of the take.'

'Al's dying. He could be dead right now.'

'Is that right. Well Al always was a success at whatever he attempted. And if he's doing that now he won't fail. Give him my regards from Broadway when you see him will you. I'm adding five thousand. Not a cent more. One five five.'

'Three percent of the gross.'

'Hey what the hell are you out of your mind kid. Three percent is what I pay the director the choreographer, the designer combined.'

'Three percent of the gross.'

'Jesus kid nobody this side of Jerusalem will give you three percent of the gross, not even for the world rights to the last supper and crucifixion.'

'Three percent.'

'OK kid, three.'

'Plus I want.'

'Stop, stop kid. Hey hasn't five flops in a row taught you anything. Now you got one temporary hit.'

'This hit is permanent. And it was three flops in a row.'

'OK three, you sound proud of it kid. But you know, let me tell you something. Greed is a necessary evil in all of us. But greed is a mean spirited characteristic in a human being that can crush somebody else's heartfelt generous optimism in the future. And your greed could break this show. And I wouldn't wait two seconds after it lost two nickels to close it down if it starts losing money. But let me tell you something else. There is nobody on Broadway who would do more than I would to make a success of a show. I'll get up and wag my own prick at the audience and get arrested for it and get thrown into prison. Just to make publicity to make the fucking show go.'

'OK Joe. OK give me a day to think about it.'

'You have five seconds to think about it kid and this time I'm not kidding when this phone goes down.'

'Hey don't try to put a gun to my head.'

'Kid, I'm just putting numbers in your ear. And I'm counting five seconds. So listen. One. Two.'

'Joe I got other bids coming.'

'Well you take them then kid. There are other shows I can buy cheaper and pay somebody one and a half percent of the gross and maybe make even bigger hits out of them. So I'm counting. Three. Four. Because when I say five. This bid you don't have no more.'

'It's a deal.'

'Jesus kid. Who taught you this kind of cliff hanging ruthless tactics.'

'People like you Joe. That's who taught me.'

'I'm a romantic kid. Stage struck. That's why I let you get away with this. What do you want all this money for. This deal is a disgrace to the whole industry. And they better never hear about it. My lawyers will have the papers on the plane to London tonight. Goodbye.'

Schultz's stately black gleaming limousine passing slowly round the ancient soaring plane trees of Berkeley Square. The snow swirling in bigger flakes. Never can forget that the roots of these trees are down deep nourished all these years by victims of the bubonic plague. Christ we survive and build on catastrophe. All you got to do is keep on fighting and never give up. At last for sure I'm sitting on top of a real smasheroo hit spreading its tentacles across the globe. The only fucking Englishman in the ointment is Binky. Imagine such words, the unapologetically upper crust Mr Sunningdale. So upper crust he's got silver spoons rattling out his ass. Mustn't jump to conclusions, these trumped up interviews always usually amount to a load of shit. And that avaricious bastard Jewels. Didn't even notice I said Al was dying. Jesus, maybe he did. And he's going to feature the event on Broadway. The Resurrection. Al Duke Goes To Heaven. One thing I know, never trust anybody or anything in show biz. But at least now in the last five minutes and right at the number five, Joe Jewels capitulated. Five could now be my lucky number. Five quid in the church box for candles. Pity for the sake of this number my full hard on is six inches long. But it's just exactly that extra inch that women fall in love with. Pricilla before we got married used to measure it seven inches from the hilt, but it was cheating. Christ marriage and they suddenly start thinking they got a fucking work horse butler under their thumb who polishes the princess throne they sit on. And bottles their farts for posterity. Jesus I'm going to become a Catholic. Come out of that church and five minutes later there's one hundred and fifty five thousand dollars comes clanking into the till. Holy shit I don't want to be superstitious which I fucking already am but maybe I should go back and put the fifty I originally promised in the offering box. Jesus, I guess it's a form of lying like one does saying all the beautiful things you say to women in a cold fuck when you don't believe a word of it and are ready to put on your pants and leave in five minutes.

'Hey take us home first Jorricks. I got to get a couple of contracts I got to look at.'

The limousine heading around Hyde Park Corner. Jesus thank god Al's not in St George's hospital here where he'd be so near I could hear him croaking out his last. In that arch there they got hidden a police station. I know. One evening strolling home from the theatre I innocently pissed on the lawn and a dozen bobbies waving truncheons jumped out to arrest me for indecent exposure. Adding yet one more time my prick nearly got me into trouble, only this time, for the first time it was flaccid. Told each of the bobbies they could collect a free ticket for two to the show. Or else I might have been in the dock pleading a necessary call of nature to the judge. So much for taking a piss. God doesn't everything look so beautiful in the snow. Even the prison looking walls of the Queen's palace. That's another plus. And something Binky doesn't know. The Lord Chamberlain called me over to his office. Jesus got to admire these guys. Even though I was feeling fucking superior it was wonderful the way he was able to treat me as an equal. Royalty is planning to confidentially and privately attend at the show. And I'm the one who's going to be there greeting them in the royal retiring room and showing them to the royal box. And they are all going to get a royal private family confidentiality they ain't never seen before. With an army of photographers and reporters descending upon their majesties when I confidentially and privately leak the news to Fleet Street. Show could run for centuries. Every social climber would have to see it. Which means nearly every god damn one in the country. So many things to be joyous over why do I even have to mind that fucker Binky. Stealing his pathetic little piece of limelight. Look at this wonderful crescent of houses in this beautiful whiteness everywhere. Maybe no fish shop on the doorstep and you can't piss on the grass, but there's not much else wrong with Belgravia let me tell you. Who needs a tax dodgers' towers. Who even needs her. Shit I need her. But soon now, just like his Lordship and fucking Binky, I'm going to have one of those god damn exceptional, luxuriously appointed country residences they advertise. Exquisite miniature estate. Beautifully equipped to satisfy the most exacting standards. Maybe it won't be like as big as his Lordship's castle but it will have everything I need. Like a tennis court and swimming pool. And voom, right after Al's cremation at the crematorium I'm going to propose to Louella marriage that can come right after my divorce. Jesus, this is a dreadful insight I'm having. How do I know Al didn't explode one of his premature ejaculations in front of Priscilla my wife before he claims he hired her as a temporary secretary. Or jesus while she even worked for him. He could have been asking her for blow jobs under his big mahogany desk. Well who the fuck cares. My dream boat just docked with another one five five on board. With Joe Jewels, the biggest most successful impresario of them all. Crawling on his knees to me with his tongue hanging out as I shove an extra half percent of the gross up his ass that's going to make him squeal in agony for months to come. So much for pure unadulterated justice. Jesus, show biz is thousands of guys like lemming hordes as they go rushing crawling up on some deal that they think is finally going to make them their fortune, each biting each other's ass. And the teeth of nearly all of them end up in sunk deep a flop.

'Hey Jorricks. What's it a jam. What's that up there blocking the whole god damn road.'

'It looks like the fire brigade sir.'

'Jesus they should pull over a bit and let traffic through don't they know some people have got to get somewhere.'

'Sir I believe they are in front of the house.'

'They what. Holy cow. Not my house.'

'I'm afraid so sir, it looks awfully like it.'

'Jesus let's get up there. Hey let me out, christ.'

Schultz jumping out of the car. Wading knee deep in a snowdrift on the sidewalk. At least that's a help. The fucking snow has just frozen my ankles so I can't feel one of them is broke. Jesus both my loafers have just come off. Hey jesus where did they go deep in this snow. And leaving me with wet fucking socks already. Fuck my loafers, shit my house. Jesus, it couldn't be me that's burning. My god. It is. A hose is up the fucking steps through my front door. With nobody in there all afternoon minding it. Jesus my ten thousand quid in foreign currency could burn, plus my private hoard of tax dodged cash. Never mind the heirloom letters my Prague great great grandmother wrote my Prague great great grandfather in Czech I could never read.

Schultz limping, skidding and falling in his snow encrusted socks. Getting up again and licking snow from his lips and shaking out the snow from jacket cuffs and sleeves. Lights flashing. The gleam of the fire apparatus reflecting shiny red on the snow. Jesus not one, two hoses are in the front door.

'Back sir, back please. If you will.'

'Hey that's my house you're in.'

'Who might still be in there, sir.'

'Nobody nobody. Hey but what the hell is happening.'

'Your house is on fire sir. Have you any dangerous inflammables inside sir.'

'Yeah. If perfume burns. My wife's got two hundred varieties. You name the brand and she's got it. In a big bottle. And I got contracts and cash in there.'

'Well sir any minute now you might only have ashes and charcoal, please don't attempt to enter.'

'O my god I should live so long.'

'Just a moment sir. If you will. What is it John.'

'The kitchen, sir. Suits, clothes, shirts, pictures, papers all piled up on the table and burning like an inferno. Smell of paraffin oil. Too early to say. But we may be dealing with suspicious circumstances. We've nearly got it now under control. We're lifting up the floorboards above in what looks like a library.'

'You're what. Stop. Don't tear my house apart for christ's sake. Stop. Let me in there.'

'Please. Get back sir. No one is allowed in the house till we know the fire is under control.'

'John, this is the owner here.'

'How do you do sir. We certainly will avoid doing any unnecessary damage. But the fire was eating into the kitchen ceiling. We'll let you know when it's safe to go in.'

'Hey jesus guys cut down on the damage will you and I'll give you reduced reductions to a West End show.'

'I'm afraid sir we can't accept any kind of gratuity however well meant. And be assured we will avoid doing any unnecessary damage.'

'O K, O K. Christ we brought back fish to cook for dinner.'

'Well the only cooking you'll be doing in there at the moment sir is on the embers of your kitchen table.'

'O momma meeo.'

'And if it hadn't been for the prompt action of a neighbour living behind you sir, the entire building would now be a shell.'

'Christ when can I go back into my house.'

'Not for a little while sir, not till the whole premises is checked. Meanwhile sir can we give you something to put on your feet.'

'Holy christ my shoes. Back there in the snow drift.'

'Well at least your socks sir, fire engine red, are of an appropriate colour.'

Schultz returning to the limousine. Tiptoeing in his frozen woollen footwear along the pavement past the long line of stopped cars. Watched by black faces in all the embassy windows across the street. O my god. He's smiling and waving at me. Jesus that's wonderful. The Ambassador's back. He must have survived the fucking coup in Zumzimzamgazi. At least that's a spark of cheerfulness in this abyss. Yet what did I do to deserve this. When everything was suddenly going so smooth for two seconds. Petrol. Jesus arson. It's fucking her again. I got to change the locks for the third time. And put iron bars for a door on the house. Jesus my last emotional trauma is not fifteen minutes old yet when I got another already to torture me.

'Jorricks it's us.'

'O dear sir. Can I do anything.'

'Play Ave Maria will you. I got to soothe my nerves. And find my shoes they're planted in the snow out there somewhere between here and the kerb.'

The side window shades of his limousine drawn. Schultz with bare feet propped up on the jump seat. The soothing strains of Gounod's Ave Maria. Close my eyes. Not even erotic images are blinding out this latest disaster in my life. With the only thing that I can imagine that's worth imagining, is Louella. And that one and only night. O god the soft pouting magic between her legs. Her cunt tasting like the sweetest nectar. Not since Izzy Goldstein's pineapple soda he made back in his drug store in Woonsocket, have I ever savoured anything as beautiful as that ambrosia. Holy jeeze I swear if I ever get near her again I'm going to give her a sample of teenage premature ejaculation that will knock her over. Even if I have to blow a gasket like Al. She'll get an astonishment she'll never forget. The very first time I ever clapped eyes on her I wanted to clap my wide open mouth straight on her crotch. And once when she wore satin tight moss green slacks over her two long tapering thighs, I was left drooling for days. Jesus I'm abreacting and going sex crazed nuts out of my mind. How am I able to think of such things when my house has just nearly burned down. Procreation must be stronger than cremation if you're not cremated first. Someone's knocking on the door of the crematorium. Holy shit I must have fallen asleep. What the fuck is that.

Schultz bolting awake. The fire brigade officer tapping on the limousine window. Schultz pressing the window switch. The glass gliding down. The fire officer removing his helmet, leaning forward to speak in.

'Sir, it's all right for you to return to your premises. However there are some questions we'll be having to ask, but we can come back later when you've settled in.'

Jorricks pulling up in front of number four Arabesque Street. The limousine parking in the wake of the flattened snowdrifts left by the departed vehicles of the London fire brigade. Jorricks in his black suit and peaked black cap, following his barefooted master up the steps carrying his snow encrusted loafers and red socks and entering the Sigmund Franz Isadore Schultz townhouse. The front door askew on its hinges and with its broken locks and latches.

'Jorricks this is horrible. Unbelievably horrible. Tell the Dorchester Hotel I'm coming over.'

'Very good sir.'

In the hall, Schultz righting an overturned table and picking up the ceramic pieces of the lamp previously resting there. The library door open where I left it locked. Jesus my safe door too is open. The foreign currency gone. All the Hungarian forints, German marks, Swiss francs. My poor money, my poor house. Which jesus has, now that I'm counting again what's left of what I have, has sixteen windows in front instead of the fourteen I thought I had. This is all worse than the scorched smell of dead bodies. Once more remind myself for the umpteenth time, expect the worst and that's what you'll get only it will be much worse. The sooner I escape to a residence of charm and character in the countryside surrounded by a fifty foot high stone wall and a fifty foot deep moat, the better. Here I am with my first ever hit on my hands, a chauffeured limousine I'm not hysterical about affording and I end up walking around London in a snowstorm in my socks, which of all fucking days, I had to pick out a pair to match the fire trucks while my house is burning down. The red carnation in my buttonhole might just as well be sticking out my ass. Today's code name at the Dorchester is going to be changed the moment I get there to being double barrelled. So anyone calling can ask to speak to Mr Attulah Shattered Shambles. My life has got to the point now where the only thing to do is disguise myself as an Arab.

'I'm afraid sir, the Dorchester is fully booked.'

'What. My suite too.'

'Yes sir.'

'Holy shit now even the Dorchester is leaving me destitute.'

'Not to worry sir. I'll air out the bedroom, build a fire and we'll be as right as rain in a jiffy.'

'Jesus Jorricks don't talk about building another fire. Just turn up the thermostat for the central heating.'

'Very good sir. And I can, you know, use the pantry upstairs for a little cooking.'

'You do that. I'm going to see how bad the damage is down there.'

'It's bad sir.'

'Thanks for the warning.'

Barefooted Schultz descending the stairs to the kitchen. Stepping on top of the door smashed flat and floating in the water an inch deep on the floor. Look at this total loss. Up through the ceiling I'm looking into my own sacred library with books I was even planning to read one day. Smoke through the whole house. Not a penny of insurance was I carrying on my personal effects. Why waste money and a fortune in premiums. And a fortune in my chattels promptly get burned up. Hold my nose in this rising stinking steam. Jesus I can't, I got to catch my breath and give my heart a chance to start beating again. Not only every single solitary pair of shoes but every suit, jacket, shirt, tie of mine, fucking burned into charred remnants. This could make you cry. Plus make me have to go barefoot to the shoemaker in St James. Christ I am crying. Every one of my six new silk polka dot bathrobes I bought at the Harrods sale reduced to a couple of polka dots. O god what's this. Pictures of actresses. And my débutante dancing star Margot who signed her picture to me with a welcome suggestive remark as well as with love. And who I always wanted desperately to fuck. And who just moved in across the garden from his Lordship. Jeeze even my casting volumes of Spotlight. Isn't there anything personal of mine that that bitch has left undamaged. Any second don't tell me that in this mess is going to be unearthed the charred edges of my foreign currency. If that's destroyed it is going to break my heart. Only that I know she took it. Two thousand quid of which is the French francs I was going to go to Paris with. I'll be asked questions. Police will arrest her. Could be the answer to all my prayers. Only holy shit. She is the mother of my children. Two innocent sweet little babies with their mother a jailbird. Plus here I am their father. Two gorgeous little twin daughters who could be débutantes one day. Hanging out at Ascot. Marrying the top most acceptable people like his Lordship in the peerage. With a beautiful wedding just like his in Westminster Abbey. O K God. So keep giving me disaster on a platter and pieces of ass on a spoon. I don't give a fuck about anything else so long as I get Louella as dessert. But jesus, if you leave me on this sexually deprived desert any longer I swear I might fall in love with Jorricks first. He's been a godsend in at least keeping away that black cloud of a wife with her voodoo hanging over my life. Nothing I ever did to her could deserve this terrible awful catastrophe she's done to me. And O no. I don't believe it. At times like this you wish to god you were deprived of your eyesight and sense of smell. Right under these bloody charred remains of my first genuine Savile Row suit, only a month old, are both of my gold watches from my father. Given him by his father who got them from his father who made the fucking things up a side street in Prague before people in the rest of the world even knew anything about fancy horologically perfect gold watches that could ring with tiny chimes. Look. My cufflinks. With the big diamonds from Uncle Werb dug out of the centre and gone. Why didn't she just steal the cufflinks whole. How could she stoop so low. Shit she could. Look. My silver letter opener given me by my parents on my high school graduation. Bent like a pretzel. The engraving scorched. For Sigmund.

Wishing him success always as we know will come with every letter he opens. Mom and dad I got a surprise for you. That letter opener just recently opened up the beginning of a big fucking legal action from my wife. She had a household of stuff she could have incinerated of sentimental value. Instead the bitch threw everything of financial worth she could find of mine into the conflagration. To leave me barefoot shivering and cold. Smoked out of house and home. While she, jesus I can't stand the thought of the expense, has an eight room flat in Kensington. Not counting a big fucking front hall you could graze sheep in, plus a kitchen, pantry and four bathrooms with a nannie, a housekeeper and daily help running around them. And she's chiselling diamonds out of my cufflinks I was going to wear to receive the Queen.

Schultz climbing up on a chair. Standing on his bare soaked cold toes to peer and reach into a cupboard and open a board inside. Got to get higher on my one good ankle. Jesus, she's got it. This too. Holy god. Eleven and a half thousand quid sterling tax free. Another nice lesson how to save money by not opening the biggest safety deposit box they got in London. Where I should have installed a mattress and slept in it. What did she do this to me for. I need a second now to gather up my guts after they have been emptied out in my arms by an Arab scimitar swipe. There could be strychnine now put in everything. Like there was rat poison last time she broke into this house. Hey jesus what's this stuff hidden up here in the secret cupboard I'm sniffing. It's fucking kerosene oil.

'Holy living crucified shit.'

Schultz slipping on the chair his nose stuck in the vessel of oil and loosing his one footed balance backwards, clutching the container as he falls splashing ass first in the water. Sending waves lapping across the floor. Now I need a row boat. While I'm soaked in kerosene oil which I've just now fucking dumped all over me and she must have dumped to start the fire. Just so she could make sure no trace was left of stealing my money. My present Harris tweed jacket and my flannel trousers could explode now in flames like a torch. The only clothes in the world I got left to wear. I may not have seen much action in the Coast Guard but this is fucking battle stations. After for christ's sake, the ship has fucking sunk. And she's like a circling shark in the water. Waiting to strike to take off my legs after she has made an appetizer out of nipping off my cock and balls. But she better remember one fucking thing though. I made what I made out of my fucking sweated blood. And with my sweat and blood I'll keep every penny of what I've got left. And I'll fight to the fucking end. Through thick, through thin, and through paraffin. But jesus, this is getting to be a full day. Which has already taken the permanent wave permanently out of my pubic hair.

And is
Driving me straight
To Jerusalem
To the
Wailing wall
Wet assed
And all

5 'Ah, good morning Schultz, and what brings you yet once more, early dawn to the offices of our rapidly expanding theatrical empire. But of course, you've rushed in to sign what appear to be top priority contracts just arrived by messenger. Rebecca here and I were just at this very moment discussing a little gossip column item about you in today's early edition of the evening newspaper. With a picture of your town-house no less. Dare one imagine there could have been a fire in such an attractively elegant abode.'

'Yeah Binky. A fire. But that's nothing compared to what I've been reading about you. And about which I want a retraction printed in no unminced fucking words.'

'You'd better hold my calls Rebecca. Seems our most favourite fellow director of Sperm Productions is about to call one of his extraordinary general fucking meetings. And Rebecca, I do think we may require a little coffee and chocolate doughnuts for elevenses.'

'Milk or cream Mr Schultz.'

'Just bloody plain black for me.'

'Ah but Schultz dear me aren't you going to put down your armful of parcels. Upon which I do declare that I see royal warrants emblazoned. And from the best of London's haberdasher's. And upon my word, what on earth have you got on. By my perceptions it appears as if you are in an old pervert's mackintosh. And a pair of, yes, the more usual blue green striped pyjamas very much favoured by the more prurient of such desperate gentlemen when making their visits to the remoter located gents' conveniences in our better London parks.'

'Just tell me when you're finished with your usual shit Binky.'

'And, good gracious me, slippers, too. Do we owe all this to, O no. Not to your fire I hope. A débâcle about which I understand you had our publicity agent busy an entire evening acquainting every paper in Fleet Street.'

'You have your fucking nerve. Talking about publicity.'

'Well of course we do from time to time get a little notice here and there. To which I must confess we're not entirely opposed. But speaking of publicity, Al's picture was in the paper this morning without his toupee. Tell me what fresh news is there of our dear friend. We tried to visit and had sent over some exotics in both fruit and flowers for the poor dear old chap. Last information was that he was hourly sinking and not expected to remain long with us. We volunteered our help in the matter to his little lady. Indeed she seemed already bereaved. And I do hope Schultz you don't intend appearing like that at the funeral.'

'When it's official I'll be wearing plenty. And don't worry he hasn't sunk out of sight yet.'

'Schultz you do speak as if you wished he might do just that. Surely you haven't forgotten that noble man got you most if not all of your investment money. While at the same time gaining you entrée to London's more rarefied celebrity circles. And you know Schultz, the picture is becoming quite clear. What in fact have you yourself actually invested and risked in cash in our little smash hit.'

'I put my whole life in that fucking production never mind money. That's why you're going to print a fucking retraction that you're the producer. Or I go see my fucking lawyers about it. And let me tell you something else. You Binky are going to sink one of these days. And out of sight.'

'Ah the coffee thank god has come. Dear Rebecca, thank you. Our fellow director Izzy here at this ungodly hour of the morning, is not only just about to cast curses upon me but is threatening to sue me. Surely Schultz you don't mind my calling you Izzy short for Isadore.'

'You call me what you want. I want a retraction.'

'As you will notice Schultz we have doughnuts with the nice big holes. Especially for you and your lawyers to indulge your proclivities. Now dear me. Pray speak sir. Do tell me. How shall I sink out of sight. Could be a most preferred condition I assure you. I'm always doing it in the deepest chair in the furthest corner of my club. By the way must propose you as a member Schultz.'

'Shit if the place is full of guys like you why should I want to join.'

'Ah but for you to keep ready track of your publicity, all the papers are there. No wives. Just other similar gents taking their peace and solitude. Club servants ever watchful to one's little needs and comforts. Why we have chaps who take up their vigils eleven in the morning till eleven at night. Chaps sit in the same chair, read the same papers. Grunt the same grunts. Take a pee every two hours. Wash their hands every three. Of course you Schultz couldn't appear like that bare of ankle in your slippers. Nice comfortable looking slippers by the way. And I say Rebecca. Do we have a blanket Mr Schultz might wear if he prefers to remove his mackintosh.'

'Yes in fact we have several.'

'Don't bother. My raincoat's fine. OK Binky I ain't got time to waste, what's this further shit about this all time biggest musical.'

'Ah I thought you'd never ask. Do Schultz have another third doughnut. Although you've actually had four. But who's counting. And yes Schultz, you read right. Nice little item I thought wasn't it. Pretty little girl she was. Smart and sharp, wasn't she, Rebecca. With the sort of nice well bred bosoms of the sort you would have liked Schultz and of the distinct sort that we favour to cast in our shows. Indeed the lady in question is in fact from a well bred family in Suffolk. Good old county that. O dear but we are, in your Americanly democratic company Schultz, talking much too much about good breeding. In short, the lady journalist was a perky little creature. Suggested I come shooting on her family's estate. Ah how nice I thought. Bang bang. One does love that cacophony of the shotguns. Nice rhythmn don't you think Schultz. Bang bang bang.'

'You're going to bang bang bang Binky let me tell you. Only meanwhile I got plenty more important to attend to.'

'Ah but Schultz you haven't yet heard all. She also invited his Royal Grace, our dear Lord Nectarine, who is arguably the greatest shot in these islands.'

'Yeah so I heard. So he's going to go bang bang too.'

'Yes Schultz, bang bang. But you haven't heard about the fishing our little lady has as well, on another little stretch of land and river her nice family has on the Spey in Scotland.'

'Come on, what's suddenly this big musical. God damn it what the fuck is it you and his Lordship are trying to pull behind my back this time.'

'Dear me Schultz. Temper. Raised voice. Surely not on such a pleasantly sunny snow thawing day such as this. Do drink your coffee and do try another one of the holes in those nice doughnuts there. Now as to the little slip of the lady reporter's pen. Making poor little me, sole producer. Ah I knew you'd be mightily aggrieved by that. She of course made such assumption with so many autographed photographs of so many of our international stars on the walls here. But do please remember Schultz before hysterically imploring your lawyers to sue me that I am I believe a not insubstantial owner of the show.'

'Nobody is going to steal my fucking credit, Binky.'

'Credit. Dear boy, I think you better consult certain words in our little contract according to which not only am I accurately termed one of the show's producers but indeed could sue you for printing my name too small. Not to mention other contributory matters however minor, of your wheedling your way into these little offices of ours, besieging us for investment, using our good will, our mailing lists, making countless long distance telephone calls, reading all our daily newspapers, trade journals, using our secretaries, notepaper, arse paper, electricity, stamps and dare I say it, even our staff luncheon vouchers.'

'Hey shit let me see the billing clause in that contract. Rebecca is that in it.'

'Yes Mr Schultz.'

'Hey someone must have changed the wording. I never signed anything even remotely like that. And if my fucking cheque book didn't get burned up in my fire I'd give you a god damn cheque right now Binky for every god damn penny you have dreamed up I owe you.'

'Ah very kind. Thoughtful, not to even say generous of you. Let's see. But dream. Nay Schultz. No dream. I do think we even have it written down right here. In the drawer. Indeed here we are. Yes. In the usual nicely distinct colours of black and white. Ten thousand eight hundred and twenty six pounds fourteen shillings. But let us make it a more forgiving rounder figure. Of ten thousand.'

'Ten thousand. What. Are you kidding.'

'Sit down Schultz, not only are your pyjamas but your privates are visible.'

'I never used one fucking fraction of ten thousand or anything like it. I called Tokyo and Peru a couple of times, that's all.'

'His Lordship did the figures Schultz. And you know what a stickler he is on fractions of anything. We included of course your shoes. And that's why I am especially surprised to see you shuffling about in your slippers. And glad you mentioned Tokyo. And indeed even Peru. I think his Lordship may have overlooked those calls entirely. What do you say to a couple of hundred quid being fair to add to our little debt. We can then jump up to an even rounder figure with a nice extra nought on the end of eleven thousand.'

'You add what the fuck you like. And make it as round as you need to shove it up your ass. I'm paying nothing to nobody. And that's final. But I'm a director of this company and you just tell me now, what's all this further fucking bullshit you're bandying around about this most expensive star studded lavish musical ever.'

'Ah yes. O dear Schultz you truly are a dilemma. And I'm glad we've got to that little matter of our future plans. O dear. Eleven thousand is quite a lot. But ho hum, I suppose in the light of our new production, it's peanuts. Of course one hesitates to use words like the biggest, the most expensive, the most lavish musical in the history of the British theatre. Far from our original intention. However I believe it is.'

'You're cutting me in for a piece.'

'Is that a demand Schultz or do I perceive a hint of request.'

'It's a fucking demand. To know what the fuck goes on here behind my back.'

'Dear me Schultz the options to invest were snapped up before one had a chance to say cock robin. Cock robin. Notice how quickly one can say that. Mind you I haven't yet looked, but knowing how Lord Nectarine is most meticulous, you may even find if you refer to our agreements Schultz, that we have no need to include you at all.'

'You're fucking well doing this to spite me Binky aren't you. Excluding me. Behind my back. You can't stand it that I've got a hit can you and that your name isn't up top there alone on top of mine in neon lights.'

'Yes. Quite true Schultz, quite true. I can't stand it. Positively painful it is. Seeing Sigmund Franz Schultz plastered in large letters everywhere all over London. Even I understand, in the underground tube stations, although I haven't been down there recently to look for myself. But you see, aside from my personal aggrievement, truth of the matter is, that every option to invest has been seized, and to all practical intents and purposes we are fully capitalized. I may say too that I did tell many of our hopefully intending investors holding options that shares were scarce. Ah but just let me take a little peek here on my desk. Ah yes. The final share to the show has just been taken up by, ah, yes, a Mr Joe Jewels investing out of New York. That last expression, out of New York, put as you might put it Schultz.'

'I don't believe one single word of any of this. Why the fuck would Joe Jewels to whom it so happens I was recently speaking in New York, want to invest in a show nobody knows nothing about, except that it's going to cost and could lose fucking more money than anything else in history.'

'Ah but we shall be glad to, in just a moment give further and better particulars upon that point. But first there is, as yet, one other tiny little insignificant item to attend to. Our Lordship and I have struck off this little salary you pay out of our little show's running expenses, and listed under Miscellaneous. A certain Mr Jorricks.'

'You what. Struck it off.'

'Yes Schultz, struck it off.'

'What the fuck for.'

'May I at this little juncture, Schultz, make an observation. You were you know, in your previous flop orientated innocence much more fun to be with. Now it is all greed, profit, and publicity and getting your credit in the billing.'

'I don't believe what I'm hearing.'

'Ah my dear Schultz, but to get back to that mysterious weekly wage debited to the production. Although we have heard it from the most unreliable of sources, it is alleged that your Mr Jorricks, who it appears personally ministrates to you, is in fact a raving out of control homosexualist well known to frequent in some of the seamier haunts of Soho's night life. And we wonder why he is on our payroll.'

'You fucking guys. What am I your public punching bag. You're not going to get away with another one of your schemes to try to create humour for yourselves out of my private god damn life and slander one of the most gorgeous behaved human beings, who wouldn't even show the disrespect of sneezing in front of his own dead grandmother's portrait, and is the fucking nearest thing to being a saint. So this is going to be a knockdown fucking battle is it Binky.'

'Nae dear fellow. Nae. Not unless you make it so. Join us for lunch Schultz, only a few old lobster claws and a spot of simple chablis but of a rather special culinary calibre which Mario has devised. You see, you must not take these matters we attempt to conscientiously administrate in this office, quite so seriously. In the light of your Jorricks not deigning even to sneeze in front of his grandmother's portrait I retract entirely my previous rumoured aspersion. But naturally we should desire for you to pay up the eleven thousand quid you owe us, in round figures of course.'

'Jesus, I couldn't even brush my teeth this morning because all the toothpaste and my toothbrushes got thrown in the fire. And I come in here to listen to all this.'

'But all money aside my dear Schultz, and as to private and personal matters, how could one ever dare cast, and dear me one is having again to use this word, an aspersion upon your manhood. With so many ladies either running into or out of your clutches all over London. And far be it for me, to cast stones, slung by condom sling shot, as we were fond of doing at school, at other homosexualists. For you see Schultz, I, in the innocence of one's pre puberty, did partake in the sweet idyllic little blissful dalliances of the homosexualist. Of course I was but a mere mite then, however, as I was accused of being the most beautiful boy in the school I naturally fell in love with the other most beautiful boy. We were positively obsessively devoted to one another. When if we didn't wank alone then we did with other beautiful boys all wank wank wank together. O yes there were occasional ugly boys too. Very democratic. Who were encouraged to take up a chorus to the tune accompanying us. Which was by the way, the school boating song. Indeed it's been traditional for the chaps to so sing when they were so pulling Schultz. Ah but let us Schultz get back to your toothpaste and house, the former of which was cremated and the latter nearly conflagrated. Here have one of our toothpicks. Perhaps this is why you seem so duly distressed.'

'Jesus everything Binky is the same joke to you. You don't even have one fucking principle do you.'

'Well if it may be loosely regarded as a principle of course one's school has given one a certain self sufficiency for which you Americans substitute your brashness.'

'Oh yeah. Well if you want to really know, Jorricks is my official assistant. And acts as my talent and casting scout.'

'Ah then that little matter is at last cleared up. We'll put down production assistant and casting scout. Soon as I clear it with his Royal Grace we shall reinstate this little salary. You know Schultz just to mention something a little more cheerfully different. I couldn't help noticing from the picture of your house in the paper which we understand you have bought from your landlord that you and I, fellow company directors of the same company have something else in common. Each of us has sixteen windows with five floors above the basement in our respective townhouses. Now is that not one jolly coincidence, don't you think. Atop my third fourth and fifth floor I have pink window drapes. What colour do you have.'

'They are all fucking soot stained from the fire.'

'O dear I was going to suggest it would be nice if we all matched. Set an example. You see Schultz the proletariat world at large does not give any thought to the more dispiriting aspects of the affluent upper class way of life, how in the isolation of our comfortable riches we suffer to feel that the common man is only out to use us if he can. When we ourselves maintain our compassion for others less blessed. I mean damn it. That's why so many of us spend so much time in the sad isolation of our clubs.'

'Come on cut the shit Binky. I got to change my clothes. And it so happens I got a big colour supplement interview coming up. Where for a change my two fucking cents of the truth is going to be blasted all over newspaper pages.'

'Dear me. How nice for you Schultz. Please mention, if not me, at least his Royal Grace.'

68

'You bet your ass I will. He's the only one I trust. And so now what's this shit of the final share being taken up by Joe Jewels in a fucking myth of a production.'

'Myth Schultz. Nae. No myth.'

'Yeah. Well then who wrote the book, who's doing the lyrics and choreography, who's starring. Jewels wouldn't put a penny in something nobody knows nothing about and doesn't look like a potential hit.'

'Indeed Schultz there's quite a lot to know about our new little show. Ah and on our little calendar here. Yes rehearsals start in just two months and fourteen days. And our little agreements for our stars are duly signed. Our director, designer. And our composer and choreographer.'

'Well who the fuck are they.'

'Dear me Schultz I think you may be surprised.'

'Yeah well I got a surprise for you.'

'I think it's time for a spot of sherry. Rebecca have Mario attend upon us. It might do to have something to steady our nerves. As dear me, Schultz and I seem both poised on the brink of our surprises. You do please go first Schultz with yours.'

'You bet I will. In these contracts right there I sold the show in an agreed deal to Jewels in New York for one hundred and fifty five thousand and three full fucking percent of the gross.'

'You what Schultz.'

'You heard me. And he was gasping for mercy.'

'Well you do I must confess surprise me Schultz. Especially as I have a cable here in front of me not more than a few hours old from Goliath and Goliath Productions of New York, offering one hundred and ninety thousand and four full fucking percent of the gross.'

'What. Let me see that cable.'

'And well you might say what. You silly little twit Schultz. That dear old cobra Joe Jewels has snapped his fangs upon you and brilliantly taken you to the cleaners.'

'Holy shit I don't believe what's happening.'

'Well then I think you ought to get ready Schultz to believe my small surprise. Regarding our little extravaganza. Provisionally entitled Ecstasy in Extremis for the Leisure Classes. Little optimistic as a title perhaps. But will attract a general public. And did you know Schultz that our now famed Terence Magillacurdy can actually play the piano with his toes while singing an aria. He's to be our star. Teamed up with our talented débutante who's being billed under her new name of

Virgin Virginia. Both thespians at double their present salaries of course. Good god Schultz you've gone absolutely puce in the face. Well I better tell you the rest quickly before you turn blue. And faint. Or worse have a heart attack like Al.'

'I don't believe this.'

'The director Schultz is the director you fired. The one whom Magillacurdy threw off the stage into the third row of the stalls. We thought that taught him his lesson. Of course we have retained Kiss It Don't Hold It It's Too Hot's brilliant designer and last but certainly not least, we have just duly signed up that husband and wife composer and choreographer team Herbie and Sylvia both of whom I believe you anally cohabited with at the Dorchester. O dear you have gone blue Schultz. And do forgive the implications of my language Rebecca, required I fear while Izzy and I are being forthright in giving each other surprises. Ah Mario just in time with the sherry, pour some for our esteemed company director here. He's breathing rather heavily.'

'I should be glad to Mr Sunningdale, this fino is dry, fresh and young, with an especially delightful finesse.'

'Ah, exactly as Mr Schultz prefers his ladies.'

'Boy let me tell you, I'll have a sherry. But I'm going straight to my lawyers. You're out not only to destroy my show but me. You've been plotting this behind my back. For months.'

'Dear me Schultz, don't be paranoid. I signed up all of these talented people who I thought were about to trip on their faces in your biggest flop ever. And I did so as an act of charity and as a genuine theatre lover to save such thespians from an acute unhappiness which at the time, appeared about to dawn on them.'

'You're never in a million years going to get away with this. Never. That's gospel by Schultz. And I'm getting the fuck out of here.'

'Wait wait, there's more Schultz. Rebecca bring in to Mr Schultz the poster design.'

'Jesus if I stay around here any longer my life could soon be getting like my parents who had to hold a closing down sale nearly every month. Well let me tell you. I'm not closing down. And boy, so help me god Binky this is one thing you're not going to get away with. I got binding contracts with Magillacurdy and the débutante.'

'Of course you have Schultz for six months and which expire in two months and fourteen days.'

'Right in five seconds after I put on this new pair of pants I just bought and have a piss, I'm calling up first my lawyers and next the biggest estate agents in town and I'm going to move the fuck right out of here.'

'Trousers is the expression we use in England Schultz. Pants are for ladies. But Schultz, we should so hate to see you go. I do really mean it, all joking aside. Rebecca please. Tell Mr Schultz how we should miss him were he to leave us.'

'We would be very sad, Mr Schultz.'

The sun warmly in through the windows. Sound of a pigeon cooing on the sill. Drips of thawing snow outside splattering. Binky Sunningdale raising his glass of sherry to the light. Schultz turning to Rebecca.

'Rebecca I believe you. But I don't believe him. Out of him I'm going to sue the living fucking shit.'

'Ah here I am distrusted once again. How does one make oneself convincing that I have no evil intent. Have a spot more sherry. And dear me Schultz the loneliness would be distressing after you were gone. No one tearing their hair out. Slamming down and breaking phones. No screams and shouts. No long distance calls to Antarctica concerning Eskimo touring rights. I mean how little we have here anyway to occupy our minds except counting the presently bountiful box office money.'

'You're going to be counting writs Binky from now on. Believe me. And the fucking world is going to know that nobody but nobody chisels Sigmund Franz Isadore Schultz and gets away with it.'

'Don't Schultz trip over the carpet.'

Rebecca handing over the mid day mail to Binky as Schultz on his feet, parcels cradled in his arm heads towards the open door, and swings it shut with a slam. His slippered feet pounding away down the hall. Distant phones ringing. Another door slamming. And suddenly an agonized loud scream. Binky and Rebecca rushing out into the hall. And a cry coming out through the door of the water closet.

'My god Rebecca what's this now reverberating through our little firm of Sperm Productions. It does sound awfully like our esteemed fellow director Izzy Schultz is screaming in the chairman's crapper.'

'You bet your fucking ass it's me in here.'

'Good lord Rebecca and it sounds as if he may have fallen down the toilet bowl. And is being sucked away by the flush. Dear me even echoes are coming back from the buildings across the street.'

'It's coming from out of in here you fucker.'

'O my dear, he does still go on screaming. Do get the first aid kit. Here we go again.'

Rebecca running down the hall. Past three secretaries wide eyed in the reception room doorway. Binky pressing his ear to the lavatory door.

'Is that really you Schultz in there, screaming. In this highly feminine manner.'

'It's fucking well me Binky. I'm in agony, I can't move.'

'Dear me. You mean your bowels are stuck.'

'I don't mean my fucking bowels are stuck.'

'What then on earth may I enquire is the difficulty.'

'My balls are stuck. Caught in the fucking zipper of my fly. Of these god damn fucking new pants I just bought in Jermyn Street. I'll sue the fuckers who made a zip like this like a guillotine. I can't get my balls free. The skin's caught. Every time I move a fraction of an inch the pain is killing me.'

'Stand your ground my dear man. Be brave. Hold tight to your testicles. We are to the rescue. I did think by your screaming you were conferring with your lawyers in there.'

'Come on Binky. I'm in agony.'

'The door my dear chap. Get away from the door. So we may open it. And view the little problem.'

'I told you already I can't move.'

'The door Schultz opens inwards.'

'I know it opens inwards.'

'Well you must then get back out of the way. Or else we shall have to pull it down. I say Rebecca. This is a bit of devilment isn't it. You don't suppose our Schultz is in there presuming upon our sympathies and having a joke upon us.'

'You fucking bastard Binky I hear you out there. I got to have relief you fucker. These are my jewels, there's blood dripping already with the fucking zip caught in them.'

'Rebecca do summon the stage carpenters from the theatre. Don't tell them it's old Schultzy boy who's got his testicles in a mangle as that might delay them rejoicing and also mean they may not come.'

'They better come. And hey jesus meanwhile I got to wait in here in pain and agony.'

'Be British Schultz. Stop whining in there.'

'I could lose my fucking balls.'

'Dear me, Schultz you mustn't worry so. With organ transplanting these days, chaps will knit a new pair on you in what, as his Lordship might say, is commonly known as a jiffy. They of course may not jangle and ring with the pure tone of your originals but should be entirely serviceable. Who knows they might have a spare pair in the organ bank discarded by a member of the peerage. Imagine a pair soon of lordly balls. And what they might do for your love life. Not to mention your social status. And dear me also imagine we could end up having to refer to you as Lord Schultz. Bang bang and your wife could have little honourables. Indeed you could go bang bang bang all over the ruddy place, as lords are rarely denied indulging their appetites.'

'O boy have I got a lot to get even with you for. Jesus added up it goes to the skies. Get Rebecca to ring my lawyer and get him over here as a witness. These tailor sons of bitches who did this to me are not going to get away with this, whoever invented fucking zippers in the first place.'

'Surely Schultz it's you who have zippered your own balls up. One is beginning to think that you may yet soon catch your inflated prick in a tiny paper clip. Ah but you can at least depend upon me to witness this mischief for you. Amazing to say this office has just made a purchase of the most marvellous video camera.'

'Like shit am I going to let you witness anything or take moving pictures of my fucking private parts.'

'Have it your own way Schultz but we could show all in full action replay. Our assistant stage carpenter, who should be here any second, ripping the door out. Then with our wide angled lens zooming in to the testicles for an appropriate close up shot of the zipper locked securely upon your gonads. Even have an appropriate sound track of your agonized screams. Very effective in court. And wonderful head-lines Schultz. In the first edition evening paper. Zipper Zaps Balls of the Producer of Kiss It Don't Hold It It's Too Hot. Or should the show be renamed, Kiss It Don't Zipper It, It's Too Painful. You know we did have a boy at school who was trying to fuck a milk bottle. Like you he got stuck. Poor little chap had to be removed to hospital to get it off him.'

'This is no joke Binky in here. I'm serious. I'll sue this fucking office for this door opening the wrong way and will wipe that laugh out of your throat. There's blood. O god this is terrible in here.'

'Ah and we're not joking Schultz. In fact we're reorganizing our office. We're coming to grips in the recognition that certain situations and company structure require a clarity of decision making in order to accomplish objectives. And especially to avoid such things as selling to the lowest bidder. And meanwhile I'm afraid bad news Schultz, your lawyer's already in court for the day. Shall we call for an ambulance.'

'No I need Jorricks. Get Jorricks.'

'Ah Schultz of course. We should have thought of that. Just the chap to lovingly and gently bandage up your balls for you. We'll tell him to bring plenty of celluloid tape. But hold on now our number one assistant carpenter is here. Ran all the way from the theatre. Good job he was on the job.'

His fingertips pressed in prayer Binky surveying the carpenter laying out his tools on the floor. Taking a saw serrated at the end and beginning to saw through the door along the door frame of the water closet. Schultz hanging on to the edge of the sink. Blood on the fingertips. O my god Rabbi save me. Save my testicles I beseech you. Jesus and they get a carpenter who would have to be the most smart alec little son of a bitch to saw down the door.

'Mr Schultz if you can just move an inch further back I can saw out a hole so we can reach you.'

'Hurry. Hurry. I'm contorted bent over in agony in here.'

The front entrance hall of Sperm Productions now crowded with secretaries, assistants and the day's supply of ventriloquists, singers, actresses, magicians and musicologists and the usual plethora of female theatrical hopefuls several of whom were accompanied by their mothers. His Lordship entering, shotgun cases in either hand and stopping at his own adjacent office door.

'Dear me, what's going on Binky.'

'Ah Lord Nectarine. How nice to see you. Yes a spot of bother I'm afraid. In there in the water closet has occurred a little difficulty. I fear the door shall have to be pulled out. Hope it won't inconvenience you.'

'Seems a perfectly good door Binky why doesn't someone simply open it.'

'Ah good question your Royal Grace. But the fact of the matter is, old Schultzy boy poor chap, is inside there and has irretrievably caught up his balls in a zipper and can't pee, shit or apparently move.'

'And, you bastards out there. I'm going fucking blind from the pain.'

Lord Nectarine, wearing two ties, one knotted on top of another, dropping both shotgun cases and grabbing his hands to his stomach as he slowly sinks to the floor on his knees. An eruption of laughter from his lips, and gasping out words between guffaws.

'Oh my god, O my god, Schultz you do, you do really, take the fucking cake.'

We really must
Must
Find a
Zoo
For you

6

The cut out centre of the sawn grey panelled water closet door falling out into the front main hall of Sperm Productions. A gathering of show biz hopefuls clustering around. Binky peering in at Schultz in his green striped pyjama top, bare arsed bent over double. One supporting bloody hand clutched on the wash basin and the other propped back on the lavatory seat. Binky leaning further in over the bulkhead.

'O my god Schultz. It does appear you really are in a dilemma. A doctor and an ambulance should be here any second. Indeed I hear a gong in the street. That may be them already.'

'O jesus they got to get to me before I'm dead from suffering.'

'They will, they will my dear chap. If you can but be British about it and sustain for another few moments. And my word what attractive looking trousers.'

Two white coated ambulance men arriving puffing up the stairs, a stretcher in tow. A young doctor following. Several frightened mothers and their starlet daughters squeezing in a crunch to rapidly exit out the door as someone in the crowded reception room said a murder had been committed and the corpse was being removed.

The ambulance men and the doctor making a bee line for his contorted Lordship still on the floor half way in and half out of his office door. Still holding his stomach, both shotgun cases clutched between his knees. The medical men struggling to unravel him as more guffaws emitted from the lordly lips, being that his Royal Grace was ticklish in the extreme. Binky turning around from the water closet to the new higher pitch of laughter.

'Dear me no, my good chaps. Not him. That's our dear old Lord Nectarine. This way. In there. Him.'

Jorricks's raincoat blanketing Schultz in his new tight tapered trousers, contorted knees up on the stretcher, being lugged out the hall. Rebecca alongside carrying his remaining parcels. A still convulsed Lord Nectarine now in his office draped across the top of his desk clutching his stomach. Binky filming with his video camera. Schultz groaning, a blood drenched hand held up over his eyes as the ambulance men manoeuvred him slowly down around the narrow four flights of stairs. Binky descending in the lift and waiting on the pavement, stationing himself with the little crowd gathered on the street to watch this anonymous celebrity be carried towards the blue light flashing on the ambulance and its back doors waiting open.

'Come on Schultz don't be a meanie, before they take you away, smile once for the camera.'

76

'Don't think I'll forget this, Binky.'

'Dear me Schultz it's why I'm going to all this trouble to make this superbly directed film of you that we may watch again and again.'

Binky waving a fingertip goodbye to Schultz disappearing head first into this vehicle of mercy. The doors shutting and klaxon blaring as it turns the corner and speeds away. Rumbling over the melting bumps of ice. Oxygen tanks and blankets. Jeeze maybe it's not compassion but at least this doctor seems to have a smile of encouraging sympathy on his face. Fucking Binky and his Lordship couldn't control their joy. And just like Al they're taking me away. Only that bastard probably had his old withered balls still on. O my god recently I come out of a conflagration and now I promptly enter straight into utter humiliation. Lesson thirteen in my life. Never pull a zipper in anger. What the fuck is happening to my existence to reduce it to such a shambles. That money should now be overflowing out of my pockets and this gets to happen to me. When living on my wits having no money did nothing to me anywhere near as bad. Except I committed suicide getting married. Binky is out to ruin me and the show. I'll murder the cunt if he thinks he's going to hire away talent that I found and nurtured and made into fêted West End stars. He better remember I fucking well found Magillacurdy sleeping in a graveyard when he had only the urn on the next grave to piss in. I can't believe it. Joe Jewels that cobra. Swallowed me like a god damn innocent mouse. Maybe success has blinded me to man's inhumanity to man. Could have got another one percent out of him plus another forty five thousand. Holy shit, given their chance every human being in the world will pull a fast one and then turn against you. It makes you fucking wonder how you can survive to grow up even to be only twelve years old when I first got desperate to get laid, and all I could do was to go on pulling it, not realizing you could shove it somewhere softer than your hand. But this battle is not over yet. And the winners are going to be different let me tell you in no shit terms. And one winner is known by the middle names of Franz Isadore. And that's fucking gospel by Schultz.

The ambulance arriving at the curved entrance under the portico, of Celestial Pavilion Hospital. The attendants lifting out the stretcher to put it on a trolley and wheeling it into Casualty. Amid the disinfecting smells, moans and groans. O my god back in this place again who would believe it. This is how a trolley ride could start to the crematorium as it's already done for Al. Christ even going down the same hall. Christ it must be bad. They're taking me straight to an operating room. At least this looks like a nice dark complexioned

Indian doc. Ought to ask him if he can find me an Indian wife who might not ever love me but if I feed, clothe and give her a place to sleep at least she might work, screw, keep her mouth shut and obey. And failing that I think the time has come I got to urgent find a psychiatrist who can cure me of fucking.

'Will you sign this sir.'

'Jesus what is it.'

'We are giving you an anaesthetic sir to operate. Now if you'll just let us put this over your mouth and count to ten sir.'

'Jesus no.'

'It will only be a little gas sir. I'm afraid you have caught a considerable amount of flesh in the zip. And in such a sensitive area it could be quite painful.'

'I'm not going to be unconscious if it's the last thing I do.'

'Believe me Mr Schultz it's going to be much better that way. We have to make a cut.'

'Holy jeeze a cut.'

'Yes. To incise the skin free.'

'Can't you tear the zipper apart and release me to freedom.'

'I'm afraid Mr Schultz it would also tear your scrotum.'

'This is a choice like do you want to die by guillotine or hanging.'

'I'm afraid so Mr Schultz.'

'O K hang me.'

Sound of washing. Rubber gloves snapping on. A figure entering the room. A voice vaguely familiar. Or in this terrible panic am I losing my mind. And Jorricks was meeting me with the car and will wonder where the fuck I am. The word incise could also mean in any decent dictionary, cleave, split or gash. These lights are blinding. Christ almighty. Who's this looking at me now. It can't be. But shit and shinola it is. The Matron.

'Good heavens not you again.'

'It's me Matron.'

'And to what do we owe this little surprise.'

'Oh jesus Matron do I have to say it in so many words.'

'Not if you don't want to. Mr Kahn will supply details when he is finished scrubbing up.'

'They're going to give me gas.'

'Ah Mr Kahn what's our little trouble here.'

'Well Matron I'm afraid the patient has rather unfortunately caught part of his lower region in a zipper.'

'Oh dear let me see.'

'Jesus Matron this is embarrassing.'

'You mustn't be embarrassed, it isn't as if yours are the first testicles I've ever seen. And it is isn't it, the Mr Schultz, the impresario. That one has the honour of speaking to.'

'Jesus Matron don't call me names. Maybe you should be dealing with Mr Duke.'

Schultz lifting up a hand over his eyes. Gentle fingers touching and lifting aside an uninjured part. What's happening to me now never in a thousand years could I ever believe would be true. Matron's voice is sending a shiver of lust from one end of me to the other. I may have lost a lot of blood but jesus I can feel the arteries going like trip hammers engorging with every ounce of the blood I got left. Giving me the last thing I want which is now the most embarrassing massive hard on of my entire life. Holy cow how can I stop the fucking thing springing up and hitting her in the face. Hey come on doc. Let's not wait. Give me gas. Or give me death. Before I die of embarrassment.

'Well doctor I do think Mr Schultz is already showing incontro-vertible signs of a rapid recovery. Ah and by the way Mr Schultz, our Mr Duke is sadly no longer with us.'

'O jesus, when did he die. I missed that.'

'He was flown to Los Angeles.'

'O christ I knew it. Just so his old friends couldn't be at the crem-atorium. Poor guy couldn't resist, he had to have his funeral in the celebrity limelight at that fancy crypt of his in front of all those Hollywood creeps in that big mausoleum they got out there. Sorry Matron, you wouldn't understand, I'm just talking to myself.'

'Mr Duke is not dead Mr Schultz.'

'What. You mean he's living.'

'Yes perhaps not quite as vigorously as you appear to be, but in fact from the brink of death, his condition improved sufficiently for him to be flown out to be operated on in California.'

'You mean he could get cured healthy again.'

'It's entirely possible. Mr Duke has a remarkable fighting spirit. Might one assume this to come from the world of show business Mr Schultz.'

'You bet it does. Or you ain't in that world long.'

'Mention of your description to him seemed to suddenly stir him back into life. Although I can't say that he was pleased to hear of your visit.'

'Holy shit. Excuse the language Matron.'

'Of course. We occasionally hear such four letter word used in this hospital, but not usually preceded by the word holy. And now may we get back to our rather present difficulty which I see, is an extremely awkward matter indeed. And how on earth could you have done this Mr Schultz. What do you propose to do Mr Kahn.'

'Make an incision in the scrotum wall either side along the zipper which has caused severe abrasion to the dartos and external spermatic fascia. And thus with a cut, remove the undamaged skin from the zipper. There appears no penetration to the testicle spheres. There's slight oedema. And suture.'

'I've got a few moments Mr Kahn perhaps you wouldn't mind if I observed.'

'I'd be most grateful and honoured Matron if you would.'

'Holy jeeze I'm losing skin. And if suture means god damn sewing is there any risk to my balls with needles sticking in them.'

'Not to worry Mr Schultz. We're referring to a cut in a thin layer of the loose reddish tissue here which is amply endowed with contractility and which is of a very elastic and stretchable nature. And you can afford to lose some. In fact very much more than one could lose in a face lift which would resemble this operation. Please don't be alarmed.'

'Hey Matron pardon my conversation but christ you're not going to face lift my testicles, my whole life is located down there.'

'Mr Kahn I think you might be better able to discuss this with Mr Schultz.'

'Yes Matron. Now Mr Schultz. Many of us are in the same position with our organs of regeneration. And I assure you that I will treat yours with the same respect as I would treat my own. Indeed a little tightening up will do no harm at all except for the testes being slightly more snug and hanging a little higher. Just as one might pull one's socks up so to speak as they say in England.'

'As Matron of this hospital, Mr Schultz I also assure you Mr Kahn is one of our very best suturers. Now put your head back. We put this mask over your face and you just count to ten. Who knows if you do as you're told I might even have that previously suggested glass of champagne with you.'

'OK Matron. It's a deal. I obey.'

An anaesthetist placing the mask over Schultz's nose and mouth as he counts. One. Two. Three. Four. Five. Holy jesus five again. Another deal I got. This time for a glass of champagne. Which I'm going to really need after I get over all this painful shit. Plus my cock also badly needs a sympathetic sucking. While I'm listening to Ave Maria. And

80

there ain't a single mouth left in the world I can find to either sing or suck. Al Duke on the third day rose again from the dead. And ascended to Hollywood while I'm twenty four hours later nearly where he was with the privacy of my privates invaded. And everyone looking at my testicles. Some grinning. Fuck it. Ignominy is becoming second nature to me. And the Matron's face more alluring every second. Or maybe I'm just unbelievably hard up. Holy shit is she holding a big scissors. That looks like a fucking garden shears. Hey christ my brand new grey flannel pants they're fucking cutting holes in. While I go out like a light they could miss the zipper and go snip off not only my prick but both my balls. After that who needs to wake up. My gonads could then go transplant in some duke. Add my prick for length and turn a useless old aristocratic fucker into a vital go getting impresario. Christ I'm still nearly conscious. Jesus I'm gathering an audience. A mob. And all you fucking English bastards better remember I'm an American. Hey Matron, you're no West End beauty but without even a trace of makeup on your face, jesus you've got fucking attractive grey eyes. The way the lids drop down on them is gorgeous. I like even the starch of your uniform. Boss of this whole big monstrous hospital you could be ruling over hundreds of lives. Christ what fantastic authority. To have underneath you whimpering and groaning in bed. Could even make you my general stage manager. What's gone wrong that I should think now of plugging my prick in women with power. Guaranteed to give you a fucking electric shock. Women naturally just have got the power over you anyway. The moment you start panting after their asses they can then start kicking you in the face. Till you go panting after someone else's ass and then they try to kick you even harder in the face. Holy jeeze. The nearest face. There she is. Matron. Among all the others looking down as if I'm some big hospital experiment. God. I'd love to fuck you. Hey goodbye. I'm going somewhere. Hey I hear a beautiful children's choir singing. The lights are going out. Jesus with deals to do I'm now getting gassed unconscious. Hello excuse me, is this death. I'm fading. In a nude court case. Jesus there's Priscilla waving a writ at me. Get her off my back. Her ass at least to others looks like sheer pleasure. But is one big fucking pain up mine. All she ever liked to do was sun on the beach by the ocean waves. Voices. The stitching is coming nicely doctor. Stitches. Holy shit. A wrench is unscrewing my balls. Hey where am I. In church. Who's that. On the altar. Fucking Binky is there the cunt with a fire extinguisher. O there you are Louella. In veils. Holy cow you're not getting married to Al. With his prick being wheeled up to the altar in a wheelbarrow. And with all these candles burning all over the place. Hey it can't be me walking naked up the aisle behind you. Jesus it is. I'm going to protest and object. Can't you see me. Hey Louella. I love you. Jesus hey I've died already. And I forgot to order underwear. With all these haberdasher fuckers dancing around me with sample materials. This is what they're wearing this season Mr Schultz. Well fuck you guys. With everyone imitating my show all over town, it's what I'm wearing this season that counts. And I'm going to sport spats and two tone pointy shoes. And a double tie like his absent minded Lordship who sometimes puts three on. Am I waking up. Jesus am I still living. Or am I bare assed heading for hell. Voices. Seven stitches. Suture. Clamp please. Cut this away entirely. What. Jesus what are you cutting. Leave something left to fuck a duck with. Matron has just begun to take off her clothes. God. Now that's really beautiful. Watching her hands undo those buttons. Opening up her shirt. Lifting up her skirt. Reaching behind to unfasten her bra. Got to get her to the smoke filled bedroom of number four Arabesque Street. Her pearly white back. Can see the sweetly curved sloping side of her tit. What. Jesus I just thought I was just going to get laid. After weeks of celibacy. And here I am running up the fucking main street of Woonsocket. In the finish of a cross country race last year I won and now I'm losing in front of a whole god damn gang of high school classmates. What's that. The scent of jasmine and mimosa. I'm going slowly sexually insane. His Lordship with his dozen castles with hundreds of empty rooms is going to waste time finding me a zoo. Fuck that. If I can't find a palace of my own I'm going to go join the chimpanzees out free swinging in the trees of the jungle. Throw frenzied hysterical fucks and tantrums among the monkey proletariat. How the hell did I ever deserve to get born to struggling parents in Woonsocket in the first place. I could instead have been the contented son of a duke instead of having Irish giving me fucking looks from the stoop of their houses and whose kids I beat the shit out of when they attacked me in a whole gang of micks. It was Zionism in action. They never knew what hit them when I beat the hell out of three of them and the rest of them ran. Put snakes pouring in one of their parents' bedroom window for calling me a Jew one day. Christ when I said thank you they fucking look dumbfounded at each other. Imagine fucking primitive cro magnon Irish calling me a Jew. I didn't know what the fuck they were talking about. Said the first thing that came into my head. Hey didn't you know the Jews invented the world. While the Irish still thought their pricks were amputated crow bars to lever stones out of the ground with. Twenty six garter snakes and a couple of big ones looked like copperheads.

What a scene that was. They turned the lights on and started screaming at the snakes everywhere. From the moment I saw that happening on that bedroom stage I got interested in the theatre. Just from standing there on an orange crate looking in through the screen window. It was like listening to operatic music. Jesus fight back. Fight back. Gee Mom. Hey Dad. You fought the competition so hard over your lingerie, you nearly even got prosecuted for obscenity. Struggling to get profits out of fire sales, closing down sales, Easter sales, Christmas sales, even Passover sales. And all just to send me to at least a college that nearly somebody had heard of. But which was no fucking good I discovered after I graduated. It was tragic awful disappointment. To find out you're behind the eight ball after four years of blissful dreaming that the fucking world ahead is lying at your feet just to walk over. I said, Uncle Werb my poor innocent fucking parents sent me to the wrong college. Uncle Werb drags two pieces of tissue paper out of his pocket opens them up and says see these, five could build a college, so who needs a college if you know how to buy and sell diamonds. Anyway in spirit I became an ivy leaguer. Plus putting on clothing I saw advertised in a magazine. And who in this rush rush world has time to ask anyway if you went to Harvard. Plus nobody but nobody gangs up on or pushes around Sigmund Franz Isadore Schultz and gets away with it. Plus I'm descended from some of the best rabbis that ever wore a yarmulka in Prague. Holy fuck who's got me by the balls. Who. Who. Stop. Let go. You fuckers. Let go of me.

'You're all right Mr Schultz. Everything's all right. Please now. Just lie back. Everything's going to be all right. The zipper has been removed with complete success.'

Schultz struggling to sit up. Hands holding him back. The Matron over him, a little gap between her front protruding teeth. Nice little lines around her mouth where she smiles.

'Hello Mr Schultz. Do you know where you are.'

'Jesus. Holy christ. O boy. Hello. Matron. Never mind me. My balls, my balls. Where are they. All I feel is bandage.'

'You're all right, Mr Schultz your testicles are securely and entirely intact. Mr Kahn has them exquisitely sewn up.'

'Hey let me get up. I got to go. I got serious things to attend to.'

'Mr Schultz please you must lie back for at least a while in Recovery.'

'No. Let me up.'

Schultz propping himself up, pulling away from the restraining hands. Levering his legs slowly over the side of the operating table.

Remnants on the floor of a pair of charcoal grey ivy league flannel trousers. Schultz standing unsteady on his feet. And peeking down in the direction of his private parts. A groan emitting at the sight of the large bundle of bandage over his balls with a circumcised prick perched on top. Jesus just like Al has decorations on top of his chocolate cakes.

'I'm OK Matron. I can manage.'

'I'm sure you can't Mr Schultz.'

'Hey Matron just let me go will you. My balls may be bandaged up in a bundle but I'm no cripple. Come on. I got to learn to walk again. Let go.'

Schultz taking a swaying step forward. And suddenly reeling, keeling over backwards. His hand grabbing as he falls. A tray of instruments dumped with a crash scattering over the operating theatre floor. Upon which Schultz lands with a head cracking thump. What's that big noise. Hello again darkness. I'm glad to be back. In nice calm oblivion. So gentle and kind. How did I get to this Greek island so fast. The pure crystal clear water. You can see all the way to the bottom. Louella sunning in her bikini. Gee I got to try to see all the way to her bottom too. Maybe I'm near Athens.

'Mr Schultz. Mr Schultz. You're here. In Celestial Pavilion Hospital. Now don't move. I'm afraid we've got to have an X ray.'

'Oh my god what happened.'

'You got up off the operating table when you shouldn't have.'

'Hey this is the end of me, Matron. No shit it is. Sorry about the language. I feel I died about eight times already. All I can hear in my head are the howls of the lost spirits in hell. Is my skull busted or something.'

'I don't think so. Your pupils have returned to normal. But we're taking these X rays just in case. We'll have you right as rain.'

'Jesus my butler said that recently after my house nearly burned down.'

'Oh well, I'm sure your butler knew what he was talking about. I must go now.'

'Matron. For christ's sake. Don't leave me.'

'I'll be back, don't worry. We're going to keep you at least a day for observation. We have in fact Mr Duke's room available.'

Schultz under the X ray machine. Staring up into this knob staring right down. Now my brain is going to get rays through it. Jesus that Matron. Christ now she's left me abandoned. She could save me from any new disease I could get. Having money was never meant to do this to me. Jesus I better lie back. Shut up. And try to get calm. And rise again. Like Al did from the dead.

Schultz wheeled out of the door of the X ray room and passing down this familiar hall. A door with a sign reading Autopsy. The back of the hospital porter emerging pulling his wheeled cart and blocking the hall. Proceeding again on his round collecting bodies. Turning his trolley and doing a double and then a triple take, and scratching his head as Schultz supine goes by to disappear upwards in the elevator.

Inside this door with letter A, Schultz propped up on pillows. Centre of a pale green wall, a photograph of the Queen on top of her horse. Christ now I got to receive royalty with my crotch out like a balloon. This place feels haunted with the ghost of Al. I feel like sleeping ten years and already the phone is ringing.

'O Mr Schultz, it's me Jorricks. Mr Sunningdale phoned to tell me. I've been worried sick.'

'I'm all right. I'll be leaving first thing in the morning. Buy me a couple of pairs of pants with buttons in the fly. Thirty two waist.'

'How long in the leg, sir.'

'Plenty long. And an extra bulge around the crotch.'

'Very good sir.'

Schultz sinking his head back on the pillows. An aeroplane crossing the sky. Whistle of train from the station. Here I am where Al was. How did the fucker ever get up and escape. And I'm down and hoping I ain't out. Got to catch my breath before I ring Louella and either give her a laugh or a heart attack. The bump on the back of my head is as big as a baseball. Haven't been to the box office for two days. They could be chiselling on the bookings and seats. That's the difference between box office money and all other kinds of money. It is its utter purity. That comes out of people laughing and enjoying themselves watching a bunch of talented egomaniac exhibitionists getting up on a stage to be egomaniac exhibitionists while enjoying themselves. Jesus now that I think of it. I got to get out of that traitorous environment. Who in Sperm Productions ever did anything but fuck me up. With the exception of Rebecca. She's a gem. With a fantastic figure. I should have made a bee line for her. You always can't but fail to fall a little bit in love with faithful secretaries. Especially in the doom situations when you watch the rats run for their holes. And there she always was. Pencil poised ready even in the shambles of battle to go on. Even his Lordship who keeps his emotions to the minimum except when he's breaking his guts laughing at me, said that he was deeply fond of her. And jesus I am even more so. One evening let me tell you, after the banks were closed, when the gross on the brink of disaster had already teetered the wrong way, the theatre lobby entrance vacant, not a phone ringing in the box office. And I sat there up in Sperm Productions, my ass literally and figuratively in a slough of depression, a lonely night descending, my elbows on the desk, my head in my hands. I thought holy fuck even my mouth's gone dry with terror all the way to the bottom of my spine. The office like a morgue, and everyone I thought gone home. I was nearly too worried to even go out into the outside world again. Even to find a pinball machine to play. Thinking any second that maybe, just maybe the phone could ring which could change the disaster already around my neck dragging me under the waves. To break the pall I got up and went down the hall to take a pee. Which I did without zipping up my fucking balls. And jesus, I got a fright. There was a light left on in an office. And I tiptoed and looked in and there was Rebecca. Christ her words to me are forever emblazoned on my mind. What can I get for you Mr Schultz. Is what she said. I fucking well went and kissed her on the forehead. Nothing honey, nothing, I said. Don't be here, go home. She said no, I'd rather wait, I know things are so bad. A girl in a fucking million. With only one thing wrong with her. She worships every fucking inch of carpet that Binky goes up and down on his toes on and every paper clip he touches. And that son of a bitch doesn't deserve even one fucking iota of her beautiful lovely attention. Jesus that's a knock on the door.

'Come in.'

'Hello Mr Schultz.'

'Jesus Rebecca. I was just this second thinking of you, no kidding.'

'We have some things for you.'

'Boy I'll say.'

Binky's chauffeur Swithins followed by two nurses, all their arms laden. Followed, holy cow, by the hospital porter who takes out the dead. Christ and he's got a great massive cascade of flowers. Dozens of red, pink and yellow roses. Glass jars of chicken in aspic from Fortnum's. Exotic fruits. Apples, oranges, tangerines and bananas. Figs. Marzipan. Jesus a whole piece of Gorgonzola cheese. A picture of a sturgeon on that nice big jar. Nobody has to guess what's in there. Especially not me. Yummy. What a feast. I can't believe my eyes. Could that be a little box of fraises des bois. It could. A humidor of cigars. Bottles of champagne and brandy and Madeira. A note on a card.

To our dearest beloved fellow director Sigmund Isadorable Schultz from his two old pals back at the office, and with all fervent wishes that his balls will soon be ringing again.

Binky and Basil

Tears streaming down Schultz's face. Holy shit. What kind of guys are they. I could open up a fancy retail grocery. Heap fucking ignominy all over you and then drown me in presents. And now suddenly lying in a lonely room in front of everybody I can't control my fucking sobbing tears when out of nowhere someone has been after all these fucking days of horror, nice to me.

Kindness
Is the worst
Cruelty
When it breaks
Your heart
And
Holy jesus
And I might even
Have to be
Nice right back

7 Big Ben tolling seven. Sound of a train whistle. Everybody rushing for the stations. London has gone home. All except those ticket holders who are getting a cut price meal with two tickets to Kiss It Don't Hold It It's Too Hot. The most electrodynamic show in town. Ought to put that word in the classified ads. And jesus so much to do. And all that's happened is it's all being done to me. Just as my black eyes are fading back to normal and my ankle allows me to hobble further, I guillotine my gonads. Then have a breakdown. For five seconds. Long enough for tears to come out of my eyes in front of everyone before I could stop them. Emotions wreck all rules, principles and regulations. And seriously undermine revenge. Christ news like that gets around to fuckers like Joe Jewels, and he'll think he'll be able to pull an even worse deal on me. Jesus this isn't so fucking bad just lying here like this nearly the dead centre of London. At least the ceiling hasn't fallen down on me. Yet. Push a button for a nurse if I need one. Amazing how these uniforms make even the plainest nurse look invitingly nice. That's how Al once from a previous brink of death got brought back to health by a dedicated nurse giving him midnight blow jobs in the hospital. The surest and most beautiful way to recover from anything. Maybe that's how he regained the strength to fly to L A. Jesus I got to ask if my testicles still work and request the same therapy. Wow, even now wishful thinking has got me somewhere. Here's a nurse already.

'Are you quite comfortable Mr Schultz. Can I get you anything.'

'Nurse I'm fine. Don't worry. I'm just trying to decide which of these delicacies I'm going to eat.'

'Well do let me know if I can be of help.'

'Sure. Thanks.'

With the bulge at my crotch I'm going to need help not to look like a potential rapist. But with my balls the way they are I couldn't fuck a flea. I can't go nowhere now without wearing Jorricks's raincoat. Or Arab robes when I have to receive the Royal Family at the theatre. Then have some Zionist trying to kill me. Now how much longer is this going to add to my fucking celibacy no more of which I can stand. Beautiful, the roses. But jesus in this box these are just ordinary strawberries. It's the wrong time of the year for fraises des bois. But I know exactly who I should get over to have them with some champagne. And she will never believe this in one million years.

Schultz dialling on the phone. Waiting through the rings. Jesus keep ringing. Christ Louella. Don't have gone to California. Not while at least the road's been cleared of Al. Be there I'm begging you, pick up and answer the fucking phone.

'Hello.'

'Hello, it's me Louella.'

'Goodbye.'

'Jesus I beg of you don't hang up. Please.'

'Why shouldn't I. I don't want you calling me anymore.'

'Hey come on honey. Al's now six thousand fucking miles away. And you need someone to take care of you. O christ if you knew how much I just want to cup the palm of my right hand around the left cheek of your ass. When are you going to believe me. For christ's sake, honey I love you.'

'If you loved me as you profess to do, you'd leave me alone as I ask.'

'Why honey. Why.'

'Because if Al ever found out we were still seeing each other it would devastate him. And it's why I'm now begging you, never please, never come back again.'

'Honey relax, at the moment I can't go nowhere.'

'Why.'

'Because honey. You won't believe this. But I'm in the hospital.'

'Are you. Why.'

'Hey honey, it's a story that's highly personal and I don't want to talk about it right now. But you won't believe this. I'm in Al's same hospital room. Hey honey. You still there. O shit don't hang up.'

Schultz dialling again. Ringing and ringing. Maybe she's gone to have a bath. All girls go to have baths. Loll around in the tub. Lathering all over their tits. As if they weren't clean enough. Jesus if only she'd let me foam up the soap all over her I'd die happy. Jesus that's thirty rings I've counted. She must be in the bath. Christ. She's answering. There's human breathing on the other end of this line.

'Honey please don't hang up. Just listen a second. O K I was seriously kidding.'

'Well I think that's a very sick joke.'

'O K honey. Yeah it is. But look I'm going to give you a telephone number and you ring it. Because honey, it's no shit. I had an accident and I'm in the hospital.'

'Are you really there then. In the hospital.'

'Yeah. A car hit me. I'm O K. Just kind of bruises and fractures.'

'Your voice sounds normal.'

'Well yeah it is. But there's a suspected skull fracture. Couple of cracks in the pelvis. With my sprained ankle I couldn't jump out of the way.'

'I don't know whether to believe you or not. And I don't think I do.'

'Honey the best way to believe me is come witness. Come and visit me.'

'No I can't.'

'Why.'

'Because I'm waiting for a phone call from California. Al's operation was last night.'

'Then what is this honey. It's contra fucking diction is what it is. I only got off the operating table a few hours ago.'

'I've told you please don't go on with that sickening joke.'

'Jesus honey I don't understand all this. O K I could understand why you stay with Al. There's no denying he gave you everything while the rest of us were struggling. But honey I got a proven hit now. The show has paid back its whole investment. I mean I'm sitting perched on top of a financial miracle. And these days that's a miracle. His Lordship and I are throwing the biggest show biz party this town has ever seen. Right on stage in the theatre. I receive the Queen next week. I don't want to sound crassly materialistic but the sky's the limit. The Riviera, Paris, Palm Springs, you name it. Not only my, well I won't mention it, but my limousine's bigger than Al's got or ever had. Plus now I'm not joking I am an accident victim.'

'You're showing off. And stop saying you're an accident victim if it isn't true. I've already told you. You think those things mean something to me don't you. Well they don't. They mean nothing whatever. Like they do to Al's wives present and previous. Those vultures. Al means something to me. His kindness and thoughtfulness. And that's why I'm here. He's been a father, a good father to me. And you certainly don't sound like you're an accident victim.'

'O K honey. O K I heard. You don't have to tell me. I know he's over twice your age. And O K honey you want to be loved by a father. I'm beginning to believe you. So who needs this continued suffering frustration. I got to take an injection now for some pain. Anyway thanks for the conversation. My accident made me have to cancel a haircut and chiropodist's appointment plus a publicity interview. A whole film crew and interviewer was going to be at the Dorchester later. I guess that's the only kind of attention I'm ever going to get in life. Let's just say goodbye. And you got my vow. Right now. Never to come back and see you later.'

'Excuse me there's the other phone. I must answer it. You'll wait a moment won't you.'

'Sure go answer it, honey. Hey instead just ring back while I get my injection.'

'Stop pretending or else I won't speak to you again.'

'OK honey. You got my word. No more pretending.'

Schultz hanging up. Two cold pigeons landing on the window sill. They must be hungry in this weather and looking in through at all this food in this room. If my fucking balls would let me I'd give them a few strawberries. I got to go move to the country. I could have gardeners like his Lordship's growing things. And enjoy nature. And the wild creatures that are in the meadows instead of the ones singing and dancing on stage. Holy shit, a knock on the door. Right while I'm testing to see if my prick can still get a hard on.

'May I come in.'

'Hi Matron.'

'How are you feeling Mr Schultz.'

'Little weak but OK.'

'We had to cut away more skin than we anticipated but Mr Kahn did a wonderful job of sewing.'

'Jesus Matron I guess I don't really feel that good.'

'Well Mr Schultz you've had a bit of a trauma. But dear me. We are rather being treated well aren't we. Mr Duke certainly had his admirers and flowers, but I've never seen so many beautiful roses.'

'Yeah. A few people back at my office sent a few over. And Matron. Hey thanks. For coming to see me. Jesus come in. Come in. Close the door. Come and sit down. It's good to see you like this.'

'Good to see you too, Mr Schultz. Following our first little contretemps.'

'Hey look. I really am sorry how I behaved the other day.'

'O not to worry, Mr Schultz. It was entirely understandable.'

'Matron. I really do have a favour to ask you now.'

'What is that and I'll see if I can oblige.'

'Please. I really mean it. Come and have dinner with me. We'll have it in Paris. Will you please. Jesus don't laugh. I'm serious.'

'I'm sorry. I'm not usually asked to go out by someone just recovering from the operating table. Especially by someone who has previously threatened to sue the hospital. And then asks me to go all the way to Paris. And how do you know I'm not married. And have a husband and children to take care of.'

'I don't know if you're not married but how could you take care of anyone if you're taking care of this whole massive hospital. But don't worry I'm not going to sue. And you'd like it there. In Paris.'

'I know I would Mr Schultz. But you're in no condition to go suddenly off to Paris.'

'O jesus Matron I'd adore to be there right now in some side street cafe over a glass of Alsatian beer. But I'm going to be up, two fisted into the battle once again in a second.'

'No. No. Now Mr Schultz. Lie back.'

'Hey how long do I have to be like this. I got to fly to New York in a day or two too.'

'No. Mr Schultz. Too soon. For you to fly anywhere. We will need you here at least another day.'

'Jesus Matron. You've got nice nostrils. And an exquisite nose. Where did you get those grey eyes. I could look into them forever.'

'My, Mr Schultz I am flattered but I must also ask is this how young ladies are led to the casting couch.'

'Jesus Matron you do me a disservice you really do. You're a fucking beautiful woman to me. Jeeze sorry about the language. It's kind of show biz vernacular you get in the habit of.'

'I certainly don't mind Mr Schultz being called fucking beautiful. In fact it's rather fucking beautiful to hear it said.'

'Holy shit Matron. Holy shit. Jesus. Hey come here. Come closer. Come on. Let me kiss you. Please.'

'I can't Mr Schultz. I'd quite like to kiss you. But I've got to set an example for every nurse in this hospital. And I hardly think kissing patients is the behaviour to be exemplified. But provided you keep your hands under the cover I will give you just a little peck on the cheek. There. And I'll be back to see you, I must go now.'

'Hey jesus don't go. You're the loveliest thing that's happened to me in years.'

'Dear me. Mr Schultz. Dear me. I hardly think that I am. But thank you. And now I really do have to go.'

'Matron. Is it a date. Dinner.'

'All right. It's a date. It will have to be a Tuesday.'

'You got it Matron. A Tuesday. Here have this nice red rose. No have two.'

'Thank you.'

'To remember me by.'

'Be assured Mr Schultz I'll remember you.'

Schultz staring at the ceiling. A small cobweb on the green shaded light fitting. Christ a spider is up there in a web. Must be hungry too for a summer fly. The two windows rattling in a gust of wind. They open out into the darkness across a panorama of adjacent slate roof tops where the hospital lights now glisten. Jesus the poor pigeons are still there. This is like being isolated at the end of the world. Who'll ever believe this. Because I don't believe it. In fucking Al's death bed. I must be on the same god damn mattress. Off which the fucker has miraculously risen. As if to spite me and prolong my agony. As if someone is designing my fucking life to be a parody of his. Jesus it's twenty minutes, it's time to ring her back on this phone.

'Hello.'

'Hello.'

'Louella. It's me.'

'I know who it is.'

'Well I just thought I'd call you back. And I know I said it's no more pretending. Are you listening.'

'Yes I'm listening.'

'Well listen. Don't you believe I'm in Al's bed in the hospital.'

'You are a ghoul. Goodbye.'

Schultz holding the phone away from his ear. Holy shit my fucking ear. She slammed the phone down so hard it must have sent splinters all over tax dodgers' towers. Nearly deafened me. Now what do I do. Tell her again I'm kidding. And wear out my finger dialling once more.

'Hello. It's me. I apologize. Look please for christ's sake just don't hang up for a second.'

'I'm in no mood to play games with you. Al is again in critical condition. I've just spoken to California. He's had a serious relapse after his operation.'

'O jeeze honey. Sorry to hear that.'

'You are not sorry.'

'I am honey. How many times do I have to tell you I love Al. So please tell me what's happened to him now.'

'They operated all through the night. And now complications have set in.'

'Honey Al's tough, he's going to be up at bat again, don't worry.'

'And now I suppose you're going to tell me you're all bandaged up.'

'No honey. No. Fine. I'm fine. Sorry about the sick joke about the hospital. I was just desperate for your sympathy. Really I'm just sitting home here in front of my own fire watching a little television in the library. I mean there's a hole in the rug and floor from my fire you must have read about in the papers but it makes a nice cooling draught up from the kitchen. Jorricks has just made me dinner on a tray. With fish we got over at your nearby fish shop. Lemon sole and a spot of nice old chablis. Got my polka dot dressing gown on. I guess the whole world is my oyster. Which I am also having a few of. I'd ask you over only I know you don't want to come.'

'I'll come.'

'Holy shit. What.'

'Yes I'll come.'

'Hey wait honey. Jesus wait a second. You've got me in a fucking dilemma.'

'Why.'

'O shit. Jesus. I fucking well am at the hospital. And I am in Al's bed.'

'Goodbye.'

'Don't hang up. Don't honey.'

Holy jeeze she hung up. So much for truth. Never again will I tell it to any female and maybe even to anybody. I'll press the button and ring back that nurse. And tell her a whole fucking pack of endless fucking god damn lies. Lies. Lies. Lies. To everybody from here fucking well all the way into the hereafter. Jeeze in the middle of that outburst I got a hard on and it hurts like agony. Christ if they hear me in here like this they could take me next in a straight jacket to the fucking looney bin. Where I may be headed anyway. If I go up any more emotional blind fucking alleys. Fucking women are designed to do exactly what you can't predict. I tell her I'm in the hospital and she blows a gasket. Tell her I'm home where I ain't and she says she'll hurry right over. Tell her where I really am and she slams the phone down. Matron. Matron. I need you. I really do. You could run my life without ruining it. Efficiently and officially the way you do this hospital. Once I recover from all this. Then there are really going to be changes. You could be the first woman I've ever met who isn't insanely obsessed by herself. Who isn't always on her way to powder her nose, paint her toenails orange, have a hairdo, or have a facial looking like they've been out baked in the desert, or take a steaming hot perfumed bubble bursting bath for an hour and a half. Holy mackerel. And in between they ask a tiny sentence how are you. And if you say more than six words their minds go blank till they can get back talking about themselves again. Then if you fuck them. They go straight to sleep and don't want to move or get you a glass of water like they're in a coma. Jesus. I used to love and worship women. Maybe it's because I don't have enough of them at my mercy anymore. Where you can listen to their bullshit for half an hour, get a fuck, leave them sleeping and then change to jump on another one. Like the nightmare at number four

Arabesque Street of three at once, one on each floor of the house. Or was it two at once while one was locked in the cellar. Too complicated to remember. Plus I remember two of the girls I was trying to fuck at once started to fuck each other and left me out. With my prick sticking like a sore lonesome thumb pointing in their entwined heavy breathing direction. Nurse. Nurse. Come quickly. I need to open the fucking champagne. Also I need to ring the box office and find out how the standing room is doing tonight.

'You rang Mr Schultz.'

'Yeah. Could you hand me over a bottle of that champagne. And take a few of those strawberries and put them out on the window sill. The pigeons will really appreciate them out of season.'

'Why of course.'

'Hey and while I open this we may need an extra glass from the bathroom.'

The window opening. The nurse putting a handful of strawberries out on the window sill. Schultz unzipping a strip of gold lead foil from around the top of the champagne bottle. Twisting the little wire loop to unfasten the wire cap. Grasping the cork and twisting. Jesus it's in tight. Give it every ounce of strength or else this nurse who is no beauty but not half bad either is going to think I'm some kind of weakling.

'My god, Mr Schultz. O dear.'

The cork exploding out of the bottle hitting Schultz in the eye. His head rocked back on the pillow with the impact. The champagne flowing out over the bedcovers. Schultz groaning hand over his eye. The nurse mopping up with a towel taking the bottle and putting it on the side table. The nurse examining Schultz's eye.

'O dear you did get a bang. Eye is a quite a little bit bloodshot. Can you see Mr Schultz.'

'Yeah, a little blurred. But the sight's slowly coming back. God damn cork is lethal. I'm O K thanks.'

Schultz reaching to the side table and two handed lifting the champagne bottle up over his head. Tipping it to pour some of the bubbling wine down on the top of his curly black locks.

'Are you all right, Mr Schultz.'

'Yeah. I'm just sloshing a bit of this over my head and baptizing myself a French Catholic from fucking Rheims. Because I need a religion to save me from any more fucking disaster. And pardon my French. And if you hold over those two glasses I'll fill them.'

'Are you sure Mr Schultz you are all right. Let me see your eye again.'

'I can thank God for one thing nurse. He's already landed me in the hospital where treatment is handy.'

'O dear I suppose your vitreous humour got rather shaken up. The eye is awfully red and it seems it's already a tiny bit black.'

'That's from a recent black eye.'

'Mr Schultz your hair is rather dripping a bit with champagne. Let me get a towel.'

'I'm OK. Just let's fill these glasses.'

'O I can't have any champagne.'

'Sure you can.'

'I can't, not on duty. Matron would be furious. Just let me dry you off a little. Goodness you do have the most marvellous thick long black silky curls. That any girl would give her eye teeth for.'

'My Prague grandfather. He had big black curls he wore down to his shoulders. It's kind of like an ancient family tradition.'

'O how nice. Are you a Czechoslovakian Mr Schultz.'

'Yeah in blood and spirit. My ancestors knocked around Prague for centuries. But I was born and brought up out of context in America, so to speak. Hey nurse. Look out the window. Look at that. There are the pigeons. Jesus. Isn't that fucking wonderful if you'll pardon my French, they're eating up them strawberries like they were insatiable. Hey put a little bit of this champagne in a saucer. We'll give them a little party to enjoy themselves.'

The nurse, with her own long curly mousy blonde locks of hair taking a saucer off a tea tray, filling it with champagne. Opening up the window. The pigeons fluttering away into the air. The sounds of London blowing into the room with a cold breeze. The window closing. The pigeons returning and picking at the strawberries again. And dipping and filling their beaks with champagne. Throwing their heads back as they gargle it savouringly down their throats.

'Mr Schultz, please let me change your pillow case. It's also wet with champagne.'

'No don't worry. The dampness is fine and I like the smell.'

'Well I'm afraid Matron wouldn't like it if she found out.'

'Hey don't worry about Matron, honey. She's a real sweetie pie.'

'No she's not quite, Mr Schultz. Matron runs this hospital with a rod of iron. With every junior doctor and even a few consultants in trembling fear of her. And I don't want her rod of iron to land across my backside.'

'Hey tell me are you married, honey.'

'No.'

'Is Matron.'

'I think she's been divorced a couple of times.'

'What. Wow. Maybe with her rod of iron she whacked the husbands across the ass. Hey come on. A little champagne never hurt anyone. This stuff's the best there is in the whole world. Look at the pigeons. They love it. Holy shit that fucking pigeon is wobbling already. It's Roederer crystal honey, and with a few grains of caviare, the vitamins alone will transform you.'

'Ah but what makes you think I need transforming Mr Schultz.'

'Jesus not you. Me. Jesus, hey let's give the pigeons a few grains of caviare. Not too much. Just a few. I don't want them to concentrate too much on the champagne. Jesus which is suddenly taking all the pain out of my life.'

'Mr Schultz I can't really stay here like this having a party.'

'Hey come on this is the private most expensive part of the hospital. You got to keep the patients comfortable and happy. Come on. It's way after eight. The hospital day is over. Here let me fill your glass, and scoop up the caviare. It's beluga, honey. That means vitamin D with a big D which stands for delicious.'

'I must admit this is the most wonderful champagne I've ever had. And this is the first caviare I ever tasted. And I do like it.'

'More where that came from. Hey jesus how them old pigeons doing. Wow. And do they love strawberries out of season. Hey isn't that sweet. They're fucking well billing and cooing in love out there. Hey jesus but wobbling drunk as skunks.'

'What's a skunk Mr Schultz.'

'That's a stinking animal we have back over there in America. Only some of them are human. Open that jar of peaches. Open the figs. And that jar, chicken in aspic. But before you do that, just pass me some more of the caviare. Go on have more. And hand me that other fucking bottle. And pardon my French again. Momma meeo honey. Don't let me knock my head off with the cork this time.'

Schultz undoing the smooth gold lead wrapper and unzipping the wire cap. Pointing the bottle at the ceiling as the cork explodes and hits the spider's web. The cork falling and bouncing off the nurse's head.

'Now I'm hit Mr Schultz. O dear. I really really mustn't have any more.'

'Come on honey. Hey jesus look at that will ya. Two more fucking pigeons have joined the party out there. Hey everybody is getting the message. O my god this is fucking miraculously good. Didn't I tell you.

Wow. Isn't this the most beautiful stuff in God's creation that these god damn guys have sent me. Six wonderful bottles.'

'What guys Mr Schultz.'

'The guys back at the office. Hey nurse you know, you're pretty. But pretty young aren't you.'

'Well I'm old enough to nearly be a nurse.'

'Hey you're not a nurse.'

'No I'm a student nurse.'

'OK let's drink to your graduation. Come on. Take more than a sip.'

'Mr Schultz this is most irregular. I'm on duty. There could be another patient buzzing me.'

'Come on be fucking irregular for christ's sake. You're only young once in your life.'

'Well let me just check and peek down the hall and see if my desk light's blinking.'

'Sure honey. Do that. Hey jesus christ the fucking pigeons. There are six hogging in on the party out there. Gate crashers. Christ don't let them run out of strawberries. Throw them a few more.'

Giggling nurse returning from the door and opening up the window. As the pigeons flutter up and away and the breeze rushes in. Putting out more strawberries. Closing the window the pigeons fluttering back again.

'Hey god look at them go gobbling them strawberries. They never could have guessed they were going to get a feast like that.'

'I've never seen pigeons eat strawberries before, Mr Schultz.'

'Sure they love delicious delicacies just like us. Jesus I wish this champagne wasn't so good or else I'd give more to the pigeons. Shit a whole cupful is enough anyway. Now honey where are you from.'

'Croydon.'

'No shit. They used to have an airport there.'

'Well long before I was born.'

'O boy don't remind me of age.'

'But you're not old Mr Schultz.'

'Well maybe not enough to be your father, honey. But I ain't no spring chicken anymore. Although boy right now I feel like a spring chicken just fucking hatched.'

'You're in the theatre, Mr Schultz.'

'Yeah. That's right.'

'We had a most famous man in here just before you in the theatre. You must know a lot of actors and actresses and exciting people.'

'Yeah well you have to rub elbows a bit.'

'Did it take you a long time to get where you are.'

'Yeah. But hey honey let's talk about you. What's a nice girl like you doing nursing in a hospital like this. I mean you could have been in ballet or something. You're a dancer.'

'How did you know that.'

'The calves of your legs honey.'

'I did. I danced. And wasn't good enough.'

'Hey come on. None of that stuff not good enough. Maybe you didn't just get your lucky break. Fill the glasses. And let's keep being generous with the champagne.'

'It's wonderful but I really am feeling this Mr Schultz in the head.'

'Come on, call me Sigmund. Or Siggy. Hold it. O my god honey. O my god. Jesus quick open up the fucking window. One of the pigeons just keeled over. Christ don't let him fall off the fucking sill to his death.'

Nurse jumping off the edge of the bed, rushing to open the window. Reaching to grab the lone, half comatose pigeon into the room. Schultz sitting bolt upright in bed, craning to see the stricken bird.

'Just put him in that empty box there, till he sobers up. Christ some poor pigeons can't hold their drink. He could have a hangover. Now honey, why not a little more caviare.'

'I'd love some more. I better wash my hands and just let me peek down the hall at my light first.'

'Hey jesus honey don't worry about how things are down the hall. We got a drunk pigeon in here now flapping around. Wrap him up in a towel before he hurts himself. Jesus, it could be two gorgeously drunk pigeons the way I'm feeling.'

'O dear, my light, it's flashing.'

'Jesus well see what the fuck's the matter honey and hurry back.'

Wow. No wonder they say champagne is medicinal. It's fucking magic. My balls feel fine. I feel fine. And that fucking conked out pigeon over there feels nothing. I'll call you Jorricks after my butler. Hey you Jorricks over there. You drank too fucking much champagne. Jesus, boy, so have I. Wow I can't read the numbers to dial the telephone. To say hello this is Schultz, and everybody is invited to the pigeon party. What an idea. His Lordship and I got to have a fucking flock of pigeons at our big party too. Jesus they could go shitting all over the upholstery of the theatre seats. Who gives a shit. Except christ that's the first theatre I'm going to buy. So I give a shit. So what's the worry we'll put diapers on the pigeons. Or we'll have a big special cage with sunflower seeds and champagne for them. But jesus if they are anything like these pigeons they'll all be sozzled anyway knocked out all over the place. Jeeze the guys sure sent me over the very unbelievable fucking best of everything. I swear on the ancient bones of my rabbi ancestors that this is all I'm ever going to drink into eternity. The gorgeous quality of this bloody vintage exquisite crystal bloody brut champagne is for the gods. And I'm the god. Who's got a drunk pigeon. And Cynthia is the student nurse. Who is sure entering into the spirit of things. And jesus whose fingers I could feel in my hair. Giving me the first recent testicular unpainful tingle. That fast gave me a rod of iron. I like her sense of hygiene, washing her hands. Holy mackerel. Nurses. Why the fuck I never thought of them before. So much for being healthy and never having to go to the hospital. And missing all the joy and fun. Because they are the most beautiful fucking class of human beings. Trained to give instead of always fucking taking. Hey old pigeon, jesus you nearly broke your ass falling off the window sill, don't try now to get up on your feet and flap. Calm down. We're all of us tight as hell in this room. Soused, canned, plastered, potted or as his Lordship would say, pissed. And in Yiddish we're shikker. Jesus, the time. The curtain at the theatre has just gone up for the second act. And I am shikker. And this is my fucking second act. And who gives a fuck anymore about Louella. Matron and I are going to have a big fucking dinner. Then a big fucking fuck. I'm going to show her such a good time she's going to drop her rod of iron right on her toes. Jesus, maybe on my fucking toes. Hey where is my pigeon friend Jorricks. Shit he got out of the towel. There he is pecking at my figs. Jesus the other pigeons have come back. They're looking in the window. They see Jorricks in here feasting. Jesus we got to be fair to pigeons everywhere and let them in. Before they start thinking we don't like them and are leaving them out there. We should have them all in here. So they don't get cold and drunk out there. That's it. It's Schultz's pigeon party. Folks. Everyone's fucking invited. Even that fucker Binky. Who's soon going to learn that nobody but nobody, you bastard, puts on a bigger or better show than Sigmund Franz Isadore. And that's gospel. By Schultz. Christ this is like sudden sunshine suddenly beaming into my life. I could live here. Only this room could be costing a fucking fortune. And more than the Dorchester. Hey jesus Al. I'm sorry to hear you could still be dying at this very second. I really do wish we were still friends. Like I'm making with the pigeons. And if you ever recovered, that we could still shoot the shit together again. If you weren't all the time such an old grandmother. And if you didn't have to have such a glorious girlfriend. That I had without warning had to end up adoring. Jesus that's all fucking water under the bridge. What I need right now is more fucking champagne down the throat.

'Hey honey. What kept you so long. Jesus Jorricks the pigeon got out of his towel and he still can't walk a straight line.'

'I had to assist a patient with a bedpan across the hall. And he did smell the champagne on my breath.'

'Who honey would know that much smelling it on your breath.'

'Well he's supposed to be someone very important like an army general.'

'Well holy shit honey. I don't know about army generals but jesus help Jorricks back into his towel. Before he trips like he just did on his face again. And open the window and let his friends in. They all have fucking rejected looks on their faces.'

'My god Mr Schultz I can't let all these pigeons into the room.'

'Hey come on it's a winter cold fucking night out there. Let the guys in. And there are a few strawberries left.'

'How do you know they are all guys Mr Schultz. They could be all girls.'

'Jesus touché honey touché, you're right. I could have a harem in here. Hey come over here a second. That's it. Sit down. The way I see it right now, this is the pigeon party honey. And I'm giving another big party soon and I'd like you to come. Hey, do a few steps and movements for me.'

'O I couldn't. I'm even slightly dizzy.'

'Come on. Give this old half sozzled boy a treat.'

'Well all right. Let me jam the back of the chair under the door knob in case somebody comes.'

'You do that honey. Hey. Hey. Boy jesus honey. That's all right. You've got your own nice individual style. Maybe it's a little more modern than it is classic. But I like it. Very nice that very delicate shift of the hip. And dipping the leg like that is what we call in show biz, the icing on the frisson. You couldn't show me that a little better, giving you a little more freedom of movement with that uniform off could you. Hey I know already. Regulations and Matron says you can't take off your uniform in front of the patients, else you get your ass whacked with her rod of iron.'

'Well. Maybe. I guess I could commit sacrilege. Maybe I'll just have another little sip of this lovely champagne first.'

'Sure. That's it. We'll both drink up. And commit sacrilege. This is Sigmund Franz Schultz's pigeon party. Holy shit. Hold it honey. Jesus another fucking pigeon has just keeled over out on the window sill. Quick get him in. Quick. The fucker will plummet. Sorry maybe it's a lady pigeon. Jesus another one too has just capsized. That's three drunk fucking pigeons. Get them in. To safety.'

'Mr Schultz. No I really can't. I'll get sacked, filling the room with pigeons.'

'Honey you're already hired. By me. I've just cast you in the chorus line of my show. We'll have you an Equity card in no time. Don't worry about being sacked. What's your name.'

'Cynthia. And are you really really in the theatre.'

'Believe me. That's why my balls are all bandaged up. O K Cynthia. We're going to have a good fucking time. Sorry I mean a fucking good time. Just you and me. Douse the lights. Hey wrap up Jorricks again, he's loose. Now be a good wonderful girl. While I fill your glass, take in the other two pigeons and wrap them up.'

Cynthia taking in the pigeons. Wrapping them in face towels with their heads out. Washing her hands in the bathroom. Tiptoeing to the door taking the chair away, opening it and looking down the hall. Closing the door. Dousing the lights. The night glow of London coming in the window. Three pigeons wrapped up cosy in the corner. Three still left looking bleary eyed in the window. Cynthia undoing her uniform. Lifting up her white slip over the blue cap on her head. White long stockings on a pair of long muscled legs. Unlacing and kicking off her white shoes.

'Hey honey. That's lovely. Lovely. You got gorgeous rhythms. Style. Life. Holy jesus christ. You're a really jolly sweetie pie. I know just the spot for you in the chorus line. Come on just take the rest off.'

'O god Mr Schultz. This is a hospital. I sit my finals in just two months.'

'I know honey it's a hospital. To cure people. And shit honey, jeeze, am I getting cured. In fact I am fucking cured. Of everything.'

'And I'm disgracing the profession of nursing.'

'Honey you're lovely, disgracing nobody and nothing. You're a fucking wonderful credit to nursing. Wow. Hey shit. Fuck a duck. You can dance, really dance. Magic. Bravo. Just do that pirouette en point once more. Whew. Hey jesus watch it. Fucking Jorricks. Don't step on him. He's loose again. Sorry honey. Just go back now. Where you were. That's it. That's fucking it. Wow. Fantastic. Son of a bitch. You got control of every single muscle in your body. Like I've never seen before even in a prima ballerina.'

'O my god Mr Schultz. Did I hear my emergency buzzer. Let me look out.'

'Go look out honey. But I heard nothing.'

'O my god. It's the General. He's out of his room looking for me down the hall.'

'Take it easy honey. Don't panic. Just put your uniform back on. Hey christ don't go without your shoes.'

'O no. O god. I stepped on a pigeon.'

'Holy jeeze is he all right.'

'Yes.'

'Hey lace up your shoes. And tell the old fucking geezer he ain't the only one in this hospital that needs attention. And fucking come back. Come back. Invite another student nurse. And jeeze, why not, the General too. There's still a whole bloody five bottles of champagne left to drink. No. Shit. Only four. But who's counting.'

This is
The gala night
Of Sigmund Franz Schultz's
Personal
Pigeon party
Going on
In here

8

'And who are you, sir.'

'I'm Schultz. Sigmund Franz Isadore. And who are you.'

'I'm Field Marshal Leathers.'

'Holy shit. Excuse my French. Not of Alumette.'

'Well yes. I rather still think and hope so.'

'My god. Come in, Field Marshal. I don't believe this is happening. But join the party. Cynthia get a chair. Hey this is an honour. A real honour. Let me tell you.'

'I hope you'll excuse my pyjamas, sir.'

'Hey gee don't call me sir. Cynthia. Fill up a glass for the Field Marshal.'

'Well I do appreciate a man who drinks the best champagne. And to drink it myself. Especially while one is in a damn hospital having one's rear end fixed. Isn't that right nurse. Didn't I tell you what you were drinking when I smelled it on your breath.'

'Yes sir. You did.'

'And then damn well had to go searching for you down the hall.'

'I'm sorry sir. I really do apologize.'

'Well girl. Off your station. We shoot people in the army for that.'

'Holy cow Field Marshal, we're not going to shoot Cynthia. At least ha ha, not while she's pouring the champagne.'

'No sir, we're not, not while she's pouring this champagne. And we'll have done for the moment with discipline. Bad manners to shoot ladies anyway. Much more fun to throw stones at sitting ducks. And by jove sir, you'll forgive my observing, you've got yourself your own private bloody bathroom here. While I've got a ruddy bedpan over there.'

'Jesus Field Marshal any time you want to rush over here and use my bathroom. I'd consider it a privilege. And have a cigar. Best Havanas. Sorry I can't get out of bed. Cynthia in the humidor. Get the Field Marshal a cigar. Just snap the clips off the jar. Hey and some caviare Field Marshal.'

'Well sir you're well outfitted in here I can see that. I'd be delighted to have some caviare. And what on earth are they. Not pigeons.'

'Yeah. Pigeons.'

'Damn useful bird sir, I have always kept a few tumblers. The Sultan of Baghdad had a pigeon post system long back as 1150. Faithful to each other in love they are. Never trusted the telephone myself to send messages. Give me a good racing pigeon all the time. No bloody batteries going flat.'

The room filling with cigar smoke. The Field Marshal munching down caviare on a biscuit and draining off a glass of champagne. Gold braided artillery pieces crossed emblazoned on his black slippers. Cynthia opening the wrapping on the fruits. Schultz popping another cork off another bottle of champagne. The Field Marshal smacking his lips and smiling and brushing a speck of biscuit off the lapel of his woolly dressing gown. Holy shit here I am facing one of the all time living legends only six feet away. Who fought fucking overwhelming enemy armies to defeat in all kinds of terrains including deserts. And who knows every fucking thing there is to know about pigeons. And jesus who likes his caviare, cigars and champagne as much as I do. And now my balls don't even hurt. Nothing hurts. Holy shit that is if my balls are still there. And talking about deserts, Cynthia gave me such a hard on with her dancing it turned the bedcovers into a bedouin's tent.

'Ah but I thank you sir for this but I think it's enough champagne for the moment and time I got back to bed. Damn nice. Very hospitable of you.'

'Field Marshal let me tell you, you made this one of the great moments of my whole life.'

'Well sir, you've improved mine as well. I'll just swallow back this little remaining bit of champagne and have done with it. And smoke my cigar back in my room. Got a few papers to attend to. And Cynthia. You be on the job. You know Matron wouldn't like it one bit, would she, patients having to run down the corridor.'

'No sir, she wouldn't.'

'Come back again. Field Marshal. Any time. Feel free.'

'I shall sir. Especially when you've vacated and I can use a nearby toilet. Thank you. Goodnight.'

Door closing. Schultz sitting straight up in bed. Cynthia rewrapping the pigeons. Echoing alarm of the fire brigade somewhere out in the London streets. Jesus the stripes down the Field Marshal's pyjamas are identical to mine. Shit imagine having a confrontation like this with a living legend who's been my idol for years. Got to give him half price tickets any time he wants to go to the show.

'Hey Cynthia, let's finish off what's left in the bottle. Jesus we were for that few minutes sitting in on world history.'

'How.'

'Hey don't you know who that was.'

'Well I don't know. I may have heard of him.'

'Heard of him. Hey honey you just had sitting two inches from you one of the greatest military commanders who ever lived. I mean even fucking Caesar would have to take his cap off to him. Christ he can shit in my toilet bowl any time. This I swear has been the biggest most wonderful night of my entire life. I know verbatim that guy's battles. I studied them. He was a genius with guts. Hey jesus imagine, he was chasing you down the fucking hall. Something you could tell your grandchildren. Honey, there's just us now. And look. They're all of them. Fucking sweet looking. The pigeons. Hey what time is it. Christ around now the curtain is just due to go down at the theatre. Hey. How about a few more of those steps you were doing.'

'You heard what the Field Marshal said. That I should be on the job.'

'I heard honey. But he's on our side now. And you are on the job. Come on. Just give us a tiny little treat. You got a fantastic figure there all hidden away by that uniform. Just a few pas de deux.'

'All right. But it's got to be fast. I'm keeping my friend on duty for me at my desk.'

'Jesus, honey that's swell. But don't rush things. Bring her for a glass of champagne.'

'O god I'm breaking nursing rules of this hospital enough as it is.'

'Beautiful honey. That's beautiful. What lovely gorgeous tits you've got. Gems hidden. My god. Where did you learn to do that. Jesus honey you're too expert for words. Doing a turn like that you fucking well could be earning money in a stripper club.'

'I was.'

'Holy christ, will wonders never cease. You mean you were a stripper. Did your mother and father let you do that.'

'They didn't know.'

'Well boy honey their darling daughter is one big surprise. Wonderful, wonderful body. Right down to your bloody insteps.'

'Do you really think so.'

'Honey I got something here in bed with me that's living upstanding proof. The Field Marshal just left here is the world's greatest expert on battles and pigeons. And you honey are performing right now in front of the world's greatest expert on female bodies. Especially those that dance. Holy shit. Who's that. At the door. Where christ the chair ain't propped anymore. Who is it out there. Don't come in.'

Cynthia grabbing up her uniform, slip and underwear from the floor. Hopping in and closing the bathroom door. Opening it again and reaching out to grab her shoes. A pigeon cooing from a towel.

'It's me sir.'

'Who's me.'

'I am the hospital porter sir with whom you were previously acquainted.'

'Holy shit. Well I'm previously engaged in here, fella.'

'I was wondering your honour if I could be of any further assistance to you.'

'Yeah jesus come to think of it, just hold it a minute. In fact you're just the man I'm looking for.'

The grinning porter entering, buttoning up his soiled once white coat, and tugging at a forelock. His eyes quickly darting around the room.

'Ah your honour I don't want to intrude upon your peace and quiet but I thought it was you I saw passing in the corridor.'

'Yeah you did. But don't expect to come back and haul me out of here with your cart.'

'Now with the optimistic looks of things and the perfume of the roses in here there's no worry about that, your honour. By the way me name's Daniel, your honour. And lo and behold. What do we have there your honour.'

'You have pigeons there, Daniel. You take them and keep them for me.'

'Right your honour. Fine fat pigeons they are too. But by god now. What's this, they can't stand up.'

'Jesus keep them in the towel. They're drunk.'

'Ah god now, I thought I'd seen everything in this hospital. Except fluthered pigeons. Sure I'll sober them up in a nice warm comfortable spot down in the basement.'

Daniel exiting, the pigeons hidden under his coat wrapped up in a towel. Cynthia peeking and tiptoeing out of the bathroom, all her curvaceous ample proportions, in another towel. As she twirls unwrapping herself spinning like a top across the floor and plucking and taking two roses to hold up in each hand in a shimmying grand finale.

'Olé honey. Olé. Jesus baby, the beautiful bloody way you did that. You must have some artistic parents.'

'Well I do, one half. My mother is a violinist. And plays the harp too.'

'Hey. That's swell. What's the other half.'

'My father is an income tax inspector.'

'What's that you said honey.'

'My father is an income tax inspector. O Mr Schultz are you all right.'

'Holy jeeze sorry honey. I just swallowed my champagne the wrong way and jesus blew it all over the room, and on you.'

'I don't mind. My skin's waterproof.'

'Come over a second I got the towel. O christ honey. Let's stop talking. And jesus wiping. Lean over and let me plant a kiss or two on those sweet young gorgeous tits of yours. You're built beautiful. Jesus honey have you got a boyfriend.'

'Yes I have two.'

'Now you got three, but who's counting. And hey honey. I like anonymity. If we get to know each other better like we're doing, let's use code names for each other. You can call me, say, something cheerful like Sunningdale. Yeah exactly that. Sigmund Sunningdale who's in the lingerie trade. You know if you ever want to discuss me with anybody.'

'O Mr Schultz. Like everybody you're terrified out of your wits that my father is an income tax inspector. You needn't worry, ha ha, if you behave yourself.'

'Well shit honey I'm not, right now am I. Behaving myself. Nor are you. And by the way jesus, be careful of my balls.'

'I love your hair, Siggy I wish mine were long black and silky like yours. It's sticky too from the champagne.'

'You know honey you're a fucking bloody surprise I never thought I was ever going to get in a million years.'

'I can give you plenty more. Let me pull down the covers.'

Cynthia lifting down the covers. Unbuttoning Schultz in his striped pyjama top. Her fingers touching his rigid prick sticking up out of its bundles of white bandage and gently slapping it back and forth. Schultz slumping down on the pillows, and holding on to the sides of the bed. A roller coaster. I feel I'm on. Hey honey and now. I may not be able to fuck. But I sure have got something for you to kiss. Because don't hold it it's too hot. Ha ha. The nice irreverent way you are with patients. Honey. Why the fuck do I, right smack in the middle of my big income, have to get mixed up with you, of all people. With all the kinds of jobs for fathers in this world. And now have to spend the rest of my paranoid life telling you to forget my name is Schultz. And that my middle initials are H.D.P.A.T. Which stands for he don't pay any taxes. And the initials after my name are B.H.D.B.I.T. Which stands for because he don't believe in taxes. Fuck taxes a second. Fuck them for two seconds. Jesus just fuck them. Don't pay them. They're too high. Because the way things are going on in here how the fuck do I know this sweetie pie wasn't taking care of fucking Al and giving him his premature ejaculations in this bed. Because never in the ancient long history of blow jobs, even Jewish ones, have there ever been any like this. Holy christ this is nursing down to a fine art. No wonder cocksucking is rampant backstage. Where did this tender young girl learn what she's doing to me. On the slightest invitation. Comes a visitation without hesitation. The only hindrance is my poor old balls. Not only does she dance, but she must be a genius on the saxophone. Fuck the Field Marshal. Much as I admire him and have sympathy for his comfort, I'm never moving out of this wonderful place. My last magic time like this was back in Woonsocket with a childhood love I called my campfire girl. Out ice skating in the moonlight on a lake. Roasting marshmallows by the shore. We were so fucking innocently idyllically in love. And she broke down in tears when I made her blow me. And I broke down in tears because she said she never wanted to do it again. Except to a new boyfriend she just met. Always the fucking girl you think you've got, you ain't got. O christ Cynthia honey. Talk about the bliss of vespers. Where the two of us could go to Farm Street Church to listen. Even that stab of pain your elbow just gave me feels like good pain in my bandaged balls. This is the worst day of my life I now don't want ever to end. Honey talk about a cobra's tongue. Or any tongue. Lift your head up here a second. Kissing your mouth. Is liquid excitement. Now go back down there. And kiss you later. Even the smartest wife of the wisest rabbi who ever lived couldn't teach you such perfection in sucking. Although maybe Rabbi Löw's wife could. Meaning no disrespect to rabbis' wives centuries ago. Jesus I can't even remember if rabbis have wives. But all the best rabbis are supposed to know everything there is to know about fancy fucking. Even though it says nothing about it in the Talmud. So who shouldn't believe them if they teach too about fancy sucking. Like it was meant to be oral law. Torah by mouth. Right in the old Jewish cemetery of Prague I had one of the most important insights of my life. Loneliness is a step towards death. Rabbi Löw hello. It's Schultz here speaking in a delirium. I got a problem. A special situation. Supposing you tell me the answer. If I ever let Cynthia and her fleshly assets into my life would her father come too. And give me paranoia. And worse, start smelling and tracing my hidden tax free resources. Hello Mr Schultz. This is Rabbi Löw speaking. The answer is. Money before pleasure. Or you could get no pleasure. Cynthia. I'm going to take a risk. Momma meeo. With lips like yours. Who needs a mouth. Or with such a mouth. Who needs a throat. Or with income who needs tax. But this special night I'm glad Cynthia you have all three working. Thou shalt not covet thy neighbour's pigeons. Holy shit there's a stray thought. Flew wings flapping right across my brain. O jesus, holy cow. Out the window. Three fucking more of the pigeons are keeled over drunk. Sorry guys or ladies I can't do anything about it now. This is the fucking countdown that's begun. In ten, nine, eight, seven seconds from now it could be goodbye to weeks of celibacy. And hello to a tornado coming to tear my head off with rapture. Cynthia, welcome into my life. And hello to paranoia. My name is not Schultz it's Sunningdale. Fucking christ a chair ain't there to hold the door closed for five, five seconds more. Honey you are a magic genius. Poetry in motion. Holy shit. What. The fucking phone is ringing. Jesus this is a disaster. On the verge of my gorgeous apoplexy. It could be Hollywood. With an offer so fucking big for the movie rights that I could buy a two hundred foot yacht to go sailing back and forth for the rest of my life on the Riviera with tits wagging everywhere. Honey don't let me disturb you. But I just got to answer this. Holy shit. Wow. Get my mind back to doing business on an even keel. Thirty percent of the profits off the top. Twenty down the sides. And five off the bottom. Holy jeeze honey. Don't stop. Just slow down a second while I answer this phone.

'Hello.'

'O Sigmund.'

'Who's this.'

'It's me. Louella. I am sorry. I really am. I simply couldn't believe it was true and I just rang the hospital. What's wrong, are you in awful pain. You really were in an accident.'

'Yeah. I'm in awful pain.'

'O dear. Forgive me for not realizing.'

'It's OK. Sure. Everything. Oooo. Sorry. It's the pain. Comes in waves. I'll call you back. O god. Oooo.'

'O dear Sigmund. Can I come over.'

'That's all right. I can stand it. Oooo. I better hang up. Don't come over. Call you right back. Goodbye.'

The women are back in my life now faster than I can handle them. One at a time unless they want to come two at a time, is the principle. And you first Cynthia. Because you you little delicious honeybun are fucking well going to kill me. And my Hebrew epitaph will read when it is translated in big capital letters into English. He died of a gorgeous sensation while the balance of his mind was beautifully disturbed. It's the first time since the show opened that by the final curtain I didn't know what the night's gross is. So who's going to concentrate counting. When a mouth like hers is sucking like gossamer silk. O jesus my balls are going to explode the suture loose. Leave blood everywhere. Like a rabbi does after a botched circumcision. In the old Jewish cemetery in Prague the wise old rabbis they lie in death wide awake. Rabbi Löw tell me. How many of my Czech ancestors had a blow job. Sigmund what a silly question. There's always strife in marriage. How else conveniently could you shut a nagging wife up. Touché Rabbi. And now let me tell you something. Tonight is going to lengthen my life. Or end it altogether. Cynthia. You should be studying for final exams. Let me ask you a question. What's a young lovely gorgeous girl like you doing this at the end of my prick. Answer that when you've finished. Because you passed already with flying colours. The top of my head is exploding off. Brains throbbing out of my temples. And voom. Cynthia. I'm in orbit. Up in this wonderful place. Hey holy shit. The world's way down there. There's Woonsocket. Those fuckers who called me a Jew after I called them Irish are welcoming me back to main street for the biggest July fourth parade they ever had. But you're making me feel a bigger hero. O Cynthia. I'm only an impresario. But you honey are a living and breathing doll. Who instead of out of fear and loathing as a wife. Is just one gorgeous tit bouncing dancing girl. And fuck a duck honey. At this pigeon party. Where a star is born.

On a
Hospital bed
Instead of on
A casting couch

9

'Jesus, what time is it Cynthia. I fell asleep.'

'It's twelve o'clock, midnight. There goes Big Ben. And I like running my hand through your hair, Siggy.'

'My mouth's dry.'

'Here's some water.'

'Thanks. Jesus wow. Hey how old are you honey.'

'I'm eighteen and a half.'

'Holy cow you're only a kid.'

'O yeah Siggy. I could teach you plenty things daddy you don't know.'

'Jesus I'll bet you could. But jesus christ. You don't want a relationship with a guy lots older.'

'Hey what's the matter with you pops, why not. I've already had a boyfriend who was as old as thirty five. And you're going to put me in the chorus line of your show remember.'

'Jesus honey with all we've had to drink let's think about this a little bit. You don't want to throw away a whole career just on the verge of being a nurse to hoof around a sweaty old dusty stage with a lot of desperate people who spend half their lives out of work.'

'How do you know I don't. I'm already hoofing around here with smelly old bedpans. Couldn't I be a star.'

'Jesus I don't know honey that's what I'm saying. To be a star takes years of just being around being nothing. You're a lovely fucking girl who's got a lot of lovely fucking talents.'

'And sucking old fashioned cocks is one of them.'

'Hey honey that's not becoming talking like that. You got to have responsibilities in your behaviour.'

'Hey maybe you're pretty famous, aren't you.'

'Jesus honey this time of night all I am is pretty foolish.'

'My girlfriend on duty has seen your show. Says it's in poor taste but occasionally good for a laugh. She'd like a part in the chorus too. She's a really good dancer and has got beautiful legs.'

'Jesus hold it honey. I can't start casting this whole hospital in a show.'

'Why not. The Field Marshal could come on banging his bedpan. Hey Siggy do I scare you.'

'Whew. Come on. It's tomorrow morning already. Get back to your desk. The Field Marshal instead of banging it may need the bedpan. See me in the morning.'

'I do scare you, don't I.'

'Hey honey. I'll be honest. You do.'

'It's just because I'm a little uninhibited. But you should take me seriously.'

'That's what's scaring me honey, I am.'

'Well you'll find me in the nurses' annex. I'm the only Cynthia. And remember it's only when guys are thirty six or seven that they're really passé. Now Siggy you fussy old pops. Watch me. How I go out this door.'

Cynthia pirouetting across the floor, taking a curtseying bow holding out the hem of her uniform, her nurse's cap askew, a lock of her hair falling forward. She steps out and her head comes back sticking around the half open door as a disembodied hand curves from behind to slowly grab and pull her head away. And the door closing with a quiet click. Jesus on top of it all, she's a comedienne. What the fuck now has suddenly dawned in my life. The night outside. A wind blowing hard. Three drunk pigeons, if they didn't fly then they must have rolled to their drunken deaths off the window sill. It's been another long day. Christ I am. I'm getting fucking old and passé. When you start trying to splash cold water on a fire that's burning in a girl like that. Holy cow. I'll be accused of robbing the cradle. Instead of with the Matron I could be accused of robbing the grave. What the hell I haven't yet tried necrophilia. But a fucking young woman full of youthful vibrant spirits I'll try any time. Especially one who doesn't yet have to be a devious bitch. Who maybe she never will be. Who knows. I've heard of crazier ideas for a musical called hospital. Could be hilarious with bedpans banging, bodies carted to the autopsy down stage. The chorus line skipping rope with extra long stethoscopes. Half price to those with one genuine broken leg. Cynthia and her girlfriend could keep the first ten rows with the guys pumping away under their raincoats. The gorgeous thick luxurious crop of hair between Cynthia's legs. Jesus. The apoplexy I got when she danced with a red rose sticking out of there. Even her hands are beautifully graceful. Fingers fluttering suddenly like a butterfly. Even when she didn't move a muscle magic was flowing through the line of every limb. Rabbi Löw. Are you there. Listen. I already got pigeons but jesus tell me is this maybe what I need. A young vibrant fearless outspoken girl in my life. Mr Schultz. It's Rabbi Löw answering. Let me tell you. In five words. It's what we all need. But in two words too. Watch out. Goodnight Rabbi Löw. I heard you. Thanks for the favour of the answer. See you soon in Prague. I'll put a pebble on your gravestone.

Dawn creeping through the dark over London. Big Ben booming seven bells. The sound of traffic coming back into the streets. The echoing rumble of the big red buses. Schultz waking to a knock at the door. A smiling grey old lady in a green smock wheeling breakfast in. Two boiled eggs. One brown, one white. Porridge. Tea. Slices of toasted soggy buttered bread. Holy cow, upon this earth upon this hospital bed, I got a splitting hangover headache. If I didn't have a concussion yesterday I got one now. My balls are throbbing. What's happened to me. From the heights and joy of last night I had a nightmare after falling into a drunken sleep. That someone was shouting right out in front of my house back in Woonsocket in big fucking words you could hear all over the neighbourhood. Bring this tax dodger out into the limelight. Let the internal revenue service shine their flashlights upon him. Jesus. That could be in a fucking short time. If Cynthia's father who's bound to be anti semitic, starts investigating me around the globe. He could be holding up the placard. We've got him. This Jewish fucker who took advantage of my chaste daughter. Only a child. O my god. I just know I'm not going to be able to resist in my present desperate celibate circumstances getting in touch with her again after I escape from this hospital. She's the sweetest fucking thing I would ever hope to fuck, as wildly licentious as anything I've ever met. Any girl who likes running her hand through your hair is bound to be bliss in bed. I think of such things while I should be thinking about paying attention to keeping stable. O no. O god. I never called Louella back. O christ. I got to up and get out of here. Like my whole life has been one long pigeon party. Push my buzzer. Then ring his Lordship. He's always up early in the morning. He's no rabbi but he's bound to have good sensible English aristocratic advice handed down through generations. Which I could, if I could only think straight, nearly give myself. And which I am now giving. Don't whatever you do, ever ever have a fucking thing to do with any girl whose father could put you behind bars. And who could send a message to your wife's lawyers who would love to know how the fuck much further they can embarrass and blackmail me out of my fucking money that's left after I maintain my wife in a palatial style in Kensington, and after what my wife has stolen already. O shit. How do I rise up out of this depression. Grab the rungs hand over hand and climb. Don't nosedive into paranoia. Stay optimistic. Claw your way through the jungle of pessimism. Let's go Schultz. Let's go.

'You rang Mr Schultz.'

'Yeah, nurse. Have you got anything to kill some pain.'

'Are you hurting in your testicles.'

'No in my head.'

'I'll get something.'

Jesus, she's nice enough but with a hatchet face and grey hair. Where have all the young student nurses gone. Maybe they only come out at night. Meanwhile on a piece of paper. I got to write out my priorities. Headlined first with a principle to behave by. Always remember. I conquered previously and I can conquer again. Binky's trying to dismantle my show and bury me. Jesus you kill yourself with something new and in two seconds everyone is treating a hit like it's old hat. Recent events have nearly blotted all my show biz worries right out of my mind. Voom. I got now to get to New York. And if my balls don't get speared on the sharp pointed top of the Chrysler building, then voom. Also to Hollywood. But before I even go take a piss in a bedpan I got now to fly to fucking Zurich to a bank with my luggage stuffed with notes to put in a secret account before I'm stripped naked. Uncle Werb used to say. To escape inhuman bondage, if you don't have at least a few diamonds stored away then always keep a few shekels in the lining of your coat you never take off. Maybe I need a convalescing rest cure in Prague. A little lonely holiday. With just money and myself. Stay at the Three Ostriches Hotel next to the quiet flowing Vltava River. Stare at the ancient painted ceiling. But first I got to stop my show from being demolished. Life slaps you in the face every five minutes with its inexhaustible disasters. My wife's lawyers trying to get injunctions. Against me even coming within six hundred yards of where she lives. And she comes within six inches of me and socks me in both eyes. You got to come back fighting. Get the fuckers like Binky. Get the zipper perpetrators. Who done this to me. And maybe even meanwhile Al might have at last croaked. Although give me a few Cynthias and who needs Louella. Faithful to that old fart. Holy shit I can't start hating her now just because I love her. But Cynthia's dynamic personality hidden under that nurse's uniform sure gave me a release from all previous spiritual pain. To find her full of beans. That now I want to count at my leisure. Bad as marriage was, at least with two twin daughters growing up to say da da, made me feel I had two little defenceless creatures to care and fight for. A stable optimistic relationship is what I need soon and fucking bad. I've got to be contented for at least the whole of one week in my existence. Rabbi Löw here's another question. With all the money pouring into my life where's the fucking happiness I've been waiting for. Mr Schultz. Remember good manure grows beautiful flowers. So happiness is up your ass. And that's why you say holy shit so much.

'Hey nurse you're not going to stab me with that long needle.'

'Well you'll feel no pain. Let me move your tray. Just roll on your side and expose your buttock.'

'Holy cow.'

Jesus will I ever get out of this hospital alive. Any second I could have Daniel calling for me. Before like all good impresarios I go to live it up on the Côte d'Azur. But maybe first I hope I'll be blinded by the glare of publicity of old Al's funeral. He'll be with a rigor mortis erection, wearing a pair of Bermuda shorts, sunglasses and sandals in his coffin. Imagine at last he seems to be dying. If I can only get there in time. It's bound to bring Hollywood to a standstill. In every restaurant everybody will stop eating. For three seconds. As people take off their own sunglasses in memory. To say he was the biggest premature ejaculator of this or any age. Holy cow, I got to control the thoughts in my mind over breakfast. The pain in my head and the throbbing in my balls is at last disappearing. The nurse must have given me an elixir. Got to call again his Lordship. His private phone is busy busy busy. Jesus these are really hard boiled eggs. When I asked for soft poached.

'Hello. Basil. Is this you your Lordship.'

'Who is daring to use my Christian name at this ungodly hour in the morning. Not you I hope Schultz. Your balls must be all right.'

'I'm sorry your Lordship. Did I wake you. And my balls are O K.'

'Well as a matter of fact Schultz over a spot of breakfast, I was reading my breviary and meditating on the lives of the saints.'

'Your Lordship you're trying to be a comedian but you fail utterly. I just wanted to thank you guys for sending all this stuff over.'

'Stuff, Schultz. Surely I think it deserves to be referred to as something a little more appealing than that.'

'O K. The exotic cornucopia. The wonderful fantastic champagne. Thanks a lot. It really made my day. Or rather my night. And may have changed my life. But also has given me the most terrible hangover of my whole existence. This is the highly confidential question I want to ask. My wife stole money out of my house. Can I have her arrested without anyone knowing publicly what she stole. Hello. Hello. Your Lordship are you still there.'

'I'm here Schultz. And I can't believe what I'm hearing. Certainly no one can accuse you of lacking cold calculation. And it is not one of your greater endearments. The normal practice Schultz, in this land where chivalry found its origins and where we trust vestiges of it still remain, is to send your wife a conspicuously expensive gift, as this points up her misdeed and her resulting feelings of reproachfulness may cause her to make restitution.'

116

'Holy shit that could leave me fucked two ways from Sunday.'

'And I'm afraid Schultz at this exact moment from this Tuesday I've got to attend upon the lavatory and have a crap.'

'Hey your Lordship you're no fucking help in looking for justice. I'll call you back after you've finished your toilet.'

Holy jeeze. Everyone is either going to take a shit, or running down halls looking for bedpans. Got to get Binky's film of my rescue. To sue those fucking haberdashers like they've never dreamed anyone could be sued. Get the best lawyers in town. O jesus, I knew there was something missing. The fucking evidence. The pants the pants. Snipped to ribbons. On the operating theatre floor. I got to get them. And the zipper. The trouser length. All the measurements. Just like the ones we made one day against the office wall. When Binky claimed he was taller than me. The fucker standing on his toes behind his desk announcing. I am verily I believe Schultz, a shade over the six foot one mark. That fucker has tried to best me in everything. He couldn't stand it to find I was six foot and three quarter inches tall and a full half inch taller than he was. Jesus they talk of chivalry. Towards someone who wants to see you dead. And who wants to have every penny off you that you ever made which is worse than being dead. I'm never in two hundred years going to send that bitch an expensive gift. Unless it's an electric chair to sit in. And that's gospel. Written upon the Wailing Wall. By Schultz. And by now his Lordship should have had his crap.

'Good god. It's you again Schultz.'

'Yeah.'

'Well as a matter of fact you have just interrupted me at my ablutions. I should never have given you my private number.'

'Jesus, sorry, your Lordship.'

'And Schultz before I hang up. I must let you know that as an amusement you are first rate, as a business partner you are second rate, but as a person, you are extremely third rate.'

'Jesus christ you guys. You're obsessed by principles of morality and so called upper class behaviour. And you know why, because people like Binky would rat on his own mother like he's already done to me.'

'Ah Schultz you could not have heard. Binky's mother died last night. In fact that's why my phone has been busy. She was possibly one of the most magnificently beautiful women who has ever lived. Certainly the most charming.'

'Holy christ what happened. I met her at your wedding.'

'She walked out her French drawing room door after dinner.'

'So what.'

'The doors Schultz open upon a cliff ledge and it is a sixteen hundred foot drop into the ravine at the bottom.'

'O jesus no. Your Lordship. Shit. Jesus, will tragedy never cease. Fuck a duck.'

'Your response Schultz is characteristically suitably sentimental and you may of course Schultz fuck a duck but while you are I do hope you will excuse me while I fucking well go back and complete my washing and brushing up.'

Schultz hanging up the phone. Staring out across the slate roof tops. Jesus what am I expected to do if someone's mother dies, throw a fit of sorrow. I'm already in a deep enough fit of hangover depression. Christ maybe that's a suitable funeral I could go to to test to see how my balls look in a new suit with buttons on the fly. And without the bandages making them appear bulging hanging over the grave side. O god the bump on my head is even bigger. The blow job last night blew my brains out. Like a defenestration that they used to do in the old days in Prague. She was insatiable eating me alive. Her head going up and down like a pump on top of a Texas oil well. Sucking every drop out till there could be no sperm left in me at all. Like a woman does who's teetering on the edge of the menopause. Jesus I'm getting worked up even thinking about it again. Even this champagne cork looks like a foreshortened phallic symbol. That kid with a mouth like that, could have me at her mercy. Begging her for a suck. Jesus put her in the chorus line and she'll join all the other fellatrices back stage. And her violinist mother and tax inspector father with his nose sniffing for dodgers, have got to come and see her in the show. And then back stage meet the producer. How do you do. Well for a start I don't pay my taxes. Taxation without relaxation is tyranny. And is American history they taught us in high school. Or was it taxation without representation they taught us. O jeeze I've got to stop the hypothetically terrifying conjecturing from entering my brain. Of a computer stopping in its tracks, ringing bells, blaring bugles and blinking lights when it sees my name and makes a sudden print out with numerals so numerous and astronomical it breaks the fucking machine and attracts even more attention to me. Christ you think you're winning. A fucking incredible gifted girl turns up on my plate in whom in two minutes and a couple of bottles of champagne I find solace. A sweet but not so innocent young girl. Till the awful complications begin to well up and explode in a doom laden cloud that's closing down over your life. I got to get out of here. Even if I have to go out by

118

the window and crawling over the slate roof tops. And bring my pigeons with me. Dial myself out of the fucking dilemma.

'Jorricks, it's me. Come to the hospital. Right away. Bring the new pants. I'm coming home to convalesce.'

'That is good news, sir. I'm delighted. And shall be there directly.'

O god. How the fuck do I arrange right after my divorce, to marry my butler. And with our pigeons exist in a paradisiacal garden. Never, never is he not ready to do what I want. Imagine. How once in maybe every ten thousand years some good things can occasionally happen. When Jorricks first came into my life. He was standing there dignified in the alleyway of a stage door. And you couldn't have known that he was literally starving silently to death. Without a penny, just a sliver of soap and a comb in his pocket. But everything about him immaculately clean and neat. Jesus what sad obsession gets in people's heads to be on the stage. Or worse to try to stay there when they get there. And Jorricks stops me as I pass, to ask was he at the right place for the auditions. I was nearly in one of the worst hurries in my life, on my way out the stage door alley ready to jump into my car with my hired chauffeur to go to Victoria to catch the train to Brighton and just as it begins to rain. Poor Jorricks late to audition for of all things, the walk on part of a butler, because he had to walk from Camden Town without bus fare all the way to St Martin's Lane. A part that just was cast five minutes earlier. When I told him, his face fell a mile and tears came into his eyes. And as I tried to gracefully tear myself away, it was a total joke I thought I was making to cheer him up to say I needed a butler at home. And he follows me out the alley.

'Sir you are Mr Schultz, aren't you.'

'Yeah I am.'

'Sir permit me to offer my services. I can assure you of my every attention for the most modest of emoluments. I am long experienced in the theatre. But have in fact also done a spare time bit of butlering. I can provide you with any reference you may require.'

I was dumbfounded that he meant every fucking word he was saying. I thought shit. The theatre is my life. And for this guy for whom the theatre was his life as well, I can at least wait another half hour for the next train. I even vaguely knew his picture from Spotlight. A respected journeyman actor. Here he was in front of me five foot eight with light brown eyes with all kinds of credits and years of playing in the provinces. And as the rain was now pouring down in buckets on both our heads, I couldn't believe what I was doing until it was too late. Because jesus, once you start being charitable in the theatre, it's endless and

119

knows no bounds. My rented chauffeur has the door of the rented car open. Jorricks just stood there. As if a guillotine was about to come down on his head and that I was going to tell him to fuck off. And christ what a smile broke out on his rain dripping face when I said when can you take up duties. The chauffeur was gnashing his teeth getting wet in the rain. And Jorricks just like the best boatswain's mate I ever knew in the Coast Guard squared himself up to attention.

'Sir from this moment as I am standing here now, I am at your service.'

Christ that fucking afternoon, I can't help it, it still brings tears to my eyes. Somehow you see the bravery of the theatre in people's blood. The fucking courage of going on when it's a goose egg around you everywhere. His only problem was he had to vacate his room in an hour or else pay another week's rent. I gave him five quid, a set of keys to the house, put him in the rented car to take him to get his stuff to bring to Arabesque Street and I took a taxi to the station. When I got back from Brighton two days later at midnight I was so tired that all I noticed was the house smelled beautiful. And then when I woke up late the next morning to find my room immaculate and the cleaning done, the shopping completed and not a vegetable or a fruit with a bruise on it. The garbage put out. The vines and shrubs in the garden trimmed. But my first lovely perception, as I am hobbling out in my pyjamas in the hall, was the aromatic smell of freshly brewed coffee. And on his way up the stairs past the bust of Justinian on the landing, is Jorricks with a tray full of breakfast and all the mail and morning newspapers. Jesus for a second I thought I'd made some fucking mistake and was locked out of my room at the Dorchester. I took a piss and got straight back into bed. To face a big tall glass of freshly squeezed orange juice. To find the coffee just as delicious as it smelled. The hot croissants just perfect. The marmalade he bought as good as my own mother made. Normandy butter looking that lovely pale gold from France. The eggs soft boiled to exactly how I always dreamed I might like them if some fucking person could ever boil them that way. Hello, Rabbi Löw. Are you listening. Yes Mr Schultz. It sounds like some breakfast. But I hope it did not include ham. Rabbi Löw it included bacon, three slices. It was four you had Mr Schultz and I'm counting. Rabbi it included toast just toasted with not a fraction burned and wrapped in a hot linen napkin. You should have had matzos, Mr Schultz. Rabbi Löw, listen. No English butler worries to bring you matzos and at the door Jorricks is bowing.

'Bon appétit, sir.'

Let me tell you Rabbi Löw I can still taste that breakfast. Then I couldn't believe it. I had to that afternoon go to Liverpool to see a show and Jorricks had already worked out the weather report and had filled my suitcase with exactly what I needed to wear. For three weeks straight he never even took one single hour off. And to top it all, with the miracle of miracles he even knew the names of people to whom one could go to raise money. Plus the cast and what was playing in every West End theatre and could reel off the current gross of every enemy show in London. So much for the bliss and now for a few faint blots. His only little drawback, which could when you think of it be a fucking big advantage was, he got moody and irritated the moment a female was around, and curt to any woman calling on the phone. Then sullen if she turned up at the house. Even when I was pretending it was business with an assistant stage manager I had over from the theatre who had only half a kidney and part of a lung missing but was completely two titted and as sensuous as a cobra, and into whom I was contemplating throwing a full hearted fuck. Of course she tried to do something helpfully domestic which was suggesting she'd make tea and that was the non fucking end. Jorricks growled her straight out of the kitchen. But O god. The day Priscilla came. And Jorricks answered the door in his cutaway coat and striped trousers he just put on for the first time that morning. He jumped back. To find this tigress screaming at him on the front stoop.

'You fag. You couple of homosexual fags, living together in there in this house in my matrimonial home.'

Jesus Jorricks really got a jolt. But so did Priscilla in her big purple hat. Jorricks lets you know even though he's closing the door quietly that he really is slamming it. But that day he slammed it right in Priscilla's face. The whole embassy from across the street were watching the whole thing. One guy through his binoculars. Priscilla kicked the door and screamed and ranted more homosexual abuse. And I must say it was the first time it was ever put as a possibility in my mind. My god maybe they wouldn't let you into Westminster Abbey to consecrate the union like it all happened at his Lordship's wedding that beautiful day I attended. But if you want comfort and convenience that's the solution, marry your butler. With the only problem of wondering which one of us would wear the wig and gown going up the aisle. Wilt thou have this factotum to thy wedded wife, to live together in matrimony. And in sickness and in wealth forsaking all others, keep thee only unto him or her till death do you part. I do. And do you Jorricks. Take this fucker Siggy, as his business partners affectionately refer to

121

him. And with his split balls still in a sling, wilt thou obey him and serve him as your master. For all the days remaining. That his avaricious wife does not get her hands on his house. I do. Holy god do something fast.

Deliver me
When my balls again
Swing free
A true beloved piece
Of ass
Before I go
Queer

Upon that late February day, a mild breeze blowing over London. The sun out, the snow melted away. A photographer and reporter on the steps of Celestial Pavilion Hospital taking a picture as Schultz was handed his three pigeons wrapped in a towel. And draped in Jorricks's raincoat was assisted by that gentleman's gentleman in his black suit and cap, across the pavement into the waiting limousine. Schultz presenting a bottle of champagne to the Matron and two nurses loading the remains of the cornucopia and they stood smiling and waving as the gleaming black vehicle's wheels whirred away down the road.

10

'Is sir comfortable back there.'

'Fine Jorricks, fine.'

Schultz slippered feet up on the jump seat and a plaid rug over the knees. The limousine circling Piccadilly Circus and motoring westwards past Fortnum's emporium of exotics. The white stone elevations of these clubs and odd hotels looking out over the now green again little rolling wooded hills of St James Park. A gorgeous day. Out among the healthy and the living once more. With only the last disastrous thing I have to learn from Daniel who was just in to check to see if I was by any chance ready for the last round up, and I find that they have sent the remnants of my pants together with the zipper and the remnant of my testicular flesh to the incinerator.

'Jesus, I need them pants and zipper as evidence.'

'Ah now sir I could go sifting among the ashes and can't guarantee to find the cloth but the zipper might be there.'

'OK find it and you've made a fiver. And hey Daniel, would you like an occasional job which might require physical strength. How tall are you.'

'Six foot four in me stockinged feet.'

'And how heavy.'

'I am without socks at all every bit of sixteen stone. And have lifted single handed a fat dead man twice that weight.'

'How would you like to once in a while work for me. For a fee.'

'Certainly your honour and what would I have the privilege of doing.'

'Scaring people.'

'Ah now since I do that naturally and for no extra remuneration whatever, I'd not object to being paid for it. And as sure as I am known as Daniel the Dangerous I would even include without further fee the breaking of faces, legs, arms and neck of any man, any time, any where upon whom there was an incumbency so to act. So help me God. And he who dares to sigh loudly in your presence shall forever thereafter be in his trepidation trembling in his tracks for fear of my surefire vengeance.'

'Daniel it might be a woman who might be screaming and scratching.'

'Ah in that case, I'll smother her in kisses and render her ecstactically comatose with an injection of me own personal tranquillizer. And after that she won't need the life frightened out of her. But I might stand accused of being the father of the unborn.'

'Here take this number I think you're the man I'm looking for. Keep in touch.'

'Right your honour.'

The size of the Irishman. Nearly as big as Magillacurdy and filling the whole doorway. And with him coming into your hospital room with his cart, if you were still living, he'd be collecting you anyway having scared you to death. Jesus, as a bodyguard he could make my life safe again in London. Where I could go everywhere freely enjoying myself. Without having to look over my shoulder every two seconds for some private detective. Like I am now. Looking out the window making sure we're not being followed. By one of these fifty cars going now around Hyde Park Corner. Where all was white two days ago under the piles of snow. Holy shit Rabbi Löw, whoever invented the torture of marriage. He should get desecrated. Mr Schultz, listen, it was a woman who invented a wedding as the highest price you can pay for a fuck. Touché Rabbi Löw. I should know. Because I'm paying. But god it's wonderful to be out in the world again under a presently blue sky. The only thing is I hope I don't have to depend upon Binky and his film evidence. The damages I win when I sue the fuckers who did this to me and maimed my balls could be tax free. Plus the award for punitive damages for the mental cruelty added by the prolonged anticipation I now have of getting the stitches ripped out. Then add the damages for interruption of my sexual rights. I could make more money this way than I'm making in show biz. Holy jeeze we're only just getting to Belgravia and just thinking of all the legal actions I got to implement is tiring me out already. But I got to do a complete reconnoitre of the contracts that that fucker Binky thinks he has signed with my stars. It'll be a good time to do it while he's bereaved. Give me a chance to catch up to any further treachery he's been doing to me while I've been out of action two whole days. Without being able to call up a single person to make a quick deal. And now with only a few days left to get to the tailors to look good for the Queen. And jesus I must remember not to call that pigeon by the name of Jorricks.

'Sir, you'll be pleased to hear the house is again in apple pie order, the stage manager as requested sent over the designer, carpenters and painters. And they quite wrought a miracle working until four a.m. But I'm afraid that Mr Sunningdale has sent you a rather large bill.'

'That dirty fucker.'

'Begging your pardon, sir but that's exactly the sentiment I had in mind myself, sir.'

The limousine circling Belgrave Square and the trees towering over the shrubbery hidden lawns in its little park. Embassy flags flying. Christ maybe this is getting to be a dangerous place to live with all the international coups going on. Jeeze when we passed the Ritz Hotel I was already thinking of taking Cynthia in there under the cherubs painted on the ceiling. Only christ she might before I rushed her back to Arabesque Street, get up between courses and strip for a nude dance and call me pops in front of the waiters. But after that blow job she can call me anything. Holy jeeze how do I put that evidence before the judge. Your worshipful honour I couldn't go for a normal fuck and so couldn't control the wonderful explosion and that's how in blowing my load it undone my stitches. It'll sound much better in an English accent delivered by Queen's Counsel. My Lord I am sure will appreciate that Mr Schultz's private part could not be inserted in the usual manner and therefore was being sucked in such fashion that in so exciting him, it caused an involuntary eruption in Mr Schultz's testicles leading to a fracture of the suture thread holding his scrotum together and I am sure your Lordship will further appreciate that this led to more anguish than you could shake a gavel at. O jeeze, the tabloids could have a field day with the testimony. Balls of Impresario Caught In Court Uproar Following Zipper Zapping Gonads. Anyway, one thing's for sure, that blow job ended the plan to take the grey eyed Matron to Paris. Plus for the first time ever knocked Louella out of my consciousness. Or was I just knocked out. Don't even know Cynthia's last name. And for the sake of her father, I hope the fuck she knows next to nothing about me. But by the way she blew proves she has an unquenchable thirst for knowledge. To be added to what she already savvies. Which is plenty that she's already learned in eighteen and a half years. Maybe in addition to my black long curly locks she even likes me for what I am. Being for five minutes famous and rich. Which I became honey, after five years of much persistent practice of being wholly insignificant and penniless. Or am I deluding myself. Into being dumbfounded listening to fucking insights about life which are mostly glaring fucking oversights mostly about women which you don't want to know about anyway. Because if you did, the consequences of such knowledge would never ever let you get an erection again. And that's today's Torah. By Schultz.

'Jesus Jorricks someone's on our stoop. Don't stop.'

'Shall I drive around the block sir.'

'Yeah.'

Schultz crouched down in the back of the limousine. On the third circuit the way finally clear. And the possibility of peace reigns once more. That was the behemoth. And she even had an umbrella like she did once before to beat me over the head while the Ambassador laughed his off while watching from across the street. When are they ever going to let me alone. Already they must have heard I was in the hospital. Jesus vulnerable as I presently am, what her nineteen fleshy stone of her could do to me. Always amazed me how fast she could move. Holy shit I should have hired Daniel on the spot.

Schultz helped step by step up the steps of number four Arabesque Street. To a brightly gleaming newly painted door flanked by the boxwood shrubs in their yellow bright barrels. Jorricks unlocking three locks and helping Schultz into a fresh clean spotless hall. And under the chandelier, a wide bodied apparition standing waiting. Of Mrs Prune, Sigmund Franz Schultz's still legal mother in law.

'You pansy. You miserable pansy. You're forcing us to drag our good family name through the courts.'

'Hey jesus christ you tub of lard. What the hell do you want. How did you break into my house. Get out.'

'My daughter has a legal right to be presented to the Queen. We're going to be there whether you like it or not. Marrying my daughter was how you got the money for that rubbishy show in the first place.'

'Hey what the fuck are you talking about.'

'Don't think we don't know that you were promised investment money by Al Duke as a wedding present.'

'Hey what are you kidding. Get out of here. You're trespassing breaking and entering. How did you get in.'

'To half our legal house we've got keys.'

'The pair of you bitches have already done enough damage to me as god damn thieves, vandals and arsonists. Your daughter has already served me with a writ. So our miserable relationship is sub judice terminated.'

'Terminated, my foot. We've got claims. Who do you think you are, someone. Riding around in a big car. We're British subjects. You're nothing but a blow in American. And this is our Queen not yours.'

'Excuse me sir I shall go and prepare a late lunch.'

Jorricks gently making his sideward way past the mountainous presence and dirty looks of the behemoth and towards the kitchen staircase and looking back over his shoulder at this massive female clothed in the biggest mink coat of all time in which four normal women could fit at once. That's where my money has gone. Holy shit when I need him most Jorricks leaves me now. Jeeze late lunch. Which if I don't get rid of this bitch I won't be able to have late dinner or even a late late breakfast. Left with a person known not only to be violent but one sworn to castrate me. And when with my bandaged up balls I can't protect myself, all she's got to do as she even tried once before is give one tug on my testicles and I'm going to faint in agony. But jesus as I do I'm going to pull that new wig off her head and over that face that I can't believe was good looking once. Holy jeeze and also I can't believe she has the nerve now to demand to be presented to the Queen, no less. Jesus that's all people like her and the black cloud want out of life is to be in glad rags to go glitter somewhere in front of flash bulbs and cameras rubbing elbows with nonchalant celebrities like me and the Queen to whom all it is, is hard fucking and sweating work letting the public see us in person.

'You get the hell out of here.'

'This house belongs as much to my daughter as it does to you and don't you think you're going to get away with going on living here in fifteen rooms, putting on your fancy airs as if you were important. My daughter is going to be presented to the Queen otherwise our lawyers are informing the Lord Chamberlain that you are a tax dodging practising peeping tom adulterer. Her Majesty shouldn't be allowed to meet people like you.'

'I don't believe this.'

'You better believe it because it's the last day you've got before we go straight to St James's Palace.'

'The pair of you, would do this kind of criminal slandering blackmail wouldn't you.'

'You bet we would. Because it's the truth about an upstart like you. Who belongs back in the place Woonsocket you come from and back in the bargain pornographic lingerie trade your parents engage in. We're respectable people. We have standards. My daughter wasn't brought up to marry someone as lower class crass as you.'

'The procuring pair of you are fully maintained living in luxury stealing and spending my fucking money nearly twenty thousand pounds of which was just stolen out of this house.'

'Prove it.'

'I'll prove it.'

'Go ahead and prove it Romeo.'

'You bet I'll prove it you big fat bitch.'

'Don't you call me a big fat bitch. Don't you use that language to me. You dirty Jew boy.'

'Hey you stay where you are. Don't come near me you big fat anti semitic monster.'

'I'll come near you. You damn adulterer.'

'I've just got out of the hospital. Don't you put your hands on me.'

'I'll put you back in the hospital where your balls should be kept in a jar, you Romeo you.'

'Holy shit. Jorricks. Jorricks. Come quick. For christ's sakes get up here. I'm being attacked.'

'I'll show you. In your pervert's raincoat. Frightened of me now are you Romeo.'

'Jorricks. Jorricks.'

'Need your fag butler do you.'

'Fucking slandering bitch I need only to get rid of you and that other big black cloud out of my life that's what I need. Holy jeeze don't touch me. I'm an injured person. Jesus stop. Stop.'

Schultz backing up, his left fist feinting out in the face of the behemoth and a right hand cupped over the bulge of his privates as this oncoming freight train throws him back against the hall table. The lamp capsizing to the floor and the behemoth's foot crushing the shade and bulb. Holy jeeze, how many more times does the fine art have to be risked and that fucking light and a brand new shade have to be broken in the battles that have taken place in this battle scarred hall. This is just like she attacked me once before like some kind of two ton walrus with her tits heaving like ocean waves in a hurricane.

'You bitch you're attacking a defenceless hospital patient who is already damaged, and is convalescing.'

'Don't worry, Romeo when I'm finished with you you'll be pushing up daisies.'

Jorricks at the swing hall door, a rolling pin to hand as he rushes forward to grab at the behemoth's shoulders to pull her back. The behemoth swinging round her arm, the weight of it landing across Jorricks's face, laying him out backwards on his arse on the floor. Holy shit what a haymaker, he didn't keep his guard up. And jesus she's even gained weight since she last assaulted me and is now like a fucking army tank and battleship combined. Jorricks get up, get up. Shit he's gone down again, up ended stepping on the rolling pin. Jesus as good as he is at butlering, he's a dead fucking loss in a fight. O my god this is the slaughter of the innocents. Help. Deliver me from this new Arab Israeli war. I am getting another object lesson. Only I don't know what the fuck I'm learning. Except to get as far away as possible forever from these two scheming witches. Last time of her attack I at least had my naked blatant erection to distract her. When then she tried with a brass lamp to smash my prick together with my balls into a non kosher coleslaw of cold cuts.

'Jorricks get up, get up. Welt her one behind the ear with the rolling pin.'

Schultz shoved by the shoulders crashing backwards to the floor, his head banging against the umbrella stand. Mrs Prune advancing on the supine raincoated figure, her hands outstretched like giant pincers of a lobster. Her great heaving belly pressing into her knees as she struggles to bend over to descend her claws down on Schultz's throat. Slippers dislodging from his feet. Sound of tearing. Holy cow my new trousers are not only already losing their crease but have just ripped up the seam.

'Stop. Stop.'

'Call me a fat bitch will you, Romeo.'

'I'll call you an even fatter bitch, you witch.'

'I'll fix you Jew boy.'

'You bloody big bitch bigot, my ancestors made philosophy for the world to follow before yours could even drink water out of a cup.'

The three pigeons escaping from their wrapping. The behemoth stopping in her tracks waving her arms around her head, as the pigeons in a panic flapped and beat their wings about her. At last something has put terror in her face. I'd rip her wig off if only I could stand the shock of seeing that bald head again which gave me nightmares for weeks after I first saw it. Holy jeeze the pigeons are diving at the behemoth's wig attacking her all over the face. Go guys. Go. Show her what Jewish pigeons can do trained on the best champagne money can buy. Jesus thank you Rabbi Löw. I've got three friends at last.

'Attack. Attack. Attack.'

'Get these birds off me. Get them off.'

'Attack. Attack.'

The mink befurred behemoth screaming, punching her arms in all directions and making for the door, pulling it open and jumping out on the stoop. A concussion shaking the house and rattling the windows as the door slams. The pigeons flying up the stairs to the landing, one perched on the skull top of the bust of Justinian. Jorricks slowly sitting up, and getting to his knees. Brushing himself off, blood seeping from his nose and taking a handkerchief from his sleeve to wipe his face. The embattled Schultz swivelling round on his arse and pulling himself up pressing his hands for support against the table. Jorricks bolting the door.

'Sir are you all right.'

'Yeah Jorricks, are you all right.'

'Yes I am sir. But has something happened to your forehead.'

'Jesus feels like I got blood there. O my god, it's a load of pigeon shit.'

'Very good luck, sir.'

'Boy I needed it. And thanks Jorricks for the assistance.'

'I'm sorry sir that unlike the pigeons I couldn't have been of greater help. I'm afraid I occasionally do suffer a slight fibrillation of the heart muscles which can bring on a dizzy spell.'

'Well let me tell you that bitch should be prime time wrestling to be seen on television.'

'I couldn't agree with you more, sir. But the door is securely bolted top and bottom and luncheon will be ready in fifteen minutes. Shall I serve it in the dining room.'

'No just give me a tray in the drawing room. That way I can keep an eye on the street.'

'I'll light the fire sir.'

Schultz hobbling into the drawing room to peek out the window. The behemoth on the pavement shaking her fist at the house. Jeeze that a beautiful girl could be born out of such a monster must be a miracle of nature. But it's no miracle her daughter turned into such a bitch just like her mother. Holy jeeze she's kicking the fenders and doors of the car. And the Ambassador, with his big white teeth is grinning in his big black mouth thinking it's so fucking funny. No wonder his bloody country is always throwing a coup and catching him and his dictator off guard when all he's ever doing is watching this house with his binoculars. Jesus there's another saga I might have learned a lesson from. Why didn't Priscilla go marry that big African black gorilla King Buggybooiamcheesetoo who was chasing her ass all over London and then she could have got herself presented all over the jungles as a queen. O christ at last, a taxi is coming to the rescue if that bitch can ever fit in the door. Holy jeeze the Ambassador is waving at

130

me. Maybe he's glad to see I'm still alive. Of course some kind of attempted coup is going on in here nearly every fucking five minutes. Maybe that's how he learned to survive so many coups of his own.

Schultz wrapped in a blanket finishing his lemon sole and chablis and with a coffee and an Armagnac reading the morning's papers in front of the blazing drawing room fire. Holy jeeze here it all is. Binky's mother's obituary. Measured with the metacarpel of my thumb, two whole column inches.

Lady Doris Ottoline Fitzherbert Crawford Sunningdale of Radiator Castle, near Perth, Scotland, who has died at the age of 49, was the daughter of the sixteenth Marquess of Radiator. Educated at Heatherdown and Roedean, she served as a nurse in the Second World War and married the industrial magnate R. D. F. Sunningdale who, before his death, presided over a worldwide business in textiles, oil and meat processing. Regarded as a great society beauty, Lady Ottoline, as she preferred to be known, successfully ran several large estates inherited from her father and was an accomplished shot and horse woman who hunted with the Pithquick. She is survived by a daughter, Catherine, and a son, Binky Sunningdale, the well-known theatrical producer.

She had a title no less, while Binky the shrewd cunt goes around pretending he's a commoner, no doubt because show biz has such a long reputation of fleecing the aristocracy. Holy cow what the fuck was she doing walking out her door after dinner to plummet to her death. With everything, except a wonderful, honest trustworthy son, to live for. When I saw her at his Lordship's wedding she was even eminently fuckable. Christ with a beautiful mother you must think sometimes of fucking her. Even though I wouldn't go near mine with a barge pole. I don't even know where I got my good looks from. My father, lines harrowed deep by business worries into his face, sure didn't resemble any movie star. Holy jeeze maybe this isn't really the ripe time to get Binky the son of a bitch. But I could vet every damn contract and deal he's got in that office. Christ if my own mother died I'd expect everybody who could to rat on me. And here I am standing on sentiment. When in this business with so much happening on every single battle front, treachery is the inevitable norm. Binky's out to crush me. While money is pouring out of the fucker's trust funds a mile long, if that's how they measure the fucking things. And he's no doubt now inheriting a million acres and five castles like his Lordship does from some aunt every few months. But this afternoon and tonight I really got to in these few hours to convalesce. And by the law of averages and by the pigeon shit dropped on me, something wonderful has got to happen. I'm counting on it. Jesus maybe I should do what I shouldn't do. Fuck it. Don't. Stop. Why can't I keep my fingers out of dialling certain god damn numbers on the phone.

'Hello.'

'Louella it's Sigmund.'

'How many times do I have to tell you I know who it is. There's nobody else with a voice like yours.'

'Hey jeeze honey that don't sound like any compliment.'

'It's not supposed to be a compliment it's a simple matter of fact. Why didn't you call me back from the hospital.'

'They had to suddenly redress my wounds honey. I was leaking blood.'

'O god. Are you all right.'

'O yeah, fine, fine.'

'I've just been trying to urgently ring you. The hospital said you'd checked out. And the exchange told me your number in Arabesque Street is changed and ex directory.'

'Yeah. I had to change it for security reasons. And it was getting a little claustrophobic over there at the hospital. Did the funeral happen. Is it over.'

'Al is not dead yet.'

'O jeeze sorry. I thought you said last time you were telling me that his life was ebbing away after his operation.'

'I did not say his life was ebbing away. I said complications had set in.'

'O sorry. O shit I mean sorry there were complications. Hey jesus. Look. Just while you're waiting through the new crisis why don't you come over and see me. Before more complications set into my life. I'm home. Having a nice Armagnac by the fire.'

'Your wife this morning was on the telephone to me. Saying among her other unpleasant accusations that she was on her way to jump in the river.'

'At high tide.'

'Yes. As a matter of fact. How did you know.'

'Well she always waits for high tide on the Thames to jump off. To make sure it's deep enough. She looks it up in the papers. Here wait I'll tell you the exact time she would have phoned you. Got it right here. Eleven seventeen. Isn't that right.'

'Yes.'

132

'The tide's at eleven forty two. And she would have calculated the taxi took twenty five minutes to get from Kensington to a bridge. She used to be a high diving champ. Also held some record for the one hundred yard backstroke.'

'I see.'

'Well come on over honey. Let's have a little fucking fun in life. I got a big fire roaring here. The place is all looking beautiful. Not a trace left of it being wrecked in the fire.'

'Your wife sounded so serious as if she meant what she said. Don't you have any sympathy for her.'

'No I don't. We are totally fucking well fatally estranged. Hey look, a dozen times she's done this, either a fainting fit on a floor or sitting on a window sill. Ask Al. I used to have to telephone him what to do. Even to holding a mirror in front of her mouth to see if she was breathing. Her own mother was just here a while ago trying to murder me. The family is just like that. They got some idea I'm some kind of ore deposit they dip into to pull out handfuls of gold nuggets. They're a bunch of hysterics. By whom I'm being systematically tortured into my grave.'

'Don't be such a big cry baby.'

'Cry baby. Hey honey. Only a little while ago I was knocked down in my front hall. Not only do I need companionship but I need protection.'

'O K can you give me a couple of hours.'

'O jesus honey, that means at least two hours, are you really coming.'

'I'll be there in three hours. I have to wait to phone the hospital in Los Angeles.'

'Jesus honey, don't get my hopes up and then not show up. My spiritual resilience isn't up to abject disappointment. I'm a little bit hors de combat here.'

'How bad was your accident.'

'Honey, just let me tell you all about it when you arrive. O K Jesus. This is the best news I've had. No shit. Or rather no pigeon shit, which was recently shat on me. And which I know from now on is going to bring me good luck. I'll give you a glass of the best champagne you ever had. And you can even meet my new faithful companions.'

Schultz falling asleep, a hand still round his glass of Armagnac. Jorricks covering him in a blanket. Darkness settling on Arabesque Street. Late afternoon traffic purring by. Tiny hail stones tapping the window panes as a wintry squall blows over London. Five thirty bells booming of Big Ben. Jeeze. I fell asleep. Where am I. Woonsocket.

What time is it. Christ it's late. And I was dreaming it was three o'clock after school back in Woonsocket. When I ran all the way home to be down my mother and father's basement lingerie store. My suicidal job coming home every day was to be stationed at the brassière counter to politely as I could, ask the customers please don't handle the merchandise with dirty hands. No memory do I hate more. And holy shit let me tell you the dirty looks you get for doing that. And even worse when one afternoon a big black woman nearly the size of the behemoth punches me square right in the nose nearly busting it and right while I was minding the cash register alone in the store. I had to run up the stairs to escape and try to find a cop. And the black bitch went out of the place stealing not only a couple of dozen brassières that didn't fit her but every brand of stockings, bloomers every colour, panties every shape, scanties every size, even boudoir caps we were featuring in a sale. Jesus the awful things big grown up people do to little children half their size. The ordeal left me shaking all over and I pissed in my short pants. Everyone could see the piss down my leg. That day Uncle Werb came to visit, found me crying. He made me a present of a tiny diamond I still got to this day carried in my wallet. Jesus what a kind man he was. In contrast to the miserable violent types we had more than a few times coming into the store. He said, Sigmund never cry standing by the cash register in case people think business is bad. Always even though you're crying keep smiling as if business was good. Even though it's bad.

'Sir excuse me putting on the light, but there is a person at the door enquiring after you, who gives her name as Louella.'

'O jeeze Jorricks. Christ show her in. I meant to tell you she was coming but I fell asleep. Put some of that champagne we brought back from the hospital in a bucket. And we'll have a little smoked salmon on the side.'

'Very good sir.'

Louella stopping in the drawing room doorway in a black sweater and string of pearls. Her long tapering legs in her snug satin blue slacks. A shy uncertain smile on her face as she pushes back the sleeves of her sweater. That strip of flesh of her ankle showing under a stocking and between the cuff of trouser and her shoe. Her hair combed slanting over one eye.

'Hey honey. You got here.'

'Yes. I got here.'

Louella stepping in, glancing around the room. A lamp alight in the corner and the fire glowing a pink light on the walls. Schultz attempting to get up from the armchair, suddenly tensing and grimacing in pain.

'O please don't get up Sigmund.'

'Jesus maybe I won't. Christ maybe I can't. But honey come in. Come in. Sit down. Right over there. Get toasty by the fire.'

'It's nice and warm in here. And it looks as if nothing has happened.'

'We had the painters and carpenters over from the theatre. They did some beautiful job fixing up and cleaning everywhere. Hey what can I get Jorricks to get you. We'll have a little champagne. Is that all right.'

'That would be fine.'

'O jesus honey it's really good to see you. How's Al.'

'You really don't have to ask about Al you know.'

'But I'd like to know.'

'They say his condition is stabilized whatever that means. He wants me to go to California to be with him. At least there we're free of all his awful past wives. And what about you. How are you. What happened to you.'

'Jeeze honey, you know right at this exact time I'd like not to get into the whole fickle chain of circumstances that led to the complicated story. It was something that happened between my legs. Suffice to say sort of like a break in a vulnerable place sort of thing. Hey christ you look really great.'

'Thank you. Gosh this house is big. I'd forgotten how elegantly beautiful Belgravia is.'

'Yeah honey, it's pretty nice around here. Just a handful of very private people. We even have got a couple of nice old pubs down the mews over there.'

'I know. I have been in one. And whenever I've walked down this street I've always thought it one of the most pleasant streets in all of London.'

'Honey, when you go past number four remember the welcome mat is always out.'

Another squall sending hailstones sprinkling the drawing room window panes. Jorricks wheeling in a table under a white tablecloth. Two plates of sliced smoked salmon in a rosette, and a wooden bucket of champagne and two gleaming tulip glasses.

'Shall I open the champagne now sir or leave it a moment further to chill.'

'That's all right Jorricks, we'll have a little sip now.'

Jorricks undoing the wine cap and wrapping the bottle in a towel and gently twisting out the cork with a soft pop. Alternately filling the glasses and handing the first one full to Louella with a smile. Holy jeeze what's this. The first time Jorricks has ever smiled at a woman come into this house. Christ he's even fussing over her opening her napkin across her lap. Fuck a duck. Will wonders and surprises never cease. Here I am waiting tense on tenterhooks to get him fast out of the room so as not to throw a pall over proceedings and he's dancing solicitous attendance all over her. Christ and she fucking loves it like a purring cat. Holy shit that's something anyway, if she doesn't want to come live with me she at least might want to come and be waited on by my butler.

'I'll draw the curtains and will that be all sir.'

'Yeah, that's swell Jorricks. Thanks.'

Jorricks turning back at the door and inclining his head to one side and slightly bowing forward from the waist, a wide smile on his face.

'Bon appétit madam.'

'Thank you Jorricks, very much.'

Schultz as the door quietly closed, sitting his mouth agape. The firelight dancing on the ceiling. Wow. Did you see that. No maître d' in no hotel I've ever been in ever did a gesture as beautifully perfect as that. Talk of religious ceremonies. And making an obeisance to a goddess. And jesus even Jorricks recognizes that this is the most gorgeous one. And O boy even following my hangover, my craving for this champagne has come back. O christ why do I have to be confronted again with this woman. Why couldn't she just be a fucking bitch like the others which could reduce the pain substantially of loving her. And make it easy to suppress the constant panting longing to have my prick deep inside her. Wow and I adore the way she adores her champagne and the way her pearly white teeth smilingly bite through her orange pink salmon. Nothing on this earth is there as beautiful as a slender beautiful woman who's really hungry and who's gobbling down food and drink with a good healthy appetite.

'My goodness Sigmund. You're not exactly slumming here are you. What utterly lovely champagne. And look, the lemon tied in gauze.'

'Yeah so it doesn't squirt in the eye.'

'How did you ever find anyone like Jorricks. He's positively wonderful.'

'Kind of long story I won't go into right now but he is wonderful. There's not one fucking thing that comes into this house and then goes into my mouth that isn't perfection.'

136

'Yes, the bread, the butter and this smoked salmon are perfectly splendid even though one hates saying anything is perfectly splendid.'

'Have more, honey, have more. Go ahead. Pour yourself. It might be better I don't move.'

'Gosh I might too. And you.'

'Well just a token bit to keep you company. O boy. Just let me sigh. Whew. Come home to roost. It's like having climbed to a mountain top these last few days. You get to the summit finally after all the struggle. Up out of all the chaos. And suddenly there's the view. Utterly beautifully lying out there all around you. And you honey are the very fantastic most gorgeous centre of attraction.'

'Ha ha. I'll bet you say that to all the girls you've probably put sitting exactly where I'm sitting and drinking champagne. But of course I'm not complaining.'

A rapid knock, the drawing room door opening. Jorricks holding it ajar, his tongue nervously licking his lips. A napkin stuck in his collar hanging down his front as he suddenly pulls it down and crumples it up in his hand.

'Excuse me sir, pardon me very much for interrupting, but there is something I think you should see just on now on the television which I've been watching in the kitchen.'

'Jesus Jorricks. What the hell is it. The Russians.'

'No sir.'

'Christ not the theatre on fire.'

'No. But sir, I think you should put the television straight on. Let me do it for you. And excuse me madam. And sir I'll be in the kitchen if you need me.'

'Jesus honey you don't mind if we watch the six o'clock news do you. It must be something about my partner Binky's mother's death. Maybe it was murder or something.'

Jorricks in a headlong rush out of the room, closing the door with a louder noise than is his discreet usual. The colour coming into the big glass tube. A reporter with a microphone as he stands near a wall embankment the wind blowing through his hair. Hailstones coming down out of the shafts of floodlit darkness. A pair of looming twin towers in the background rising from glistening lights on the river. The reporter shouting over the roar of a helicopter low overhead.

'We are here outside this ancient fortress on the bank of the river Thames where the Crown Jewels are kept and where it is said that Henry the Sixth met his death while at prayer. The woman now perched on the west upstream tower of Tower Bridge was seen early afternoon climbing out from a window and onto the ledge where she now sits high above the water. Since that time today Tower Bridge has been closed to traffic and a vigil kept on this just identified lady threatening to jump down at least a hundred and fifty feet into the water. From where I'm standing now police patrol boats are on the ebb tide waiting to rescue should the lady jump as she's all afternoon threatened to do. Her identity was still a question up till only a moment ago when the lady shouted to police that she is a celebrity and her name is Mrs Schultz.'

'My god. What's this. Holy gefilte fish, I can't watch. Jesus I got to watch.'

'The lady who has accepted blankets and food has refused all requests to leave her almost inaccessible perch. And has continued her threat to jump should she be approached too close. Should there be any further developments during the present newscast our cameras will return to Tower Bridge. From Traitor's Gate, on Tower Wharf we now hand you back to the studio.'

Schultz sitting upright in his chair his glass of champagne clutched tightly in his hand and a crescent bite gone out of his salmon adorned piece of brown bread.

'Jesus Louella turn it off before the studio newscaster announces the fucking bound to be insignificant world news.'

'O dear Sigmund. O dear.'

'Holy jeeze she had to choose the most conspicuous bridge in all of London to jump off when there are a dozen other bridges to choose from ten minutes away from her house. Holy christ. What made her do this.'

'She loves you Sigmund.'

'Holy fucking shit honey. How the fuck can you say anything as psychopathic sounding as that. All she's ever loved is to see that I don't ever get another piece of ass. Jesus christ, sorry I put it like that. But I'm fucking distraught.'

'Well Sigmund think what Priscilla's feeling like in the wind and hail out there overhanging the Thames.'

'Don't worry she's loving the attention of the whole fucking nation she's getting.'

'But Sigmund she could get killed or drowned.'

'Boy that'll be the day it happens to her with nine bloody lives. Jesus what's that now. I knew it. In two seconds the door bell is ringing and banging. O jesus go peek out the drapes and see if you can see who it is Louella. Sorry about this.'

'O my god Sigmund. You're right. The street is full of reporters and cameras.'

'Jesus honey. This just ain't my day.'

Schultz getting to his feet and flopping back again in his seat and staring across the room. Three invitations on the mantelpiece. One gold engraved. With the words that someone was having the pleasure of inviting me. Christ here I am on the verge of a prominent social position in London. People who've never even met me inviting me as if I were an elite asset to their parties. Just to get their picture taken with me sipping a cocktail. And christ here I am jumping up and down in my seat as if nothing is wrong in my balls. Shows what a powerful local anaesthetic utter panic is. O god Rabbi Löw, are you listening tuned to this new saga unfolding. When for the first time in my life for five minutes at least, I'm not looking for publicity. And two seconds it takes them to get here. This is it. My fucking goose is cooked. I'm never going to be able to meet the Queen. That's just how they planned it like this.

My social
Image
Is ruined

▼
11
▲

'Sir, Lord Nectarine is on the phone.'

'Bring it in and plug it in here, Jorricks.'

And on the double Jorricks carrying the phone and placing the receiver on Schultz's lap as he takes the cord across the room and kneels on a knee to plug it into the skirting board. Jorricks back again lifting the champagne from the ice bucket and with a towel wiping the moisture from the bottle as he pours to replenish Louella's and Schultz's glass. Holy jeeze pouring champagne at a time of action stations with the bullets flying. Boy if that ain't fucking grace under pressure. And elegance in adversity. Then he nice as you please bows Louella out to go to the ladies' room. And at a time like this we all need to take a piss. And be lucky if something else much more unpleasant isn't darkening our drawers.

'Schultz. Have you seen the six o'clock news.'

'I've seen it. And I've gone into purdah.'

'Why aren't you there.'

'I'm not there because I'm trying to give my balls a tiny bit of recuperation and plus according to the news traffic's blocked. Plus I've been through these situations too many times before.'

'Good god Schultz you're still your wife's husband. And I do believe she must be in some distress. To put it mildly.'

'Hey she's suing and her behemoth mother is assaulting me.'

'That's no excuse Schultz. The woman is the mother of your children.'

'Don't tell me. I know it. And she has a fucking injunction out against me to keep me six hundred yards away from them. But look, I can't already get out my door, the Press with notebooks out have got the street jammed with their cameras. Anyway all I have to do is wait for the nine o'clock news for the latest and by that time she's probably done a nude jig along the parapet.'

'Schultz you're a fucking cad. And should be excluded forever from the rank of gentleman.'

'Cad you call me for christ's sake. Hey jesus exclude. Just before you say more let me include what I've already been through without this present cliff hanging event even happening. And when I should be in New York and Hollywood with deals concluded already.'

'Well Schultz I've got to go to Scotland on the train later tonight to be at Binky's mother's funeral tomorrow. But if you don't go down to Tower Bridge to be of assistance to your wife, I shall.'

'Stop. Stop your Lordship. What you maybe don't know is she's a high diving and swimming champion. She was born practically on a beach. It's nothing to her to be sitting up there.'

'In the sleet, icy cold and wind Schultz.'

'I heard it on the news, they gave her blankets and food. And she could go smooth as an arrow down to pierce the water as if it was part of a swimming follies. Hey shit by the way, what train you taking.'

'The eleven fifteen overnight sleeper from King's Cross Station. A train perhaps better known as the Flying Scotsman.'

'Shit, if my balls don't drop off meanwhile I'm going to go flying with you. I'll meet you there. That way we're not that far from Tower Bridge. And maybe on the drive over I might stop by the action and see what's happening. That is if I am ever able to escape through the reporters surrounding this house.'

'Schultz you really do take the fucking cake, sometimes. This is no time for joking. When someone's life is at stake.'

'Look believe me your Lordship. Truly believe me. I did everything possible to make that woman's life happy. And let me tell you, provided the money was in abundance she didn't even care if I was there. Shit I can think of no place better to be at this moment than up in them fucking bereft deserted highlands with the goats sheep and deer. Jesus I think I can hear the fucking drums and bagpipes already.'

'Well Schultz if you're not joking and on that train, you'll certainly hear them in the morning. But you're not exactly a friend of the deceased.'

'Sure I am, I met her at your wedding reception while you were busy with a dentist and a doctor or something examining your inflamed tooth you got at the time. And if you also remember at that reception, your security guards who thought I gate crashed tackled and jumped on top of me in front of the whole place and all the other guests.'

'Do you know Schultz such events have entirely slipped my mind. God how time flies.'

'Well the busted ass I got at the time hasn't slipped mine. Jesus your Lordship, how do I get rid of the reporters to be able to get out my door.'

'Schultz you merely go and simply give what is commonly referred to as a press conference.'

'A press conference. Are you crazy. About my wife trying to jump off a bridge. I should be denying my fucking connection.'

'Clearly Schultz since reporters are already there, the connection has already been made.'

'O my god. Jesus I'm in no condition to stand on my stoop, my balls still bulging under bandages to give a fucking press conference on a subject which has got the whole fucking entire nation embroiled.'

'Well for once Schultz the words shrinking violet may be at least, and at last, said of you.'

'Boy I'm shrinking. And let me tell you I think I am going violet enough to be a pansy soon. Right down to my toenails. Plus right now I have a dear lady friend in my house as a private guest. So I am going to publicly deny everything.'

'And Schultz be warned that if you do, you'll appear on all the wrong inside pages of every periodical in England saying exactly that and the page opposite will produce a marriage certificate and wedding photographs plus a picture of your lady guest, hopefully not in the nude.'

'Jesus, your Lordship what the fuck do you think I should do then.'

'I suggest that you suggest to your lady friend that she make herself as discreetly scarce as possible and that you own up to the bridge situation entirely. Simple lies told in the avoidance of public truth have brought entire British governments down.'

'O jesus, goodbye, your Lordship. At least you've been one fucking friend who's made an effort to remain one. Hey do they serve breakfast on this train.'

'If they don't Schultz I assure you that you can get the very best you're ever likely to get at the station terminus in the morning.'

'OK right up till the last second, don't let the train go without me. I am now about to plunge into the stress situation of my life.'

'Well Schultz, in all the current directions in which you may venture let me wish you bon voyage.'

'Thanks. I'm presently first going to try to jump on a balloon ascending into heaven.'

Schultz hanging up the phone. Shifting gently in his seat in his chair and adjusting his thighs. Ominous sounds from the street. The phone on my other line ringing down in the kitchen. Jesus, someone has broken through my security curtain. O god, before recognition comes which you never think is going to come you struggle and struggle your whole fucking life against obscurity and rejection. And people closing doors in your face. Just like my Uncle Isadore did in my father's face, his own brother. As we as a family stood on their stoop calling uninvited at their house one day on the eve of Yom Kippur. They owned a fucking path up between lawns to their front door. We owned just a fucking door. They owned a car which stood in its own fucking garage. We owned a jalopy with the springs broke which stood rusting in the street. They had six bedrooms. We had two. O christ the ignominy of that visit. They told us to go away and go home, don't bother us. We were poor. Uncle Isadore was rich. I got named after him when I was born, my father thinking the name a good omen. And Uncle Isadore, said why have you done that nuisance to me when I already call my own son Isadore, who with your recent impersonator means two Isadore Schultzs in the vicinity of Woonsocket. And suddenly I'm called Sigmund and Franz and Isadore is my third name to always remind me of such humiliation and shame. And on that day our tails between our legs, we had to go visit Uncle Ezekiel who was a tailor in two rooms like us and who had a smart assed fat little fucker son called Saul. Holy christ I sit here now. Head hung in hands. Sweat under my armpits and at the topmost gross income of my life which could buy and sell Uncle Isadore and his fucking son ten times over. Plus I stand poised on the stepping stone into the celestial perfection and presence of the Queen. And yet here I am fucked and finished.

'O Sigmund. O Sigmund. There there now. It's going to be all right.'

Louella coming back into the room putting her hand gently down on the black curly tresses of Schultz's bent head. The musky smell of her perfume. Her thigh shining blue under the satin as she kneels her knee on the arm rest of the chair. The bell ringing and the knocker rapping at the front door. Rabbi Löw hello. Quick. Come in. I need your advice not to mention maybe even moral assistance. Before all this happened to me I was just this evening going to settle down to read about the care and feeding of pigeons in my encyclopaedia. Everything for a change was calm and comfort. Then after a dozen phone calls trying, I finally get the woman I love and the scent of her lovely body right by my side and nearly in my clutches. So tell me why suddenly this precious situation has to be invaded by what must now be world wide television coverage entertaining everyone from Zanzibar to Prague. All, excepting you, who I know is too sensible to waste time watching such a situation comedy starring yours truly. Who hasn't even for the third day running, checked the box office. Or even seen to the Royal retiring room at the theatre where I am having the most sumptuous setting appropriately made ready to receive the·Queen. Are you listening Rabbi Löw. He's listening, Sigmund. And he'll tell you about the condition you've encountered in two words which is known in the Torah, and which loosely translated from the Hebrew means, tough shit. The kind that even with a hammer and chisel you can't take chips out of and if it drops can break your toe. Jesus Rabbi

Löw, stop. There's a turd already that's landed on my skull to send me reeling. So now let me tell you something. One thing show business teaches you, is the five second rule. Which is do what you have to do in the first two seconds. Or run the risk of being fucked for eternity.

'Sigmund, I know there isn't much I can do, but if I can, I'd like to be of help.'

'Honey you already are, just being here. His Lordship says I should go face the music and go give a conference to the Press.'

'Sigmund I really don't think so. Some of those reporters can be like tigers when they're after a story and will keep digging and never let up.'

'Fuck honey what am I going to do trapped in here. Just the thought of what the Rhode Island papers and television could do with this international incident. I'm an American for christ's sake from the smallest state in the Union which automatically makes everything larger than life, and it's going to give my poor defenceless parents who haven't even seen their priceless twin granddaughters, a heart attack. Shit that bitch is now involving innocent people. My parents out there in their respectable suburban community and at last out of the ghetto and now with decent neighbours. I mean it's all so fucking awful, that's what it is.'

'Sigmund, Sigmund, you mustn't let it get you down though. Surely we're exaggerating this out of all proportion.'

'Well honey not if you consider that every internal revenue and income tax inspector keeping files on me around the world is going to be watching and listening. But don't worry I'll be O K at least I can hold out the two and a half hours till the nine o'clock news.'

'Here Sigmund at least let me make you more comfortable. And you'll feel better, sip some champagne.'

'Honey, thanks. You know I can chew fucking lawyers up for breakfast and light my cigars with their writs, but suddenly this bloody thing like a fucking bad dream has really hit me. How could I ever even imagine this could happen. Jesus so many show biz crises have come at me from every angle and direction for so many years you think you're fielding everything just like catching baseballs on the fly with the glove held behind your back as I used to be able to do and kids would come from miles around to watch me do it. But jesus now, wham. This ain't no baseball, it's a meteor the size of a football field that's coming at me. And it's no longer me I'm worried about. It's two innocent children. And my mother and father who aren't ready for this.'

'But she might have already come down Sigmund. How do you know.'

'Because I know she hasn't. But hey jesus honey, thinking about you. If Al sees this on television in his hospital bedroom in Los Angeles, if he's got even one working gasket left, he's either going to once and for all conk out or put his fist or foot through his TV screen. And O jesus, what's worse is.'

'Yes I know. If it's ever made known I'm here.'

'O god honey I am sorry. Jesus maybe go ring and tell the hospital to black out all international news from him. But jesus knowing Al that would only make him get two sets to watch in case he thought he was missing something. O K I got to, like in the Coast Guard call action stations.'

Schultz lifting himself up out of the chair to reach for one last sliver of smoked salmon, rolling it up and anointing it with lemon and putting it in his mouth. Louella nervously licking her lips. O god when she does that. Which even in all this personal catastrophe is giving me a hard on.

'Honey, remember, whatever else ever happens. I, Sigmund Franz Isadore Schultz, truly fucking swear upon the life of my mother, that I love you.'

'O god Sigmund. Please. Can't we just be good and trusting friends.'

'Honey no. Because when my balls are better I want to fuck you.'

'What's wrong with your balls.'

'O jesus honey don't get alarmed that was just a slip of the tongue I just said. And we can't get into that right now. Let's just say they're sort of in a state of suspended animation, resting.'

Schultz sending Jorricks to hang a towel over the number four on the front door. Another bottle of champagne opened. And supper of macaroni and cheese served on trays. The fire blazing in the grate. The drawing room drapes tight closed. The street noises increasing. Even to a fist fight between two motorists trying to see who was going to drive first through a space wide enough for only one car. Floodlights now, illumining the door. No need to call the police who are already there. But with this attention, there's no doubt at all that every actress that I didn't give a part to that I promised after I fucked her in an anonymous hotel, is going to know where I live. Jesus maybe I really got to catch that train to Scotland. If I can ever get out of here. After my whole house if not my face, ends up on the nine o'clock news. With them still ringing and knocking and Jorricks telling them to go away.

'I guess with their being so insistent you could speak off the record or something to them Sigmund couldn't you.'

'Honey at this stage and in this electronic age, everything, and I mean everything, is on the record and coming out of everyone's mouth live and recorded for repeat replay transmission for all time. Shit here we go. Honey. Hold on to your hat. It's time for the nine o'clock news. And time for me to walk the fucking plank.'

A face of a clock, the second hand ticking away the seconds as a bell tolls nine. The face of the bespectacled commentator coming on screen. Louella reaching her hand to pat Schultz on the shoulder as he grabs the arm rests and shifts forward to the front edge of his chair.

'Good evening, this is the nine o'clock news. The Israeli forces this evening, making large advances on a wide front across their borders into Syria, Jordan and Lebanon, continued their several concerted lightning attacks, which has now again involved the Middle East in a potential conflict which some political quarters consider could renew a Middle Eastern war and spread further. The Prime Minister has called an emergency meeting in Downing Street to assess the situation.'

Schultz in his chair taking a deep breath and blowing his breath out between his lips in a loud sigh. On the TV screen tanks, sending the sand flying in their tracks, and roaring over desert terrain, their guns blazing as aircraft scream overhead.

'Holy shit honey imagine all this going on that I didn't even know was happening. Look at that, our fucking guys are showing them something. Look christ at that rapid fire from those 75 millimetres. Boy those things can knock your fucking hat off. Wham. Bang bang. They're fucking wonderful. Jesus they're not only keeping Israel safe but also distracting the public attention from my fucking life. Thank you, guys. Even though I haven't had a chance yet to contribute help or money I'm behind you all the way and long live Zionism and Israel.'

The commentator back on screen, his voice coming over as a picture of a nuclear bomb detonates underground in Nevada. A spiel about Russian objection. Another picture of the North Sea and an oil rig capsizing in a storm. And a spiel about the boost such rigs and their oil were giving to the British economy.

'Well honey, touch wood. Jesus where is some real wood to touch. Never mind I'll touch some in a second. At least this looks like peace will reign in our time. She must have come quietly down. Jesus let's send down to Jorricks for another bottle of champagne.'

The commentator voice over as in the distance Tower Bridge comes into focus. Its tall tip top spires illuminated and the graceful cables sweeping down to shore on either side.

'Now back to London.'

'O my god no, she's not still on the fucking bridge.'

'The drama which began this afternoon on Tower Bridge continued to unfold this evening when a woman professing to be a Mrs Schultz and the wife of the well known impresario, remained perched on a parapet threatening to jump. We are now for the latest developments with our outside broadcast cameras at Tower Bridge.'

Its two spans suspended between the shadowy elevations of the twin towers, figures up on the end of extension ladders from a fire brigade vehicle parked on the overpass. The camera panning to Priscilla standing up on the parapet and glancing at her wrist and removing a blanket from her shoulders and taking off her coat, revealing jeans and a tight sweater, her mouth mouthing shouts. A reporter in front of battlements his voice coming over as the camera focuses again high on a tower.

'And at this very moment as you can see from our camera, the woman has removed her coat and is. O my god. She is. She has. Jumped. Or rather taken a dive.'

Priscilla springing forward from the parapet in a graceful arched arc, her hands balletically mid air touching her toes and her body straightening like an arrow as she plummets fingertips first down into the rippling black water to disappear in a neat white foaming splash. The idling police launches moving towards the spot. Two deep sea divers flopping backwards into the water as a few feet away, a dark head pops up. The motor police boats closing in and hands reaching to pull Priscilla from the glistening black river into a launch.

Schultz covering his eyes. And uncovering them again. Holy jesus christ, I don't even know how much of that descent I was watching but what an olympic medal winning performance. Jesus I hope no one else could hear what she was saying before she jumped, because even if it wasn't broadcast I certainly could read her lips. She was shouting, my husband is a tax dodging adulterer. Just so the Lord Chamberlain could hear, and cancel my reception of the Queen. Here I am struggling years paying good money to publicity agents and badgering them into giving newsflash handouts for international immediate release and all we then get if we're fucking lucky is the ass end of a column mention buried somewhere near the obituaries in the middle of some provincial newspaper. And now in the two and a half seconds it takes for her to hit the water she makes news headlines and prime time T V coverage

which is probably already around the world. Sending neighbours
running up the front path to my mother's and father's house who now
semi retired to the borders of Connecticut have got not only a path just
like Uncle Isadore's up to their front door but a duck pond with
ducks. And their new next door acquaintances, who have ponds of
their own with more ducks, will be shouting, hey Mr and Mrs Schultz,
hurry and watch the TV there's something you should see, because we
know your son is a big wheel in London from the posters you got
hanging up in your front hall and we figure that how many Schultzs
are there in this world could there be, that there isn't some connection.
And so now my mother and father can hear and watch. In the special
nice little den they built on the back of the house for peace and quiet
with the big picture window for watching their ducks. And where now
they can blow their gaskets in every heart valve they have. And I'll be
back tomorrow in Rhode Island making arrangements for their funeral
to bury them.

After
I have just sworn
On the life
Of my mother
That I love
Louella

The milling noise of reporters and photographers outside of
number four Arabesque Street. The front door swinging
open and Schultz behind his silvered impenetrable sunglasses, stepping out in Jorricks's bathrobe and slippers. TV
floodlights illuminating all sixteen windows on the five floors
of this townhouse even to the three peeking over the attic
eaves. Clapping erupting. Schultz's mirrored spectacles glinting with
the flash and glare of camera bulbs. Photographers jostling on the
pavement and climbing up the stoop.

12

'That's it Mr Schultz, a little more profile. Can you smile.'

Policemen guiding cars past the crowd of reporters and camera
crews blocking the thoroughfare. The hooting of horns and a traffic
jam in the surrounding streets. Every window in the Ambassador's
house across the way occupied with a black face or two, watching. A
reporter spokesman shouting above the noise.

'Sir are you the husband of the lady who jumped from Tower
Bridge.'

'I thought she dived but otherwise no comment.'

'Mr Schultz we understand you are the producer of London's biggest
smash hit, will you comment for us on that.'

'Well yeah. It's a smash hit and everybody should see it.'

'Mr Schultz is it true that you and your wife are presently estranged
and that you have ignored your wife's request to meet the Queen
rumoured to be coming to attend a performance of your production
Kiss It Don't Hold It It's Too Hot.'

'No comment.'

'Mr Schultz presuming that you are the lady's husband as she claims
aren't you very upset that she has chosen to threaten all afternoon to
jump off a bridge, and then jumps.'

'No comment that's all I've got to say. And it's goodbye for now.
And thank you for coming gentlemen.'

'One more question please Mr Schultz. As one of London's currently
most successful impresarios, why are you here tonight behind your
disguise of sunglasses, attempting to deny any relationship instead of
being at your wife's side. And aren't you a little disturbed that as just
reported by radio from the police launch arriving at Traitor's Gate a
minute ago, your wife says she has been driven to doing this by your
cruel and inhuman treatment. Do you have any comment to that.'

'Yeah I have a comment. Go fuck yourselves you bunch of blood-
thirsty bastards. I don't have to listen to these kind of accusations on
my own front door step.'

'Thank you for your comments. And for taking off your sunglasses. And for being such a diplomat Mr Schultz.'

'Yeah, the same to you, that's what I am, goodnight, goodbye.'

Schultz stepping back in the door and slamming it shut. Putting on his sunglasses once more and Jorricks solicitously offering an arm to escort his master back into the drawing room. Schultz slowly levering himself again into his chair. Perspiration on the brow. Utter shambles in the heart.

'Sir, I took the liberty of showing the young lady to the pink bedroom.'

'Jesus Jorricks is she all right.'

'I think madam has a migraine.'

'Thanks, Jorricks, this is a pretty bad time.'

'Well sir, they got what they were looking for, your very forthright chastisement.'

'Jesus Jorricks did you hear me in here.'

'It was live on the television sir.'

Schultz slumping back deeper in his chair and shaking the big black curls back and forth on his head. Clenching a fist and pounding it on his knee. Holy jeeze now I've done it. As soon as I saw her two fucking hired detectives right out there in the middle of all the journalists, I couldn't control my temper. The whole fucking thing is a put up job. To inflame the Press against me. With lies and innuendo. At what is now becoming before I know it, the most crucial time of my existence. That will go live by satellite to the USA. Be networked coast to coast so that every fucking station across the nation can make capital out of my fucking life. While right here in London they are scaring the woman I love away to bed without me. What new girlfriend is ever going to be convinced I'm a genius. After I've just made a public imbecile out of myself being honest. Rabbi Löw. You must have got a load of this latest. And being the great astronomer of life's vicissitudes, tell me please through your telescope where the fuck am I orbiting now. Ah Sigmund, hello. I have a prediction. There are comets coming. You are orbiting into trouble. And it is because you are a rube. Hey christ Rabbi. Who are you calling a rube. And comets have already come. Two in the shape of busted balls. But I ain't no rube. No. Because Sigmund is going to win. And one of these days go float on his backside in the sunshine of the Riviera. How can you be so sure Sigmund. Sigmund is sure because this old Schultzy boy has money for a change, that's why. But jesus that black cloud bitch is out to destroy exactly the thing that's putting the bread and butter into her mouth. Royalty's presence could have added two whole years to the run. And make the subsidiary rights worth an absolute fortune. Even if Binky did steal my stars. I'm so confused tonight I don't even know whether I'm unhappy. Only a world war starting now could take the public's mind off me for a second. But at the rate I'm going maybe I could sell the TV rights to my whole life story in thirteen hair raising and prick depressing episodes. Starting with a full screen zoom in close up of my bandaged balls and a technicolor flashback all the way to a banjaxed youth trying to mind the brassière counter in lingerie. Christ if a few laughs could be introduced somewhere in between the continual calamity, it would make fucking good slapstick black humour and for its obscenity get publicity being banned everywhere. Only maybe the comedian star shouldn't be as good looking and charming and as willing to please women as I am.

'Excuse me sir, will you take a call from Mr Magillacurdy at the theatre who is on the line.'

'Yeah Jorricks thanks. And Jorricks. I may have to take a train to Edinburgh. Hello.'

'Ah me boyo. A great wife you have. She's beautiful. Now that's what I call great theatre. At the final curtain tonight in celebration I am going to cause another short circuit pissing into the footlights.'

'Jesus christ almighty Terence. Please don't. Leave the fucking footlights alone will you.'

'But you have put us on the world stage me boyo.'

'Terence please. Just bow and take your usual thunderous applause. And just by the way, Terence, before I speak to your agent, I hear you've signed up in another production.'

'Ah you heard right.'

'So you're fucking well going to close me down.'

'Never my dear boyo. I've wiped my arse silly with that contract, broken it over my knee, kicked it in the clauses, ripped out all the notwithstandings and wheretofores and chewed and shat out of me every word of it so as you wouldn't ever, even if you were a mind reader, recognize one letter of the alphabet and they be capitals.'

'OK Terence. You've convinced me.'

'That contract me boyo is so fucking unenforceable that the substance left of it wouldn't be recognizable enough even to flush down the loo.'

'OK we'll get it down in writing with your agent.'

'You have me word me boyo. Never mind agents and writing.

Terence Magillacurdy deserts no man with a wife like yours with her poise, her elegance, her bravery.'

'Well thanks a bunch, Terence. But my fucking wife just ain't only poise, elegance and bravery. She can be other things too. Like an enormous pain in the ass.'

'Ah now what you need me boyo is a good Irish lass who is trained to be obedient with just an occasional fist in the gob and boot up the hole.'

'You're fucking right Terence.'

'Now tell me, me boyo. We understand around the theatre here, not having seen you lately, that your goolies as we call them back in the old country, got in a bit of a pickle. Now the great magic cure for all afflictions of the testicles me boyo is take a peek at any bull in any meadow. You'll see that he swings them side to side and lets the fresh air blow upon them freely. Ah but I've got to run now. The second act's been called. Keep up the good publicity me boyo. Kiss your wife on the ass for me. And we'll both be sitting on the Monarch's knee. And remember I'll continue to march hand in hand with you with our suitcases full of our bullion to the biggest banks in Switzerland. Up the Republic. And down with begrudgers.'

Schultz, thighs apart, a hand pulling himself upwards along the bannisters, slowly climbing the stairs to the third floor. Tiptoeing to the back pink bedroom suite. Pushing the door gently ajar. The curtains drawn on the window. The hall light casting a shadow across the floor. The mantelpiece with my twin daughters' music box that the bridge jumper forgot to take away. Louella on the bed, a pink towel over her eyes. The patchwork quilt my mother made, drawn up to her chin. Jesus should I lie down beside her. And christ wake her up into another potential nightmare in her life and mine. Which I've already had in this room. Fighting for my own nude life with a nude erection wagging at a nearly nude wigless bald mother in law. When finally at last I at least have got the woman I love where I want her, trapped in this house. And wouldn't you ironically know, with my prick hardening, it would have to be with the glare of world publicity outside trying to get in the chinks between every drawn curtain to blast our privacy to matzo crumbs.

'Is that you Sigmund.'

'Hey yeah honey, it's me. How are you.'

'I'll be all right. Could you call me a taxi.'

'Gee honey, why don't you please stay here till you feel a little better.'

'No I can't.'

'The Press honey. They're bound to be out there still. Hiding behind garbage cans all night ready to jump out and take your picture.'

'Do please Sigmund just call a taxi.'

'OK honey. But let me go see if the coast's clear.'

Schultz levering himself back down the stairs to the library. Dialling on the telephone. Silence at last in this house. At least I can leave the window curtains open on the back garden. Hey jesus. What's that. Wow. She's undressing in that window. Wow. This I got to watch. At least it's a change of scene. Hey baby, you're built. Would that everything was as pleasant to see out of the windows of this house.

'Hi your Excellency, sorry to disturb you so late like this. This is Mr Schultz from across the street. I guess you noticed this evening's little bit of action on our stoop.'

'Ah yes, Mr Schultz I did so wonder what the difficulty was but of course I also watched you on the television.'

'Gee Ambassador they really caught me at the wrong time. And as you saw I get no medal for diplomacy. But you at least know first hand how my wife behaves.'

'Ah Mr Schultz, indeed. And such a stunningly charming woman too. But in any event diplomacy is so frequently a matter of being artfully undiplomatic. May I be of any help in any way.'

'Gee as a matter of fact, maybe you can. Can you see from your side any reporters lurking over my side. I'm trying to get out of this house and I have a young lady here who needs to confidentially go with me without being identified.'

'Ah my dear Mr Schultz, no problem. It is one we ourselves face frequently when our ladies are not in purdah. Leave it entirely in my hands and we will see to what extent we might avail you of our diplomatic immunity so to speak. At what time would you like to depart.'

'In an hour.'

'I shall attend to the problem. How tall are you. And how tall is your lady friend.'

'I'm six foot one. She's five foot nine or so.'

'In perhaps half an hour someone will knock fifteen times in series of five on your door. Let them in.'

'Jesus thanks your Excellency. And jesus let me tell you, it really is nice to see you back again in action across the street again.'

'I am most happy to be back and to see you in action too Mr Schultz. I brought a party to the theatre the other night and we all did

153

so thoroughly enjoy it, so nice. And Mr Schultz you must come to our next little gathering. And we must soon have tea. And I am glad Islam has been able to come to your aid.'

'Yeah. And for that thanks a bunch your Excellency.'

Schultz slowly putting down the phone, missing the cradle as he watches out across the back gardens. The woman in the window. Stark naked scratching under her bosoms and examining them in her mirror. Jesus fuck a duck. A little ample but what a fucking figure. I've never clapped eyes on her before. Maybe she's the one who reported the fire, christ when she's got her clothes back on some time I should thank her. But wow now she's going with her nice ample ass into her bathroom to take a bath. Jesus why do I bother to go out and chase women when I have this kind of thing right across from me in my own back garden. Giving vicarious sexual pleasure with no lifelong pain to endure afterwards. Move to a back bedroom and I can watch her through binoculars while I'm resting in bed. Jesus better than that, why the fuck don't I get her phone number. Chat to her while she's undressing. Say hey honey here's the guy you just saw on television news who's looking at you with a hard on in the middle of all his troubles. Holy shit I better get the fuck out of here before I do something really stupid exactly like that next.

Schultz descending the stairs to the kitchen. Jorricks in his blue and black striped apron at the sink. Pigeons getting fat in a cage hanging from the ceiling. The television on in the corner. The array of servants' bells up along the wall. Breakfast tray already laid for morning. Dishes gleaming, glasses in cabinets sparkling. Christ he keeps this place as neat as we did on ships in the Coast Guard.

'Ah Mr Schultz, you startled me.'

'Sorry Jorricks. Thought I'd keep exercising my legs a bit instead of ringing down. And just in case I got to really start running one of these days. The Ambassador across the street thinks he might be able to help if I go try to catch the train.'

'Very good sir. Your bags are already packed. I did find a few things for you to wear. And in anticipating your departure I was just preparing a little snack here for a hamper to accompany you. The temperature when you arrive in Edinburgh in the morning is expected to be two degrees of frost. A moderately strong east wind may bring snow. I have put in a heavy sweater.'

'Jorricks I want to apologize for getting you into all this kind of limelight we've got into.'

'No apologies needed sir. If I may be quite frank with you, sir, I in fact quite enjoy it as a challenge.'

'Jorricks you would have made a good boatswain's mate.'

'Well sir, I did in fact make my sergeant's stripes as a batman in the army. I do believe I hear knocking again at the front door.'

'If it's fifteen knocks it's the Ambassador.'

Fifteen knocks and two enrobed masked ladies admitted by Jorricks. One shown up to Louella's bedroom. The other accompanying Schultz to his. Fifteen minutes later four ladies in purdah, black skinned behind their masks, descending the stairs. Jorricks waiting open mouthed in the front hall. For the first time he is more than a little bit shattered out of his usual composure. And holy jesus christ I don't even know which fucking one is Louella. And the only way you can tell me is I'm the tallest. Wow this descending procession is the most fucking electrifying sexiest thing I've ever been in and is a lot less painful for my balls when my prick jumps into steel hard action. And for the time being lets my testicles swing free in the shady breeze. My god look at Jorricks. If he doesn't faint with surprise he's sure fit to explode with laughter.

Four ladies in purdah emerging from the front door of number four Arabesque Street. Jorricks following with suitcases. The procession proceeding to Schultz's parked limousine. Two reporters jumping out of a car with two photographers and rushing with notebooks and the flash bulbs going off.

'Are you Mr Schultz's butler escorting these ladies.'

'No comment.'

'Who are these ladies coming out of Mr Schultz's house. You're the butler you should know.'

'No comment.'

'Are these ladies part of Mr Schultz's household. We saw two go in and now four are coming out. Would this be some of the inhuman treatment Mr Schultz's wife claims she is subjected to.'

'No comment.'

Jorricks ushering the four ladies in purdah into the back of the limousine. The shades drawn on the back and side windows as Jorricks drives away. A reporter and photographer attempting to flag down a taxi to follow as two more try to start their frozen car. The limousine disappearing westwards into Knightsbridge, down Sloane Street and across to the Carriage Road through Hyde Park. Curving up Park Lane, crossing in front of the Dorchester Hotel, its flags flying in its floodlights. If my old pal the concierge ever got a load of me now in here. He'd faint dead away. Jesus this has made my night, but hasn't helped Louella's migraine. All four of us are speechless. And christ is one of these ladies next to me pressing her thigh against mine. Or am I pressing mine against hers. Strange high and low pitched mumbles coming out from behind her mask. And one fucking thing is decided in my life. I'm going to apply to become a citizen of Zumzimzamgazi. His Excellency the Ambassador is one fucking genius. Not even my wife's detectives sitting in a car suspected a thing, and the pair of buggers that I'm going to end up paying both looked fast asleep.

The limousine flying through Mayfair. Dropping off Louella in her purdah at tax dodgers' towers. The two remaining enrobed ladies waiting in the car as Schultz offloads at the station. As he follows a porter away with his bags, Jorricks smilingly coming to attention and bowing.

'Have a good trip madam.'

'Thank you Jorricks.'

A black masked Schultz in his flowing vermilion and cinnamon coloured robes and dark head veils, walking quickly behind his porter under the great grimy girders. Locomotive engines throbbing and the smell of diesel smoke. Train carriage doors slamming. Jesus I'm only here just in the nick of time. Holy shit every fucking guy is turning around giving me the eye. My god one's even following. At the rate I'm going I could make a living out of doing this. Jesus christ almighty there's his Lordship standing on the platform. Only that I just couldn't keep a straight voice and would sound like a broken victrola, I'd whisper going by that I was by appointment available to the aristocracy as a nice tall piece of black ass. And with this fucking greasepaint covering the tiny patches you can see of my face, and except for my sparkling blue eyes, I'm as black as the Ambassador. Jesus I have already done enough nutty things today that one more can only make me permanently nuts which might not be that bad if I can find a nice luxurious fortified institution. Then later I might recover. Even a crazy man has once in a while got to come back to his senses if he's about to fall into a blazing fire. If I go up and whisper now to his Lordship the worst that can happen is that he faints dead away and will just be another casualty on this day of casualties.

'Excusing me sir. You like I give you quickie nice piece of black ass for ten pound.'

'I beg your pardon. I'm afraid I didn't quite catch what you said, madam.'

'You like. I give. Special pour vous. Piece black ass. Quickie on station. Very black black ass. Ten pound.'

'Well I'm awfully sorry, thank you for your kind invitation, but I'm afraid I am madam about to jump upon the train.'

'Me go on train too. Me give you quickie. Long time cost twenty pound.'

'Well. I'm afraid I am expecting someone.'

'On train long time zig zig I give for fifteen pound. Quickie I give now seven pound.'

'Good god. It's you Schultz.'

His Lordship suddenly doubling forward clutching his stomach, and putting one foot before the other to prevent himself pitching prone on his face, as he staggers in a circle around the platform grabbing against a pillar for support. His head shaking in a helpless spasm of laughter.

'You do, you really do take the fucking cake, Schultz. O my god. O my god. And ah Schultz, as the Bishop said to the call girl, take off your lovely lace my dear and hold my amazing mace.'

'Hey holy shit your Lordship, stop, you're going to hurt yourself.'

'O Schultz, I might have known. What on earth do you think you're doing.'

'Jesus it took you fucking long enough to recognize me.'

'Only because of what you were selling. But no one could ever mistake the way you do business. And my god I hope you don't plan to appear at Binky's mother's funeral looking like that.'

'Holy shit I had you fooled you fucker. I nearly made ten pounds.'

'I was absolutely never even remotely considering the proposition. One does not, if one can avoid it, ever be rude to even such an unlawful suggestion no matter how bizarre, when such is presumed put to one by a lady.'

'Don't kid me your Lordship. You were flustered. I had you convinced.'

'Well you certainly have me convinced of one thing Schultz. I had no idea you could pitch your voice so high. And looking like that you ought to go on the game.'

'Hey you really think.'

'Yes I do. Except for your very blue eyes, you could easily pass as a Sudanese transvestite.'

'Well let me tell you, your Lordship, it would be nice for a change to be paid instead of paying.'

'Ah yes Schultz. And as the call girl further said to the Bishop that will be two and sixpence to polish your mace your Grace.'

Schultz regarding himself and fluttering out the folds of his silk sari and executing a sudden whirl on his toes. The porter stepping down from the train behind him, pausing for his moment to elicit an emolument from the lady in purdah.

'Excuse me madam, but your luggage is awaiting you in your compartment X14, third door left in the corridor.'

'O yeah, hey thanks a lot. Just a second let me find a couple of quid.'

Schultz lifting his sari and reaching under. The porter's eyes widening as he steps back, his mouth open aghast, at this bare hefty hairy leg exposed up to one knee.

'Hey jesus your Lordship give me a couple of quid, will ya. Not only don't I have any pockets I forgot I don't have any fucking pants on.'

His Lordship suppressing another spasm of laughter and fumblingly selecting two brand new crisp bills from a large black sealskin wallet. The porter looking from the masked black face with the deep voiced American male accent, to that of the blondly aristocratic mirth contorted countenance of his Lordship who hands the two pounds to Schultz who hands it to the head bowing porter.

'Well thank you. Thank you. Very much obliged. Er, madam.'

Porter walking off down the platform turning around to look back. Schultz raising his hand to wave. Train doors slamming. A first class passenger taking off his spectacles urgently wiping them and putting them back on to frown out the train window.

'Good god Schultz you've put that poor porter in a state of shock.'

'Hey what's wrong I gave him two whole fucking quid.'

'Well in actual fact you gave him my two quid. But you also gave him a good look at your legs which are like a gorilla's.'

The porter increasing his departing speed and turning around once again to suddenly walk smack into a pillar, knocking off his cap, and reeling backwards holding the side of his head. As Schultz doubled up, struggles laughing in his flowing skirts to pull himself up into the train. His Lordship oscillating in another spasm of mirth limps away to the next carriage down the platform.

Schultz aseat on his bed in the locked compartment of X14, his head dress and mask off, dabbing tissues to remove the black greasepaint on his face. A whistle outside. The train lurching into movement. A soft click clack of the wheels. Just stretch back down a second on my bed. What a day. What a week. And at final last. Deliverance. Jesus my balls, even bandaged as they are, are feeling better already with the fresh air flowing around them. After the first laugh I've had in about a century. Just in the nick of time when you begin to wonder if life even for five seconds will stop being a struggle. Christ what peaceful bliss. To be on a train. And not know where in the fucking hell I'm going. Except to Edinburgh. Maybe I should jerk off. And reduce the pressure even further. After another full day. At least I won't know until tomorrow if Magillacurdy has pissed on the footlights, or worse, socked somebody into the orchestra pit as he usually does when he's celebrating. Except for my present bonanza income I sometimes wonder if I'm really suited to a show biz way of life. Never once had I ever been able to call anyone darling. And I'm never fucking well ever going to call anyone darling, either. But boy one or two guys passing me in the train station tonight were nearly on the verge of calling me endearments. Jesus this is dangerous. I'm beginning to like being in drag. Amazing how it suits me. I could have been a femme fatale in a harem. Holy shit how did I ever end up like this. Had to be cut out of my new pants. Then I'm in striped pyjamas and now I'm in silk robes. Boy transvestism is giving me an insight. Of how the theatre must have first got in my blood, before I ever even knew what a proscenium stage was.

Schultz taking off his sari. Washing his face and lifting the top of the wicker picnic hamper. Taking out a thermos of hot coffee and pouring a cup. Opening the flask of brandy and filling the snifter glass a quarter full, that Jorricks has carefully wrapped in tissue and polished gleaming. Two linen napkins. Two pieces of marzipan. And holy living and breathing shit. Look at this. Just look at it. He even has caviare, pâté and smoked oysters in here. And not only brandy but Armagnac too. Jesus what the fuck would I ever do without him. Everything he touches he leaves perfect. Everything he plans has a built in contingency for a gorgeous cornucopia. Jesus all I have to do now is lie back here with the sleeping towns and villages of England flashing by. And remembering how fucking young I was when I first got a taste of loving the sight of tits. Try as I do I can't remember my own mother's but boy I remember other udders. Where I had a hole made down in our basement lingerie store, to see the ladies' dressing booth which took my father, sweat pouring off his face, two weeks to build. Because every time he hit one of the nails too hard which was supposed to hold the whole thing together, the whole fucking thing fell down on his balding head, raising lumps on his skull and dust all over the place and merchandise. Jesus he was a pathetic sight, my poor fucking father. Before it was made a public health hazard to try on underwear, he did everything unsanitary short of murder to make a dollar. Struggling with my mother tooth and nail making sacrifices to pay the dentist's bills to straighten my buck teeth. He darned my socks, cut my hair, mended my shoes which then got polished with banana skins. With his dreams of branching out into dresses and being like the biggest department store in New York, he even had the linguistic audacity to say he was a couturier. But it was me he put all afternoon standing out in the street like they did in the Judengasse in Vienna, enticing the customers in and it was me who had to shake the debris off the lingerie merchandise and make it fit to sell again. But boy from the business we did in falsies, the young hero Schultz, was learning about women. That they care more about the size of their tits than they do about anything else. If they're small they want them big. If they're big they want them a better shape. And let me tell you the pairs of tits I've seen that no brassière in a million years could ever make look good again, were legion. I even studied the anatomy of the tit in the library. How their contours hung was my absolute obsession. Until I developed a serious interest in asses. And who knows, christ maybe my mother elbowed me in the jaw off the nipple, Rabbi. Because tits and later asses gave me my driving force to get into show biz. When I went to the Old Howard burlesque in Boston for the first time, hollering, hey take it off, I thought christ some guy's making money hiring girls to do this. I was amazed to see the distinctly better quality, albeit low slung pairs of tits prancing and bouncing around on the stage. From being a long time bargain basement amateur I became overnight a sophisticated mammary expert. To be a one day big time impresario, I knew I needed to keep my eye in training. Until holy shit I got caught. Right at the most crucial time of my father's business expansion. When he was opening another branch and left me after school minding the store. And out of the blue, like a breeze of fresh beautiful country air down in that stale fume farted atmosphere, with the worst ones laid by my fat gluttonous cousin Saul, this girl comes in who was really a lady. After weeks and weeks of a long stream of hags that I nearly no longer even bothered to watch. She was not only the best looking girl ever to come into our store but she even wore beautiful delicate perfume. My cousin Saul, being apprenticed to the lingerie trade because his father a second rate tailor was nearly as poor as us, and who I asked to mind the cash register while I was being a peeping tom, went into an apoplectic trance trembling all over. Jesus come to think of it, he was a business disaster. Even though I was only a fucking kid, I was already good at business. Knew how to take inventory, even buy stock. Maybe that was what my father was grooming me for and opening another store. He also said he would show his brother Isadore. Instead of a path, my father was going to finally one day have a driveway up to his front door. But Uncle Werb used to say to him, Herbie, no, whatever you do don't tie up money buying a house. Go instead rent an apartment on a high floor, it's cheaper and then no one can shoot you while you're mowing your lawn. Jesus Uncle Werb was a genius. And as a joke would say to me hello Sigmund, soon as your father has three stores you'll be mister merchant prince. O christ I got to stop thinking. But what delicious coffee. And exquisite brandy. Which makes the whole fucking saga of my father's struggle just too sadistically pathetic. But that day when I leave the little fat fucker Saul at the cash register. And it was even worse when finally every one of the relations thought we were headed for the big time. Shit come to think of it maybe we really were. But that little cunning fucker my cousin Saul said that my father was all cash flow and no profit and that he'd believe the success when my father could afford a new hat. And that shrewd little fat assed bastard when he made his bar mitzvah you'd think he'd just been made King of Israel. And the way he clutched even an old fashioned nickel in his clammy hand. Choking the Indian on the coin to death. Anyway I wait for the all clear and I leave Saul minding the cash register. O jesus. She's in there in the changing booth. I'm shaking like Saul is as I go tiptoeing into the adjoining dressing booth. And start staring through the partition wall. Confronting what was for me for the first time ever, true physical beauty. Her fucking blue gorgeous eyes like my own, which I and nobody else in my family had. And which every time Uncle Werb would look at me, he'd say to my poor father. Herbie he's going to grow up into a goy. Maybe I was always a Jewish fucking misfit from the start because every relative my father had has ever since held my gorgeous blue eyes against me. And it was the first time I ever knew that someone you could call patrician could ever come down our fucking dingy eighteen steps, no it was seventeen after we took away the step over the bump of the pipe which went right across the front entrance and over which two customers tripped and sued us. I even already had my first fight of the day up on the street with the big bellied grocery store neighbour off whose outside stall Saul stole fruit and who tore down our sign we always stuck up next to our doorway entrance. This big bully bastard right while I was nailing it back, pulled me over right on my ass. Jesus I was so furious when I got up that I kicked him square in the balls. He crawled back in his store and got a gun and shot at me. The hours spent battling over a couple of square feet we sneaked of his space to advertise, with this next door fucker and my father belly to belly on the sidewalk in front of this guy's over ripe bananas threatening with his fists in my father's face. An old lady passing by shook her walking stick at them and called it a Jew fight, with the grocery store owner an Italian. And that girl, whom I've remembered ever since with her long gleaming black hair hanging down over the little velvet collar of her black coat.

Loafers on her feet, which is why I treasure mine. Even her voice asking Saul if we had anything in silk was beautiful to my ears. Musical as if laughter might any second erupt. Jesus now that I know what I know about life she must have been a little down on her luck. O god here I am propped on the pillows, the towns and stations flying by the window outside and I'm sipping this wonderful brandy and drinking coffee and making even in this night alone as much as my father made in a whole month. And recalling one of the most traumatic days of my life. I must have really fallen in love. And holy shit just like Louella in her calm beautiful way, with the merest trace of a smile. The calm beautiful way she asked about her size. The fucking number I shall remember for all time. Thirty four. Thirty four. Just like the train wheels click clacking on the track. Thirty four. Jesus I might have been seeing for the first time, Louella. Who is a thirty six. O god. I'm abreacting. After all the fucking stress of this past day. And I could get off the train in Edinburgh in the morning and may have to go into purdah again with people jeering me as I come out of the station. I nearly used to get down on my knees to beg for publicity but never did I not want it so much as I do at this time. When there was the time that I could think of nothing but. Maybe an obsession comes with every stage of life. And when mine was tits, it was tits morning noon and night. And until I became highly selective I was ready to rip up sweaters or tear open blouses and jump on and kiss the nipples of nearly every customer under eighty who came into the store. Holy shit, how hard up can you get. Jesus let me tell you, you can get plenty. Till it even gets explosive. Whoosh. Blam. Kaboom. Like a rocket over the Eiffel Tower. But the lady in the black coat brought discrimination and artistic standards into my love life. I was already shaking like a leaf as I waited till she was in the dressing booth. Ready to nip into my peep hole through the partition wall where I disguised it behind a sign, which I printed in big capitals PLEASE TURN OFF THE LIGHT. Then when I finally put the small printed word fucking in front of the word light, for the first time people would turn it off. Shows you how rude words help get attention. She took off her black coat with the little velvet collar. She had on a lace blouse and a string of what I swear must have been thousands of dollars worth of real pearls. My eyeballs only eighteen inches away, I nearly fainted with the simple beauty of the lace of her blouse at her throat. I didn't know that people like this even existed who smiled serenely and spoke gently. Never mind sniffing the most beautifully delicate of perfumes that not even our stale basement fart fumed air could destroy. Although correct that.

Farts Saul laid corroded the light fixtures on the ceiling. And nearly broke the blades of the extractor fan. But her perfume I've searched the world for since, and there's not a trace of resemblance in even one of the two hundred bottles my black cloud wife owns. Through the peep hole I could just catch sight of a book, which said Wellesley College on it which was on top of her black handbag. It was pure genuine leather. Let me tell you, not only in ladies' tits but in ladies' accessories. I could always tell best quality. As were her loafers and stockings. The other thing I knew then, was about fabric. And she didn't have one single speck of rayon on her. Shit too, come to think of it, before I was even twelve, from Uncle Werb I nearly knew as much about pearls as I knew about diamonds. From pink Strombees as I liked to call them, to black Pinctada. Shit when you think of what I was taught by Uncle Werb, I was really educated about garments, jewellery and gems. And I should be on my way to Antwerp instead of Edinburgh. In school I was even selling shoelaces, belts and ties at a discount to classmates. Jesus my whole life up to that moment of that blue eyed girl in the black coat had been merchandising. I only wish Uncle Werb could have taught me something about the English upper class. Maybe that's why when this lady walked into my ghetto life every fucking thing in my psyche was changed forever. Shit, right here, right now, I'm practically an aristocrat just like his Lordship. Sailing a hundred miles an hour north on the train. Jesus, I am an aristocrat. If you miss out the degradation of my mother and father and go back to the fucking big wigs we were in Prague. And then zoom back to me right here in this compartment. I got a butler. I got a fifteen room townhouse in the best part of Belgravia. I got three gorgeous pet pigeons. And soon I'll have a body guard. But back in that dressing booth I was awe stricken. I nearly didn't know no longer as I watched out of that peep hole that I had a hard on. I guess because then all day long I had a hard on even the whole time when I made my bar mitzvah. I used to pray it wouldn't happen. And the harder each time I prayed, up it would come as stiff and harder than a steel fence post. The end poking right out of my short pants. Especially right at the time I was being introduced to relatives. O jesus the crushing ignominy that can come out of carnal enthusiasm. Hey folks, this is our good boy Sigmund who minds the store now after school with his cousin Saul. And folks please excuse his prick sticking out. Christ if I stop to think and shit tonight I'm thinking. And I guess I'm still in merchandising and minding the store. Only now I'm in the world of full blown treachery, minding egomaniacal stars. Going through scripts with a bunch of hack writers whining about the integrity of their work. When the integrity is a ticket that gets sold to something that doesn't bore you shitless. I can take the prima donna choreographers, and designers who think they know what the lyrics ought to say, but the worst of the business are the mister smooth smart ass directors in leather coats, getting down on their haunches as if all time show biz profound philosophical thunderbolts were going to come blasting out their ass. But that day down the store I was witnessing my first production with a solo incredible performance that that little fucker Saul knew was giving me the thrill of a lifetime and just to ruin my exquisite pleasure he was coughing and clearing his throat and ringing the bell on the cash register. And there's no doubt about it that the only thing that can stop people fucking up your life is money and getting really really rich. Till of course an endless mob of fuckers then try to prise it out of your clutches. But finding Louella is like finding again the girl of my dreams. Who became that girl that day down the bargain basement of my father's lingerie store, with her beautiful hands and the way she unbuttoned her coat. O christ after a day like this I'll never sleep tonight. Take one more helping of coffee and another dollop of brandy. What the fuck is wrong with me I should lose my fucking temper in public. I could be criminally prosecuted for uttering an obscenity to the whole population of England. And be for all time forbidden to meet the Queen or mingle with other members of the Royal Family. Who christ almighty I must say I really want to meet. Sipping champagne elbow to elbow in the Royal retiring room of the theatre. They're the kind of people who don't have to go rummaging around down basements of lingerie stores. Maybe I should stay in purdah and meet them with a masked face which no one can recognize. It was my white hands and legs on a black face that the porter saw that made him walk into a pillar on the station. Shit why don't I go into the first barber I see, have all my hair cut off, be shaved bald. Put on a wig and become a tall blue eyed transvestite. Holy shit, then Jorricks and I would really make a pair. Christ, the train is rocking and swaying, and we're going flying through stations drinking brandy, and quaffing coffee like at hundreds of miles a fucking hour. Can't even read the signs. I like it. Thank god his Lordship is on this train because when we stop at the last stop in the morning I'm going to be the most worried fucking man in Scotland. That's one thing about his Lordship. The guy has the most astonishing good sense and advice which maybe he never has to apply to himself having so much god damn money and possessions that jesus he couldn't even count if he started counting till the end of his days. But he says when he gets up to give his advice in the House of Lords that everybody falls asleep. But what I want to know is what the fuck does he do for fucking. Right on that couch in his library you could blissfully screw yourself out of your mind. When with shotguns, polo mallets, fishing rods, riding boots and hats there and all over the office, he's all the time off fishing, shooting or foxhunting. Shit. Come to think of it, ask me what the fuck do I do for fucking. Except for a blow job months have gone by in celibacy. And with as much money as I'm making it's a crime and a shame that some lovely doll and I are not in ecstasy with each other. O jesus don't let me sink down into the depths. Life yet is going to be good. I'm still only really making peanuts when soon any day now I'll be making coconuts. When I beat these pair of fucking guys with the silver spoons, and sell the film rights and record album of the show. They'll be taught a fucking lesson that I got taught every five minutes fighting my way in and out and up from the ghetto gutter. But jesus Rabbi. It's the next twenty four hours that I got to worry about. My mortgage on the house. They could call it in or something after what I said on the TV. Sigmund have another jolt of brandy and relax, they can't do that to you. Remember one thing about England, if you went to the right school had the right mother and father and the right accent and inherited the right amount of money to pay the right lawyers, you can expect and be damn sure to get fair minded justice from a fair minded jury and a fair minded judge. Rabbi for christ's sake you forgot I'm from parents with Yiddish accents and graduated from a no account high school and went to a no account college and come from a no account part of America no one has even heard of. And I was until tonight moving right up the social ladder. And fucking well nearly am at the last rung right at the top. So Sigmund listen, it's time to stop climbing. Hey wait a minute Rabbi. I haven't cashed in yet. I could call up anyone prominent in London and invite them to a party and they'd come running. Sigmund never forget that after they smash back your vintages and eat the food how fast guests leave dishes to wash and forget you and what you fed them even faster. Touché Rabbi. Then shit, I should just drink my fucking wonderful brandy and coffee and not think about anything else but fucking again the woman I love. Now Sigmund you're talking sensible providing she lets you like your mother let your father. O jesus Rabbi. I can't imagine my father ever screwing my mother. Or my mother ever laying on her back for my father. Sigmund how do you know they didn't do conceiving you, some fancy fucking. Because Rabbi when my mother wasn't nagging my father she was sneering that he wasn't as rich as his brother Isadore. They consistently enjoyed a nice sour silence together all their lives. But Sigmund they had dirty pictures and literature in a dresser drawer. Yeah Rabbi, jesus when I found those I got a surprise. I showed them to Saul who went apoplectic and started putting his clammy hands three miles up the dress of another twelve year old cousin whose father beat the shit out of him for his trouble. O jesus it gives me the willies, just remembering back then to my father's lingerie store devoted to the proposition that erotic underwear could get women somewhere. Imagine my father even tried to patent some of the apparel. He even designed to feature a satin striped red and black bra and G string called the Temptress. What that gorgeous woman who undid her blouse, and who only must have still been no more than just coming into her prime of full womanhood was doing in our sleazy store I'll never know. When those first two buttons on each lace encrusted sleeve cuff became undone I nearly died. Only before in samples had I ever seen such exquisite lace. And boy I knew my lace. That on her blouse collar and cuffs was Italian eighteenth century. The warp and weft of that fucking embroidery. Point de Venise à réseau. One of the most delicate of all laces. Stuff like that my father should have been importing. He did once try to feature as a pièce de résistance bras and G strings they made in a convent up in the Austrian mountains that even a queen would have been proud of. But at the price they wouldn't sell. Only did our customers care about the provocative features of the garment and didn't give a fuck about quality. Every time we tried to up market we always plummeted down nearly out of business. O jesus, the simple thoughtful gifts of lace I used to bring to give the black cloud. She threw them out in the garbage. Then I bought a beautiful stainless steel egg whisk and colander I spent hours deliberating over in the store. These she threw right fucking at me and screamed your uncle is in the diamond business you stupid fucker don't you have enough brains to bring me something I really want like diamonds. And O my god, there's no one in the world who wears determination on her face the way she does. Unless for that little know all fucker Saul, who was determined that day I wouldn't have an orgasm. With my bare hands I could have killed him. Speaking out loud he was to a new customer that both the dressing booths were occupied, but that he would go check. The fucker knowing I was right in there already going out of my mind. First over the lace and now over her beautiful Venetian tits. He had me sweating that any second he was going to pull open the flimsy door. The fucking thing had already come loose on its hinges and was already ready to collapse in dust. Real unwarped pine doors for genuine privacy and shop lifting, that was the other wonderful stroke of up market genius invention of my father's which were constantly erupting out of his merchandising dreams of grandeur. Plus calling brassières, under bodices. Hey pop, I'd tell him, get wise, no matter how high class the name of the merchandise they stuff the stuff into their handbags. And pop would put out both upturned palms in front of my face and say Sigmund, suspicion in a store can ruin business. And if we had public curtains like department stores in New York we'd still have shop lifting. Jesus you wonder how with an unsuccessful father with all his flopperoo efforts, you learn about wholesale and retail in the first place. And that's how the fuck I was learning. Just me left, after my infant dead brother and infant dead sister at the very fucking bottom of nowhere to carry on the glory of the family name. And now my mother and father on the verge of retirement. Shit maybe after all they made out all right. Until of course their gaskets blow with my recent publicity. But back then even my fucking fat assed cousin Saul with his slicked back hair parted in the middle resented we owned two stores. While the little fucker was being paid by the hour mostly practising expelling gas in a bang from his intestine. I worked a week without a penny. And boy that day was he resenting the wonderful joy I was having in the booth. But as each new thing happens. You think you've learned. And then another new thing you never expected fucking happens. If not in your face then behind your back. And then whammo slammo. And suddenly you're back to learning again after the new fucking surprise has jumped on you. But I've learned one god damn thing that goes a long way towards providing wholesale contentment. And that is where the best bloody place is to be in all the world. In elegant comfort chewing a marzipan out of golden wrappers, sipping pale old brandy, drinking coffee and lighting up a havana cigar. While flying faster than a pigeon to where you don't know where the fuck you're going except that it's on a train to a place called Scotland. Who the fuck needs tranquillizers. Holy shit. I need them. In an equal mixture of hashish, women, cocaine and heroin. But at least tonight I can get by with a glass of the best brandy and a cup of delicious coffee. O christ her pearly white skin when the lady started taking off this blouse. Never did I want to kiss a tit so much. Just to have my lips there touching on that flesh as beautiful as the smile on her face upon which I also wanted to crush my mouth. Holy shit for her I would become what every woman really wants. A slave and doormat for life. Wipe your feet on me honey. Throw kitchen utensils back in my face. Jesus that's what does it, you get desperate for a fuck, then by money consuming exhausting beguilements, you get one. Then as soon as you begin looking for another one, you're a tongue hanging out victim of even more money consumption. For her I'd be a victim, tongue, prick and all hanging out. I thought with a twinge of conscience, I shouldn't be like doing this, peeping, invading her privacy. But that was the whole fucking cliff hanging thrill. You didn't know what gorgeous curve of beauty you were going to see next. Instead of what I'd been seeing before. Nothing but new garter belts being shop lifted for the old. And some lady tickling her nipples erect so she could see what they looked like encircled in the daring bra my father called Erotic Exposure. If my father didn't win any prizes for originality he sure won them for unrelenting effort. And he would have killed me if he ever caught me ruining his business jerking off peeking at all the customers undressing. Hey shit we just then flew through an enormous station. Jesus maybe now in my life more than ever I should adapt to the money saving and emotionally less aggravating exercise of masturbation. Like the first ten rows of the stalls do with the guys pulling away under their raincoats enjoying themselves. Jesus money pouring in lets you do some really crystal clear thinking. Holy shit. Bing bang. The bells of the pinball machine of my life are ringing. And that's how it happened. My exact first moment ever in show biz. When Saul says hey Siggy you mind the cash register and let me see for twenty seconds. I said Saul it's my peep hole and this is my father's store and it will cost you a quarter for three minutes to watch. It was the first time I had the little fucker. But would you believe it he spent a whole fucking hour trying to chisel the fee down to fifteen cents at a nickel a minute. Then the little bow tied fucker wanted it in writing and an agreement signed and the nickel rate in perpetuity. Later I had to look the fucking word up in the dictionary. It said endless time. Shit I was crazy to agree in writing. Which has now made me read every agreement ten times frontwards, twice backwards and three times between the lines before I sign it. The little fucker Saul was, after short changing enough customers, having an endless gorgeous time while I ended up minding the cash register. Then that little fucking bastard sublet the agreement to neighbourhood kids at three times the rate and was telling me to go fuck myself when I tried to renegotiate and charge him a flat fee of ten bucks per day for multiple admissions. Which he insisted he get for two dollars fifty. Christ with another couple of booths we could have been making more than my father made out of his store. But then I stood firm. And shit I did everything to convince him he was missing the best show in town. I even groaned out loud in the booth which made the lady I was peeping at jump out of hers and bang with her fists on my door. Then a woman called a cop when two kids at a dollar a piece in the booth broke out laughing. And the fat little fucker Saul never budged. I ended up offering again a whole day's viewing at a dollar. He went straight down to fifty cents. At which I said Saul go get fucked and forget it. Holy shit I guess I killed a lot of deals like that in my life trying to extract the last penny. But what the little fucker had already begun doing was to say he had diarrhoea and would disappear into the storeroom where he'd drilled two holes through the nearly impenetrable concrete wall and was renting out and watching now in the dressing booth for nothing. He and kids he rented to were even now able to watch me watching. When I stopped him subletting, a whole gang of Irish kids were waiting to waylay us after we closed the store. Saul put on a pair of thick eye glasses he kept handy for such occasions and pleaded a heart condition. I got beat up. He ran. Christ, outside now it's snowing, streaking past the windows and coming down under a flash of a street lamp. But jesus I'll never forget that day of the blue eyed girl in the black coat. Thank god she came in when I had the store room at last locked. I wouldn't have sold him even two seconds at ten dollars a second to watch that lovely woman undress. And unlike the highway robbery salaries I'm paying to a production now, I was watching that beautiful creature for nothing. Not only the cheapest but the best solo cast I ever had. All happening right back there in Rhode Island. My father always so vehemently denied the state was founded as a refuge for misfits and malcontents. He would say Sigmund, give gratitude that here where we live puts food in your mouth and shoes on your feet. Holy jeeze and then with shoes on my feet I got my dreams of grandeur when one day I took a trip to Newport. And saw these fucking marble palaces built overlooking the sea. And I found out what being rich was. And the dirty looks you got looking as if you didn't belong going down the street. The police even stopped me to ask what I was doing there. I said I was dreaming of being rich. They didn't think it was funny and told me to go dream back where I came from. I don't give a fuck what anybody says but nobody is ever going to stop Sigmund Franz Schultz again. But what a fatal moment in my life. That I should be afflicted forever after not only with worshipping big houses but with adoring elegance in a woman. And when her tits came blazing in front of my blue eyes. After all the unappetizingly distorted pairs I'd seen. I couldn't believe the beautiful way she watched her own in the mirror, small and delicate, but big enough to be gorgeous. Hello Rabbi Löw. Are you listening. Sigmund let me tell you, my ears have been burning all night and you should be ashamed. And please for all rabbis' sake, don't continue about tits. Your pal Al was right who said you should be stopped fucking until you settle down to a steady diet of the same girl. No wonder watching ladies undress you grew up horny and trying to screw everything looking screwable you see and getting hard ons in front of aunts uncles and cousins. If you were a rabbi in your grave you would be now sending it up through the coffin lid and knocking over your tombstone with it. But Rabbi, horniness has got to be chronic while eighty percent of women going by on the street are not ready for a fast fuck when asked. So to get laid once you got to ask five. And you could get your jaw broke three times. Sigmund in my day it could get you a spear up the roozel four times. So Rabbi that's what I'm saying imagine the risk to get laid just once a week for a month you got to ask twenty. Leaving in most months twenty six days of celibacy. Well Sigmund, in such days you can take a psychological rest and hold your breath you didn't catch the venereal plague. Rabbi thank you. And don't worry, those fuckers Binky and Basil already scared me enough with that affliction. So in the past a fucking opportunity came my way for every four times I got slapped in the face, and I didn't care then about the rest who told me to go fuck myself. But Sigmund according to the first principles of phallic philosophy, only twice in a fifty year lifetime does a woman come along who makes up for fucking everybody else. And Rabbi down my father's store was that one other woman besides Louella who on that beautiful day on the eve before Rosh Hashanah when business was slow and when Saul the little fucker was making unnecessary noises with the cash register. Jesus that little fucker had unbelievable nerve, not hesitating to ruin my father's business reputation cheating the customers and pocketing the change. That's one thing now I know, don't ever put the sons of relatives in charge of the cash register. Rabbi Löw that's how the catastrophe happened. Right in the middle of while I'm watching the girl of my dreams he astronomically short changes a customer who was size forty eight who comes red faced insane with being gypped storming back into the store. I have to, because of the noise of the shouting, peek out to see what's going on. Saul is arguing. Like a human abacus he is counting on his fingers. He is gesticulating like you never saw. Like he has five hands waving in the air and all the fingers on three of them are pointing to the sign on the wall behind his ear. The lady's shaking one single fist. Saul's shouting at the lady please read the sign, which says count your change, no refunds or redeeming of merchandise. And the one thing I know is that Saul already has the lady's change slipped down into the cuff of his pants. It's not his fucking store. It's not his ass in a sling. He should worry. He could always go apprentice to be a third rate tailor like his father. But my father would disown me for disobeying his first commandment in business. Always satisfy an unsatisfied customer, even when they're stealing or wiping their feet in the merchandise. Remember they could become honest decent citizens with money to spend again one day. And I'm fucking well there at the peep hole hanging on the edge of an orgasm. When the short changed woman takes the merchandise out of her bag, grabs with one hand Saul by his greasy hair lotion drenched hair and yanks a pink pair of bloomers that had gone out of style years ago, right down over Saul's head. He starts screaming for me. Can you imagine, he wants help. And from me who he hates and resents with a vengeance. Jesus what a yellow little son of a bitch he could be in the face of physical violence. But boy did he have the fucking courage of his clauses when he was hiding behind a contract. But right now he's scared shitless and can't see from under the bloomers which got entangled around his neck and over his big white ears. But he knows right where the fire alarm is, breaks the glass and gives it a yank. The woman tries to grab a fistful of cash out of the register to compensate herself. Saul slams it closed on her fingers. She screams even louder. Holy shit. I'm looking through the crack of the door of the dressing booth, and trying to slip out of the fucking flimsy booth without making a sound. The automatic sprinkler system is already sprinkling water from the ceiling. I jump out, going bananas at the sight of the water ruination of all the lingerie. And wouldn't my coat get caught on a nail my father left working loose and sticking from the partition. I was a foot beyond the door already travelling as fast as this train tonight, and moving towards the sound of Saul who still under the bloomers now thinks he's seriously being murdered. Everything was slow motion in my mind except the water spraying down on us. I could feel the coat tighten on my shoulders. It couldn't have made that much noise but it was like the biggest thunderclap in my life and the end forever of my youth. The whole fucking two rickety dressing booths collapsed. The walls slamming flat on the floor raising a cloud of dust and seven years bad luck with two big and two small mirrors smashing. The booth collapsed around her, this wonderful elegant lady now naked to the waist standing there, watching me. While I was stunned immovable and couldn't no matter what was happening to Saul and my father's business's future, galvanize myself to fit my engorged prick

171

back into my pants. It was just too long and the pants even with buttons on the fly were too tight. But the cruellest blow maybe even of my entire life, and let me tell you there were some real real cruel blows, was the horrified blushing red look on her face. The mortification still creeps up and all over me to this moment. And to this day I still get a hard on in a crisis. I even paid a fortune to two psychologists till I went to a psychiatrist who finally said, Mr Schultz, I'm going to send you an enormous bill, but I'm also going to tell you what to do about your erection. Go home out of this office and count your inches, we should all be so blessed to get hard ons that size at such times of extreme worry. My two little gorgeous girls. Jesus when they grow up what a mortifying fucking scrapbook they could make out of their father's life. Broken mirrors, collapsed dressing booths, hysterical customers. And that day on the eve of Rosh Hashanah you wouldn't think we could be doing more than desultory business, but two more customers came down into the store, saw the sprinkler system on without a sign of smoke or flames and turned on their heels to run back up the stairs. Thinking of course they had walked into the middle of a rape and robbery. And Rabbi, believe me. It was nothing but the purest of pure beauty when her tits came blazoning in front of my blue eyes. O jesus Rabbi. Are you still listening. Sigmund, let me tell you, out of a thousand voices talking to me at the same time, I hear you the loudest. And believe me it sounds like a shambles in the lingerie store and an ill omened way to start the new year. It was worse Rabbi. And even on a train fleeing in the night to Scotland I feel I haven't lived it down yet. Maybe that mortification lies behind why I am where I am buried under such a huge pile of unholy shit. O god Rabbi Löw this story breaks my fucking heart. Sigmund, for a change a broken heart will do you good and is always mended if you didn't throw all the pieces away. Rabbi. I'm on my way to a funeral. To death in the highlands. I might even hear pipe and drum music that I love. Even had pipers and drummers in a show. A dozen of them came into the office for auditions and I nearly got blown out of the place. The critics attacked the act like you wouldn't believe, because I had a troupe of marching nude girls they said it was an insult to Scotland. I was giving the public what I thought it wanted. And it did. Only the fucking critics are always like that. They don't want the public to have what they want. Fuck it. I finally won. Against all the odds. O K Rabbi Löw I'll tell you further what happened. Even the racial question blew up down in the store and nearly put my poor fucking henpecked hard slaving father out of business. In less than a minute later, never did I feel more Jewish than when, down the fucking stairs came two paunchy Irish motorcycle policemen. Guns drawn. And jesus that sent the lady who got short changed into a new and even more violent paroxysm of accusation against Saul. Such a sacrilege in my father's store who spent his whole life building up decent customer relationships and starting out in business with a selection of garments in a big box. Demonstrating the lingerie at front doors let me tell you, is a delicate matter. As often as not between sales he got the shit kicked out of him. And going to a back door is worse. Where my father was nearly killed by a ditch digging dago husband right in the middle of innocently taking the wife's chest measurement. My father was always predicting one day he would go up market with his own store to where women would come who didn't always speak Yiddish and broken English. And jesus the broken nose he got on that dago's back porch really made him go where what to him then was up market. Only all he could was go down a sleazy basement. And now here was this elegant lady with her nice spoken words. She was still there even forgetting she was minus the upper part of her clothes because she nearly got killed when I pulled the whole rickety booth down and buried her blouse and handbag. Saul out from underneath the bloomers is screaming blue and worse murder. Jesus I'll give that little bastard that. The smart little fucker in his striped bow tie could really scream, just like he could argue you all over the place. There we were, the two of us confronting the customers who ran out to come back as witnesses. As usual in my terror and with the special stimulation of this lady I had an unbelievably long hard on. Doing everything desperate with my brain to make it go down. I spotted the fucking woman who pulled the bloomers over Saul's head, with a fourteen dollar negligee off a counter she was maybe now ready to stick in her bag. By her shrewish pasty face I recognized her. She was a constant bargain hunter in our store. And it was a miracle anyone could ever get away with short changing her. Soon as we reduced below wholesale cost she bought. We could never get proof but she must have been running a resale business somewhere. Even one or two shop lifted fourteen dollar undergarments in those days were enough to bankrupt my father. Fucking Saul whose merchandise it wasn't didn't bother to challenge her taking property, as the police, jesus, with their revolvers pointing, thought I was the criminal by the guilty evidence of my prick. Not to mention the horrendous expression of horror on my face. The short changed woman is now shouting she was robbed waving her receipt pointing at Saul who shrugs his shoulders and backed up by the twelve private elocution lessons he'd already taken, points to me with his immortal words 'he's the one who's involved'. To that little bastard I used to say, what are you putting on that accent for Saul. And he'd say, it's for when I get out of the ghetto, people who talk good can get some place plus they don't sound like they will chisel you. Well shit at that moment we were still in the ghetto and Saul had chiselled the shouting lady and the police were saying to me keep your hands up. My fucking hands were up, and I said my prick being up too, was a medical condition I took treatment for. But I was so incensed at Saul that for the first time my prick started to go down and the police gave me permission to stick it back in my pants. The short changed woman is still shaking a fist at Saul even while she is getting soaked under the sprinkler. But gracefully, swiftly the elegant wonderful fucking lady had grabbed up a purple negligee with red spots to shield herself. Her beautiful blue eyes are there in her head watching me, a fucking peeping tom she must have known was only an eyeful away the other side of the partition in the dressing booth. I started to do the worst thing as the shambles descended. Talk about weathering storms in show biz, my immortal words were pretty fucking simple. Hey, I kept saying, I didn't do nothing. Hey, you always said as a sign of genuine surprise. Hey. And to this day I'm still saying it. Only if I didn't have my prick out I could have nonchalantly taken control of the whole situation and started to accuse everybody else. But a hard on makes it impossible to start accusing someone else of something. Ever since when I was just a tiny kid, these Irish guys the motorcycle cops were always my heroes. It was always what I wanted to be looking really fucking tough wearing sunglasses and shiny leather leggings and jumping up on those bikes like they were rockets, revving the engine, voom, voom. I thought those guys were kings of the world, going a hundred miles an hour along the highway. And here I was waiting every second in front of them for the lady's finger to point at me and say I was a peeping tom peeping at her. My heart thumping in my chest I thought would explode. Jesus when you're little, big adults can scare the shit out of you by just standing there staring at you. That's all I ever remember any fucking neighbour ever did. Pointing their fingers and growling their accusations. Until I'd squirt a water pistol full of indelible ink in their faces. Saul said to the motorcycle cops he was a prodigy on the violin. The police didn't know what the fuck that was being a prodigy but they thought since that was what Saul was it would be easier to arrest me. And jesus they had their fucking handcuffs out now and just looking around the store for the wrists to put them on. Especially mine

174

with my hands trembling on the ends of them. In fact one of the police was coming right over to me, looking at me as I stood terrified speechless. The cop then looking at the undressed customer and then at the pulled down dressing booth. Then to the lady he says, 'What did he do to you ma'am.' Everything in my past life went by in slow motion even including Uncle Werb who was always scurrying somewhere in a hurry. It was like two centuries went past instead of two seconds waiting for her to answer. And from the lady with the pale blue veins on her pale white skin I heard these beautiful words, 'No officer, that young man was most helpfully assisting me.' God I think it is whatever since has let me overcome the depressing despair I feel at the treachery I automatically expect from everybody and automatically then get as soon as I trust them. Her blazing blue kindly sympathetic eyes there forgiving me. And I couldn't even in front of Saul stop my tears. She explained to the police how it was all an accident. Even the short changed customer with her fingers maimed by Saul calmed down at the sound of her voice. And Saul who in the mêlée of the collapsed dressing booths now had the pink bloomers off his head clutching in his fingers, also had his mouth gaping wide open. Plus I noticed a roll of bills fall out of his sleeve onto the floor. Rabbi Löw are you listening. I heard, Sigmund. Over brandy and coffee it's a nice story. But the pair of you were a nice disgrace to young Jewish gentlemen. And in front of someone who must have been a beautiful person. Maybe that's why for the rest of your life, with binoculars you're a peeping tom. Expecting the person you're watching to be glad you're watching. Holy jeeze Rabbi. Your remark is giving me more than just a little sudden sober reflection. Maybe I am a voyeur. But I watched Louella through binoculars because I am also convicted in love. Nor do I ever want to blot my copy book with real nice elegant people. Whoever the fuck they are these days. And let me further confess. That when I was growing up tall dark handsome like I am with my own blazing blue eyes, down a dark side street on the way home from the store a bunch of dirty Irish micks jumped on me so they could kick the shit out of a Jew. And I convinced them I was Irish. Hey don't worry Sigmund. After the dumb way you've been behaving all your life, that's a good identity for you to assume. You think so. Yes Sigmund I think so. Well thanks a bunch Rabbi. That better be then all the news I tell you tonight. Wait a second before you sign off, Sigmund. Tell me did Saul give back to the other lady her money he short changed. No Rabbi, he kept it. O K Sigmund I just wanted to know.

Hey Rabbi
Maybe you should also know
That that little shit
Now owns
A whole street
In midtown
Manhattan

Jesus every lousy thing I ever experienced is crowding back into my life tonight. It's the sound of these wheels on the track. And the whole black night flashing by outside. God I'm going to have another big coffee and Armagnac. A big fucking Armagnac. Wake up Schultz. Wake up. Rabbi Löw if I did wrong. From now on I swear I'm going to do right. Sigmund don't be too hasty. The other thing in life I didn't tell you about, is to avoid regret. With all the disease and sorrow out in the world already. All it does is blind you so that you go stumbling into a new disaster. Got it. Rabbi. I'm glad you said that. And that I'm getting drunk enough to listen. Imagine. What could be now so ironic. That after weeks and weeks and thousands of besieging words, I got Louella. Right inside my house. Even to lying on a bed. And out we all go in purdah and in continued celibacy and I'm by now a hundred and fifty miles away. Lonely as hell and getting drunk as a skunk as no Jew should. Rabbi if I didn't have you who else would I have to turn to in this world. And I got a question. Answer me Rabbi Löw. Why did my parents have to fuck and make me a Jew in the first place with standards of morality to keep up. I suppose it's no worse than being an Eskimo having to live on the Equator. Jesus all hell is breaking loose in my brain.

Tiny dots of light out across the countryside sweeping by. Schultz pulling himself up on pillows looking out the train window. I must have conked out awhile. O my god this is wonderful. To wake up still on the move. My god the Flying Scotsman. Everything neat and smelling crystal clean. On the floor before one's bed, a drugget. His Lordship told me it was so your feet had something clean to step on when you take off your shoes. Jesus the life he leads. His butler is already planning what will go in the hamper for Henley. But right here and now I'm going to open up the thermos still half full of coffee, and pour another brandy out of my nearly empty flask. Beautiful the way Jorricks has everything laid out. I'm going to sample a bit of caviare, smoked oysters and pâté, in that order. What a fucking momentary relief to lie back on this bunk dozing through the night, and stare at the ceiling and then at the backs of the houses and the night time windows flashing by with the people in there fast asleep. The train swaying on the rails, rocking roaring through the stations, under bridges, through tunnels. Here I am now in my life escaping from under the black cloud, scrabbling up the beach on my hands and knees hoping to crawl back up out of the ocean depths clutching my fingers into the sand. While the big fucking waves of adversity are still beating on my ass. Wake up from the nightmare down the lingerie store. Hey christ. It's getting bright outside with the full fucking moon. Cattle in fields. And what's that. A castle. Right on the shores a gorgeous loch stretching out into the beautiful sea. Jesus we're in the highlands. Lovely as it is lonely. Who the fuck is Scotland. They say Scotland the brave. And I'm any minute now going to find out. Who the fuck Scotland is. Jesus was there anything ever anywhere like a Scottish Jew. There must be. Looking for peace and prosperity we had to find anywhere we could. Even places as terrible as Glasgow. In bad situations, never look for hope. Instead cling to what there is of reality. And then get dispossessed out of your fucking mind with worry. How could my life in just a few innocent days trying to mind my own prosperous business, turn into that of a cornered rat. Because Sigmund at all times when you're thinking things are OK, they're not. Rabbi Löw you said something. And this time it's me who's listening. With a top smash hit I thought I finally won. And here I am having to win again like I thought I'd never ever fucking have to win before. OK Schultz, go back to sleep now. But in the morning you walk out of this train and out of this station with your head held up high. The world's going to know you're not Sigmund Franz Isadore Schultz for nothing. O jesus. Here I am recalling that little fucker my cousin Saul. Imagine that there could come the time years later when that little fat bow tied fucker with his smarmy slicked backed hair becomes a big fucker too busy to see me or even return my telephone calls leaving me days pacing a room waiting that he might ring. When in an utter last ditch desperation holding the threads of a production together, I was trying to get an investment out of him. Voom. I went to New York and there I was marooned in the most desperately depressing hotel room of all time. Unable to pay the fucking bill to get out. Saul's suddenly away in Chicago. He gets back to New York. And then nearly after two weeks waiting, a secretary keeps me further waiting fifteen minutes on a line and then another secretary keeps me on another line another twenty minutes till at last he comes on. Right away I hear him asking his secretary, hey who's this I'm talking to. And I say, Hello Saul, this is Sigmund.

'Sigmund who.'

'Saul it's me. Have you forgotten my father's lingerie store.'

'O hey hi ya kiddo, how you doing. Heard you went to Europe. Long long time no hear. What are you doing.'

Holy shit I didn't tell him I was waiting in the fucking sweltering heat two weeks just waiting for his fucking call and for him not to call me kiddo. Pacing a mangey puke green room with flaking paint and broken tiles and a leaky shower in the bathroom keeping me awake at night. Haunted like murders had been committed there. And Saul the fucker up in his air conditioned penthouse office somewhere on the top of a skyscraper and now sounding with a long casual drawl as if he graduated from Harvard.

'Saul, I'm in show business.'

'Hey that's really great old buddy boy. That's great. Long way from lingerie. Ha ha.'

'Yeah Saul I have a nice large special opportunity available for an investment in my latest show.'

'To be sure old buddy boy, to be sure. That's great. Give the details to my secretary. I got a call on the other line. Have a nice day.'

Twenty fucking words I said to him and never heard another fucking thing. I spent half an hour giving some stenographer over the phone details of the production and nearly of my whole life plus I was tempted to mention, just to remind Saul, of the prize for mathematics I won on my high school graduation. It was all like speaking Greek to a stone and yet I couldn't stop so enthusiastic was I to save my fucking life which was sinking faster with each second into an abyss of looming eternal poverty. Never mind the present ignominy. Having from the first moment I heard from my parents that Saul had made it, I confess I then planned to reserve him for the exact right time of a desperation moment and to hit him hard then for a whopping great investment. He was even demolishing a theatre in a building he was now tearing down, to erect a luxury condominium, on top of which he was going to provide himself with a twelve room triplex. When I couldn't at the time afford the fucking hamburger I ordered on the half assed room service that took two hours to get to me in that sleazy hotel. And O my god to have come three thousand miles pretending I was just casually stopping by in town. After endlessly reciting my casual approach the whole way coming on the plane. And then boy was it casual. I was like a comma in a conversation to him. Every time trying to call him he was involved in a meeting. If he wasn't in Houston or Minneapolis for the day. Then I wake up over a putrid breakfast to read in the morning paper that the little upstart fucker had bought two skyscrapers in Chicago. Imagine. Fat Saul with the bow tie. How did such a schlemiel ever make it. I was nearly fucking well tempted to ask him, hey Saul, just give me back with interest the money you stuffed up your sleeve from my father's store. That's right. You heard me. I want it back at two and a half percent over the prime rate obtaining over all these fucking years you've had it in your clutches. Jesus that afternoon I walked down Broadway between the pimps, whores and pushers and past porno joints and topless bars like I was wandering on a desert trying to sell shoelaces to Arabs. I walked along Forty Seventh Street seeing all those guys in their little cubicles getting haemorrhoids examining and selling gems and jewellery. Like Uncle Werb wanted me to do. And imagine, at such a crucial low time Uncle Werb was in Amsterdam. Then I met two guys who knew him. There they are under their black homburgs and I mention an investment in the show. They say, hey are there girls we could meet. I say yeah. No problem. Beautiful girls are a dime a dozen in show biz. Especially if you're rubbing elbows with a big impresario producer. They say count us in for a piece of the action. I had investor agreements right there with me drawn up on the finest paper. And jesus I ruin the agreements printing in their names before I find these two fucking shrewd cheapskate rabbinical cunts wanted to put up fifty dollars apiece and meet the girls. They probably each had at least a hundred thousand dollars in diamonds in their pockets. I tore up the agreements and said, hey look don't overspend for girls, you can for less than ten dollars buy at bargain prices around the corner. Everyone wants glamour for nothing but show biz is the most costly way in the world to get a piece of ass. Then I was on my way planning to go to Providence and to catch a bus at the Port Authority bus station. I'm on the upper level. And bang a gun shot. I duck. And a girl ten yards in front of me blew her brains out with a pistol held to her head, blood and gore everywhere. There she lay. Not much more than twenty years old. I nearly cracked. I needed to talk to somebody. I didn't know who to call up. But at that moment boy did I need something spiritually bolstering like a fuck. And I knew a gorgeous glamorous starlet who to me was always a personally pleasant friend in spite of me never casting her in anything but who now was going to break her way into serious acting and had a few months previous come from London to New York trying to get a part in a play. Shit she sounded so glad to hear from me I should have been suspicious. In London she had a string of rich boyfriends to take her all over the place. Then she said she wanted to be recognized in the legitimate theatre and to be independent of men. Holy shit did she get her independence. She invited me over. I nearly got mugged twice in her street. Up some mangey stairs in Hell's Kitchen in a shoebox cold water flat with a window out on an air shaft with cockroaches crawling all over her pillows. I brought a bottle of wine. She had a couple of avocados and some spaghetti she cooked. The two of us putting a

180

brave face on both our fucked up situations. Compared to how she was in London she was crushed to such insignificance. Her face seemed like a mask ready to crumble in a million pieces. We were even trying to impress each other. Then to forget horror for a second, the two of us tried to have a fuck. Going through the motions. A little kiss here a little kiss there. And then. Wham. Suddenly we both collapsed in commiseration. Throwing our arms around each other and sobbing. Shit I hope you're not listening to this Rabbi Löw. She had no money for the rent or for her voice lessons and acting classes. Her phone recently put in was going to be cut off. She had a drunken uncle in Chicago's skid row and no other family to turn to. She'd spent every penny she'd borrowed from the string of guys she then ditched back in London. And in the middle of it all it was her birthday. Her age a secret but two candles for each half of the years stuck out of a tiny cake. My hands trembled lighting them with a match. She'd turned herself into a new person. Her first name was Frederica and friends back in London called her Freddie. And imagine, her middle name was Joy by which she now wished to be known in her future career. And far from singing it, I could hardly say it on my lips to say happy birthday Joy. I thought maybe she was going nuts. But it was at that moment a moot question as to which of us was more bewildered in our desolation. I had some remnants of confidence left to bolster hers, but nothing is worse than having to be a nursemaid to women. You make the big whacking bloody mistake of thinking they need you. As you sincerely advise that their lives can be cured by their lying back and giving you one big almighty fuck. And holy jesus all it does is put them snoring to sleep and stretching out their limbs, taking up all the fucking room in the bed. Out of her still pretty beautiful body maybe showing a sign of a sag in a couple of out of the way places, she'd been selling her blood to get food and the car fare to her auditions. I could tell by the way she talked about him that she was being screwed by her hairdresser who did her hair free. She had the most beautiful fucking nose in all the world that you could stare at for hours even trying to figure out why it was so beautiful, and even this she was thinking of having reconditioned. I couldn't believe it. Holy shit where do you ever find a pure simple uncomplicated woman who accepts being herself. Let me tell you one place you don't find her is in show biz. In the sultry heat we had our feet on the bare boards of her floor. Eerie sounds of groans, moans, coughs and crying coming in through the airshaft window and beyond from the walls and ceilings which looked like they were any second going to fall down. Shit this was a girl I used to see climbing in and out of the biggest limousines and going in and out of the best hotels and making every head turn in the most elegant restaurants all over London. Even Binky and Basil tried to date her and to Al she gave apoplexy. And the fucking utter incongruity when I went to take a piss in her sink curtained off with her evening gowns and silk dresses, and a shelf of the most expensive London fashion house face creams and cosmetics. Sooty grime everywhere with cockroaches running in and out between the bottles and jars. Even in my own dismal circumstances I was struck numb with the disaster of her situation. Because I knew, beautiful as she was from the top of her head to her toes, I knew she couldn't act her way out the automatic doors of the crosstown bus I took to get here. And that instead of a happy birthday I really should have been saying have a not too unhappy horror. And I hope it's over soon and then you go do just what should be no problem and marry a guy with a few million dollars. The crime was, that beneath all the tough persistent ambition she was a lovely person. And would do you any favour so long as you weren't annoying her panting after her cunt. But all she had left in this world to get her through tight spots was her ass and that, if she was like this much longer, could start drooping fast. Then she said, Sigmund, tell me, seriously, do you think I can make it as a serious actress. Amazing thing was she could have made it as an unserious actress. But I said sure honey, sure. Because let me tell you, we did not need any extra pessimism, for already, for both of us, that evening was a fucking requiem. After the final fiasco with Saul I went to see Joe Jewels. And at least he was someone who would at least fucking well see me. And I tried desperately to do a deal. Him behind his big desk as I ended up standing right out in the middle of his big carpet. Christ you have to hand it to him, the guy's with snake eyes in the back of his head and with three fangs sticking out of his tail. But you could tell he loved show business and respected the battle scars that we both wore. Also that he could smell a mile in the distance I was desperate. It was all over in no more than a couple of minutes. It was figures and money in cut throat syllables like sword blades swiping fractions of an inch away from your jugular vein. And shit he sliced through mine and I went wobbling bleeding to death out of there. Only I was going to make fucking sure I would die out of his sight. I wasn't going to give him that satisfaction. But before I got back down to the street I vowed that one day I'd shrink his balls in a deal to the size of a flea's. And of course the fucker has yet once more taken me in a deal. While my balls got swollen up into grapefruits. And there I was a couple of hours later in Freddie Joy's unjoyous company, utterly shattered and trying to get distracted looking at her beautiful legs. And heard myself saying to myself in her cracked mirror, you've just about had it you poor son of a bitch. But even in the most dire of times always the one thing I could still do was fuck. That evening I couldn't even sustain a semi hard on. When with Freddie there didn't have to be any fuss, no fanfare no song and dance. No saying I truly love you. Because we simply liked each other, and for old time's sake, she was just going to unhesitatingly open up her legs for a simple old fashioned straightforward fuck. O christ correct that. Fucks may be old fashioned but no fuck is simple. And especially not straightforward. It is the most fucking complicated thing mankind can do with each other in the so called civilized parts of this earth. And maybe it's even complicated in the jungles of Zumzimzamgazi and in King Buggybooiamcheesetoo's harem. But this night, the prospect of this fuck was at least as simple as it could get. I just gently held her. A hand softly on her hair and head. But my hormones just wouldn't react. And hers must have got grounded as well. I told her of a play I knew was looking for a female lead and gave her a couple of phone numbers she could call. O fucking god. Hey what am I doing. Reliving all this dirge. All out of the distant horrible past. O jesus. I know Rabbi you're listening to this. And I hope I'm dreaming. And O jesus I'm not. I'm remembering like it happened yesterday. With the world as it was then those New York City sultry days, so fucking lonely. In which I felt so fucking crushed and awful. And in which I had nothing left except the creeps and willies. How I ever got through that night I'll never know. I chewed back the avocado and spaghetti and drank the wine out of a broken cup. But all I could feel was death. I wanted to fly like a bat out of hell out of that place. Even so I hated to leave her there alone. But that's what she wanted. Not to depend upon guys. I made her take a few dollars of the few I had left. At least to stop her selling her blood. I could see the needles' holes in her once immaculate arm. My fist was locked to throw a punch at the first looming shadow as I went back down those four flights of stairs. I tripped over a wino curled up unconscious inside the front door. I got out on the street, the death and doom just reeking in the air. The few people passing in the darkness were like the living dead. As I hurried towards Tenth Avenue I hoped like I'd never hoped before in my life for a taxi. I could tell that the block across the avenue was no place to go. And suddenly near the corner I found myself stranded in front of a funeral parlour. A vase of ceramic flowers illuminated by a green neon light in the window. I couldn't believe the power of the premonition that hit me. I just somehow fucking well knew that Freddie Joy's funeral was going to be in there. All five foot eight and a half inches of her spectacular beauty and those exquisite ballet dancer's legs stretched in a coffin. I even felt a tear in my eye. All I knew was I had to get out back across the ocean. Back to the sanity and even the treacherous aristocracy of London. To a pair of business partners who half the time were trying just to pull tricks on me, and had entangled me in a production looped around my neck to hang me. In the morning someone pretending they had a message tried to bluff their way into my hotel room to rob me. I said if you don't fucking well get away from that door in two seconds I'll kill you. There wasn't even the sound of the guy running away, so fast did he get out of there. Shit it was the first opportunity I got in the whole city to fight back. When I went out that morning on the street I was even looking for a mugger so I could flatten the fucker in his tracks. Because my fist was ready to flash to his jaw three times faster than his knife or gun could come out. And then just as more of my fighting spirit was seeping back into me. More horror. On the subway station a girl got deliberately pushed into the tracks. And in the screams, her bones crunched and flying, she was turned into mincemeat. I reeled back up to the street, sick. Everywhere. On every side there was nothing but pure spiritually crushing disaster. Never mind my whole future in jeopardy. It was like my next hour was in jeopardy. I hardly could buy a newspaper or even a pineapple soda. Somehow something in the voice gives you away. When you're talking to somebody who's on top of the world and you're clinging by your fingertips to the cliff edge and he knows exactly without even looking and stepping backwards where to crunch his heels down on your knuckles to send you plunging to the bottom of the chasm. And I came fucking well three thousand miles to what I thought was my ace in the hole, and a sure fire thing after all the deals we done as peeping toms, to just hear Saul say to me. Have a nice day. And some fucking nice day I swear on the Torah, if it is the last thing I ever do, I'll show him. At least the one consolation in show biz is, it's so tough that final failure is a relief. The only trouble is you get so beaten getting beaten you don't have enough sense left to know you're finished and you go on twisting in the anguish and agony. Till, if you're lucky and alive enough, you wake up bankrupt in the street and at least able to look for a fellow bankrupt's pocket to piss in. Momma meeo. Which if nothing else sure fucking well makes you look out where you're going in the future which you no longer have. And I didn't look out heading into mine and into the black cloud of marriage. A sneering wife snarling at you. A flop producing buffoon she called me. Jesus she was right. While meanwhile she's become an international high diving sensation. But hey now honey. Hear me good. The wind is changed. It's blowing perfume up and perfume out my fucking ass. My sails are full. You go fucking well now and you listen to the jingle and jangle of a box office cash register and to the applause and bravoes at that final curtain. But don't you or your mother ever again ever go sticking your noses into my private life. Because those meddling protuberances will get amputated off. And that applies to the minuscule pricks of your lawyers too who will find their limp appendages on my chopping block. O god. I may be soon facing the horror of another courtroom. I guess somehow that disastrous trip to America set the course of my life. Sailing resolutely steering towards bullion. But whatever else it did for me I can do without. And holy mackerel I'd totally forgotten it till now. I walked into St Patrick's Cathedral on Fifth Avenue and lit a votive candle just like I did in Farm Street Church. Momma meeo. Freddie Joy was a Catholic. And I was just saying a little prayer for her soul. And if God could, to help her career. Me. Who doesn't believe in anything. And certainly not God. Except that one who looks down over the box office. Sorry about that Rabbi. Back in London a couple of months later, I get a postcard of pretty little flowers from her with just the words. Forget Me Not. And signed Freddie in her hardly legible scrawl. A few days later I pick up a copy of Variety lying in a beam of warm sunshine on Binky's desk. I'm in his office having a cup of coffee and I'm reading through the pages. I'm already making fists furious to discover that Joe Jewels has three plays running simultaneously to packed houses on Broadway. And then flipping through the back pages, always, I admit, hoping to find Al's death notice and as I close the paper, the name Joy and Frederica suddenly catches my eye. I turn back to the last inside page. There she is. Listed second. In the obituaries. The tears just fell plop on top of the bland report and the matter of fact words. Which said that police discovering the body of the screen actress and dancer reported that she seemed virtually penniless and without known relatives. I was amazed at the space she got. Giving a potted biography and the names of all the grade B pictures she was in and even mention of a couple of grade C. Like she was a fucking star that she dreamed of being. And that obviously the show biz trade already thought she was. Holy jesus christ will such insane anomalies never cease. Said she was killed in an unexplained fall. And I'll explain it. Her beauty was just too much for her. She could

185

do anything with it. It could get her anything she wanted. Except make her into a great actress. Had she just stayed a starlet or a chorus girl she could have after a career retired to a house in the country and had six kids and a couple of millionaire husbands. I guess if she was there on the market to sell herself, she wanted, not the highest, but the longest lasting price. This once gorgeous girl who if nothing else was at least fucking understanding, thoughtful and kind and could crack you up laughing at some of her brutally cynical remarks that would drop on your toe like a sledgehammer. And who could blow up a restaurant by just walking in the door. Holy good god. I could have been and probably was in love with her. One of the phone numbers I gave her was Joe Jewels. And get ready for this Rabbi. I later discover it was he who paid for her funeral. Held right exactly in the place where I knew it was going to happen. And whatever it was, I don't know what he did to her, or what, more likely, she did to him, but I guess that's why, after all the vicious cut throat deals, I don't begrudge Jewels and even respect him and even very very slightly like the guy. He got her a grave I never now fail to visit when I'm in New York. The one really still secret thing I'm going to keep secret that I do in my life. The headstone there looking so lonely on a little knoll. I kept that postcard. Looked, looked and looked at it. A year later I went for the first time to her grave and there carved in the stone under her name, the words Forget Me Not. Jesus honey I won't. And I don't. And even tonight I spare a thought for you. And for women. In all their battles with men. God I'm tired. And the fucking tears now are streaming down my cheeks. Here's a kiss Freddie Joy, honey, I didn't give you back that sad night then. Holy fuck. What am I crying and talking about. After what's being done to me. In an international incident a few hours ago. Fuck women in all their battles with men, they don't need any sympathy. Not even in their graves. And certainly not while they're sitting in their spiders' webs. Fuck Joe Jewels. Especially fuck Saul. I've got now on this train to go back to slumber-land. And wake up in Edinburgh alive and sane. And ready for another funeral. Here's with this swallow back of Armagnac, finally goodnight Rabbi. Sigmund. Let me tell you, after what I've just heard. I'm pleased at least you're going to sleep.

Rabbi
You ain't heard
Nothing
Yet

Yeah Rabbi. Like I said there's a lot more. But meanwhile I'm going to make loud snores and going to curl up nice and safe in a foetal crouch to comfort my bandaged balls, and cover up my head to keep warm. And just hope that some gaiety comes back into my life. Goodnight Rabbi. Thanks for listening. Hello blissful darkness. You're all I've got now to entwine around to make love. But who's that rapping and knocking louder on the door of my soul to get in. Hey who's touching me. Hey who's pushing harder on my shoulder. And shaking me. I got to fight. Schultz has got to fight. Schultz has got to win.

14

'Attack. Attack. Pigeons. Get the behemoth. Attack.'

'Good god sir, my throat sir, you've got my throat.'

'Don't jump. Go ahead jump you bitch, jump.'

'Sir. Let go of me.'

'Shit. Where am I.'

'You're in Edinburgh sir. For the last three hours. Please let go of me.'

The train attendant straightening his collar and tie and picking up his eyeglasses from the compartment floor. Schultz sitting up out of bed. A loudspeaker announcing a train for Glasgow. Doors banging. The sound of a train whistle, and the puffing of an engine leaving the station.

'Jesus I'm sorry. I must have been in a dream. Or a nightmare I guess.'

'I guess you were sir. Perhaps I can get a porter to help you off the train. All passengers must be off now sir.'

Schultz splashing cold water on his face and dressing. Holding up a jacket in the light. For the funeral, my suit belonging to Jorricks is going to look if not the wrong colour then absolutely the wrong fucking size in every direction. And especially too short in the sleeves and legs. Plus his tie he's loaning me is going to be no bloody help to my social acceptance. That's one thing the upper class English know is your fucking tailoring. They can spot the cloth and the hand stitching a mile away. And all the time they talk to you they are staring at your lapels. And if they're the wrong lapels they hold it against you like a criminal offence. While they try to figure out what direction is fastest to get away from you. How the hell do I tell them my vindictive wife burned my suits and I borrowed one from my butler. Hey shit. That sounds good. That's exactly what I'll tell them. Jesus one thing is certain. This is better than being back in the bowels of New York. Groping around in the black abyss of my vocation. O momma meeo I pray don't let the willies get me again.

A porter with Schultz's bags and picnic hamper preceding him along the platform. Past passengers hurrying to catch the train for Glasgow. Schultz employing a wide footed walk to make room for his bandaged balls. The porter stopping to wait as Schultz pauses to look around the station in the chill morning mist. Where the fuck do I now go. Doors there which jesus at least look as if they go somewhere warm. Out of this fucking cold. Now I've missed his Lordship wherever he was. After last night with no one else to blame but the brandy and Armagnac, I feel as if an atom bomb has exploded in my brain. And I don't even know where to find the funeral. Go Schultz. Put your body behind the punch. Go. Fuck I'm going. Towards the North Pole. Last night at a hundred miles an hour and this morning at two miles an hour.

Schultz exiting out from the barrier. Hobbling to a standstill in the middle of the station. Looking around again as people turn to look back. And one or two do a double take. A gentleman walking by suddenly stopping Schultz by the sleeve.

'Excuse me sir, you are aren't you Mr Schultz I saw on telly last night. Well I'd like to well and truly shake your hand. I have never heard a sentiment better put. It's about time someone had the public courage to put these scandalmongers in their place.'

'Thanks.'

'Don't thank me, Mr Schultz, thank you. But what brings you to Edinburgh.'

'I'm on my way to a funeral.'

'Well sir please let me say you certainly showed them who was being buried.'

A great throbbing diesel roar filling the station and blast of a whistle, as the Edinburgh train leaves for Glasgow. Holy shit imagine. I'm being appreciated. This is unbelievable. And I'm being complimented. Christ maybe instead of a heel, I'm a hero. But meanwhile I wonder where the fuck his Lordship is. If having his own private railway station at one of his castles is anything to go by, he may have his own private railway car I could have been in. Holy jeeze I really am being recognized way up here miles away in Edinburgh. I just saw the station master look at me as if I were a ghost or what is more likely a split second TV star who said a four letter word on the national network. Why didn't I put my fucking foot in my mouth and shut myself up. Maybe there'll be a replay I can watch. Get a video tape to view in private. I've got to go full total tilt into the fucking long term possibilities of my future. Into which at the moment I don't even want to peek. Since everybody now whether I like it or not, seems to want to know what the fuck's going on in my life. So along with the prolonged sexual yearning and pain I also got the sweat and strain of conspicuousness. When at this time of my existence I should be starting to become an elder statesman of show biz. Jesus maybe it's a principle of life that never can you ever let yourself be beguiled by the fucking tendency to relax.

Schultz, followed by the porter with his baggage entering the doors from the station into this high ceilinged elegant lobby and scratching his head and running his fingers through his black curly locks. Opening up Jorricks's raincoat in the soothingly warm morning air of this palatial hotel. Tall pillars, painted panels along the corridors. Holy shit. I've really done it now. Seven thirty in the morning. Hungry. Stranded. Plus I feel my bowels are in a state of impenetrable constipation. And jesus I can't even remember if his Lordship said there was breakfast on the train. And if there was I missed it having my nightmare. Here I am in the middle of nowhere. Nearly killing the train attendant. I sincerely think the next thing I do after I hire Daniel the bodyguard is to hire a psychiatrist. But before I do that and try to shit, at least I'd better eat.

Schultz entering this great high ceilinged dining room. Waiters to and fro amid the white tablecloths. Industrious sound of voices, delft and clattering cutlery. And there along the wall, a newspaper propped up in front of him. His Lordship. Jesus there he is eating with a massive plate of bacon and eggs.

'Ah Schultz. At last. You're here.'

'Hey jesus I overslept. You could have woke me up. I was waiting on the platform looking for you.'

'Good god Schultz. I was certainly not going to run the risk of confronting you in purdah again.'

'Yeah well I should be in purdah after the nightmare I had last night.'

'Well Schultz you may have another one in store. Have you seen this morning's papers.'

'No.'

'You are I fear an item of national attention.'

'Holy shit no. Not again.'

'It would appear your four letter word uttered to the Press has rather put you on the map.'

'Don't say anymore. I can't look. Don't show me. Just let me see the menu.'

'Well you always wanted publicity Schultz and now you've got it. Especially as I see headlined here that your wife is selling what appears to be her life story to a major newspaper. My god sit down Schultz, sit down.'

'I don't believe it. Let me see that fucking thing. Holy jesus christ. This is too fucking much. It's unbelievable. That bitch is pillorying me in public. How could she do this, make me the subject of ridicule. I'll sue this fucking rag for libel. Jesus where's the phone I'm going to call my lawyers right now.'

'For god's sake Schultz sit down and order breakfast. You can't sue until you are libelled. And your wife jumping off a bridge hasn't libelled you. Just made you seem a bit of a shit, that's all.'

'I'm going to be libelled, I know it. I know the fucking kinds of things that bitch is going to say. And things she's already said. I got to get an injunction.'

'Sit down and get your bloody breakfast Schultz and shut up. And do please remember that we are on the way to a funeral.'

'I can't stand anymore. Jesus with all this fucking worry descending on me do you know I don't even know what the gross was at the theatre last night. Or even for nearly three previous nights.'

'Well last night Schultz it was two thousand two hundred and twenty seven pounds eighteen shillings and three pence, up a total of seventy three pounds over last week with the four seats sold behind the pillars, and thirteen more squeezed into standing room. And the advance stands at over one hundred and twenty seven thousand and building by the hour I understand. That news seems to have relaxed you somewhat Schultz.'

'Yeah it has. Jesus if the money keeps coming in like this maybe I can face anything. It's amazing how in a few seconds a few blissful figures on the credit side soothe the spirit.'

'Well then for god's sake have breakfast Schultz. And accept the fact that your wife is a national heroine. And looks, even you must admit, quite commendably attractive in bathing costume. Or to use one of your favourite expressions, absolutely gorgeous. Indeed Schultz, with such legs I'm surprised you haven't tried to cast her in something.'

Schultz taking off his coat and slumping back down in his chair. The smiling waiter laying out a napkin across Schultz's knees and handing him a menu as he brushes a crumb from the edge of the tablecloth and tilts his wavy black haired head and ruddy complexioned face to the side.

190

'And what can I get for you Mr Schultz. Start with a little freshly squeezed orange juice. The kippers are very good this morning. I can recommend them. Preceded with a little porridge perhaps. Very nice.'

'Yeah. Swell. And some toast and strong coffee.'

The waiter clicking his heels bowing and departing with his order. Another waiter weaving his way quickly between the tables, taps an associate on the shoulder, who both turn to look at Schultz along with two breakfasting businessmen breaking into broad grins. Nectarine leaning forward across his plate of bacon and eggs holding open the newspaper for Schultz to see.

'Did you just hear that Schultz. That waiter knows who you are.'

'O god. Yeah. And by the looks of it, so does everybody else. Hey don't show me that paper for christ's sake. I don't want to read or see another fucking thing about it.'

'Ah but Schultz such instant notoriety must have something to do with your wife's promise to bare all.'

'What. What do you mean bare all.'

'This paper uses the expression topless.'

'What. Let me see that. O holy shit. I got to get an injunction. She's not going to get away with exposing herself to the fucking British public.'

'Schultz these scandal sheets are known to pay top prices for such exposures and Schultz I fear that since your wife's bosoms are her own property she's entitled to lawfully exploit them as she wishes.'

'Like hell she is. She's assumed my fucking name. They're Schultz's wife's tits.'

'Ah you might indeed have a point or two there Schultz. No pun intended of course.'

'You bet I got a point. I got a fucking decent public reputation to keep up. It's taken me years fucking cliff hanging on the verge of disaster to get where I am and to meet real royalty. I've even been practising bowing my head to address Her Majesty as ma'am. Rehearsing to have all the right small talk ready as soon as she says she liked the show.'

'Dear me Schultz you do I think take this royal business a little more seriously than it merits. The Queen meets dozens of people every day, of whom, only the tiniest fraction will she ever see again. Admittedly most will not be quite as memorable to Her Majesty as you. And although she certainly will not say so, she may certainly think the show's the most absolutely awful old rubbish she's ever seen.'

191

'Holy shit your Lordship. Royalty are a normal everyday occurrence in your lives. It's easy for you and Binky. The pair of you are already up there constantly fucking around in those circles.'

'I should hardly put it like that Schultz.'

'Well I put it like that. Members of the Royal Family coming to the show could add two years to the run. I'm having the Royal retiring room at the theatre entirely refurbished. It's got a beautiful fireplace I'm going to have a real fire in. I mean this was my fucking dream for christ's sake, shattered to a million pieces last night.'

'And several more million pieces this morning Schultz. Your publicly uttering to the entire nation at peak viewing time what is commonly considered to be the most obscene word in the language, has driven even a major ministerial call girl scandal off the front pages. Hardly entitling you to a decent reputation encouraging to the Lord Chamberlain to have you officiate receiving members of the Royal Family.'

'Hey come on who doesn't use the word fuck sometimes in exasperation.'

'Well for your private information Schultz, vexation in royal circles is invariably expressed by the words, drat or dash. As in, dash it all. And in extreme cases of annoyance, the expression O pish and pother is permitted.'

'Thanks a bunch for telling me. O K from now on it's O pish and pother. Only the fucking words just don't say what I fucking feel.'

'Well Schultz one way or another your wife has certainly succeeded in putting you conspicuously on the map.'

'Don't worry. That bitch isn't going to get away with doing this to me. This is going to be a battle to the finish.'

'She's already got away with it Schultz. As indeed these days it must be said ladies are taking the forefront in many matters, leaving men to get rather the raw end of the carrot or is it stick. What you need Schultz is to find a loyal witty and willing lady friend who will welcome you into her arms without intrigue or treachery. And O dear.'

'O dear what.'

'I do hesitate to read this Schultz which has just caught my eye. It appears the first instalment of your wife's series is to be entitled "Impresario A Smash Hit On Stage But A Flop In Bed".'

Schultz grabbing the newspaper across the table out of his Lordship's hands. Schultz smoothing out the crumples as he holds open the paper to read and rises up out of his chair. And flops back down again, taking a deep breath and letting out a long sigh. The waiter arriving at the table side with a trolley and kippers warming on a hot plate. And placing in front of Schultz a steaming bowl of porridge.

'Bon appétit Mr Schultz.'

Schultz staring down at his breakfast. The waiter smilingly bowingly retreating from the presence. As Schultz pushes back his chair from the table and slowly rises from his seat.

'Now what's wrong Schultz. You've gone absolutely as white as a sheet.'

'Oh my god. I can't eat. I'm sick. My whole stomach is in turmoil. I walk in here ten minutes ago utterly constipated and now I got to get to the lavatory with the fucking shits.'

'Schultz don't stay shitting too long. Binky's sent a motor to be here in front of the hotel prompt at nine and there's a long drive ahead.'

The snow turning to sleet outside. Nectarine assisting Schultz bent over holding his stomach and helped by the hotel porter out the lobby door to a waiting ancient long black Daimler motorcar. Nectarine attempting to point out sights of interest as they drive through Edinburgh along Princes Street and Queensbury Road.

'This is Schultz a city of some considerable if austere dignity that it is a pity for you to miss seeing.'

'Don't worry I can miss seeing it. I don't want to ruin anything beautiful to look at with the way I'm feeling.'

North beyond the waters of the Firth of Forth, Schultz, head under a blanket, now snoring asleep. An eye opening occasionally to peek at snow covered mountains and glens and at blue black lochs and lakes. The passing empty moorlands mile upon mile. The air getting colder. The wheels skidding on these winding icy roads through forests and up through dales and valleys. A flash of morning sun brightening the dark greens along the steep banks of the tumbling bog brown waters of a burn. Nectarine reading in a tome open across his lap and pressing the switch to lower the glass division to ask the grey haired ancient chauffeur to stop at the next village. Schultz waking and stepping out of the motorcar as Nectarine goes for a pee and returns with another newspaper. A full front page picture of Tower Bridge. Schultz moaning in the cold air and putting his hands up over his eyes.

'Not to worry Schultz just a provincial version of the same old hackneyed stuff carried by the national dailies. But up here where of course there is not much in the way of scandal, papers do tend to use considerably larger pictures and headlines on the front page.'

'O god. I want to be from now on just a private bloody person. Why does this all have to happen to me in the middle of while I'm making all this money.'

'Buck up Schultz. Get back in the car. Take a few lungfuls of this fresh air with you. And blow those old cobwebs of paranoia out of your brain. In just a short while we'll be there.'

The motor pulling out again on the road. The sheep grazed countryside hills ascending in the distance to whitened granite mountains which loom and bulge with boulders strewn on their slopes. Schultz sitting back in the corner, knees covered by the plaid rug. Nectarine his foot nervously jigging up and down, again reading in his book.

'Holy cow I didn't know it was this far all the way up here miles from nowhere.'

'You had but to refer to a map Schultz.'

'Jesus you want me to look at maps while I'm besieged.'

'Surely you knew where Scotland was.'

'We haven't seen a house for half an hour. Hey in this isolation are there likely to be any women up here suffering from the disease of nymphomania. That I always hope every girl I meet will have.'

'It would appear Schultz that the fresh air has revived you and that in spite of your emotional turmoil and difficulties you seem to have regained your abnormal amative appetite.'

'I never lost it. And as strong as that appetite is thank god there is no law in England that can ever compel me to fuck my wife again.'

'Good god Schultz you're the limit beyond which women are driven I think when they murder men.'

'Hey thanks a bunch your Lordship that's real nice and encouraging for my confidence what you just said.'

'Your confidence Schultz needs little encouragement in that quarter. Indeed one might suggest that with your recently sewn up balls and national celebrity you might go fuck on the top of the mid span across Tower Bridge while all England watches. Cheer the nation up as well.'

'Jesus your Lordship, this really is miles and miles from civilization and I'm the one who should be getting fucking well cheered up. Where the hell are we, there's nothing, nothing anywhere except this bereft landscape. Which you're not even bothering to look at.'

'In order not to be ignorant of the obsequies we are about to attend,

194

I am in fact reading the order for the burial of the dead. And Schultz it would not hurt were you to heed psalm thirty nine.'

'Holy christ up in the ass end of nowhere I'm also getting biblical lectures.'

'Well Schultz you really should have stayed in London, you know, and faced your music.'

'O K your Lordship what's psalm thirty nine.'

'I will take heed to my ways that I offend not in my tongue.'

'O boy. I'll say. Hey your Lordship seriously tell me what do you do for fucking these days. I really got to know what to do with my life which women are wrecking.'

'I've told you many a time that what I do for my fucking Schultz is no concern of yours. And it really would be more appropriate if you were to realize that we are on our way to a most solemnly sad occasion, and while we are attending, it would be more suitable were you not to address me as your Lordship. I do have Christian names you know. Which include Basil, Andrew, George, Albert.'

'O K Basil, my dear, as Binky might say. You are no longer your Lordship. Hey and let me see that book. Jeeze. The Book of Common Prayer and Administration of the Sacraments and Other Rites and Ceremonies of the Church According to the Use of the United Church of England and Ireland. And hey listen to these bullshit words. We brought nothing into this world and it is certain we can carry nothing out. Like your ancestors brought you with millions into this world. And shit who worries then about carrying anything out.'

A castellated bridge over a river in this lonely remoteness. Grey pebbles and stones in a narrow ravine rising to mossy banks. Winterish yellow leaves of a strange tree against the backdrop of snowy mountains. And the motor turning between massive gates and gate houses and between clumps of shiny leaved rhododendrons. A ray of sunshine breaking through the clouds, speckles of dandruff white on the ancient chauffeur's shoulders. The motor ascending a winding narrow road up this mountain side mile after mile and emerging around an outcrop of rock. Ahead, silhouetted against a misty sky, a soaring turreted castle perched precipitously on the cliff side. And on a rising hillside meadow shaggy long haired cattle grazing.

'Holy jeeze your Lordship are we here. This place looks as if it's out of some fairy tale.'

'Schultz you'll forgive me if I further suggest that you do not continue shouting holy jeeze, it might be more appropriate, if, in the present circumstances you simply say it under your breath. And please, may I remind you again, I am not your Lordship. Call me old boy, old sport, or old anything.'

'How about you old tart.'

'Ah I see that a slight element of comedy of a very anglicized nature is making its feeble attempt to seep back into your spirit.'

On the rust coloured pebbles the black Daimler car coming to a stop between two cannons flanking the massive fortified entrance. The walls, buttresses, battlements and towers of this castle disappearing high into the cold mist. Stepping from an open oak door, two moss green liveried footmen descending the steps. And a black suited red eyed butler bowing to his Lordship.

'We are very sad milord, to have to welcome you on such a very sad occasion.'

'Yes Warrick. Yes.'

'Ah and I don't think I've had the pleasure before milord to meet your Mr Noble.'

'O in fact this is a Mr Schultz, a friend of Mr Sunningdale's.'

'O I am sorry sir, do please forgive me. Mr Schultz.'

The little group entering the portals. The echoes of voices in the great front hall. Schultz following a footman with his baggage up four flights of stone stairs and along a vaulted corridor. Spears fanning out over the walls, suits of armour stationed on every landing. Ancestral portraits and one life sized of Binky's mother in a black evening gown, a red rose at her bodice. Long pale yellow gloves held in her hand. Imagine anybody as beautiful as that being dead. Christ I've never, never felt so conspicuous in my life. Boy has this trip already started out on the wrong foot. Shit. Imagine I'm already in this suit being taken as a butler. What is it that these people and their servants have got which stops you right in your tracks, leaving you, if you're not on your American guard, dumbfounded with inferiority. Then if ever you try getting to know them it's like big iron gates are shut in your face that you have to talk through. Jesus I got to keep as close to his Lordship as possible and hide through all of this. Binky did at least say thanks to me for coming. But he and his Lordship never even spoke. They said not even a word to each other, not even of greeting, just a glance and the merest nod of the head. Such close friends they know what the other is thinking. And the only real close life long friend I ever had was Al. Shit I wonder what he'd say if I ever did get to his bedside and said forgive me Al for what I done to you. Jesus he might take off his oxygen mask and hit me over the fucking head. The cunt. Christ I was nearly always half glad when someone came along to take a faithful girlfriend off my hands. And Al had been fucking other guys' girlfriends not to mention their wives, all his life. Why does he have to throw such an unreasonable fit when it's done to him. O god I know why. There's never never ever going to be another one of Louella.

'If there's anything at all sir, the buttons to press are there at the side of the chimney piece. Mourners are to assemble sir in exactly twenty minutes in the front main hall.'

'Thanks. It'll give me time to catch my breath up all those stairs.'

Schultz going to the narrow window. Opening it to peer hundreds of feet into the glen below. An eagle circling above a river entering the loch between the steep cliffs plunging into the valley. Schultz crossing the bedroom to look out another turret window. Down upon formal gardens, stone statues, pebble paths, clipped hedges, and lily pond. Great crags and a tiny cottage. And inside here a canopied bed. Hangings embroidered with red roses. Paintings and drawings of birds on the wall. A still life with flowers. Painted by Antonio Ponce. Could be one of Binky's jokes. And jesus, a priceless tapestry of these butterfly wings. I've seen enough in half of this room already to buy and sell my poor father. Just two square inches of the ceiling of this room you could stare at for an hour wondering why, like Freddie Joy's nose, it's so beautiful. Here I am a kid from Woonsocket. Growing up working down a dingy basement with Saul while Binky must have been living in all this. As if I have to remind myself, it really makes sense to make money. And these people must have been stacking it up for centuries. And at least it's providing me with a peaceful change from a night on the train. Recalling as if I needed them, past catastrophes. While the lonely lights went by like shooting stars. Even lamp standards and station clocks I counted trying to go to sleep. The click clack and the clank of the sounds of coupling trains. Figures at a road crossing, with a horse that I swear reared with a fantastic erection in a flash of moonlight. Jesus even the bathroom in here is like a private living room. Hey Rabbi Löw, not that I'm exactly starving for the company but one thing is for sure, so far there isn't another single Jew in sight up here. So be exclusive Sigmund, with you there who needs another. Touché Rabbi. I'm convinced I'm fine alone. Hey and this is a miracle of coincidence, right here in this painting on the wall, my most favourite food and taste in all the world. Fucking fraises des bois on a fucking nice blue plate next to a glass of champagne. Rabbi Löw I just got an insight. All I need is a good butler, a good cook and a good secretary and I can tell every woman in the world to go fuck themselves and for a start I'm going to tell three of them in a row. Sigmund, you're optimistic, you're going to have to go find them first. And I have news, they'll all be busy fucking someone else.

In the chill castle air Schultz returning down the deeply worn stone steps between the cold stone walls and pillars holding up the vaulted arches of the staircase. Stopping at a landing to open up one side of a pair of massive mahogany doors and peek in. Good fucking god. It's a room a mile long. With a carpet that looks two miles long. All this space doing nothing except being here. This is another Shangri La, just like his Lordship's castle. Where he would prostrate himself in depression inside because outside he thought his grass was the wrong colour green. I guess you got to cultivate a style of living to accommodate this kind of life. Boy and I got to revise my own style of living simply to include remaining alive.

People assembled in the vast front hall. Pink light from the blazing fire glinting from the silvery suits of armour, spears and swords. Binky black jacketed in a kilt, a silver buckle on his belt flashing as he descended the curving stone staircase. The gathering moving down a long corridor and disappearing into a doorway of the chapel filled to overflowing. Supine upon a tomb, a marble effigy of a knight in armour next to his wife, their hands joined pointing upwards in prayer, and at their feet, two smaller effigies of their children kneeling. The stained glass window over the altar, insignias and coats of arms in hues of green, blue, yellow, gold and crimson. The draped coffin centre of the chapel. Schultz and his Lordship taking their places in the polished oak pews carved with lions and stags rampant. As Schultz trips with an echoing clatter and grabs a candlestick to hold on. The lit candle breaking and with it clutched in his fist, wax dripping down on Schultz's face as he lies supine at his Lordship's feet.

'Good god Schultz, any moment now we'll be burying you next.'

The distant snow capped mountains shining bright above the shadows of their valleys. The slow hesitant beating of a distant drum. A piper in his kilt, taking his slow steps down a narrow stony path of the hillside. Lady Ottoline's coffin atop the shoulders of estate workers. The blue black shiny waters of the loch far below. The wind blowing the pipe strains across the valley and echoing them back from the mountain cliff sides. Binky his blond curly locks blowing in the breeze, walking next to a figure in a black cape and cowl. An eagle wheeling high above in the sky.

'Schultz can you make it.'

'Yeah just let me hold on to your arm. Jesus I'm half a cripple looking devastated, while Binky walks like a soldier.'

'Schultz, believe me, Binky despite his implacable military air, is utterly struck down with sorrow. She was a lady loved by at least a hundred men and was Scottish loveliness at its most supreme. So fond she was of wearing black. And did have the most beautiful exquisitely white eyeballs.'

'Jesus now that you mention, christ yes that I remember too. Plus she had a fantastic figure for her age. And amen. I guess you say.'

The damp chill and biting bitter wind turning hands and faces blue with cold. The long winding stream of mourners, making their way through the iron gates of a small cemetery carved out of the side of the mountain. A tiny chapel built into the rock of the cliff side. Sheep, like tiny maggots on the snowless patches on the lower slopes of the distant hills. Shaggy long haired highland cattle with great curving horns grazing the pasture below the cemetery.

'Jesus your Lordship how much longer now the fuck is this routine. I'm freezing bloody well to death.'

'For god's sake Schultz be quiet.'

'Jesus you don't need to be in this wind. I wish like you I could think beautiful well behaved thoughts instead of thinking the real thoughts I am forced to think especially that everyone's out to get me in this life. My leg feels broke.'

'Your neck will feel broke soon Schultz. You really are, to put it mildly, the original court jester.'

A sprig of heather dropped on the coffin as it lowers into a crypt in the floor of the chapel. A bishop from a slip of paper reading words. The steam of his breath in the cold air. The bowed heads and tearful eyes. The sound of a cough and a muffled sob. A nose being blown. The wind gusting in the chapel door. Footsteps crunch out again on the gravel forecourt. And as the dark line of figures climb back up the narrow path, a flurry of snow falls.

'I'm choked up your Lordship. Jesus, there goes more beauty by its own hand wasted just like that. I mean how bad can life get that you just don't want to live anymore.'

'The imagination Schultz can quickly make life far worse than death, and she was an extremely imaginative lady.'

The funeral gathering assembled back in the castle's vast dining room echoing loud with voices. Under its high ceiling, vaulted with ribs of stone and beams of oak, a minstrel's gallery. Two fires blazing massive logs under white marble chimney pieces. A long table covered with smoked salmon, ham, roast beef. Glasses and silverware glinting from the fading shaft of light coming in the tall narrow gothic windows. Servants to and fro with trays of drinks and canapés. Family portraits, tapestries and flags hung high on the walls.

'God your Lordship, I mean Basil, I'm hungry and freezing. I got to get something down my throat. And I've got to give the people credit. Except for the fucker who just asked me to go get him some Angostura Bitters, they are just too polite to take any notice of me. Or maybe way the fuck up here in this isolation they don't know they've got a national celebrity mingling in the midst.'

'I don't suppose Schultz that it has occurred to you that rather than thinking they have a national celebrity mingling in their midst they might instead think they've got a national embarrassment invading their privacy.'

'Hey shit your Lordship, come on, don't ruin, will you, the fucking momentary enchantment I'm enjoying for just two whole seconds. Hey but hold it. Holy jeeze, who the fuck is that. My god. What a face, hair and figure. Holy christ that creature is a devastating apparition I've never seen anything like before. And she's talking to that guy in the clerical garb with wrappings around his legs. Jesus I just got the first real glow of pleasure through my balls since they got zapped by a zipper.'

'Ah how nice for you Schultz.'

'Hey look at that jet black long wavy hair. Her eyes have got to absolutely be a magic green. Jesus what am I doing in my life, wasting time with old past disasters, when such opportunity springs eternal. Wasn't she the one wearing a cape and hood over her head in the chapel.'

'Schultz I have no intention of procuring for you but I will say, some colour has come back into your cheeks.'

'Jesus your Lordship you bet it has. I can't believe what I'm seeing. Just look at that over there standing at the fireplace. Wow. Who, my god is she.'

'She lives I fear some many valleys away.'

'Jesus show me the fucking stony path over the mountains that leads there will you.'

'No I won't Schultz.'

'Hey wait a second, like fuck she does live many valleys away. Look. She's even giving the butler instructions and behaves as if she belongs here. Right in this house.'

'Schultz you are a bit of a detective aren't you but I do think you have enough on your plate for the moment. And I most certainly don't think you should at this precise time start any of your lady killing antics.'

'Well who is she.'

'She was in fact at Oxford. Double first in Classics. And is now happily married with seven children.'

'Now I know you're a god damn liar. And the way you say that word Oxford. Like it was supposed to be natural and normal. You sons of bitches. It's like a garden party your fucking lives.'

'I'm sure Schultz you hardly mean to call this a garden party. If it is, there has rarely ever been a sadder one.'

'Yeah holy christ you're right I guess I'm just getting carried away by confronting all this. And to change the subject a second, what's this.'

'A silver cruet set.'

'Is it solid.'

'I should be awfully surprised if it weren't Schultz.'

'Shit it could weigh a ton.'

'Well I'm certainly sure it weighs considerably as I believe I have one resembling it.'

'Jesus, can you just imagine there on the table, five fucking thousand pure ounces of silver. Do you know silver is really selling at the moment. Jesus the value of that could be realizing interest in a bank.'

'Or Schultz, the considerable pleasure one gets out of its perfection.'

His Lordship wandering off. Schultz rubbing elbows amid the lofty accents and staring across the room at the apparition of beauty in black. These craggy faced people. Their superior chins raised. A lady regally seated there with a countenance of an eagle. What a collection. Because their ancestors made a profit, pleasure comes first. Principle of the upper classes which yours truly has just adopted. Until holy christ. Did you hear that. Some guy says, excuse me waiter, I wonder would you mind awfully getting me another glass of champagne. Fuck you buster.

Through the door under the minstrels' gallery, Binky entering the room. Nodding his head. Shaking hands here and there and the pleats of his kilt swirling about his knees, making his way across the massive gold and crimson carpet towards Schultz sipping a glass of champagne.

'How do Schultz. You're looking awfully pretty this evening even though it's only the afternoon. In our latitudes up here, the darkness of winter descends early as you will see out there through the window behind you. Sorry not to be able to look after you, a few private family matters to attend to. Are you enjoying yourself.'

'Yeah, fine.'

'Between a pause in my organ playing I did hear the noise of your not quite breaking your arse in the chapel. I do hope your balls weren't further aggrieved thereby. And I especially do hope you're not contemplating suing us.'

'Holy shit Binky, no, I'm not.'

'Ah such a relief. Of course having had a view of the video of your zipper inconvenience I believe you are going to be able to give a good account of the event. My zoom in close ups should be especially choice and I'm sure the damages awarded you from your tailors will be severe and should I think have them already quaking in their tracks and their own balls trembling in their crotches. Now must go to attend to the bishop over there, having it appears a joke with my half sister. And by the way I did enjoy reading in one of the more sensational papers this morning and in the most screaming of headlines, news of your harem in Belgravia. Ladies in purdah no less. Ah Schultz I do think we might take lessons from you in seeking the best in the otherworldly pleasures in which clearly you indulge. See you seven thirty for drinks in the armoury when we can before dinner chat a little longer. And if you're short on togs we can I'm sure fit you up. And do let Warrick know if he can make your stay any more comfortable. And we do hope you'll not be rushing away immediately and stay on a little. Ta ta. I must go and have a word in Lord Nectarine's ear.'

A black uniformed and haired maid with a magnum bottle replenishing Schultz's champagne. Schultz putting the glass to his lips and swallowing it back and holding it out for a refill. Christ I'm going to get Jorricks to order a couple of dozen cases, this stuff called Möet & Chandon on the bottle clears the head in a hurry of any hangover from last night. And that maid, had a nice musky smell. Jesus. You'd never know Binky just five minutes ago buried his mother. There he is, gliding from person to person, a merry quip here, a merry quip there. The guy is inhumanly urbane. No wonder I don't trust him. What a waste of time it was pretending I did. And the few times I tried being honest he disembowelled me with a double cross. And you'd think now to listen to him that he wasn't in the middle of one again to ruin me. But holy fuck. It's his half sister. Jesus she's got to be listed in my line up of who I got to fuck next. Now I got to wait till I can talk again to his Lordship, with christ everyone seeming to be genuflecting around him.

202

Schultz spying the apparition of beauty suddenly left standing alone. Schultz making his way across the room. Through the babbling voices and perfumes and the smell of smoke from the blazing fires. And halfway there. My god. Five guys have already closed in. Right when I'm going to make my move. Holy shit it's only when you begin feeling the first pangs of real love that it gives you a god damn chance to forget all the god damn misery you had since you last thought you were feeling the first pangs of love. Jesus there's his Lordship sitting on a tapestried chair near that massive chimney piece flanked by two niches with two large blues vases that I'm bloody sure are bound to be priceless. A sad faraway look in his eyes as he taps the ash into the grate off those god damn good cigars he smokes.

'Ten quid for your thoughts your Lordship.'

'Ah it's you Schultz. I was in fact just thinking upon the five wounds of Christ on the cross.'

'Holy jesus as if there wasn't enough already going wrong with the world. Hey but I thought it was only four wounds, but who's counting. O but hey that's right. They got him in both feet, both hands and once in the side.'

'Yes now please give me the ten quid.'

'Hey holy shit I was only kidding.'

'I'm afraid Schultz that you ought to know by now, and especially having regard for your national celebrity status, and suing and being sued, that money and the mention thereof unless it be a sum de minimis, precludes kidding in any semblance.'

'Hey shit you're serious. Holy fuck here. Take it. You just gave me the fifth wound of Christ.'

'Graphically put Schultz, as usual.'

'Sure why not call a wound a wound. I get them round the clock.'

'The money, Schultz will be duly donated to the Royal National Lifeboat Institution fund.'

'In that case here's another twenty. Hey you know this is really a good feeling giving away money like this. It's crazy isn't it. It's the first time in my life I ever had this sensation.'

'Well then you must keep up giving Schultz, keep it up. Indeed I'll give your name to a few deserving charities. And may I remark that the occasion reveals something absolutely deeply endearing about you, previously hidden.'

'Hey. Really. Here's another five. Jesus you're right. I feel fucking wonderful. It's amazing. It's like magic.'

'Ah. But you must remain aware too Schultz that you have just consumed your second glass of champagne.'

'Third. But who's counting. But I really do. I feel fucking wonderful. Like it's welcome to Shangri La. Hey here's another quid. Jesus, this is, isn't it. Up here in the towering fucking mists. I just wish to fuck I wasn't dressed like a butler with people actually asking me to get them drinks.'

'Schultz have you noticed, the sums you're giving are getting progressively smaller. That could result in diminishing the wonderful feeling you're feeling.'

'Jesus you're fucking absolutely right. Here let me give you another twenty. God I'm glad you said that. I really was, no kidding wondering why I was beginning to feel kind of sheepish. Jesus live and learn. I'm getting a fucking education up here. But hey you know all in all it didn't take that long through the ceremony. Jesus it was impressive but why was it all so short.'

'The religious office for burial of the dead cannot be used for those who are thought to have laid violent hands upon themselves.'

'Hey jesus why does everyone think suicide, if that's what it was, is such a terrible thing.'

'Well Schultz it's very much the same as someone in the middle of your conversation getting up and leaving the room without telling you why or where they are going. You feel an awful silly old fool just sitting there left in your own company. And I do think you are likely to at least mildly resent it.'

'But what about somebody you'd like to see the last of.'

'Well in such case one presumes you wouldn't be comfortably talking to them in the first place.'

'Hey Basil, old sport let's toast a drink to each other. This is the best funeral I've ever been at. But now what I want to know is where do you get all these sensible observations from.'

'Ah Schultz. You old transvestite, you. I've probably told you a dozen times already. But why not, as we appear to be getting tight tell you yet again. One is inclined to glean it from a grumpy old grandfather whose false teeth were constantly falling into the soup after finding it served too hot. And he was likely to utter impatient if not angry remarks which would often reflect the verities of life and as a small terrified boy one would be much inclined to listen and one would hear many memorable pronouncements made while servants rushed to take the sugar tongs to retrieve the teeth out of the hot soup so that when cooled enough on the sideboard my grandfather could put them back in again.'

'Jesus christ no wonder I've been deprived, all your good sense came from someone dropping their false teeth in the soup.'

'Yes Schultz, dentures both upper and lower. Of course at such troubled times my grandfather would in his toothless mumbling manner call for port. And such edict would galvanize the entire household from end to end as boy apprentice butlers would be sent scurrying off to fetch same from the cellars which were some considerable distance away. Such boys were trained to sacredly carry the port in the most horizontally gentle manner possible. But of course after decanting in the pantry if too much evidence of the lees were found to be in the bottom of my grandfather's glass after he downed it, there would be more angry voluble matters expressed concerning man's besetments in life, and another call would be made for another bottle of port while the remainder of the first bottle was allowed to settle. However it was thought by Noble, whom you've met Schultz, and who served my grandfather most of his life, that a certain amount of lees were always to be left discerned in the glass so that my grandfather could complain and order a second bottle decanted and have at his disposal throughout lunch two bottles of port both of which he would systematically polish off, making sure that in the course of doing so, the other guests got as little of it as possible. He firmly believed that taking port in this manner, between his sips of claret of course, prevented him having his seizures which indeed seemed to be the case, for he would then repair calmly with a cigar to the west facing conservatory and take his nap after lunch, not waking until just prior to tea which allowed him a few minutes stroll in the gardens and deer park at which time he was fond of letting off a few shotgun salvos at stray pigeons, hares and indeed poachers. Or failing those previous three, and as he especially eschewed idlers, he would severely enjoy to bestir any lackadaisical gardener leaning on a shovel, by stealing up close behind and without a pigeon or hare in sight, letting off a shotgun blast. Into the sky of course and while pretending he was having a shot at an overhead duck. He always claimed to have hit the duck and would send the poor idler off searching and demand he find it.'

'Holy shit, you know your Lordship, somehow that little story sort of explains everything to me in life.'

'Ah so glad to hear that Schultz.'

'Just tell me where's the best place I can go to buy some port.'

'You'll find there are a couple of rather popular places in and around St James.'

'Jesus I'm sending Jorricks for a few cases.'

'You know Schultz, can I tell you something. I've gradually grown extremely fond of you.'

'O yeah.'

'You listen to me with such awe and take what I say so instantly to heart that it is entirely flattering.'

'Well jesus, maybe on that pleasant note and now that I am minus fifty six quid and if I can ever find the way back to my bedroom, I'm going to get rid of all the travel grime and try to go take a bath without getting my balls wet.'

'Well Schultz the way this castle is built at least you have no need to worry about the crucial gymnastics that that exercise is bound to require.'

Schultz taking a series of wrong turnings. Along corridors and up and down stairs. And ending up ascending to the top of the keep and stepping out on to an embattlement with the wind tearing at his clothes. Darkness falling and the last pink rays of a sinking sun fanning up on the grey blue sky. The faint silhouette of the mountains in the distance enclosing the black flatness of the loch. Just one single far away tiny speck of light. Jesus no wonder that from here you can look down on top of those soaring eagles and touch the clouds going by. Holy god what a place. The wind evaporates the worries right out of your mind. You may feel insignificant walking along a street mid town Manhattan but this let me tell you takes the cake. Right over this edge is an abyss of darkness. Jesus no question that a fucking jump off here would end any conversation.

Schultz feeling his way back down the spiral stair of the keep again. In the faint light, stepping through a door into a picture gallery and into another hall finally ending in a cul de sac. Retracing his steps and midway confronting a heavy oaken door in a gothic arch with open tomes carved in the stone. Entering a sombre long chamber. Jesus this must be the library. Twice as big as the one we had where I went to college. O boy, will ignominy ever cease. Palatial like a fucking palace in here. Galleries of books a mile long. Couches to sit on. If Binky read even a fraction of what was in here on one shelf he'd be an all time champion scholar. Although shit, I just thought of it, one thing this trip is doing for me, is knocking my wife's publicity right out of my mind. And then just knocking me out.

Schultz pulling out a book. Riffling through the pages of a zoological text. Jesus no wonder people risked life and limb all over the centuries, just to be able to sit down like this and look at these beautiful coloured drawings. Of bloody molluscs no less. O boy, and that's an insight. We're fucking well put on this earth, our heads snooping forward to just go around smelling which cunts can be got into. After a meal or two out in an expensive restaurant. And then waiting to get sooner or later kicked in the snozzle either before or after. Holy shit when it used to be that all my efforts had to be how to kick the girls out of the house after they started sewing and cooking. And it is just one big reminder just looking at this. That such a pity we ever lost that fucking shell from one of these origins of the species. The latter evolved types among which all I am searching for is a warm hearted woman. Rabbi is that bad. That at least now in my life I should have some hope after all the stony hearted bunch of calculating bitches I've had the misery of confronting these past years of my life. That now maybe I have found what I am looking for. Sigmund listen, you will also find that what you are looking for, will after you find it, be like every other woman, and worse be just like your wife. So just make sure they can cook, clean and sew. Thanks a bunch Rabbi for the info, you've just bowed my head once more again in despair. Shattering me. Like when small and growing up I was crazy and unJewish enough with some of the Irish bastards I made friends with to believe in Christmas. And they used to kid me. By saying Santa Claus came in the summer time. Exactly on July fourth. And they hand me a present in a shoe box which blew up my dreams with a cherry bomb firecracker. Jesus by the time you learn all about life the fucking thing is all over.

Schultz entering a door under the library balcony and with faint strains of organ music, ascending another secretive spiral staircase and finding his way back to his bedroom. His baggage unpacked and clothing neatly in the drawers of the dresser. Dinner jacket, shirt and trousers laid out on the bed. Black silk socks and evening slippers embroidered with coronets. Jesus at least and at last here are a few nice things done under Binky's aegis while my back is turned. It's what you need in life. Something, anything that for a moment is kindly. But one thing I'm at least sure of. I'm going from now on, right through all worry, to force myself to enjoy myself. I'm going to stick my face in the sunshine somewhere and let the hot beams bathe my closed eyes and body in some bliss instead of hanging around in any more horror. And not ever let myself again be thrown into a turmoil of depression. Get out of the hardship of stage production into the glamour world of pictures and Hollywood. Get in on some of those gala highlights. Where all the action is at film festivals and premières. Where none of the awful damage is done to you that the legitimate stage has always lying in wait. Where the cast can be bought out from under you. And if you don't let them get bought they get sick. At least in the movie business the cast is on celluloid and the whole thing is a package under your arm you can walk around with. Now in all this medieval and primitive place, I'm going to take advantage of the modern convenience of a luxurious bathroom. And bandaged balls permitting, take a bath. While the wind moans at these lancet windows. One second I'm thinking, how can I ever forgive Binky for what he is now trying to do to me. And yet in two seconds downstairs I forgive him. Even love him. For the way he never gives anything away. Which why should he with his massive money he only has to snap his fingers or write his name on a cheque and any production he dreams up on the spur of the moment is financed. Whereas I had to go cap in hand ass kissing my way from door to door which were all nearly closed in my face. Jesus did I say nearly. Christ all. All were slammed in my face. Until Al blackmailed me with an investment into a life's disaster of marriage. Which has now become an international explosion of publicity all over the world. Thanks a bunch Al. And hope your gaskets aren't still leaking. Well anyway. For the moment. My only worry is, after a bath, how do I find the armoury.

Schultz undressed entering the bathroom. The wind whining and whistling about the turret windows. And in the sudden silence, the screech of an owl out somewhere in the night. The flames of the turf fire reflecting on the side of the tub as Schultz leans to twist on these two great brass taps. The faded white and stained tops of their ceramic knobs marked chaud and froid. At least I know enough French to tell which is hot and which is cold. Feel the flow of water with a finger. Jesus there's plenty coming out of the froid but not enough coming out of the chaud.

Schultz stepping into the tub, getting his feet wet in the lukewarm water. Soaking the wash cloth to wipe himself down. Reaching to twist the hot tap further open. Taking two hands to it. Twisting it harder. Leaning in with his full weight and groaning arching his back to turn the ancient brass fixture. A sudden snap. The tap coming away in Schultz's hand as he stares at it held up in his fist, reading the French for hot. O my fucking god. Now I've done it. Tore the whole fucking thing off its rusted iron joint. Leaving just a hole in the bathtub. With a fountain of hot water cascading a mile high and coming down like a thunderstorm.

Schultz grabbing a towel. Pressing it down over the jet of water. The fluffy white cotton cloth saturated as the flow seeps from underneath and floods in a deluge out over the bathroom floor. Schultz lifting the towel away and sticking his finger in the hole. Jesus I'm pushing my innocent appendage in up to the hilt and water's still pouring all over the place. Now when I don't need it, it's really getting hot. And I'm going to get scalded.

Schultz pulling his finger out. And jumping back as the fountain erupts spouting up to hit the ceiling. Schultz holding his bandaged balls as he runs out of the bathroom. Across the bedroom. Kaboom. Tripping over the dressing table chair. Landing asprawl on his hands and knees. Crawling the rest of the way to open the door into the hall. Raising one hand cupped to his mouth to shout.

'Help, help, help. Please come somebody. Fast. The place is being flooded. Help.'

Schultz under the cover of an eiderdown, crawling back into the bathroom. Plunging the tips of three fingers back into the hole. The water still spraying and seeping out to flow down the side of the bath and out over the floor. Steam clouding mirrors and windows. Water landing hissing on the turf fire flames. Towels drenched. Carpets soaked. Toilet paper sodden. A flash of electricity. The overhead light short circuiting. Momma meo and now we're plunged into darkness.

The sound of feet approaching. Schultz with his free hand grabbing up the soaked eiderdown back over his shoulders and bandaged balls. Light from the hall casting a shadow across the bedroom. A female voice. And a beam of light shining on Schultz as he stands up. And the eiderdown falls down.

'I do beg your pardon but is there someone in here who was shouting for help. O dear me. There's a flood!'

'Yeah, yeah. Me. I'm shouting. The place is flooding. A plumber's needed. Or a wrench. Or a champagne cork.'

'O dear, how quite extraordinary, you are aren't you, absolutely naked.'

'Hey don't go away for christ's sake.'

Schultz, still with the tips of his middle index fingers pressed into the hole of the broken pipe. The ends of his fingers burning. Time to hold the good hand I've got left over my eyes in grief. O god. And O Rabbi. After the calmest most peaceful brief half hour period of my life I now face the most awful crisis situation in Christendom. And only one thing I can do. Is to wait till the avalanche of water cascades down the staircases and someone else who doesn't run away, has the sense to go see where it's coming from. And christ if someone soon doesn't come quick this whole fucking castle is going to be washed right off this cliff side.

And now meanwhile maybe
I should just
Get in a canoe
And have fun
Going down the rapids

Schultz stopped in his wet tracks by a man in a grey overall arriving with a pack of tools to cap the bathroom hot spout. And Schultz assisted by maids and footmen moved to another bedroom. Where louder winds were howling at the castle windows as he bathed in a perfume scented bath. Laid out on his bed, a dinner jacket, silk shirt, evening slippers and a note.

15

Mr Sunningdale hopes Mr Schultz following his impromptu shower may find these suitable to make use of or come as you are, or indeed as Lord Nectarine describes your being recently rigged in ladies' Islamic dress.

Schultz at a tall mirror on a staircase landing, making an examination of the almost perfect dinner jacket fit. Embroidered in gold on each foot, an earl's coronet. Holy jeeze. A wonderful feeling to feel like an aristocrat. Everybody beneath you. The only effort you ever have to make is to make people think you ain't putting on airs. While you have airs flying all over the place. Primitive as it is, I could fall in love with this life. A few crossbows at the various slits, and voom, voom, arrows sent right up my wife's lawyers' asses. My only problem being how do I find my way to the armoury.

The leather heels of Schultz's evening slippers a shade too large, clacking across the front great hall. Where a footman directs him along a flagstone corridor and down stone stairs into a large low ceilinged room. Suits of armour, arrows, bows, spears and swords around the circular walls. Lord Nectarine pensively standing centre of the gleamingly polished black and white tiled floor.

'Hey your Lordship I'm not going to offer you ten quid for your thoughts again, but you do look like you're having a fucking deep unfathomable cogitation.'

'Ah. I was in fact reliving an embarrassing moment of cricket. When once at bat I had tripped backwards and got a wicket up the arse. But do Schultz have a freshly poured glass of champagne. You know, despite your fucking up the plumbing and throwing the entire castle household into a panic, Binky is quite touched that you should have come.'

'Shit I'm here because I'm escaping. Hey there could be guys' eyes inside these suits of armour staring out of the slits. The fucking things are surrounding us. This whole place. Every turn I get lost. The stone stairs, the turrets, five foot thick walls. It's medieval.'

'In fact a great deal of this castle is pre Christian Schultz.'

'I don't want to bring up the wet subject of plumbing but what did they do years ago to wash their faces before they ever got the fucking pipes through this place.'

'Water men Schultz. Prior to dawn these especially strong men carried water on their backs up through the castle filling the cisterns.'

'You mean you could flush toilets. Perfect for your wife's boyfriend's invention.'

'As a matter of fact in those days Schultz they had no need for my wife's boyfriend's bloody invention. They instead used those little parapets which are built out from the wall and one placed a rear end upon such breezy hole. And while one's arse was being chilled the results such as one might have wanted rid of, simply plummeted down the side of the ramparts sixteen hundred feet into the ravine.'

'Hey jeeze from down in the valley you could look up at a whole lot of asses. Imagine jeeze a castle outbreak of diarrhoea.'

'Of course for you Schultz who are so frequently staring upwards with binoculars that is another viewpoint entirely. And no doubt as a spectator you'd be suitably attired in your heavy duty oilskins. But indeed I do believe that to this day even the most undomesticated animals give that area below a very wide berth. Where it just borders the waters of the loch. In which lurks a monster far bigger than the one supposedly seen in Loch Ness.'

'Hey boy you know life then was simple. When you think of it nothing is more complicated these days than trying to take a decent crap.'

'Ah Schultz you have for the first time in knowing you said something which at long last impresses me.'

'Jesus. You guys. Hey what do I have to do. I put the two of you on the big time show biz map. I'm the natural born aristocrat for christ's sake. You guys are artificial aristocrats, just descended from previous aristocrats one of whom maybe way way back fought and conquered and was a natural like myself. Yet everything good and beautiful happens to you guys while everything bad and gruesome happens to me. Hey where are you going your Lordship.'

'I'm going for a piss Schultz. And may even have a crap. But indeed shall be back shortly to listen to more of your delightful shit.'

'Hey don't leave me alone here, this place is spooky.'

His Lordship exiting under a banner draped doorway as Binky in his kilt pauses on the last step into this ancient room of swords, arrows, crossbows, and cannon.

212

'Ah but in spite of that you do look so nice this evening Schultz.'

'O hey hi Binky. His Lordship and I were just talking. Yeah. Just maybe the jacket's an eighth of an inch too short in the sleeves.'

'And my, you do I believe smell of a perfume of a favourite rose I recall from childhood. Sorry your hot bath rather ended up as a very hot shower.'

'Holy shit Binky, the fucking faucet came off in my hand. I swear.'

'Think nothing of it Schultz. Nothing whatever. Indeed when don't we find you in some little mishap or other. Of course the eiderdown was in fact something by the personal hand of Marie Antoinette and her seamstresses. Believe they rather spent some time sewing and embroidering it together. But I dare say a good damn soaking may do it a jolly lot of good.'

'Holy fuck I ruined it did I.'

'Ah yes Schultz I'm sure you did in addition to fucking up our plumbing and flooding two baths and bedrooms. Ah but let us pass over these trifling little domestic inconsequentials. And we mustn't dwell on anything which might trouble the digestion as we are having what hopes to be some tasty venison this evening. And Schultz I do hope that in spite of the sadder aspects of your visit, you are having what one would like to describe as a childishly uncomplicated good time in Scotland.'

'Jesus Binky this visit is affecting my whole life.'

'And dear me Schultz that is as it should be. And the public are I see, rather getting what one might describe as awfully good coverage of your activities these days. And that wife of yours. She is isn't she quite physically splendid. And her courage. To dive, what is it, one hundred and fifty feet down into the grey waters of the Thames. I understand further and better particulars of intimacies are soon to be revealed featured on the inside page of one of our popular Sunday newspapers.'

'Like hell they are. They're hearing from my lawyers.'

'But it does make one feel one would rather like to chat a bit with your wife Schultz one day. And aren't you Schultz in this room a little reminded of your own battles fought, victories won.'

'Yeah a suit of armour is exactly what I need. And although already this evening has started out on the wrong fucking foot at least on both feet I now got coronets. But jesus Binky the way you played that organ in the chapel.'

'Ah Schultz you do occasionally exhibit sensibilities which pleasantly surprise me.'

'Hey what do you mean I praised your playing the time when you played at his Lordship's castle.'

'Ah Schultz. Yes. But I do think Lord Nectarine's stops, especially the diapason bass and vox celeste needed attention.'

'Hey what about a piano. We could give you singing lessons and put you performing Sundays at the theatre. Send you on tour too. With your looks, and a band backing you, shit I would have an international pop star.'

'Ah dear me Schultz, and hope your testicles are dry and still healing nicely, and you have no idea how apt your suggestion is. This evening at least, you do make it sound as if hope will spring eternal for me. And indeed I have more than half a mind to encourage you to make me such an offer. In your immortal words we could go, voom, voom, voom. But you know all these show biz deals we go through are just like two chaps standing in the desert trying to sell each other sand. Then finally when the deal is done, you walk away from each other, and already the elusive grains are falling away between your fingers. But then of course there are these rare deals that do make profit. And Schultz you will be intrigued to hear that my little share of Kiss It Don't Hold It It's Too Hot is on the market. Yes Schultz don't turn red white and blue and keel over. You've heard correctly. Ah here just in time is my noble friend Lord Nectarine. Do I hear a bid. Did you hear that Lord Nectarine. My share of our perky little show is on the market. Now gentlemen. Surely something.'

'Hey what is this Binky.'

'It is Schultz precisely what you hear. My share of the show is for sale.'

'You sound as if you fucking well mean it. There must be something fishy somewhere. There must be.'

'Ah, a suspicious old meanie you remain, don't you Schultz. But a price. Do I hear a bid. Lord Nectarine, what about you then. Surely you're in the market if Schultz here remains suspicious and disbelieving.'

'Wait a minute Binky, you bet I remain suspiciously disbelieving but Sigmund Franz Schultz is very much in the market.'

'Well what do I hear you say.'

'You say, Binky. Give me numerals.'

'Well then let us start at two hundred thousand perhaps.'

'Jesus christ. Wait a second. Till I get my composure here. Jesus you really mean this Binky.'

'Of course I do you old silly. Have a spot more champagne in your glass.'

'Come on. What are you nuts. Two hundred thousand. After you already take Gayboy in two or was it three deals. You got your piece of the action for practically nothing.'

'That's simply not the point Schultz. I think the issue is that we are treating here of an equity of some considerable value. Come come. Don't let this crucial opportunity go by. Dear chaps my offer goes public in the morning. And my lawyers already have instructions to follow up an interested party located down Cheapside in the city of London. But of course out of regard for my long and trusted business relationship with you two gentlemen, I do give you first opportunity to snap up this tasty little financial morsel. Lord Nectarine surely you're ready to pick up a tiny something cheap.'

'Well Binky I could say one hundred and sixty five thousand.'

'Hold it, hold it you fucking guys. You're fucking well going to put my balls suddenly in a vice the pair of you, in an auction. This is a scheming plot. I should have known. This whole funeral could have been a put up job. Hey your Lordship, are you in on this fucking plot.'

'I beg your pardon Schultz I do believe I'm being slandered. I am not in the habit of conspiring. But I must confess, business apart, I sometimes do wonder following such an unthinkingly callous remark, that if you are possessed of even a vestige of the milk of human kindness, one feels sure that it would be found either sour or skimmed or curdled.'

'Hey what am I listening to. This is ridiculous. I simply want to know if I'm being set up. And conned.'

'Schultz. While you are hysterically worrying that you are being bamboozled, hoodwinked, swindled and diddled, I'm selling. Are you buying. Or not.'

'I'm buying for christ's sake. Holy shit I was just five seconds ago for the first time in weeks getting calm and contented again in my life. What do you want.'

'Two hundred thousand.'

'Fucking no. It's robbery. Or else. It's worse. That I'm going to wake up tomorrow and find out that the theatre has burned down and the cast got killed last night.'

'Very well then, Basil it's one sixty five to Lord Nectarine.'

'OK, OK Binky you bastard one seventy.'

'Lord Nectarine. It's with you now.'

'One eighty.'

'And with you now Schultz.'

'Holy shit, you fucking guys are doing it.'

'I take it Schultz, Lord Nectarine has it at one eighty. One eighty now on my left. One eighty for the second time, it's one eighty.'

'No fuck you. It's one ninety.'

'Lord Nectarine. It's against you now at one ninety.'

'Two hundred.'

'Two hundred I have now from his Royal Grace, Schultz. Do I hear two ten.'

'You dirty god damn fuckers. Jesus. Two hundred and ten.'

'No foul language, please gentlemen. It's against you your Royal Grace.'

'Two twenty five.'

'Ah we're going to shake off the timid I see. Against you Schultz. At two twenty five. Against you now. Courage.'

'O my god. I feel sick.'

'Ah my good chaps. Sip your champagne Schultz.'

'OK. Jesus I'm sweating for christ's sake. Wow with you two you got to be ready at three seconds notice then you got to act in one second.'

'Precisely. Plus in the price included to you Schultz will be all that you've accumulated in telephone and other miscellaneous items, charges and bills, of say a round ten thousand. And then do I hear anymore.'

'You fucking blackmailer you hear two fucking fifty that's what you hear.'

'Ah Schultz. We adore and love you, Lord Nectarine and I. Ever ready to trust, ever ready to give your fellow man the benefit of the doubt. Your Royal Grace. Do we hear from you. Or are we all done. At two fifty. At two fifty now. It's against you Lord Nectarine. Surely we're not finished at this reasonable price. Going now. At two fifty. At two fifty. Done at two fifty. Congratulations. A nice little bargain you've got Schultz. And ah, just as business matters have been nicely resolved, I do believe I hear the dainty sound of ladies' feet above approaching along the upstairs halls. And ah, how nice, his Royal Grace has rushed away to conduct them down to us. Good god Schultz. Whatever is the matter. I hope our little deal in which you will so wisely profit in due course, and the certified cheque which shall be required by the close of business on Friday to conclude it, hasn't upset you.'

'Don't worry you'll get your fucking cheque.'

216

'Dear me Schultz you've turned a pale shade of green.'

'I'm beginning to feel sick, where's the fucking nearest toilet.'

'Well if you are about to require a suitable receptacle, be it a bidet, trough, cuspidor, urn, sink or piss bowl, please do go through that door, and down that hall, remembering on the way to switch on the lights. Then turn to your left down the first stairs and through the door at the bottom, then across the passage, up three steps, turn left and then right and left again and there, in front of you will be two doors. Take the one to the extreme right and positively avoid the other as it exits out to the valley below, and you might wake up an impresario in heaven where departed starlets fluttering their wings gently fan your procreative appendages. However if you do take the correct door you will find substantial mauve marble sanitary fittings.'

'O my god. I'm going to get fucking lost now or killed. And hey, this isn't another trick like when a skeleton dropped down on top of me out of the ceiling when I went to take a piss at his Lordship's castle.'

'You silly old paranoid Schultz, of course not. Ah but before you depart my dear Schultz, you must not forget a principle to be utterly observed in life. Always prevent and avoid if you can permanent damage to the self in the seemingly down times, so that should the seemingly up times ever return, you remain full and able bodied and minded enough to enjoy them.'

'Yeah, you bet. But right now at this fucking moment I don't know if I'm up or down. But I do know if I don't go shit I may have to puke.'

An ashen faced Schultz finding his way back to the dining room just in time for the savoury after the soup. Three elderly maiden aunts of Binky's at table. And sitting directly across from Schultz, the candle light agleam on her black wavy hair, the devastating apparition with three ropes of pearls at her pale long neck. Jesus, Rabbi why does beauty have to hit me so hard. Why can't I get excited over some homely girl who'll love honour and obey. Plus maybe be just a gorgeous fuck once in a while. Because Sigmund the race looks awful these days and we got to breed to be more handsome. Boy I'll buy that Rabbi.

And within the great castle upon that high mountain top, a gale moaned and whined around the windows and blew puffs of smoke back down the chimneys. A subdued Schultz spilling the salt and the devastating apparition requiring him to toss a pinch over each shoulder. Following dinner, the ladies withdrawing, and Binky suddenly retiring to bed. The ladies smoking cigars under the candle flames of the Meissen candelabrum. Schultz putting his vowels and feet forward to the devastating apparition, commenting on her black evening wear and pearls and receiving only silent smiles in return. As the ladies finally took their leave Schultz with his Lordship proceeding for a restorative coffee and brandy in a circular turret room. Their voices echoing in the tall ceilinged chamber with its walls adorned with stags' heads.

'Jesus your Lordship, what do you have to do to make women take notice of you. I mean what a devastating apparition she is, plus her name is my favourite of all girls' names, Catherine.'

'Schultz I have already attempted to suggest to you to steer clear of the course of action you seem intent upon pursuing.'

'Fuck I'm pursuing nothing. Why don't anyone say what's wrong making friends with a knockout gorgeous beauty.'

'Schultz as beautiful women seem to be chased by every ugly man and plain women seem to chase good looking men, why not try one of the maiden aunts one of whom quite distinctly seems looking for a gallop.'

'Thanks a bunch but no thanks. OK let's forget women a second. What I would like to know is did you set me up. Jesus this is two hundred and fifty thousand pounds I got now to nearly borrow the whole thing from the fucking bank.'

'Schultz you do take an uncommonly poor view of your fellow man don't you.'

'Yeah I do. But I wish like you I could afford to think beautiful thoughts instead of thinking the real thoughts I am forced to think especially that everyone's out to fucking well screw me in this business. And by the way who were all those guys today with the attaché cases.'

'Lawyers from Edinburgh, Glasgow and London. And Schultz, do you see those large wine cisterns there. Lady Ottoline when they were filled with mulled wine was very fond of steeping her feet in them.'

'Holy jeeze, more aristocratic pleasures I've been recently missing. Which makes me even more wonder why did such a beautiful and rich woman go and jump. Hey wait a minute, the whole thing is suddenly fucking crystal clear to me. Maybe she jumped because like when she put her feet in there, it felt good.'

'Ah and by this analogy Schultz you think, she went out the door because she could feel no worse.'

'That's right. The overheads in this joint. I mean it's a whole production. Living here would be a maintenance worry. This place is as big as your bloody castle.'

'This place, Schultz I believe is even bigger.'

'You mean even bigger than your biggest castle.'

'Considerably.'

'How the fuck big then is your biggest castle.'

'I have, fortunately, no idea.'

'You know your Lordship sometimes I think why did I ever have to meet you guys when my life was going along so nicely. And on that note and a last swallow of this fucking delicious good brandy, I'm going to bed. Boy me, just now in my shattered shambles, maybe I wouldn't mind stopping living if you can have a death like hers in all this pomp and spacious circumstance. Goodnight your Lordship.'

Schultz stretched on his back in bed, hands folded behind his head, listening to the wind howling. And the creaking boards of the castle floors rising and falling with the pressure of the wind. Eyes opening at the noise of a chair scraping on the floor. Holy shit what's this, a shadow at the foot of the bed. Rabbi, is it a spook. No Sigmund, it's a very beautiful lady. O jesus, no more jokes Rabbi.

'Hey who. Who is this.'

'Ha. Hey who you. This is who. And I am who I am.'

'O hey hello. Christ I thought I was dreaming. Hey.'

'Hey you too.'

'Jesus christ almighty, Catherine. Hey take a seat will you.'

'I will. But first I've something to tell you.'

'Jesus honey you can tell me any fucking thing, excuse my French, you want.'

'Will you give me your shoulder. To cry on.'

'Sure, sure.'

'You see I am what is euphemistically known as mentally aberrated. And I am known euphemistically. But I'm just ordinary not extraordinary. And just ordinary aberrated. But I have this beautiful body inherited from my mother. I must keep it safe from harm you know. You see the trouble with me is that I'm not all there upstairs. Anymore that is. I was once you know. All there. Upstairs.'

'Honey sit down. For Christ's sake. And keep talking.'

'Who you. Are you him. No I'm not you. You are not. Not him. But I am. Euphemistically speaking. The teeniest weeniest little bit nuts. We are all now but for me bankrupt in this castle. You see for important occasions as when someone dies, I am let loose. But I'm not completely nuts you know. But nicely nuts. Under my dressing gown I am in my negligee. What are you in. Ha ha. Are you in the altogether. Men's private parts are their parts and their parts disturb me. I have no interest in sex per se. But I do take an interest in men's private parts.

Part of your privates of course are bandaged. I am so sorry, sorry, sorry you were hurt. Were you hurt.'

'Honey, I was hurt and don't stop talking.'

'Well I may, if I may go on just a little. A little you know. I'm not ordinary nor extraordinary. And as in fact I have only just said, I am only the teeniest weeniest bit nuts. I entrance you do I. Am I and the whites of my eyes, eyes white, are they, are they entrancing.'

'You betcha honey. And what about the whites of my eyes.'

'Yes the whites of your eyes even in the dark entrance me.'

'Hey honey, I don't know whether I'm really ready to lock mentally aberrated intellectual horns with you. But christ why don't you just get in here under the covers.'

'I would like that. I'm not nuts. Not completely nuts. Just nuts it would seem. But late at night perhaps, I'm more nuts than usual. They've forgotten to bolt my door. My windows have bars. May I get into bed. I'd just like to weep a little. Quietly weep. Weeping quietly. I'm in lots of muddles and messes but I won't make a fuss. They give me pills, I'm nuts you see. But I'm ordinary, not extraordinary. And I'm not yet pregnant by you. Am I.'

'No honey you're not but get into bed.'

You're
Just what the
Doctor ordered
For
This fucking nut

In the howling and whining winds a faint bell tolling twelve. Catherine lying next to Schultz in bed. Her profile in silhouette in the sudden shafts of moonlight coming in the window. Her limbs warm. Her hair soft. Her skin silky. Rabbi. Is that musk in my nostrils. Or is this a ghost that lies beside me. With the most beautiful profile I've ever seen in my life. Sigmund it is no ghost which lies beside you. But Rabbi this is a ruined creature, who by her own admission says she's nuts. So Sigmund you're not that nuts if you know it, it's when you don't know you're nuts that you're really nuts.

16

'What a nice name you have, Sigmund. And isn't companionship on a wild windy night, nice. I know you will understand when I say I'm not interested in sex per se. But that does not mean to say I'm not. If you gather, my meaning. Do you gather.'

'I gather, I gather, honey.'

'You say honey. Are you a bee. Be you a bee. Ha ha. You be.'

'Ha ha, ha. You're a comedienne.'

'Yes I am. I am. And I'm eccentric. I collect moths. And didn't you, didn't you think, only a moment ago, think that I was a ghost, a ghost.'

'Hey holy shit honey, pardon again my French.'

'Ah it is what you thought. Only a moment ago. Move over. No nearer, nearer. Not far away. Now you just lie there now with your head on my shoulder. Let me help you in all that you endeavour. And let me be kind, kind and sweet, sweet to you.'

'Honey I'm in your power. Jesus and what power.'

'It's nut power. And you my little boy. You. You. Are one of the most handsome men I have ever seen. Ever seen. Not never seen. Ever seen. But I saw you. You. I wanted to reach across at dinner and twirl my fingers in your big long black curls. That's why I'm here. You see it was most extraordinary. But I have seen an ordinary video of your private parts.'

'You what honey.'

'Upon the box. The box. The video box. In colour. Your parts. Caught in the zipper.'

'What. Holy cow.'

'O dear, have I distressed you.'

'O jesus I'll kill that son of a bitch.'

'I did not mean to distress you. But it was I do believe one of the funniest things I have ever seen. O but I know, I know, you were in pain, in pain. But I thought you were most appreciative that it could be used as evidence in court. Binky does so wonderfully accompany it with his commentary.'

'O my god, the fucking guy has no scruples.'

'But he does, he does, if you only knew. And you are, aren't you, so repetitively rude with your language. You see that's what's good about being nuts, you mind less what anybody says. In fact you cease minding at all. Because you know perhaps everybody's fucking nuts, n'est-ce pas. But be careful you know, I may not actually be nuts at all. Anyway put your head back resting on my kind and comforting and cradling shoulder, and why don't you just continue to say what you like to me and I'll have a little listen.'

'Jesus honey no, don't let's listen to me. Please.'

'Well listening to me and my little story of life will not be very extraordinary. Very ordinary in fact. You see, like my mother, I have been extravagant. I went to Monte Carlo. It was she who first took me there. Quite honestly, the most delicious delicious fun. We were both there. Chemin de fer. Baccarat. Hardly any roulette. But O the chemin de fer, it was so delightful. Rather barren you know under those tall tall barn like ceilings. But I had such a wonderfully wonderful expensive time. You see I really am extravagant. Not very very extravagant. Only ordinary extravagant not extraordinary extravagant. I suppose if I didn't have enough jewels I would buy jewels. Not that I love them. But you see, mother promised hers to Binky. But they, the men, they bought jewels for me too. Not so many as they bought for my dear lovely, lovely mother. Over whom they got so murderously jealous of each other waiting around in the lobby that two duels were fought. More than anything or anything more, though, they invited me to bed. Two of them forced their unwelcome attentions upon me. It seems such a long time ago but it's not that long ago you know. I listened to their silly silly conceited stories about themselves. Nothing but themselves. And how wonderful they were. I would say sotto voce, the food's divine too. I opened my windows so a breeze would blow pleasantly from the harbour. And get rid of all their pretentions. They were all so ugly. Not in body but in mind. And I never felt I was being unbeautiful when I would scream and shout and kick at them to go. I put my high heeled toe right up one chap's arse and he walked away with it sticking out of him. Silly way to lose a good shoe.'

'Holy christ honey you were having quite a time down there.'

'Yes. You see there is this wonderful hotel with this large wonderful lobby. Where I used to go and sit. And never for long. Not long. As invariably a man would stop by me to ask me to go to the casino. Before of course he would ask me to go to bed. I counted them one by one. Dear me, I dare say it does add up. Promiscuity may have been part of my problem. And I am, I am a problem you know.'

'Hey honey never mind the promiscuity or the problem. No problem. If we unlocked the bolt on your prison here. Could we go there. Like to Monte Carlo. Together.'

'O I mustn't run away now, even if mommie is dead.'

'That's why you can run away honey.'

'By the way. Your way, by the way. I know your balls may not permit you. But do you want to mount me. It's all right if you don't, but you may mount me. I would, if I may be frank, quite honestly prefer that you did. Mount me. Mount me. Do I make myself clear.'

'Honey crystal and very very clear.'

'But first, first. I like to say my prayers. Do you pray, pray.'

'Well yeah, sort of, sort of honey.'

'I do pray and more than occasionally pray. I became a Catholic. Conversion you know from Protestantism. I light my little votive candle before bedtime in front of the sacred heart of Jesus, to glow you know, through the night. Please let me be kind to you. I feel you need kindness. Someone to stroke, may I, your brow. There. Soothing. And nice isn't it.'

'Yeah honey. Jesus.'

'You know, don't you that it's within, deep within the heart that nearly all life's suffering happens. You see once I was betrothed to a laird up in these hills, whom I loved and loved ever since I had been a little girl. Then before the wedding something awful happened on the grouse moor.'

'What honey.'

'I can't speak of it just now. But when I do, do think of it it is always in the most nightmarish of ways. And I wake up if I am sleeping, weeping weeping. But by the way. Hail Mary full of grace, the Lord is with thee, blessed art thou among women and blessed is the fruit of thy womb. O dear those words. And my own wilted wilted womb. Which may never, never bear fruit.'

'O jesus honey, take it easy, don't cry, for christ's sakes. Here let me get off yours for a second, rest on my shoulder.'

'I'm sorry, I'm sorry. O dear. O dear me. You'll think me a nuisance, a nuisance.'

'No. No. No shit. No nuisance.'

'I do love your French. But I am. Just nuts and a nuisance. A problem, a problem.'

'Come on, kiddo. Hey jesus I like you.'

'Do you, do you.'

'Sure. What the hell. I don't have my watch on to see the time it is after twelve, but we've known each other now for what must be a full twenty minutes, maybe twenty five. And what the fuck you've seen a video, a video, of all there is to know about me.'

'I could you know. If I tried really really hard, be nearly sane again. You can't see me smiling but I am. Not crying. Don't you think that that's the worst thing in the world that could ever happen, if no one ever smiled again. You know when you fell in the chapel, and when you stood up, your face appearing over the top of the pew, you were all flushed red with embarrassment. And O god, I did know how you felt and that was when I first saw you. Then I saw you when I didn't think I had, and you were crossing the room towards me and my heart quickened. And then O dear, all those other chaps crowded around me after the bishop left. I don't know why I so readily admit to you that I'm nuts but I do. I don't tell everyone you know. And I pretend, O I pretend, how I pretend to all those others than I'm sane, sane. But you looked so crestfallen. There you were no one talking to you. Completely left you. And you stopped and turned around and walked away. And it was you out of that whole room, mister tall dark and handsome, that I wanted to have come and speak to me. That's how little babies get born you know. Ha ha. Someone comes up to one and stands at ease with their feet apart and speaks to one at a cocktail party.'

'Honey you're one for the books.'

'What does that mean.'

'Jesus come to think of it, I don't know. I grew up saying it.'

'I love your American accent.'

'Holy shit I didn't know it was showing.'

'It is, it is, so beautifully in every vowel. I'll bet you come from Brooklyn or the Bronx or somewhere utterly awful like that.'

'Honey Woonsocket, is the place.'

'O god that sounds even worse, like the socket of my wound. Doesn't it. Shall I ring for someone to bring us a snack.'

'Holy shit, you mean there's room service going on this time of night.'

'O yes. And I'm starving. I neglected to eat at dinner. My aunts do so put me off. And I do so feel like a thick juicy big steak with mushrooms and creamed spinach. My mother you know. I'm sure the cooks cheat and go sleep somewhere nice and comfy comfy and cosy cosy but the kitchens and the ovens are kept going full blast even at four a.m. In fact especially at four a.m. That's what I mean when I say we're extravagant. My mother was fond of saying, we are on these mountains like a ship at sea braving over the ancient waves, the engines throbbing, throbbing. But it's what no one can understand you know. The night she died, she had dinner early. And I guess if I don't call room service I could eat you couldn't I.'

'You could honey, you could.'

'I guess I'm getting like my mother. She hated for the night ever to end. I suppose that was what was the most extraordinary instead of ordinary thing about her. She lived for darkness. That's why she adored the casino so much. She literally went out of her mind, O dear there is a slip of the tongue, the tongue, when she discovered Las Vegas. I went there too, you know. I got tennis elbow from the slot machines. Of course there's nothing there other than gambling to be extravagant about. And just gambling with money per se is not extravagant n'est-ce pas. My mother in going there always thought it was a way for her to cut down on expenses. O my dear mother. My dear dear mother. She did wreck, she so wrecked so many men's lives before she wrecked her own. Those she left alive in her wake are still seething. I nearly feel that the rest are all already down there beneath the mountain broken in bone spirit and body and upon the stack of them she fell, hoping to be cushioned by them all once more. God, she was awful awful to men. What by the way would you like from the kitchen.'

'O jesus me, honey holy shit.'

'Your mind's a fucking thousand miles away, and please do pardon my French.'

'Ha ha honey. It was a thousand miles away but boy honey, you were right with me, let me tell you. Hey but christ I mean someone's going to walk in on us here. You know, maybe jesus we sort of just could kind of stay alone. I got a hamper. Right over there. No kidding. Caviare, pâté, smoked oysters. The whole works. What do you say we give it a whirl.'

Catherine lighting a candle as Schultz glides out of bed. Halfway across the floor, crashing into a chair. Falling over with a squeal of anguish, clasping his balls. In her gleamingly black negligee, Catherine at Schultz's side assisting as he hobbles back to bed.

'O my poor poor dear. How sweet. You're accident prone. Let me help you. And I'll get the hamper. And you, you. You just get back cosy, cosy and quiet. Back in bed. I may, mayn't I, call you sweetie, sweetie.'

Schultz attentive host, pointing out his foodstuffs in the hamper opened on the eiderdown. Catherine unfolding a napkin, laying it up under Schultz's chin. The tower bell tolling.

'You do come prepared don't you.'

'It's not me honey. It was my butler for the train.'

'Do you know, may I tell you something.'

'Sure, honey, shoot.'

'Would you tolerate me.'

'What do you mean honey.'

'Well aberrated as I am I need to be tolerated. And I don't want this to be the last, the very last, we are ever to see of each other. But I'd try so hard to be good. I really would. I'm not half bad looking. And my figure you haven't really seen yet is the best part of me. I know we have not even slept together yet. And you may not want me after we do. But suppose you did, you did. O dear. I have a fear. I've already said too much, too much. That what I am saying is no use, no use.'

'Honey I got a confession to make. There's a girl in London I love.'

'That's why I said no use. I knew there would be something like that. Wives. Children. And worse. Someone whom you worship and adore. Adore adore. First tell me what you'd like from the hamper.'

'I'm OK for food. Hey jesus honey, no offence to you. But maybe I could take a raincheck.'

'What is a raincheck.'

'A raincheck honey is when you're on the way to the baseball game and it rains. They cancel the game and your ticket is good for the next game.'

'I'll give you a raincheck. A raincheck I'll give you.'

'Hey jesus, this night is kind of getting a little out of hand. You know I was till only a few hours ago, in business with your brother. Now. Here is you. And as you might say. You. You. You. I'm going to be gone first thing in the morning. I got a real rush of stuff to attend to in London.'

'London. O dear London. That does mean, doesn't it. Gone, gone, gone. With your raincheck.'

'Yeah. But not forgotten, forgotten, I hope. I hope. And for us honey, there could be a sunny day.'

'Here, a nice dollop of caviare on a biscuit. And do you want to see my medical records.'

'Jesus, come on, what kind of question is that.'

'I just thought you might be interested to know just how nuts I am. I do occasionally need a nurse you know. The doctors say being nuts needn't last. Indeed, the doctors don't last. Of course they all end up asking me my advice.'

'Look anyone who feels like a big juicy steak this hour of the morning ain't nuts honey, believe me. I mean not completely nuts. I mean a good appetite in my books is the only sign of sanity. That's what a Jewish philosopher told me.'

'You're Jewish.'

'Yeah honey, I am.'

'I don't mean to sound at all superficial as I know it sounds, but O god that's what really so excites me. Jewish intellectual men.'

'Honey I'm no intellectual.'

'We could put eyeglasses on you, that would do it, with thick lenses. I'm not particularly speaking of money making men you understand. Who wear bright garters pulling up their dark silk socks. And who want you to see them standing in their striped underwear from what they think is the smartest sort of men's boutique. Not men who smoke big cigars. And who look you over shrewdly. And want you to look as if they owned your beauty they so casually exhibit by their side. Those sorts of men one can so effortlessly manipulate, manipulate. I like you because you are so straightforwardly simple and charming, charming. And when you flooded out your bathroom, panic went so easily to your head.'

'Honey would you just hand me over that glass of water a second. And just let me unleash my elbow here. I just want to scratch my head. Plus I can't even remember the fucking sort of underwear over there over the chair I'm wearing.'

'O dear, my talking too much, is too much isn't it. Has the magic moment gone. Gone gone.'

'Honey any magic moment, I sure ain't going to let go gone.'

'O it could go. Couldn't it. If it hasn't. Could go gone, gone.'

'Whew. Hold it, honey. Let me catch up. Please. I'm just savouring this last little bit of caviare.'

'Yes. I will. I'll wait. Then will you savour me. I have dreamed of pricks you know coming at me thick and fast from every direction with tons of lethal sperm. Men crawling at me on their hands and knees. Would you like to crawl at me. Would you. Across the floor. You see I'm really a trollop.'

'You're a lulu honey. And jesus, have a heart in my present condition and with only one prick, I should stay in bed.'

'You stay. While my mind races, races. You'll catch up. Puff puff puff, here you come. Catching up. Up. Let me show you in the candle-light. My body. And me. While you're climbing, climbing. You see this is what I look like. Old aberrated me.'

'Fucking god help us honey, I can't believe God made two of you like that.'

'Yes. Both my mother and me. Now there's only me. And I'm just now so ever slightly fatter than I used to be. But I'm kind. I'm considerate. And are you thinking of mounting me. Shall I say O please, please. Mount me. And can I promise that it will. It will be. I'll make it be. A great choral classic. Our limbs entwined. Thunderous and mild. I'll hold you. I'll be kind, kind. And I won't, I won't, not now, order room service. I wear a coil in my old withered womb, which is still so young. I could love you till I die, but I may die soon, soon soon. Do I, I do, see tears in your eyes. That's not extraordinary is it. That's just ordinary. That I'll die soon soon soon. Ordinary.'

'Honey at this juncture there are tears in my eyes, and I don't care what the fuck it is. Ordinary or extraordinary.'

Just
Let's go
Voom
Voom
Voom

Raining in London. The train passing the back ends of
endless houses. Steamed over evening windows of kitchens.
Into a tunnel. Roaring down between walls. Whistle
blowing. Wheels louder on the rails and diesel throbbing.
Slowing and squealing to a stop in the station.

17

Schultz in his compartment gathering up his two cases
and hamper. Smoke in the air. Fell asleep in my seat.
Slept like a log. Holy shit what a memory she's going to be. One
of my favourite names. Catherine. Call her Kate. She made me blush
all over the face. Coo coo in the head. Her magic looks of beauty.
Last seen disappearing in a flash of light as I watched her tiptoe out
the bedroom door. Now suddenly I got new pain for old. Except for
his Lordship I nearly own the whole show. Can call all the shots.
And jesus Rabbi you'd think that with all this much financial interest
to think about I'd lose all my interest in women. Ah Sigmund, you
should know by now, money is a philtre. Christ Rabbi I got to revise
all I ever knew before about females. Sigmund, what revision, you
knew nothing anyway. Thanks a bunch Rabbi for the vote of
confidence.

Approaching along the platform, Jorricks's smiling face greeting
Schultz as he steps off the train. Hurrying to take the bags as other
passengers and pedestrians turn around to stare. Schultz donning his
sunglasses. The limousine purring on the roadway adjoining the
platform, polished fenders sparkling with beads of rain. Climbing into
the dry warmth. The two plaid rugs laid out and the evening newspapers neatly folded on top. The limousine pulling away past long
queues waiting for taxi cabs.

'Home sir.'

'No. The theatre Jorricks.'

'Business is very very up sir. The advance is building twice as fast as
it was last week. I suppose due to all the fuss. I think you'll be pleased
too sir to hear that Daniel the Dangerous as he seems to prefer to be
known has been a considerable help in keeping the Press at bay. I hope
you don't mind sir but I had to fix up a bed for him in the boxroom by
the pantry. He was fired from the hospital and had nowhere to sleep. I
hope I haven't done wrong.'

'These days Jorricks who knows anymore what wrong is. Anyway
don't worry you and the Ambassador were a big help. And glad to
have Daniel around if he wants to stay. Jesus, how are the pigeons,
Jorricks.'

'O they're fine. Daniel's taking care of them and they're eating their heads off. And Mr Sunningdale sir, how is he. I'm sure he took his mother's death very hard.'

'Yeah. He took it hard.'

Windscreen wipers waving, the limousine purring through Bloomsbury past the great grey brooding buildings. Schultz grabbing up the phone. Holy shit. Louella. Got to ring her. All I've got is visions. A dream on the train. That a dozen guys were waiting panting in a line to fuck her.

'Hey gee Louella honey it's me, Sigmund. Hello. Hello.'

'I know who it is. I don't want to talk.'

'What's wrong now. I'm just back in town a second.'

'Nothing's wrong now that wasn't wrong before.'

'How's Al.'

'I'm not telling you how Al is. I just don't want to talk.'

'Come on. He's my ancient friend. And I just thought honey, with his gaskets all fixed up again, you know, that maybe he's flying back to London or something. Or did he finally gasp out his last croak in L A.'

Schultz pulling the phone away from his ear as the other end of the line slammed down. It shows you. Always follow up every potential fuck. Because every two seconds you learn someone you want to fuck isn't going to fuck or even talk. Pick up the evening newspaper. Maybe there's another Arab Israeli war broke out I can take sides on and read about. Holy shit what's this. In the Londoner's Diary.

HAREM IN BELGRAVIA

Last evening from out of the Belgravia elegant residence of the famed impresario Sigmund Franz Schultz, who is also known to intimates as 'Siggy', came three of his visitors from what is, to quote Mr Schultz's high-diving celebrity wife, her estranged husband's 'harem household'. Mr Schultz being unavailable for comment, this Islamic custom was hotly denied by Mr Schultz's butler and by his body guard who, naked to the waist and waving a fist, threatened from the servants' basement door to punch this reporter 'up the snout' and rip certain pertinent private appendages from his person.

That malicious cunt. This is more ridicule and contempt. And these journalist fuckers. I'm going to get them for libel. Show biz code. Every day that things seem good, don't believe it, and do something quick to make them seem even better so that when you find next day that they are pretty fucking awful, they might not seem to be that bad

230

after all. Are you listening Rabbi. Sigmund I am. And sometimes I think you instead of me should be down here in this ground under my slab giving advice.

The limousine cruising down this street full of theatres. Pulling up in front of the blazing lights. The front of house signs. In big letters proclaiming one of the great comic creations of our time. With all the other signs blazoning words like, Genius, Beautiful, Captivating, Marvellous, that I had the brilliant fucking nerve and wisdom to quote out of their panning context. Plus the giant photograph of Magillacurdy, his big big bullshitting mouth open as usual. Tonight at 7.45. Jesus here it is. Triumph. Nearly own the whole fucking show. Boy let me taste it just a second. Read the signs. Read those you fuckers. Sold out. House full. I'll say. You bastards. Who wouldn't back me. Who panned me and dumped the ridicule.

A young boy pushing out the lobby door. Schultz standing aside holding it open. The boy's mouth and lips pressed to cry. Tears in his eyes.

'Hey what's the matter kid.'

'Nothing sir.'

'Did you get hurt. What are you crying for. Something happen. Come on, what's the matter.'

'I wanted to buy a ticket and I don't have enough money for one.'

'Hey that's no reason to cry.'

'The man told me to go away and not waste his time.'

'He what. Hey you come this way kid with me. Come on.'

Slamming the swing door closed behind, Schultz crossing the lobby. Guiding the boy by the shoulder in front of him. Yanking open the narrow box office door. The row of telephones along the counter, receivers off the hooks. Two box office employees sitting on stools reading newspapers and chomping on sandwiches and drinking cups of tea. Their usual supercilious superior looks on their faces vanishing and pieces of lettuce sticking out, as their mouths drop open.

'O hello Mr Schultz.'

'Put down those god damn newspapers and put those receivers back on the hooks. What the hell do you think this is in here. Some kind of private club. Did you refuse to sell this kid a ticket.'

'Well. In a manner of speaking yes.'

'Well in a bloody manner of speaking I'm telling you, nobody but nobody no matter how much little money they've got, and especially not a young kid ever gets turned away from this box office. You hear what I'm saying.'

'Yes Mr Schultz.'

'Get off those fucking stools.'

'Yes Mr Schultz.'

'Now, here, here's the money. You give this kid a ticket, the best in the house for tonight's performance.'

'We're sold out sir.'

'What about the aisle seats behind the pillars.'

'Sold sir.'

'What about the boxes.'

'There's only the Royal box sir. And of course that's reserved.'

'Yeah. It's reserved. For this kid, right here. The Royal box then. You take his name.'

'But sir, the Royal retiring room.'

'You reserve that too.'

'But Mr Schultz it's being used to serve intermission drinks to very important people.'

'Well now it ain't. And you tell the manager I said to bring this young man anything he wants. And as long as this show is running and every night it lasts, this kid gets a ticket. Do you hear me. Whether he can pay or not. Now answer those ringing fucking phones.'

'Yes. Mr Schultz. And there's mail here for you, sir.'

Schultz taking the stack of envelopes. Escorting the boy back across the lobby and holding open the theatre's front swing door. The boy putting forth his hand to shake.

'Sir I never knew this was going to happen to me.'

'Well a lot of things we don't know are going to happen, happen. You like the theatre sonny.'

'Yes sir. I love the theatre.'

'Good, you keep loving it. You got a nice private room to yourself during intermission if you want to invite a friend.'

'Thank you so much sir, I am most grateful. It's so awfully kind of you.'

'Don't mention it kid, don't mention it. It's just from one theatre lover to another, that's all.'

Schultz returning across the lobby. Going down the stairs into the stalls. The curtain up on the sets of the first act. A working light on stage. Dark out across the rows of seats. Holy jeeze. I'm a theatre lover. I guess it's the truest thing I ever said in my life. And here I am, rejected in love by the woman I love. Where to go, where to go, in the world, in the world. But maybe for the first time in my life. I got choices. Because I'm actually in a theatre where everything is not going down the drain. And now suddenly, except for his Lordship's share and a few of Al's stupid investors, I nearly own the whole show. I can call all the shots. Sell all the rights. Even down a side alley in Istanbul. Holy shit. It's just dawned on me. Binky must be in trouble. Why would he sell me, the man he likes to torture most, his piece of the show. But jesus the urbane fucker. Through death, through everything, not a twinge of ever even giving the game away. Unless he's still got some hidden scheme up his sleeve to finally fuck me.

Schultz in his commandeered dressing room. The lights blazing around the mirrors, keeping at bay the years of thespian ghosts. Sitting down on a couch with a fist full of the nightly returns. Leafing through. My god. Look at these wonderful numbers. Big. Fat. Even when the house is full we can still squeeze out that fraction of an inch selling someone a piece of step to sit on in the aisle behind a pillar. And soon we'll be selling seats in people's laps. Last Tuesday an all time record for the theatre. When Priscilla nosedived off the bridge. Holy cow what next is in my life. Half these letters are from her fucking lawyers.

Schultz jumping up off the couch, ripping open letter after letter. Tearing up and throwing the pieces across the room, shouting.

'You fuckers, you're all going to get one hundred fucking percent less than fuck all out of me. Nobody, but nobody from now on ever ever threatens Sigmund Franz Schultz and gets away with it. And nobody but nobody is ever going to make mincemeat or ridicule out of his life.'

The dressing room door swinging open. A great grinning head and pair of massive naked shoulders leaning in. A bottle of whiskey held in the hand of Terence Magillacurdy.

'Ah me boyo, fine sentiments. I thought I heard someone lurking down me corridor, an hour before curtain up. Now when you're not telling us all to fuck off on television where are you hiding yourself these days. And pardon me in me undershorts and bare feet. Have a drink.'

'Jesus Terence, you gave me a shock. How are you.'

'Great me boyo. Great is the word. To me old practised eye they look to be lawyers' letters you're shredding asunder there. Ah but god you've taken the nation by storm.'

'Holy fuck Terence, I didn't want to take the fucking nation by anything. I'm just looking for a little lonely peace and quiet somewhere. Like I sometimes enjoy every once in a while in this dressing room.'

'Ah now your shrinking violet modesty will get you somewhere. And with the two of us together now, and with the theatre bursting at the seams every night, sure we walk hand in hand in fame and glory to the giant mausoleums we will be building for ourselves soon. Ah but now you'll be wondering why I had your big car out there measured end to end. Well it's only so me own I've just obtained was only that wee fraction of an inch longer that no one will notice. Ah god but it does attract attention. They see me chauffeur pulling up and getting in and out the stage door alley here of an evening now is like battling through the starving hordes of Africa while chewing a porterhouse steak. Ah but what I do is run off a sheaf of autographs and at the strategic time fling them into the air and as the fans run to get them I slip into me car and me chauffeur has me out safe in the traffic of Trafalgar Square in no time. Have a drink. Of the very best fifteen year old Irish whiskey.'

'Jesus I will Terence.'

'Now listen to me. Me wife has flung me out of the house.'

'Holy shit Terence I didn't know you were even married.'

'Ah but pure simple truth of the matter is she has a great arse on her and a pair of thighs between which there was both paradise lost and found and that I couldn't keep my hands away from and my prick out of and the battle of avoiding marriage got too much. And hung over drunk one morning and helpless in my abject misery I did the deed. To my present everlasting great regret. But me boyo it's a penance I've now paid. Sure there's an impression of my fist deep in the white smooth surface of the refrigerator which my wife took a plaster cast of to give to her lawyer when my fist missed her face one night in the kitchen. Sure it was just an instant little lesson I was giving trying to pound some obedient peace and quiet into her. That's why I was living in a cemetery when you first found me along with me own collection of lawyers' letters suing me for every belch and fart I ever uttered. But look at us now. Up into the heights me boyo we go. Me dressing room is so jammed after the show I can't bend my elbow to take off me greasepaint. And here in my pocket, a fistful of cables from Hollywood just asking me to name my price.'

'Jesus Terence you're not threatening to leave the show and threatening to fucking well close us down again.'

'Never never me dear darling boy. Wouldn't dream of it. Not even for the likes of the biggest salary in the biggest musical of all time and Binky Sunningdale who would think he had me signed up. Here let me put me arm around you. And Hollywood can go and fuck itself as it has been doing in its multitude of contortions down through the ages. How would I ever dream of deserting the brilliant likes of you with whom I have such civilized intellectual rapport. Sure just let's settle on a certain percent of the gross.'

'Holy shit Terence no gross, net profit maybe.'

'Ah the word gross has a nice agricultural sound to it. Like golden wheat ripening in the field.'

'Wheat growing doesn't make a sound Terence.'

'Ah it does, it does me boyo, like heavenly harps, once heard never forgotten. But drink up. And fill you up again. Women are there to be fucked and only fear keeps them faithful. We have to break hearts me boyo. And get our own broken in return. But why should we take shit from any woman or any man.'

'Amen Terence. Amen. And holy fuck you're as profound as you are incorrigible.'

'Sure let me render you a little of Mother McCrea and a bit of O Danny Boy when the pipes were fucking calling him from West Hampstead to Camden Town. Ah but the sophisticated likes of you now I'm sure would prefer a bit of Puccini. And so here we go, from La Bohème.'

Magillacurdy jumping up on the dressing table, his bottle of whiskey swinging and smashing a light bulb as arms outstretched he takes in a lungful of air. His mellow resonant tenor voice rattling the window panes. Till the tannoy was announcing five minutes to curtain and an hysterical stage manager was pounding on the door.

'Jesus Terence, the curtain's going up for christ's sake and you're not even in costume.'

Out in the hallway a grinning Magillacurdy with his hand and arm contorted behind his head, pulling his own head away around the door frame. Magillacurdy goosing his waiting dressing lady jumping for safety with a giggling squeal.

'Now there's a pair of rear cheeks for you me boyo on this lass and never mind me costume. Naked tonight. No costume on Magillacurdy me dear darling boy. Naked. Give them an ancient Gaelic treat.'

'Jesus christ Terence put on your fucking costume, you're going to get the Lord Chamberlain to close us down.'

'I tumesce as I sing me new song me boyo, called As Nature Did Intend.'

'Holy shit, sounds familiar but that's a fucking good title.'

'Ah me boyo give me death or publicity for by god for a long time previous did I cower in ignominious obscurity. But I knew that together with our big pricks distended and your testicles in a sling and with our copyrights under our arms we could ascend into orbit together. And sure wouldn't it be appropriate if I took with me that little extra percentage of the gross.'

The dressing room door closing. Magillacurdy singing away down the hall. Urgent calls of his name coming over the tannoy. Schultz taking another swallow of whiskey and opening a pink and perfumed envelope.

Dear old Siggy or is it Ziggy,

I hope you remember me and forgive me if I'm getting in touch too soon. Me and my girlfriend were watching when you drove away that day in that big fantastic car. Is that really yours. Pardon the question. But actually I really would like to see you soon. I haven't got your address nor has my father the tax collector, ha ha. (That's a joke just in case you're worried that I forgot you were Sigmund Sunningdale in the lingerie trade.) So I am hoping that this reaches you at the theatre.

> Yours faithfully and truly
> your old cocksucking friend
> Cynth.

P.S. One of my previous boyfriends (22 years old) who once was an electrician but short circuited too many people's houses, once worked at the theatre. How do you like that for a coincidence. Plus pops I'm looking forward to you giving me a little more of what you've got big boy.

P.P.S And hey pops. Wow are you in the headlines. I really like well known people. I think they are real dinky. And hey I can't wait till you push my belly button and ring my bell of love.

And bellies, buttons and bells and a postscript to you too kid. And I may just go and ring that bell. And give you what you're ready to take. Holy jeeze Rabbi. Advice. Advice. Here I am shaken to the spiritual core in Scotland, now back suddenly in London reality. Trying to cut down on the coincidences in my life. Louella giving me the cold shoulder and still all I want to do is fuck her. And now there's suddenly more women to choose from than I can shake my prick at. It's now for a change, who am I going to reject. And send tearfully away. I don't want to hurt anybody's feelings. But being utterly fair to everybody isn't exactly what I do best. Rabbi maybe I'm heartily sorry for what I've done to women but I am more heartily sorry for what they've done to me. As sure as my momma gave me matzos, Cynthia's got beautiful legs, belly and tits but she's being so fucking indiscreet that it's stopping my heart in its tracks. This letter could have fallen into the hands of my wife's lawyers who are trying to get every corroborating letter from every girl I ever threw a corroborating fuck into. They're even dying to get documentary evidence I grimaced and stuck my tongue out and to photostat it fifty times and circulate it to my mother, father, the principal of my high school, and who knows, even the president of the half assed college I went to. Christ every newspaper editor in London has his tongue hanging out in his eagerness to expose my guts spilling in the street, so it could end me up being in the holocaust, the inquisition and all the pogroms that ever happened all put together. And then surrounded by my Arab semitic brethren standing with spears ready to all shove them up my ass at once. Plus Cynthia, your fucking previous boyfriend electrician must still be working at the theatre by the way some of the fucking stage lights are still fucked up. Anyway jesus, I can't complain a trip to the hospital plus a quick detour to Scotland has brought me a lot of new contacts. And one unforgettable, one, extraordinary not ordinary. O jesus what am I doing. Teetering on the brink again of true love. And now I hope it's not with someone who's multi orgasmic with multi guys and maybe with fucking multi microbes she could be giving me and I should need such terror and horror to rip me asunder in my prime. Maybe I could take it in my declining years when I'm already walking wobbly kneed towards the embrace of death. Like my parents who in their struggles even made my own shoes when other kids bought theirs new and shiny in the store while my father with my shoes, to save on leather always made them too tight. He said Sigmund, nothing you wear should you ever buy even wholesale. And now the lawyers of the fucking woman I made the mistake of marrying are accusing me of owning a dozen different companies I've set up everywhere from the Isle of Man to Switzerland in order to keep their clutches off my money. Which you greedy grasping fuckers is exactly what I've done. And you can scream all you want but you can do fuck all about it. And now at least for a while buying out Binky I can show them I'm a quarter of a million pounds in debt. Holy Rabbi, how do I just survive and move that big black cloud out of my life and get to become a bachelor in one piece again so that I can savour the prime time of my existence which is just dawning. Sigmund, no problem. Do like I told you before, and if I didn't tell you. I should have. Just keep your prick in your pants. And for relief just pull.

Schultz sitting back on the green upholstered couch catching sight of another postscript on the back of Cynthia's envelope. Holy shit, more unadulterated indiscretion. In big capital letters she's asking when big boy are you coming back to have your stitches out. And can I watch. And now christ somebody else has found out where I am and knocking on the door.

'Yeah who is it.'

'It's urgent sir. I'm the assistant stage manager. Robert.'

'Well what the fuck is it. Bob. Open the door.'

'I'm sorry sir to disturb you like this. But members of the Royal Family and a party of friends have just been received by the manager Mr Valentine in front of house.'

'So invite them in. Bob.'

'But sir, we were only alerted to their arrival ten minutes ago. And there's a boy who with your permission is up in the royal box occupying the royal retiring room, and there's not a seat free in the house. And Mr Valentine the manager wants you to have him vacate.'

'Holy shit. Like hell that kid's vacating. Nobody but nobody not even members of the Royal Family are going to move that kid.'

'O my god sir, confidentially this is terrible, terrible.'

'So what's confidential and what's terrible. It's not like it's the Queen. Get chairs, Bob. Put pillows on them. Here are fucking cushions and chairs in here. The seamstress can quick sew on some gold braid. Put the blue bloods sitting in the standing room back of the stalls.'

'Sir that's strictly against fire regulations. And Mr Valentine has already asked the boy to leave. And the trouble is, the boy's crying.'

'He what.'

Schultz jumping up from the couch, rushing out into the hall and through a steel fire door to the stage. Running behind the scenery backdrop. Dust up the nose from all the dancing feet. And this way out another steel fire door, in and out passage ways and up a narrow stair through another steel door, and down and up another set of stairs. Holy christ they must be at least really getting better, I forgot all about my balls.

Schultz stopping. Suddenly looking up. In the faint glow of lights, the manager Valentine standing at the top of the landing.

'O there you are Mr Schultz. I was just on my way to find you. I heard you were backstage.'

'I'm backstage all right.'

'You're invited by His Royal Highness to have a drink with the royal party at intermission. And I've put that boy out.'

'You what.'

'Out. I've put him out.'

'I'll break your fucking ass.'

'I beg your pardon. How dare you threaten and use that language to me.'

'You bet I'll use it. You put that boy back in.'

'I will not, ducky. The royal box and royal retiring room are reserved for members of the Royal Family at all times without prior notice and as you are only a lessee of this theatre you are not entitled to pre empt their prerogative.'

'Get fuck out of my way. I'll show you who's a lessee and who the fuck is entitled. And who you can pre empt.'

'Look ducky, I've already had my fill of that big Irish lout of yours Magillacurdy pissing on the footlights, don't you come another inch closer. And your private life has already publicly scandalized this theatre, which till you came along had an illustrious history. You ducky are a flash in the pan. And an American interloper who doesn't understand what he's doing. And I'm certainly not getting out of your way to have members of the Royal Family inconvenienced and caused embarrassment by someone who thinks he's somebody because he's keeping a harem in Belgravia.'

The bow tied manager holding his arms out across the narrow stairway and pressing his large stomach forward. Schultz climbing up a step and raising his fist.

'Don't you dare put your hands on me ducky.'

'You fucking well get out of the way or I'll knock your teeth down into your pansy socks you fucking imbecile.'

Schultz advancing another step. The manager backing up the narrow stairs to the landing at the top. The pounding sound of the chorus tap dancing on stage. A burst of applause from the audience.

'I'm getting one of the royal detectives to deal with you ducky and you'll find yourself with a ball and chain around your neck in the Tower of London near where your conspicuous wife had occasion to jump. And no wonder. You're nothing but an upstart Jew.'

Schultz leaping the last step to the landing. Unleashing a straight right fist plunging between the manager's upraised hands and landing smack mid nose. The theatre manager reeling backwards grabbing out at the walls as he falls. The loud clang of the fire alarm bell suddenly ringing out. The orchestra stopping mid phase, and the dancing chorus in mid tap. Voices raised all over the theatre. In the audience screams. A bomb. Terrorists. Another voice from on stage shouting out. Calm please. There's no danger. No terrorists. The exits are clearly marked. Take your time. Walk don't push. Magillacurdy's singing and shouting voice rising above all.

'Let the peerage go first and let the middle classes go second. And let the working classes stay and keep the home fires burning.'

The pavement jammed outside the theatre. People packed on the balcony above. In the drizzle of rain the audience standing shivering, their programmes clutched in hand. Men in evening jackets and ladies in backless gowns. Understudies, wardrobe mistresses, stage hands and a half nude chorus and cast pouring out into the street from the stage door alley. The wail of sirens out across London and the sound of approaching fire apparatus. Schultz's car moving forward at the behest of a beckoning policeman. The royal party climbing into their waiting limousines with their blue lights lit above the windscreen, quickly pulling away down the street towards the square celebrating the previous battle of Trafalgar. And holy shit are you by any fucking chance Rabbi listening to this. I should have stayed up in the windswept chilly wilderness of Scotland. Because any second now some of these bastards are going to ask for their money back.

And like
My fat cousin Saul
I'm not
Giving it

An assistant stage manager shining the brass plate with Terence Magillacurdy's name on his dressing suite door. Inside corks popping, the room jammed and awash with champagne, whiskey and beer. Hooray revellers in evening dress, surround Magillacurdy in his jock strap. Ladies hugging and gentlemen patting him on the back. Magillacurdy squeezing tits and pinching bottoms.

'No vegetable living or fruit alive was ever as tender and delicious as the flora and fauna we've got here at our fingertips tonight.'

Eruptions of laughter. Débutante squeals and screams of delight. Naked understudies clutching underclothing. Chorus of dancers in off the stage still dripping sweat. Two newspaper reporters with pencils scribbling across their pads. Magillacurdy with the boy from the royal box and retiring room propped up sitting amid vases of flowers on his dressing table. Schultz standing in the doorway. Magillacurdy raising a fist and shouting over the heads.

'Make way, make way for the genius of the hour. There he is ladies and gentlemen. The man who makes all this pandemonium possible. The one and only. Maybe even the only one. With his balls in a sling. Part the sea of humanity to let him pass. Let him brush between the arses of these prima ballerinas and into me arms for a hug. Ah it's been a great night. No bomb will ever stop this show in its tracks. Your little friend here reinstalled in his singular glory in the grandeur of the royal box and retiring room. Sending royalty off home. Ah me boyo what a great old bomb scare it was. And Mr Valentine is nursing a sore nose and saying he is consulting his solicitors. Ah but other than for that mournful reflection, you with your harem in Belgravia do seem still this evening full of piss and vinegar. Smile me boyo, smile. Wipe that look of alarmed pessimism off your face. Except for that mister smooth smart arse little bald director who just walked in behind you as if he owned the place and that poofta he has in tow, there's nothing to be pessimistic about. Now I told you what the best sound in the world is, now let me tell you what the worst is. It's the sound of the dismantling and breaking up of a stage set paid for by somebody else's money, and in front of which you have wrung your guts, emotions, and heart dry, night after night, and then, and before your ears and eyes are averted, the fucking thing is torn to bits.'

Magillacurdy handing Schultz a glass of champagne and throwing an arm around his shoulder and nuzzling his nose in Schultz's long black curls.

'Now I haven't slept a wink for two days, on a bottle of whiskey a day but how about the two of us out to a topless nightclub, for some aberrant behaviour me boyo. Where we can tell the bishops and members of the foreign office and admiralty with their heads under the tables up between the ladies' legs to bugger off and leave us brazen bulls to fuck the women and have champagne for the likes of us served free of charge.'

'Terence go home for christ's sake and get some sleep. But you were great tonight. With an utter genius and brilliance.'

'Ah me boyo your flattery does not go amiss but you didn't think I had it in me did you. Ah I'll show you now where it comes from. Off with me jockstrap and never mind my big prick but take a look at me massive balls. Hollywood is negotiating with me to make a film of my life and these testicles will feature in a single frame close up.'

Schultz leading the little boy away from Magillacurdy's back stage performance and out to Jorricks to be chauffeured home to Croydon. Schultz catching a taxi in front of the theatre. Pigeons pecking awake and roosting asleep all over Trafalgar Square. Down the Mall. Lights on in Buckingham Palace. Past the shadowy looming trees of Green Park. Up Park Lane. Towards Tyburnia. And all the centuries of execution, hanging, drawing and quartering. And let me tell you in show biz London that hasn't changed. There's the fish shop. And all the lobster and lemon sole consumed out of there. And something I never noticed before on the sign. As well as game and poultry they also sell ice. And O jesus there's still lights on up there in the tower, one on in a bedroom, one on in Al's big reception room. Dare I go up there. Unannounced. I got to. The fucking pain is even greater now of loving her after I've just fucked someone else. Correct that. No. Maybe not as great.

Schultz directing the taxi driver to turn down the garage ramp. Getting out at the bottom of tax dodgers' towers. Pressing the security code on the door. Seven four six. Some numbers you never forget. Entering this basement hall. Taking this elevator up. Stepping out on and crossing the soft carpet. Don't lose my nerve now, in this familiar alcove, ringing the doorbell. Door opening. And now being pushed closed. Right on my foot.

'O it's you.'

'Who else honey do you expect when you won't talk to me on the phone.'

'I'm sorry I'm not letting you in. It's late.'

'Honey for christ sakes. Come on. I got to see you. If it's the last thing I do in this world which in my case is in turmoil.'

242

'Take your foot out of the door.'

'No. Not till you let me in, or I'll stay here all fucking night till you do.'

Door opening wider. Louella standing in her satin blue outfit. In a cloud of musky perfume. A lace collared white blouse. Schultz walking in. Candles burning reflecting their flames on the gleaming polished wood of the table set to dine. The night time sky of London. The red green and yellow dots of pretty lights in the darkness out through the windows.

'You can't stay.'

'Honey you look gorgeous. Hey boy, what a wonderful smell. I haven't had dinner, what's cooking. O K so you won't tell me what's cooking. You don't mind if I sit here a second and look at you. Couldn't I have a drink or something.'

'I'll get you a drink.'

'I'll have a brandy. A little soda, a lot of ice.'

'And then you've got to go. You've got exactly five minutes.'

'Jesus honey what's all this timing for. You know we could have a whole long lifetime together.'

Louella disappearing out into the hall. Sound of her heels clicking on the hard kitchen floor. Schultz lounging back on the tweed sofa. The lights on an aircraft beaming across a black sky. Time to adjust the balls. And calm the alarm bells ringing in my brain. After the saga of another show biz crisis. What peace to find. Just to be here. Even if another phone is ringing like a chirping bird in another room. Red lights flashing on a console there on the desk. Al if he's still alive is set up here like it was the centre of a whole nation's war operations. Telexes and jesus let's see that's six phones in this room alone. One more than when I was here last time. No wonder he needs a light flashing to tell which one is ringing. And if all these fucking phones went ringing at once it would give anyone a heart attack. Christ that could be him calling. To announce in his own sonorously sepulchral tones that he has finally and successfully died and to get ready to read his top billed obituary in Variety. Or more likely to say he's resurrected from the grave with a hard on. But jesus to date he must have platinum coated carborundum gaskets for a heart the way he stays alive. Holy fuck it takes a long time for it to sink into people that they are a fucking nuisance in the world. As much as I did love Al and would like the old bastard in his new toupee to be my friend again. How do I knock sense into this girl I love. If she's going to be impossible to fuck now while Al's in his death throes what's it going to be like when she's overcome with grief. Dressed ready to kill, she must have secretly known I was coming to see her to have got dinner ready. The table set for two. She'll play hard to get for a half an hour. Then wilt right into my arms like a flower as I blaze on the charm. After dinner it will be bed. Slowly as fucking hell will she peel off her clothes. Slowly as fucking hell will I kiss each bare patch of flesh revealed. Slowly as hell will I tickle the tip of her nipple with the tip of my tongue. Sigmund I'm listening. Be careful you don't break the stitches on your balls. Jesus Rabbi let me tell you. Who could give a fuck about stitches. What a cunt she has. The soft lusciousness into which you so silkenly slide and glide not even knowing you're in there until you're there without even a push or a shove. Then like it's Hosanna in the fucking highest like a glove it grabs you. Even after Catherine and her nice limbs. I keep remembering back to that night up here. Sinking into the most comfortable eternal bliss. Before Al tried to chop my prick off with a bread knife looking like a meat cleaver for the occasion. Even having had a strange geometrically accommodating fuck so recently in Scotland, I'm still so hard up for another so soon. Jesus but it was even worse before my balls got zapped. I was buying a toothbrush in Harrods, and if the supervisor hadn't suddenly come along, I would have grabbed the girl assistant who was dying for it, and screwed her right there on top of the glass counter. Would have been one more added to the sad number of women I have had to fuck. Starting at my precocious age of twelve. Show me yours and I'll show you mine. By the time I was fourteen it was one, two, three, let's see. Carol, Joan, Jean, Sophie, Tania. Down the backs of alleys. Behind garbage pails. On apartment building rooftops. Even once up a tree. If I'm counting they added all up to seventeen before I was twenty two. Now I've forever lost track. Except that when I started to fuck older women I got the clap twice. And in false alarms thought I had it four times. But not one cunt out of the past has ever been like this creature who is just a few steps away in the other room tinkling a glass with ice cubes. The one night crescendo pleasure of a lifetime. But jesus look at that. What money does to women. And power. And being able to invite them somewhere to a celebrity packed gathering. Then they're all slathering at the mouth to go, and leave some other poor slob they had a date with in the lurch. And look at Al's fucking four gold discs hanging between five genuine modern impressionist wall paintings. How could she fall for someone so past his prime, if he even ever had a prime which I doubt. I guess Al's royalties on those schmaltzy compositions of his pouring in in crescendos are prime enough. God Rabbi. I'm apoplectic tonight, so desperate to fuck her. I got to be saved from this screwing. Saved. Don't worry Sigmund. This venereal plague Binky and his Lordship tried to scare the shit out of you with is now really coming. And that will do more than scare the shit out of you. You'll be lucky to be even left alive to live in celibacy. Hey Rabbi, I had that nightmare pulled on me once and I'm not falling for it again. So Sigmund, don't fall, join me soon. At least the kiss of death is sweet when it comes in the crescendo pleasure of a lifetime.

'Here's your drink, and sorry that was the phone.'

'Holy christ what's with the tears honey now what's happened.'

'Al is dying. It's certain. They expect it now at any time. The whole Hollywood Press Corps are outside the hospital.'

'Hey honey now take it easy. Al's been dying constantly like a needle caught in the groove of a broken record. That's nothing new honey. And if he hasn't croaked in all this time he's got to be getting better. Plus anyway, shit if he did die, think of the funeral. I'll fly you there first class to wherever it is. All his celebrity friends, and Hollywood notables, with the world's leaders, presidents and kings, there.'

'Please stop.'

'Honey, please, sit down. I know how you must feel. Hey what about some music or something. Try my hand on the piano there. And you know. I remember exactly back to what you were wearing that night. A brown tweed skirt and green cashmere sweater. And jesus how could I forget when I saw what was revealed when you took them off. We even played Al's Palm Beach concerto. But I like even more what you're wearing now.'

'You can't stay. I really think it would be best if you left right now.'

'Hey can't I even finish my drink. OK honey, I'm sorry I'll change the subject. And I'm not going to force my company on you. But we can't leave our lives just like this. If Al throws a seven tonight and we fly out to LA to watch him go through the curtains of the crematorium tomorrow or the next day. That's it. Just a bunch of smouldering cinders left in a burning hot oven. Then honey, you got your own life to lead. So why not start leading it now. And jesus, it's worse anyway if he ever survived. I remember I told you already you could end up pushing him around in a wheelchair, an oxygen tent over his head worried that he was going to blow himself up lighting one of his cigars. Come on honey, let's go right now in there on the bed for some nookie. I'm dying to fuck you.'

'You would wouldn't you, pull the most low down dirty trick you could ever pull on Al.'

'Hey shit honey come on, how's he ever going to know.'

'I thought your balls got knocked off.'

'What.'

'Binky Sunningdale said you were jumping up from sitting on the lavatory to answer the telephone and that your testicles got caught and had to be later surgically removed in the hospital.'

'I caught them in a zipper. That fucking cunt. The fucking things I assure you honey may be stitched up but still hang in there.'

'Well I'm glad to hear that but I want my private life to lead. You wouldn't mind would you please, soon going.'

'You know honey I think you're hiding something.'

'Whatever I choose to hide, if I am hiding anything, is none of your business.'

'Honey sure, none of my business. It's not like I'm a photographer present up here taking pictures or something for a double page centre colour spread featuring in a Sunday supplement. Which reminds me we could have had a lot of extra publicity if we had had a photographer tonight at the theatre. Hey honey you don't look interested.'

'I'm glad your show is doing well. And you do seem not to lack publicity. Your wife was interviewed on this evening's news. About selling her story to the biggest Sunday scandal sheet of all time and threatening to mention me.'

'O jesus honey, I'm sorry. But it's been nothing but onslaught, onslaught. From every side. But you know what the fuck I'm going to do. And you're the first to know it. I swear I've secretly been thinking of it for a long time. I should buy a fucking yacht. To escape for a prolonged holiday breather. Maybe go cruising on the Riviera.'

'Have a good trip.'

'Hey come on honey. I mention it because I would want you to come with me. I can afford it. I own nearly the whole show now. Take you away from all this harassment. I swear the grapevine rumours are already going around Hollywood that the film rights are going to fetch a fortune. I mean a gargantuan fortune which could buy and sell Al three times over.'

'You've actually got to go now I'm expecting someone.'

'Honey, you've not have you, actually got someone else coming up here. You mean now. Tonight. This late.'

'Yes. I have. Now tonight this late. A lover as a matter of fact. Who comes here to fuck me. And with whom I am emotionally involved.'

'Hey holy shit hold it, hold it honey. This is some kind of joke. You don't mean this do you.'

'Yes I mean it.'

'You're serious.'

'As serious as I've ever been in my life.'

'Holy shit now I've spilt my fucking drink all over me. Hey and all this time you're throwing tantrums and tears over Al croaking. And me pulling the most low down dirty trick you could ever pull on Al.'

'I love Al. And I'll get you a towel.'

'Hey honey don't bother with the towel. It sounds like you love anyone who gives you a prick or gives you money. And not necessarily in that order. What is he some multi billionaire.'

'If it's any of your business and it's not, he loves my pasta and the way I make it with my tomato sauce. He also so happens to be an assistant stage carpenter and is young vital and very ambitious.'

'A what. What are you doing, supporting him on Al's money. Hey jesus christ holy shit I can't believe all this. This is too sudden. And my pants are wet. Jesus christ. All this fucking time betraying me. Me with my tongue out in love with you. Me who's got no fucking one to turn to. No friend I trust. No nothing. Correct that. I got a smash hit. But I got no nobody I can tell something as intimate as this to and ask them what I should do. And now I can't believe this all of a sudden. I'm well and truly shattered. There was only you all the time. And now there's no you.'

'You can still remain a friend and ask me for advice.'

'How can I. Jesus, can I. Thanks a bunch baby. Boy this tonight, takes the cake. Well O K honey then give me some advice. What am I going to do. I mean loving you was spiritual. Even dreaming about holding your hand. It was just being near you. Able to think about you. Honey, you were closer to me than my own flesh and blood. It's disembowelling me with pain.'

'Well if it's that bad why don't you go get a gun and shoot yourself.'

'Hey. Hey. Wait a second. Just wait a second. You really mean that, don't you. You really really mean it.'

'Yes I do otherwise I wouldn't have said it.'

'O K honey. Wow. This I did not need at this moment of my life. And that's exactly what I'm going to do. I'm going to go and buy a gun.'

Louella raising her chin in the air and taking a deep breath. Her satin jacket opening. Her breasts pressing against her blouse. Schultz tipping back an ice cube from his drink into his mouth. Getting to his feet. The candle flames flickering against the glass of the windows. An aircraft flying overhead. Jet's engines reducing speed changing pitch.

Just as I am, going towards the door. That I'll never walk through again. And pass all the international celebrities on the walls. Jesus I got born. Out of baby eyes I saw. What did I see. Rabbi I saw a whole fucking mystery. Especially a big ghost rearing up with a pair of gorgeous succulent tits slapping me in the face.

'Hey and before I go shoot myself honey, you got any other good advice.'

'Yes. Don't miss.'

'Boy don't worry honey, I won't. Not if I'm thinking of you at the time.'

Schultz coming out around the alcove from Al's flat and crossing the foyer and waiting by the elevator. The rust coloured carpet underfoot in this faint pink hue of light. Historic moments and you notice even a hair you never saw before on your knuckle. And one thing is certain. That at the very exact moment you think everything is beginning to go all right with a woman, be sure of one thing. It ain't. Come on fucking elevator. Don't take all year, I got to get the fuck out of this building once and for all.

The lift doors opening. The light shines out. Schultz stepping in as the doors begin to close and a hand suddenly holds them back. Schultz turning around. Louella standing there. Glistening in her eyes, big tears ready to fall.

'O god Sigmund I'm sorry. You're not are you going to shoot yourself.'

'Don't worry honey I got too many other people to shoot first.'

'Don't go. Come out of the elevator. I'm sorry. For all I said.'

'Honey all such things have been said a million times before by plenty of girls to plenty of guys and the world is still here ready for more conversations just like it.'

'But you don't know the full story.'

'What's the full story.'

'He has another two girlfriends.'

'Who has honey, who has.'

'The stage carpenter. And he's late for supper. And that nearly always means he's not coming. Especially when he's had to work late when the set gets broken.'

'Hey wait a second honey. What set.'

'O god.'

'What set. Come on honey. What set. Not honey in my fucking theatre. Where it so happens a carpenter is required during the show when Magillacurdy breaks the frames punching and kicking holes every night.'

248

'O god I knew somehow you'd find out.'

'Fucking hell honey, you mean that fucking emaciated scruffy kid with the red beard. Jesus.'

'O please. His beard isn't red. It's auburn. With flecks of orange.'

'I don't give a fuck what it is. Green blue or fucking pink. With flecks of gold leaf.'

'But I needed someone, don't you understand.'

'Holy shit honey. You're promiscuous. Not only are my pants fucking wet, but this is adding insult to injury. A backstage employee. This is incest.'

'Please. You're married. And I'm not promiscuous. Your wife and her detectives have threatened me. You don't know what it's been like on this death vigil. With Al's wives trying to evict me. Please. Just come back a minute. All that wonderful food will go to waste.'

'Honey thanks but no thanks. Much as I'd like to go back and eat my employee's pasta for him and hungry as I was, my digestion now and stomach at this moment is in complete turmoil. I ain't got an appetite. I'm all a bit busted up honey.'

'O dear.'

'I'm going down on this elevator as soon as it comes up again.'

'Then will you ring me later please. I'm so upset about Al.'

'Fuck Al. I'm sick of hearing about Al. I'm trying to gather up the pieces of my soul.'

'I was saying shoot yourself only trying to be cruel and mean.'

'Honey you were cruel and mean. What the hell those are the simple facts of life. I accept them. Maybe not with good grace. But I accept them. And now that I know the full story, I sure should shoot myself. But who knows maybe at the last second with the cold end of the barrel against my temple I'll figure what the hell, with money to spend, go have a ball, and I won't pull the trigger.'

'But were you really going to buy a yacht and go on the Riviera.'

'Just an idea which is maybe more a dream honey.'

'God. That would be sunshine. I feel I need sunshine so much.'

'Well honey I'm glad to hear that. But buying a yacht is still in fantasy land. And if I did ever get one. It just so happens I might want to be on it alone with my pigeons. Here's the elevator. So long.'

Schultz descending. The floors passing as the numbers blink in the light. No thirteenth. London's getting suspicious like America. And boy, talking about suspicion. With women you never know what's coming next and when it comes, you still don't know, and all you can do is brace yourself for it. Imagine a fucking assistant stage carpenter.

Who doesn't take a bath. Working in my own fucking theatre that I'm renting. And here I am believing that the guy that wins at life is supposed to have his first choice and selection of women. And the guys that lose have to wait in line. Now here's some fucking girl who wants it both, no three ways. She's got Al panting for her on his deathbed and who although gone a little geriatric before his gaskets blew, at least was a big fucking winner. Then she's got me chasing her nearly fucking begging. And then holy shit, what is she doing, all the time she's got some kid screwing her and she's jealous because the kid's got two other girlfriends as well. And the pink bearded fucker's the worst fucking carpenter of all time and not even a fucking bonafide fully paid up member of the Union yet. Momma meo. Such moments as these require bravery. And I've got to go on as if I'm going on living. But how could she do this to me Rabbi. Sigmund easy. Some ladies think having a good fuck is good for them. And getting it frequent is even better.

Schultz walking up the garage ramp from tax dodgers' towers. Out into this overly familiar street. Jesus this is nearly as bad as the last time I crawled away from here. Maybe worse. In a cloud of doom. Which thank god had the silver lining of my show giving the first signs of becoming a hit. But my tail still between my legs. Nothing to bolster my ego. Like Jorricks cruising up and opening the door of the limo. And getting into the soft upholstery of that sanctum. At the theatre tonight a false alarm, a bomb, and royalty. But jesus just to see that little kid there so enjoying himself. Dreams of grandeur in his eyes. That to me is joy enough. And when the cast heartfelt gave the best performance ever. A final standing ovation of ten minutes. Eleven curtain calls. Tears in everybody's eyes. Fuck unfaithful women. Who needs them. With bravoes still ringing in my ears. For such moments lasting a few seconds one lives nearly a fucking lifetime. Fighting all the fights. Climbing grabbing with your fingers. Clinging on each little cliff edge of hope every time you put down the telephone or wrote a letter. Desperate that this time something good would happen like a piece of money to get you just another few days' survival. But lose your grip, panic for a second. And the fall is nearly all the way back down to the bottom of oblivion again licking wounds. And staring at a phone that doesn't ring. Then always in hope, slow, slow, rolling with the rebuffs, agonizingly climbing all the way back up again. To finally get there and have what you've always dreamed about. The summit. A smash hit. But you never never and I mean never throw in the towel. Or depend upon a woman. And hey Sigmund, let me throw in my two cents. This is Rabbi Löw tuning in. So you know plenty of struggle but who are you to talk faithfulness when already you go bang bang between so many legs all the time. O K, forgive me Rabbi. I'm reformed.

Schultz shambling down this street. Past the shops, looking in the windows. Smell of coffee. And I never even noticed that shop before. Selling beans of dozens of different varieties. Or a dogs' hairdressers. Maybe that's where Al sends his toupee to be shampooed. Hey jesus it's still raining. And I didn't even notice. I can't even raise my arm to wave for a taxi. Shows you. That a dream you dreamed can leave you finally and for all time, utterly shattered. Jesus who'd mind if the guy was somebody. Like Al at least with a gold lamé evening cloak, a few limousines and a jet. But a fucking stage carpenter on my show. No wonder I caught him a couple of times looking sideways at me. He could have been helping even to repair my house after the fire. Imagine. I should have such an appetite. Go back and eat his dinner. Fucking hell she even invites me. To a nice heaping dish of real ignominy. Instead of sticking to my principle, hold nothing against women. I should have at least shaken a fist if not my prick in her face. That's what love finally is all about, isn't it Rabbi. Proximity. With your prick out. And ah Sigmund, ladies like a lot of them around them sticking out so they can decide which one to use first.

Schultz crossing the road. Towards the shadows of all these big towering trees. A waning moon disappearing in the sky behind black clouds. Christ here comes a bobby on the beat who's any second going to say, 'ere 'ere you, move on, no loitering. Jesus and I just find a coin in the gutter. A whole half crown. A good omen I'm going to keep. Shows at least I'm not totally blinded by grief. Slip through this bit of broken fence. Take a walk I don't need. Short cut across Hyde Park. And hope I can get out the other side. But don't look back at the lights in that tower. Jesus crossing the wet grass like this I could actually be down and out. Like a bum. Cold. Walking with nowhere to go. I ain't got no coat. Soaking my shoes. And it's freezing where my crotch got wet. The water of the Serpentine shimmering. If there weren't so many ducks and seagulls shitting in it, I could throw myself in there drowning in the melancholy moonlight that's just peeked out again from behind more clouds. Boy there's a fucking word, melancholy. Jesus at least I've got reserves of an ass or two to fall softly back upon. Only I sincerely wish Cynthia's father wasn't an income tax inspector. And I could do worse, do worse, than Catherine. Said a guy's erection was like a little flag letting you know you were admired, desired, desired. And let's face it. All fucking women are mad. Why not be with one who's officially recognized and authenticated as a mile off her rocker. At least I'll say this for her. She's extraordinary not ordinary. And with her nurse in tow the three of us could go riding on the crest of my wave. Before maybe it goes to crash too soon somewhere. Leaving my fucking wife a celebrity. And me in the fucking dust. Boy do I need a friend. And a little cheering up. But jesus Rabbi you were right. Always suspect that someone else is fucking them.

When
You ain't

Schultz slowing in his tracks. Moving forward again. Jesus. I have just gone off the path and walked into a fucking tree. With now suddenly a fog landing all over the park out of the god damn sky. Not even the temperamental weather can be trusted for two seconds. Christ I'm fucking lost. I could now really walk into the Serpentine and get drowned. What's now this looming up. Holy cow it's a bandstand. Jesus go around it. To the tune of Marching Through Georgia. O my god now I've just tripped over a fence. I'm in a flowerbed. Up to my ankles. My god mud is packing around my shoes. Now something has caught the sleeve of my jacket. O christ something's ripping. Jesus taking a walk to calm my nerves has turned into a death march. Fuck keep walking. That's what I'll do walk off this fucking depression. Or crawl it off. Look at me. As if I've been sentenced to execution. Doing what I can't stop. Grinding my footsteps across the ground. Because the woman I love is being unfaithful. Without ever, when I think of it, being faithful. O jesus London. Fucking London. Lonely London. London. My town. This wonderful place I've grown to adore. And now jesus in the middle of financial joy which should have given me such utter happiness I am having a nervous breakdown. Christ I'm even weeping. I got to go on walking. She's kicked me right in the fucking heart, Rabbi. What am I going to do. She's opening up her legs for somebody else. Sigmund listen, don't be such a big cry baby. I told you. It might be better that way. You could do worse than celibacy since the venereal plague. Jesus thanks a whole generous bunch, Rabbi. But the trouble Rabbi with all this good advice you keep giving me is that in my desperation to play tickling games and get laid again, the wisdom you offer gets completely wiped out of my mind. I am hardly across Hyde Park before I am nearly crawling back on my hands and knees through the leaves thick on the ground to Louella to eat the fucking stage carpenter's dinner. And now you tell me she could be contaminated. Sigmund listen. It's you too, who could be already contaminated. Jesus Rabbi, my both feet fucking encrusted in mud and now I should need such an extra spiritual burden of killer microbes added to the mental ones already crawling around my depressed brain tonight. It's a fucking time to call battle stations. General fucking quarters. All hands on deck. And I can hardly even remember I was once a trained fucking officer in the Coast Guard. On a diver class medium endurance cutter. Fifteen hundred tons standard displacement. Two hundred and thirteen feet bow to stern. Thirty nine feet in the beam. Drawing fifteen feet of water. Three thousand horsepower spinning down two shafts sending us anchors aweigh at fifteen knots slashing through waves heaving over the depths. Jesus if we took off a stripe and the coast guard emblem it would have been exactly what I need in a yacht for the Riviera. Ah Sigmund, you get a yacht on the Côte d'Azur and even I will get out of my grave and come aboard. Aye, aye Captain Rabbi, I hear you talking. I'll be your gunnery officer. Blow the shit out of every one of my wife's fucking lawyers within miles. But holy shit, where am I, I've come in the wrong fucking direction in the fog. I'm at last out of the park. Holy jesus I'm not that far from his Lordship's. Something in his street, always makes me feel good. Christ maybe it was that moss green tweed suited lady I once saw with such beautiful knees and thighs getting into her car.

Schultz walking down this terraced familiar street of marble townhouses. Their steps up to their gleaming doors. Iron grills locked over the windows. Holy fuck I could really do with a heartfelt commiseration with his Lordship. Whose life is so perfectly contented. The way he just quietly calmly pursues his comfortable habits. He and Binky are probably out on the moors deer stalking with their gamekeepers. They marry women like they were breeding horses keeping the mares in a stable. The pair of them oblivious as they always are to the pain of love and life. And Binky even with death. Behaving like banks. With nice cold hard financial indifference. Unless you can't pay back the capital then you get colder harder attention real fast. Maybe that's the secret. Do like you're buying and selling people. And holy fuck you soon find out who can be bought and those who charge compound interest on the price. And here I am with my simple minded belief that there was a woman, just one, who I could finally get and who was somebody in whom I could trust. Maybe not with my life, but at least until I was thirty nine and on the verge of old age when it doesn't matter anymore.

The fog turned now into mist. The glittering whiteness of the lamps in this grey pedestrian deserted street. Schultz stopping to survey Lord Nectarine's mansion. Shutters closed on all the windows. Four across to my three and each is double in size. And there are six floors over the basement. What the fuck does he do living in such a great empty place and hardly ever there. At least my house small as it is compared to his, was for a short while a family home with lots of au pairs nipping in and out. Hey shit, when his staff should be asleep, there's fucking lights on behind the chinks in the shutters and curtains. Jesus on every floor. Holy fuck, his Lordship could be being robbed. The staff tied up. In there in the front hall alone he's got fucking candelabra and jars and vases from various fucking Chinese dynasties worth a fortune. Shit if I knock, they could run out of the back. I better just go up and listen. Without, jesus, looking like a robber myself.

Schultz tiptoeing up the white stone steps to the porch. Leaning over with his ear to the white gleaming door. Sound of high heels inside clicking across a marble floor. Jesus what's that crack. Like a fucking whip snapping. Holy shit. That's bloody music in there somewhere. Some fucking kind of robbery this is. Maybe I'd better get to the hotel around the corner and call his Lordship in Scotland. Jesus don't, maybe there's no time. Because by that time they could have loaded up a couple of vans. Two blue ones are parked down the street. I better call the police. Or maybe scare them out of the place. First slam the knocker and then run holding my wet balls and hide behind that next stoop where the beautiful doll came out of and so they don't shoot me while they're escaping. And then safely see from a distance who the fuck comes. Jesus let's see, get out my thin nail file pick off my knife. Shove it in to push the little cover flap aside. Maybe I can peek in. Jesus I can just see a fraction. Wow. That's Noble, the butler. He's carrying a big cake. What's he doing with a cake, it's past midnight for christ's sake. A woman behind him with Pekinese dogs. Or are the grey curly haired things poodles. Six of them on leashes. Can only see her legs and what legs. Hey christ. Maybe his staff is gone berserk. Even though it's live and let live I'm going to ring the fucking bell. Find out what the fuck is going on. And report to his Lordship, the only fucking friend I've got left in the world who I can trust just a little. Who if anything happens to him, could ruin any optimism I got left in human nature. O god. I can't. No. I got to. Got to ring this door bell. And give this knocker a few slams. At least if something's wrong I can let his Lordship know.

Schultz ringing the bell and pounding the knocker. Retreating down the steps, backing across the pavement and waiting on the kerb. The door slowly opening. The light pouring out across the stoop. Noble's head peering out.

'Hey Noble.'

'I beg your pardon.'

'Hey Noble it's me Mr Schultz.'

'Who is Mr Schultz. Would you mind stepping a little closer please.'

'Schultz, you know, his Lordship's friend. You met me once, remember. I was just going by. I was just staying with his Lordship up in Scotland.'

'I see. Are you calling upon us sir.'

'Well I'm sort of deliberating. Jesus you wouldn't have a glass of water or something would you.'

'Well I do believe that we might quite possibly provide a glass of water. And do I anticipate sir, that you are visiting.'

'Well yeah, sort of, I wasn't entirely sure of the time, I mean that's why I'm knocking.'

'O then you are expected sir.'

'Yeah, that's right I'm expected.'

'Well please do forgive this ceremony sir. But I'm afraid with this severe draught I must close the door. Do please come in. And over by the fire. Awfully foul old foggy night out there without a coat. Dear me sir. Have you encountered some difficulty. Sir's sleeve is hanging off.'

'I got lost in the fog in the park.'

'O dear dear dear, sir, how beastly for you and we are wet aren't we as well.'

'Yeah we are wet all right. As well.'

'I'm sure his Lordship can provide you with some dry clothes.'

'Hey I wouldn't want to intrude. Like going into his wardrobe or anything.'

'No problem sir I assure you. Indeed sir might then like something a little stronger than water to drink.'

'Hey I would.'

'And what sir, would you like.'

'Maybe I'll take some of that pure malt stuff from the Highlands on the rocks.'

'You mean with ice, sir.'

'Yeah ice.'

'Will you take it in the ballroom sir.'

'O no. Don't bother. Here in the hall's just fine. Get dry by the fire. I only knocked because I was worried when I saw all the lights on.'

'I don't believe I quite follow you sir.'

'Well you know there are robberies happening every second all over London. Could have been somebody was in here who shouldn't be here.'

'I beg your pardon sir.'

'You know like being a good citizen. Keep out a watchful eye. Like there was even a suspected bomb at the theatre tonight. Could you call me a taxi.'

'You are sir, going to have your drink and join his Lordship first.'

'Join him. Jesus how can I.'

'I'll show you to the ballroom sir.'

'The ballroom.'

'Yes sir. We only open it for such occasions.'

'What occasion.'

'To celebrate Madame Dipompididor's birthday sir. Which his Lordship does every year, I thought you knew.'

'You mean Basil. Is here.'

'I mean Lord Nectarine sir. Master of Foxhounds and the Earl of Eel Brook Common.'

'Yeah well that's who I mean too. One of England's all time best cricketers.'

'And if you will excuse me, sir, I was on my way to fetch something when you knocked. I just must attend to a small matter. And I shall only then be just a moment. Supper is not yet served, and Madame Dipompididor has yet to do the blowing.'

'The blowing.'

'Yes sir, thirty six candles on the cake.'

'O boy. Hey make that whisky a double. No correct that. Triple.'

'Very good sir.'

Schultz rubbing his hands in front of the blazing hall fire. Watching Noble depart across the expanse of black and white marble tiles to disappear through a door under the curving staircase. Holy shit, his poor fucking Lordship. Madame Dipompididor's birthday party. Holy cow. Jesus that's the sound of glass crashing somewhere. This is fucking awful. Doddery old guy is gone completely nuts out of his mind. While his Lordship's four hundred miles away in Scotland. Must be his age. Imagine I thought things were bad over at my house. And here they are chaos. Imagine. Basil in the ballroom. Does this place even have a ballroom. If it doesn't it at least sure has fucking dogs on a lead going by. And those legs. I never, no matter what, forget a pair of legs. And boy there was something familiar about every nice long shimmering inch of thigh to the knee, over the calf and right down to the ankle bone. Madame Dipompididor is going to blow out the candles. Maybe more likely she's blowing old Noble and sending blasts of steam out of his ears. The fucker is probably an old randy roué. Jesus. Soon as I thaw a second and down the whisky, I got to get to somewhere to call his Lordship. I got to. In spite of all this pleading poverty, death duties and taxes that he does, I know that the son of a bitch is loaded. But nobody can afford a whole gang gone totally wild in their house with such heirlooms as this place has got. Jesus I can hear girls' voices, noises and music. Sounds like there's a whole bunch of people inside. Jesus maybe I should investigate. Fuck. No. Without thawing. Without whisky, I'll get out the door fast before he gets back. And call his Lordship.

Schultz pulling open the heavy latches of this massive door. Twisting the knob. Noble emerging again from under the stairs. His trembling hand holding a glass on a silver tray.

'Dear me sir, you're not leaving are you. I've got your drink here.'

'I was just going to sort of catch a breath of fresh air. O jeeze.'

'Gesundheit, Mr Schultz.'

'O boy am I really sneezing.'

'Hardly a time to stand in a draught sir. Have your drink sir.'

'Thanks a bunch Noble. Really thanks a bunch.'

'And sir you're quite welcome a bunch as I believe it's still said in the better parts of our former colonies in the neighbourhood of Massachusetts.'

Noble giving a smiling nod of his head. Schultz putting the glass of whisky to his mouth and taking a big swig. Holy shit. Noble's a fucking card. And having a rare old time here tonight with his Lordship safely in Scotland. The cat's away, and the mice will play. Shit a woman betrays you so why not join the party and go find that god damn familiar pair of legs. By what must be going on in here it won't matter my sleeve's hanging off and I'm looking like something the cat dragged in. And my motto right now is go have a ball. I mean when I think of it what the fucking hell did his Lordship ever really do for me. Except fall over his shotguns and hold his stomach laughing when my own balls got zapped in the zipper.

Noble leading a sneezing Schultz. Blobs of mud caking off behind him on the marble floor. Through a door and along a hall past the library and dining room and to a spacious glass domed vestibule. The sound of yapping barking dogs. Noble pushing open a gleaming pair of double mahogany doors. Schultz stopping in his muddy tracks, mouth dropping open and his drink spilling from an upraised hand as he was bent double in a paroxysm of sneezing. In this vast room, a crystal chandelier hanging from a ceiling adorned with paintings of robed celestial figures, angels and heavenly cherubs. Life sized portraits inset on the walls. Men in military uniforms, ladies in gowns. At the end of a long table laid with sparkling glassware and gold gleaming dinner plates, and aseat in a massive golden chair, his sleeves rolled up and his shirt open to his navel as he scratched himself under the armpits, sprawled his Lordship. Noble at the door lifting his chin to intone.

'Milord, Mr Sigmund Schultz.'

'Good god, Schultz. You old poofta. What on earth are you doing over here down our little side street in Mayfair.'

'Jesus what are you doing here. I thought you were in Scotland.'

'Ah you silly old sod, Schultz. Can't you see we are here celebrating.'

'Well I got lost in a fog in the park. And came out the wrong way.'

'You are always coming out the wrong way Schultz. If I may say so. Or getting lost in a fog in some park. Were you searching for other pooftas. And having found them they jumped out at you and in their carnal quest bloody well ripped your clothing off. You're in déshabillé, fucking covered with mud. Sit immediately down. Everyone sit immediately down. It's full of prowling pooftas after dark that park. Or did you just merely go in there to wank in the shrubberies.'

Schultz taking a seat at the other end of the long table. Smiles from all the assembled ladies. In their various stages of high heeled titillating dress. So this is what goes on when my back is turned. He has our fucking lead dancer Margot, holy christ how could I ever not know those legs, on her unbelievable body and who with her marvellous lack of brains has only to cross the back gardens to get in here. That beautiful ass of hers invites you to bugger her. My god. This is insane. Talk about a harem. I'm accused. And it's his fucking Lordship who's guilty. Lights blazing all over this place. Women everywhere. This is bacchanalian. Jesus it's his Lordship who is the roué. Holy shit Rabbi, am I spooked. And am I seeing things. Maybe I have a fever. Jeeze, who are the figures standing around without moving a muscle. They are fucking wax. And there. O my god, there she is. That's the fucking lady next door. And boy O boy, one thing's for sure, she's not in wax. She's fucking living and breathing and looking fantastic. What a figure. In that clinging wool green dress. Hair pulled back and parted like a ballerina. And wearing an emerald pendant that with the diamonds around it could buy and sell both me and Al put together. Or else my uncle Werb never taught me nothing about gems. Hey boy, I'm not dying of heartbreak yet. Joy is again getting injected in me. This Rabbi, could be my night. My god. So this is why you never know what his Lordship's doing. Because this is what he's doing. The secret fucker has all this time got it all going for him here. Bowls of bananas. Grapes. Tangerines. And jesus nectarines. And gorgeous girls all assembled for his own private delight. Even gold engraved names at the place settings.

'Hey your Lordship I got just to catch my breath.'

'Catch your breath Schultz. Whatever for.'

'Just let's say I recently had an emotional let down.'

'Ah my dear darling Schultz, you are a silly old poofta aren't you. Not disappointed in love I hope. Of course you know women will always get away with what they can. Ah but rumour now has it that you presently have two pooftas in your house. And you do don't you, nearly always come into my house with something unfortunate adhering to your footwear. And while you catch your breath and as I see you staring in shocked surprise, let me point out our little wax collection of effigies. Always present for company when my grandfather dined here alone. Among the legendary reconstructed celebrated beauties of my grandfather's youth he has those chaps. You must recognize, Napoleon. And Nelson. And Churchill added just before my grandfather died, is over there with his cigar. Normally I keep them cool in the basement. But we bring them upstairs for Madame Dipompididor's birthday party. At which Margot has so kindly after her hectic bomb scare deigned to dance for us. Pops in the very "French" doors there from across the garden you know. That's the beauty of being in show biz. These wonderful events we have. And let one of the ladies Schultz help you to caviare.'

'And your Lordship. Just what the doctor ordered in my present state of pessimism. And my appetite which I thought I lost forever an hour ago is coming back now that I see there could be a couple of pounds of beluga in that bowl.'

'Ah Schultz you've estimated nearly to the exact ounce. Always the merchant aren't you, weighing, buying, selling, dealing. Looking for bargains. Ladies, do let me present Sigmund Schultz. And this Schultz is Bradford Myrtle. Manchester Caroline, Lilly from Lee's Place around the corner. And our dear old favourite Scouse, formerly from Birkenhead and now of Upper Norwood. And you do of course know as all London does, the lead dancer Margot from that hit show, Kick It Don't Fuck It, It's Too Morbid. Ah and we nearly overlooked, sorry my dear, this is Despicable Deirdre from Hornchurch. She resides near the borax works. Ah, and Madame Dipompididor from Paris, but originally from Swansea, and for whom we hold this celebration and whose most wonderful birthday this is. Ah but last and not least my dearest nearest neighbour. Madame Soignée who is in fact from Chantilly. But. But. Schultz. Stop stuffing your mouth and listen. We are not yet finished with the introductions.'

'I'm listening your Lordship. So's my Rabbi. But jesus such beluga.'

'Schultz. We have a lady for you, I am sure you would like to meet

260

and she is in there behind that door. Erica come out please.'

Schultz's jaw dropping a mile open. Beads of caviare stuck to the corners of his mouth. As a long blonde haired toweringly tall girl steps smiling forth into the room attired in an apron and golden high heeled sandals. Her long arms propped out from each hip.

'Ah Skyscraper Erica Schultz, with those curvaceously graceful fishing rod arms. She might if you have the necessary mountain gear let you ascend her Scandinavian summit. An Olympic downhill slalom champion. Her father a professor of Sanskrit and speaks eleven languages. She speaks five but claims she can fuck in eight. And we tonight celebrate her first night on the game. Now Schultz, what do you say we get on with the party before you not quite so rudely interrupted.'

'Hey your Lordship I'm ready. I like it. Let's go in Serbo Croat. Voom. Voom.'

'Ah it would appear Schultz that that indifferent edge to your voice has vanished and you are rapidly entering into the mood of things. But you silly old poofta Schultz you should be back in your purdah. The principal question is are your bandaged balls ready to go voom. Voom voom voom. Up the Skyscraper Erica. Of course your prick is going to be like a needle in a haystack.'

'Your Lordship don't worry about my needle in any haystack, but to my production practised eye that looks like a fantastic throne you're sitting on with genuine gems embedded in it.'

'Of course it's a fucking throne Schultz. You don't think I'd sit on an ordinary chair for Madame Dipompididor's birthday party, who has long distinguished herself by having the best, albeit the most expensive string of certified healthy whores in London. Plus Despicable Deirdre there from Hornchurch is getting married to someone once prominent in the borax works but who has now wisely transferred to an artificial fertilizer plant due to his recent sex change operation.'

'Hey what's the silence, why is nobody saying nothing.'

'Club rules, Schultz. In order that one's mind be allowed to concentrate the ladies are not allowed to speak until spoken to. And then one asks them about their vegetable gardens in the green belt. And then one is told about their fucking Brussels sprouts they brought to cook for the supper tonight.'

'Holy shit, what a good fucking idea. Hey include me in the membership. Jesus that's wonderful. Nobody has to shout shut up. Wow. Just eat the Brussels sprouts.'

'Nor Schultz is smiling or laughing permitted, not even at my most amusing stories. Ladies who collapse in uncontrollable fits of mirth are asked to immediately leave the ballroom.'

'Hey. This is the cat's whiskers and the cat's pyjamas.'

'I don't know about the fucking whiskers but of course this is the cat's pyjamas Schultz. And down with small minded little fuckers is the theme of tonight's little party. Schultz you no longer look as if you're attending at a beheading.'

'Yeah. Maybe I'm not. But I just came from one. But if I look like I'm at another one right now it's only because I am about to sneeze again.'

'Ah Schultz sneeze. And god bless you. I do miss your not being in purdah, but O my god almighty. I am chuffed. Chuffed. Usually I am very careful about anyone knowing I am awfully happy. But this evening I am so happy, so very very happy, that I don't give a fuck who knows it. Schultz are you listening down there you old poofta. While pondering the imponderables one best sits on a fucking throne. And scratches one's ass as well as one's head. I'm scratching my arse Schultz. And you'd think by the stunned expression now on your face that you had never before seen someone sitting on a fucking throne, and scratching their royal arse on it. Or seen the likes of Skyscraper Erica with the butterflies, such beautiful butterflies on the front of her scanty apron.'

'Don't worry your Lordship, I'm stunned. I'm even nonplussed dumbfounded. But I'll tell you one thing. I like it. Voom.'

'And voom, voom to you Schultz. My wife's fucking boyfriend who invented the flush overflow warning device for lavatories has by accident sat on his most recent invention and the sharp end of it went up his fucking arse and he wants me, who believes devoutly in socialism, to pay for a private hospital room for him. A very dispiriting prospect indeed as rumour has it that he may require a long series of enema treatments. At which one does hope the London fire brigade who visit your house so frequently Schultz, might attend.'

Skyscraper Erica serving Schultz with biscuits and caviare. Lilly from Lee's Place around the corner, laying a napkin across Schultz's lap. Topless Manchester Caroline brushing her breast against Schultz's cheek.

'Your Lordship I can't believe this wonderful pastoral domestic scene you got going here. I just can't.'

'Ah Schultz women are so much more alluring when they keep their mouths fucking shut and fuck. And you'd think you'd never kissed a tit in passion. That's what I find most lovable about you is your innocence.

Noble take away that whisky and pour old Mr Siggy innocent Schultz a glass of our better champagne. He can't believe anything. Everyone, everyone immediately stand at attention. Until we get old ripped balls Siggy there as pissed out of his mind as I am. There Schultz, on one side Manchester Caroline is giving you bosomly comfort while on the other, our dear old favourite Scouse from the Birkenhead side of the Mersey flowing along the banks of Liverpool is also giving you the benefit of her breast. We must make him pissed, Noble. Pissed do you hear.'

'Yes milord. And supper is ready when you are milord.'

'Then bring on the lamb chops Noble. We must make Schultz believe. That this is the real fucking domestic truth he's seeing here where we strictly adhere to club rules. And where pissed out of my mind I have a good fucking time. That's what you should do with your money Schultz, have a good fucking time. Put all fucking loneliness and despair to rout.'

'I'm thinking of it your Lordship, I'm thinking of it.'

Bradford Myrtle of the long black hair entering the ballroom with a large platter of steaming lamb chops held high. Suddenly tripping over the rug and sending the lamb chops plummeting off the plate and skidding across the floor. Madame Dipompididor's poodles, descending like piranhas yapping and growling as they snap and gobble them down.

'Holy shit your Lordship, those fucking mutts took the god damn lamb chops right out of my mouth. And I'm famished starving.'

'Ah Schultz these up to the mark top hole ladies on the game seemingly make appalling waitresses, but there's a turkey yet to come. And they are about to ferry in the potatoes and the Brussels sprouts. However over these many years of acquaintanceship with these daughters of joy it is their inner good naturedness of which I am so very fond.'

'Jesus who worries about inner nature when what's outer nature couldn't be more gorgeous. I must confess I wouldn't have expected this high female standard of you your Lordship.'

'What did you expect Schultz for me to have surrounding me here, a lot of old fucking clapped out ratbags. Take your prick out and fuck one, Schultz. Because it's all coming to an end. An end. Do it on the table where we can see you. We'll move the potatoes out of the way.'

'Jesus just let me sit here a second your Lordship, hold it. Take it easy. Keep your shirt on. Let's eat. Plenty of time for fucking. Let's not rush things.'

'Ah Schultz you may have just come in out of the fog in the park but when put to the test you do fail don't you. Here you are the biggest whoremongering erotomaniac in kingdom come. And you want to eat instead of fuck. And I'm taking my shirt off. And this hanging about my neck Schultz is a sovereign case, full of sovereigns. As it is customary for me to make my disbursal in such gold coins. But for you to indulge your prick this joyous night it will cost you one hundred guineas. Of course there may be a surcharge if you require extra curricular services.'

'Jesus I'm getting enough service. It's too much already. I'm in no hurry for anything. My wet feet are nicely thawing. And with this mournful sad music. I like it. I like everything. I should have been invited before to the club. Hey and why don't you let the girls say something.'

'I give the Skyscraper, Erica the Valkyrie permission to speak in one of her languages. Erica tell Schultz there how much you are going to charge him to open up those fucking wonderful Olympic skiing legs of yours.'

'Ah you, your excellent Grace. I like how tall dark and handsome mister Schultz is. Because I am pissed maybe I charge half what I will charge you. But because maybe you would not like that and you are even more handsome than he is, and you are pissed, maybe I charge him double. Two hundred guineas on the nail as they say. Because I am Erica the Valkyrie. And I need much money. And I have a good fucking tall beautiful body which is all muscle and yet still soft. And I will be the most elegantly exquisite whore selling my ass in London. I have the most brilliant fucking mind too. You your Lordship are wrong. I speak seven languages. And I can fuck in eleven. I am champion three years downhill slalom. I am a genius at mathematics. His Lordship is wrong too. My father is a brilliant professor of astro physics. My mother is a soprano who has sung in every major opera house all over Europe. And who are you pair of fuckers. Huh. Who. Who is this Schultz. Never heard of him. And I am fucking drunk. You shits. That's why I charge double. You shits. With the money I make a wonderful film. Of an exploration up the Amazon. Have you got your purse Mr Schultz. You are a nobody. Get out your purse.'

'Yes honey I'm a nobody but no honey I ain't got no purse.'

'If you can't get your fucking purse out you nobody then write out the big cheque right now and give me. Pay in advance. No cheque, I no fuck.'

'And honey I ain't got no cheque book. And honey some fucking anaconda up the Amazon ought to wrap its fucking coils around you

264

and crush the shit out of you. Jesus your Lordship impose the fucking rule I've heard enough.'

'Ah Erica you take the fucking cake. Mr Schultz is upset. He is a man of immense sensibility. And now Erica it's time for you to shut up. He fucks only for love. He never pays for it. He's got a chorus line a mile long to fuck. He has a harem, plus two pooftas in his house. See he sits now with his head in his hands. No. Sorry. He's just sneezing.'

'Yeah. Achoo. Jesus your Lordship, somebody has got to control this I swear. What's going on here. It's dangerous.'

'Our female star performer Margot has come in her white sequins across the back garden from her flat to perform. And Schultz you know nothing about life. Of course it's dangerous. You're a fucking old stick in the mud. Let's call up the whole fucking world on the telephone. We have six lines. And I want them all talking to happy people all over the world. Here I'll get up and dance for you myself Schultz. Right up on the fucking table. You're in England Schultz. Where after dinner we in the better Guards' regiments' messes play indoor rugby.'

'Jesus your Lordship you're going to break your ass or the dishes. This is getting out of hand. Stop him somebody. Hey your Lordship stop.'

'Schultz, I was a fucking high jump champion. As well as a fucking cricketer. And am still the fucking master of fucking foxhounds.'

'Well your Lordship why don't you wait to go chase a fox or get up at fucking bat and knock one for six to mid off or something in the morning.'

'Where's my cricket bat. I'll show you. Schultz. Where are you Noble, my bloody cricket bat if you please.'

'Stop him somebody, stop him, for christ's sake.'

A flushed faced Noble entering with the turkey on a platter. Frowning as he waits for a break in the noise of the shouting voices.

'The turkey is served milord.'

'Fuck the turkey we're playing cricket.'

'Very good milord.'

Madame Dipompididor's poodles gnawing at the lamb chop bones in a corner. One dog grabbing the last meaty bone and chased by the others. Their leads flying behind them as they sail barking towards the ballroom doors. The long leather leashes entangling around Noble's legs as he totters under the heavy weight of the large roasted turkey. Its massive silver platter trembling and tipping over as he lifts it high out of reach of the jumping and snapping poodles' jaws. Gravy pouring down over his grey hair and dripping from an ear lobe. Madame

Soignée rushing to his side to hold the turkey steady. Erica taking a swig out of a champagne bottle. Margot leaning back against the wall, peeling a banana and taking a bite. Watching his shirtless Lordship seize a polo mallet out of a corner stand, and in his stockinged feet jump up on the table knocking over wine glasses, sending knives and forks flying. His gold sovereign case gleaming against the hairs of his chest as he scratches up and down. Taking a candelabrum, candle flames flickering, and placing it behind him at the end of the table.

'This is the wicket. And all I've got to defend with is a skinny shafted half arsed polo mallet. Now Schultz let's see if you forty feet away down that other end of the table, can with this orange if you can catch it and with your bandaged balls in a sling, see if you can bowl out England's all time half arsed schoolboy cricketer.'

'Don't say you didn't ask for it your Lordship, and here it comes, a fucking knuckle ball which you'll never hit in a million years.'

Schultz winding up and throwing the orange. His Lordship concussing it with the end of the mallet, sending half an orange heading for the ceiling, and the other half hitting Noble smack mid eye in the face. The turkey surrounded by basted potatoes and in its sea of gravy sliding off the platter. The poodles with canine teeth flashing, ripping it asunder before it hit the floor. Madame Soignée her hands up hiding her eyes and then dropping to cover her laughing face. Despicable Deirdre the Dyke from Hornchurch in the mêlée grabbing Lilly from Lee's Place around the corner, kissing her and throwing her to the floor and grinding her pelvis down between Lilly's open legs.

'Hey jesus your Lordship, holy christ the mutts are devouring the dinner and we're breaking the fucking heirlooms and I'm famished for something to eat and now this whole thing is getting out of hand obscene in here.'

Noble with a handkerchief wiping orange from his eyes, nose and mouth and the gravy from his hair, ears and shoulders. Margot with a leg of turkey pulling in one direction as six poodles pull in the other. The Scouse from Liverpool shovelling spoonfuls of caviare down her throat. Teenaged Bradford Myrtle and Manchester Caroline holding each other's hands in alarm beneath the portrait of Nectarine's monocled grandfather in a field marshal's uniform. Deirdre and Lilly groaning and moaning, hands clutched in each other's hair. His Lordship connecting with another orange thrown by Erica.

'Ah I am Erica the Valkyrie. I know how to bowl his fucking Lordship. And he splatter peel, pips and juice in all directions, and it go splut, splut, splut. All over the place. And you, you nobody, shut up

266

Schultz. Get back away from the table. Never mind an anaconda squeeze me, a fucking piranha should bite your prick off. And let his Excellency his Grace have a good fucking time. I bowl him now a big fat grapefruit.'

'Hear that Schultz. She bowls a wicked fucking orange too. And the Valkyrie by the look of her will fuck a wicked fucking fuck up in the bedroom I guarantee you. And right now my prick may be down but my wicket is standing up.'

'Ah I charge his Lordship three sovereigns. And if he doesn't pay me I come tomorrow to this house with my luggage to live. Now I bowl this one for a wicket.'

Noble standing rubbing his hands together, great grey eyebrows raised in some alarm as he surveys the bombarding action across the ballroom.

'I do understand it when his Lordship occasionally decides to have a bit of fun and games, but I do believe that this is going a bit over the top.'

Noble moving to collect the gold plate and cutlery from the table. His Lordship swinging and missing the grapefruit. A poodle chasing it across the floor. The polo mallet swiping two candles off the candelabrum. His Lordship's feet crushing more crystal in a tinkle of crashing glass. Waving the mallet over his head.

'No one dares to stop me Schultz. Excuse me while I belch. This is my fucking party. That is causing me wonderful happiness tonight. While civilized London sleeps. I become uncivilized. Show you bunch of whores a fucking dance. Kick the crystal ware off this fucking table. Place your bets. Later we're all going out together to the casino. To gamble the night away. Schultz you never see me in the dumps. But I do get down in the fucking dumps. But I get out again. By having a private feast and making a fucking awful fool of myself. That's why I am so fucking happy tonight. I am so fucking happy. To see you there Schultz. Your fucking sleeve hanging off your coat. Rubbing your hands worried that I'll break my own fucking furniture.'

'You bet I am. This is awful.'

'May we assume Schultz that when the nuclear holocaust comes. That you you old poofta, will be seen walking about upon that deserted landscape, a contract in your hand, standing there outside the theatre where in the smoking ruins no vestige of such place remains, and demanding to be paid from the box office embers your share of your usual sixty percent of one hundred percent of the gross off the top. And twenty percent down the sides. And fifteen percent off the bottom. O K everybody except Noble must go topless. Schultz we're on a death march. And Binky is ruined.'

'He's what.'

'Ruined Schultz.'

'O boy the joke of the night. Twenty servants or something in a castle and quarter of a million going into his coffers.'

'You don't believe anything do you Schultz. Except that you think you're a fucking genius. And of course that's what you are. Erica you fucking Valkyrie downhill slalom skier come up on the fucking table with me, the two of us will do an Irish topless fucking jig to entertain the nonbelieving likes of the fucking genius Sigmund Isadorable Ziggy Ziggy Schultz. And watch us. Schultz. Come sit up here on my throne which takes all six of these girls to carry it up out of the cellar. Erica the Valkyrie, mein Gott. Her English is not perfect but her fucking and dancing is.'

Skyscraper Erica the top half of her apron down with two pear shaped breasts bouncing high above Schultz's upturned eyes as he suddenly goes into a paroxysm of sneezing, clutching the edge of the polished mahogany. Noble seizing the birthday cake from the table, placing it in safety on the floor by the sideboard. Topless Bradford Myrtle throwing a bun across at Manchester Caroline who takes a roast potato in each hand to fire back, her right arm wind up sending the potato smashing on the side of Myrtle's head and knocking her topless right out of her chair. Madame Dipompididor rushing to descend upon Despicable Deirdre, grabbing her by the hair and yanking her back off Lilly from Lee's Place around the corner.

'You dyke stop fucking my girls.'

'Take your filthy hands off me. I'll fuck anyone I like you old hag whore.'

Deirdre upon her feet swinging a punch at Madame Dipompididor. Madame Soignée leading Margot to safety. Excited dogs snapping at ankles. Lilly up and coming from behind to grab Dipompididor's hair. Screams and screeching, blows raining, scratches gouging in all directions. Blood pouring down Dipompididor's face. Noble fainting in a heap to the floor. Margot rushing to kneel at his side resuscitating him back to life with a kiss. An angelic smile across Noble's face as he sits back up again licking his lips. Just as Deirdre lands a sock flush on the jaw of Madame Dipompididor of Swansea sending her crashing backwards into the end of the sideboard and slumping down to land sitting arse deep down in her own squashed birthday cake. Flattening thirty six pink candles in the thick cream. The ballroom doors opening.

268

His Lordship's cook peeking in. And quickly retreating, her hand held over her heart. As his Lordship on the table tries to waltz through the cutlery with a barefoot Erica.

'After this last twirl my dear Erica, we will all go fucking filming and exploring up the Amazon. Now get down the other end of the table and bowl me another bloody grapefruit. Bounce it off this mahogany pitch. Show Ziggy Schultz we can sock the ruddy thing for six. And spatter with citrus fruit the smug commanding look I so regret remains forever on my grandpapa's smug bloody face. No socialist he let me tell you.'

'O my god, your Lordship, please, I beg of you please stop. This is getting dangerous. There's thousands of quids' worth of damage already.'

'Schultz success has made you lose your charm entirely. Shut up you old Ziggy stick in the mud.'

'And there are fights going on with the girls I can't get into with my balls. Come on, these are heirlooms. And you got strangers you should be careful with here.'

'These are the most dependable wonderful most trustworthy women in the world Schultz that you will ever have the privilege to be among. You must learn how to enjoy danger in your life. Hold on to your balls Schultz. The topless oil lubricated indoor rugby is soon to start. You ain't seen nothing yet.'

Erica standing grinning above Schultz. Wagging her breasts down at his alarmed upturned face. Juggling the grapefruit from hand to hand. And now wagging her arse in a hula as she turns towards his Lordship down the other end of the table and slowly winds up.

'Ah after I bowl his excellent Grace with the grapefruit I maybe go give Schultz a free friendly waltz upstairs. Because I remember now I see him on television.'

Erica's long arm sending the grapefruit on one bounce up the table to connect with his Lordship's polo mallet. The yellow skin smashing to pieces splattering up on the glittering crystals of the chandelier.

Noble ambulatory again moving to capture the poodles on their leads. Bradford Myrtle running around the table screaming as she attacks Manchester Caroline and they sink their talons in each other's tits. Madame Dipompididor wiping the great white blobs of cream off her arse as she gets to her feet. Turning to pick up the remains of the cake. Charging back down the ballroom. Behind the wax figures of Bonaparte and Churchill, Deirdre with her arms locked again around and kissing Lilly. Madame Dipompididor two handedly shoving the remains of the cake between both their heads. Deirdre, big breasts heaving, eyes disguised under blobs of whipped cream, lashing out with a round house fist, missing Madame Dipompididor and connecting with Bonaparte. Whose jaw comes off in a chunk to fall on the floor. A new horrified face at the ballroom door. A dignified lady in slippers and dressing gown. A gold pinned white satin scarf at her throat, her grey hair coiffed, her nose sniffing suspiciously in the air and peering through a lorgnette. Noble holding tight to the last captured dog on its lead and holding one yapping under an arm and frozen still as he looks up imploringly at his Lordship and clearing his throat to announce.

'Recess milord. Recess. Shall I ring the bell. I do believe it may be time to call recess, if it may please your Lordship. And if I may so respectfully advise, Nanny is here.'

And so
Should it please
Your Lordship
The blasphemy
Should stop

The fog lowering again and thickening this night in Mayfair outside his Lordship's thirty two room mansion. With sixteen bathrooms and a rumoured dungeon down in the wine cellars. Which Madame Soignée said would some day with what already had gone on in here tonight make it a London tourist attraction. And in which commodious premises at two a.m. Nanny brought some semblance of order to the proceedings. But not for long. Wow. Because Rabbi, when Noble rings the bell for recess it was just like starting the second round. With me still starving and dipping a piece of toast in the bowl of caviare. And during these few peaceful seconds stuffing it in my mouth to chew it down so that I could fast ladle out another mouthful. Before it went wild. And it was wild. Deirdre the Dyke covered in whipped cream, kicking Napoleon's jaw she knocked off, across the floor. Now attacking the wax effigy of Churchill, knocking the cigar out of his mouth. Then shoving her hand up the gowns of the lady effigies. At the sight of which his Lordship is going shouting, entirely berserk.

'How dare you you old dyke do that up those ladies' frocks.'

Deirdre grabbing a giant crystal bowl of fruit salad and going for his Lordship as he leaned to rearrange the ruckled up hem of an effigy's gown. Dumping the lot down on top of his head. Just as the dogs are loose again. One crapping a real load on the floor. Which whoops. Madame Soignée has just stepped in it. And I can't help laughing. For the first time in days. Or is it months. O my god. She's slapped my face. With bedlam beginning all over again. And the Skyscraper trying to jump from the table and hang on to the chandelier. Her fingers only reaching to tinkle the ends of the crystals. Coming down one foot in the caviare bowl. Fuck it. Let her. The caviare still is delicious. And now jesus christ the Skyscraper is in a heap landing in my arms. And ouch my balls. Her voice may be deep but at least her breath is sweet.

'Big boy that's what I think good English parties are all about. Swing from the chandelier. They hung this one too high. What do you say big boy you show me what you've got and I give you a good fuck up in one of these bedrooms.'

A strange medieval rustic pair of hunchbacks appearing in the ballroom doorway to carry Noble away. Who finally fainted for the full count seeing his Lordship drowned in peaches, pears and apricots. Schultz taken by Erica and led by the hand. The end of a torn shirt sleeve hanging off one arm. Sneezing up the main stairs. Holding on to the banister and blowing a nose. O my god Rabbi. I feel like I'm going up these steps to more mayhem and slaughter. Sigmund it's a miracle you even got back out here to the front hall like this. I know Rabbi, I know. And I even passed an elevator I have never noticed before in the front hall disguised in the wall. Into which that pair of hunchbacks dragged Noble. And into which Nanny disappeared. And I only got to the balcony landing and looking down, what do I see but his Lordship trying to escape out the front door. With the greatest struggle of all time taking place. As he kept shouting. I must go to the casino. The hunchbacks returning out of the elevator to grab him. And I felt as they dragged him away backwards across the tiles and into the elevator screaming and kicking that I was betraying my best friend. But jesus when you're in a loonybin why not also be loony and go up these fucking stairs. And how could I resist these endless long beautiful legs in front of me. Slalom should be a good Hebrew word for instead of downhill going upstairs. It was like I was going to climb Mount Everest. And holy jeeze, I swear, I really was for only the second time in my sex life intimidated. From the top of that long wonderful body she just kept turning around and looking back down at me with that sultry smile. A fucking beauty she is too. If only she had washed her hair recently. I thought I could even vaguely hear coming through the chimney his Lordship still bellowing.

'Come get me the fuck out of here Schultz.'

The Skyscraper removing her apron and lighting a candle on the mantelpiece of this exquisite bedroom. Lace everywhere. Icons on the walls. Tapestries either side of the massive four poster bed. I tell you Rabbi I've had long nights in my life before. But this is already after the long train ride down from Scotland, the longest night of all the long nights in my life. With right now the worst of worst things happening just as I drop my drawers. With my prick suddenly hanging down ashamed like an overcooked piece of spaghetti.

'Hey big boy what happened to your testicles.'

'Nothing. They just got a couple of scratches.'

'I love maimed men.'

'Honey I'm not maimed.'

'Hey big boy that's too bad. It excites me.'

'Sorry to disappoint you honey.'

'Hey I like you, you little squirt. Usually I scare the shit out of guys like you.'

'Well honey I don't know what you're doing but you're sure not scaring the shit out of me.'

'Well then come on big boy let's see it get up.'

'As a matter of fact honey talking about elevation how tall are you.'

'I am six foot eight and one half inches and do not make the joke to ask how it is up here in the clouds. Because on my back I am as you are on your back on the same pillow, the same height.'

'Touché honey. Touché.'

'Hey parlez vous français.'

'Honey, my French is a little rusty, all I'm fluent in is a little Yiddish but maybe just so we keep track of things tonight what do you say we keep talking English.'

'You betcha buster. Hey you got a nice body.'

'Yeah, it's not too bad is it.'

'Hey big boy, you know Kierkegaard and Rilke.'

'Hey honey I've kind of had a long sort of day and I don't know if I'm up to getting into intellectual areas tonight.'

Rabbi I never thought it could happen. My prick as limp as a piece of lox. And I was dying famished to have a hot pastrami on rye with coleslaw and a pickle. Standing there wondering if the candles gave enough light and if I should look in the mirror sideways to see how my profile was doing. Jesus I couldn't for the life of me stop staring at her big massive bare feet spread out on the floor. Her fucking pinky toes were as big as my big toe. O my god and between her toes there's a whole bunch of caviare sticking. How do I suggest licking her feet. And then jesus you'd think I had enough surprises already this last twenty four hours. When suddenly without warning this fucking big slender beautiful dame bursts into tears sobbing like Niagara Falls. Holy fuck. I mean like uncontrollably. She collapses back down to sit on the side of the bed. Taking her head in her hands. Jesus. Rabbi. Next tell me about physiology will you. I suddenly had another surprising surprise. The top profile of my prick which when I looked down on it had a horizontal hard on which was two miles long. I was so embarrassed. Like I was only twice before, having an erection which wouldn't go down at my aunt Rachael's funeral. Uncle Werb told me go have a pee. But my other aunt Naomi wouldn't take her eyes off it. But tonight I must admit it's giving me a frisson of confidence. Like I was standing on the steps high school graduation back in Woonsocket giving as I did once the valedictory address on behalf of my school classmates. And I got a hard on. Had to side step back behind the lectern. But parents were so enthralled in their seats that they all stood up at the end to give me a standing ovation which amazingly, increased the angle of elevation of my prick two more inches. With my cousin Saul's parents so hot under the collar with resentment and jealousy. Which reminds me when Saul and I were eleven he bragged he could get a six second hard on, till I beat him with five seconds. But shit tonight Rabbi my prick came up in three seconds. Sigmund it was four seconds but who's counting.

'You shits. You shits. All of you are fucking shits.'

'Hey honey. I just knocked on the door of this house tonight to see if there was a robbery going on. Don't include me in the moral judgement will you.'

'You big millionaires in rich mansions exploiting the lower classes. I come from an equal society.'

'Honey you were having fun downstairs for christ's sakes and you got gold sovereigns for it.'

'Debauched aristocrats.'

'Honey I may be debauched. But I'm no bloody aristocrat. I'm an American.'

'Shits. Shits. That's all you are.'

'Honey join the sunny side of life for a second will you. This is his Lordship's laugh clinic. And he's just a happy eccentric.'

Erica hanging her head convulsed in another paroxysm of sobbing. Her shoulders folded forward like wings. Her lungs heaving catching her breath. Schultz crossing the soft carpet to her and putting a hand on her shoulder. And had to stand sideways so the erection does not wave in her face.

'Hey kid, jesus don't cry. Everything's going to be all right.'

'Get your hands off me. I am a prostitute.'

'Well, overlooking the contradiction in terms, no you're not kid. You couldn't be if it worries you. It's all in the mind.'

'I am. I have sold myself. To get money.'

'So honey what could be better than selling it. It's an all cash business with low overhead. With the plant and machinery already available. Plus it's a proud tradition honey. The first form of paid entertainment.'

'Don't you fucking try to give me any romantics big boy.'

'Hey come on. I'm not giving you romantics. I'm giving you economics. Women do worse things than this to get money.'

'What's worse.'

'Honey they fucking well marry guys, that's worse. Shit kid how old are you.'

'None of your fucking business.'

'Hey come on you don't have to take up morals right now, I'll put a few quid investment in your film up the Amazon. Hey come on, what is it a documentary. Maybe even get his tightwad Lordship to take a piece of the action if we make him production manager. I'll go talk to him right now where the hunchbacks have him chained up down in the dungeon.'

'Don't joke. I'm a serious artist. I have already half the film in the can.'

'Kid I'm a serious investor believe me. For the other half of the film to go in the can. This is what I call a special investment situation. Shit piranhas. Anacondas. Cannibals. Showing the real natural world in its glorious normal habitat. It's a real big possibility for big family entertainment in all media.'

'I need forty five thousand dollars. So don't kid me.'

'Honey that's peanuts for something that could be for big family entertainment in all media. Unless honey it's all close up action of you fucking the wild jungle Indians. Then we could be X rated with restricted viewing.'

'I tell you please don't joke me. I need the forty five more thousands of dollars.'

'No problem honey. No joke. We could spread the risk. And advance you a little at a time. Fuck honey by radio telephone right from on the fucking banks of the Amazon I could set this up with Hollywood and do presale distribution deals. But let's keep the atmosphere go ahead honey like in the word voom. Honey look what I got here for you. It's up a mile long.'

'I don't want that while we're talking business. I know you fucking guys. And all the big talk. Don't shit me big boy. I've been in St Tropez with these wops, krauts and all kinds of fuckers, big yachts, big helicopters talking this big talk. All they wanted was to fuck me for novelty.'

'Holy shit honey, forget I said anything. But I'll fuck you for your charm. If you'll just be charming for a second. And then all the novelty will come naturally.'

'Hey what's all about this show. This Margot dancer says she's in. You got a show.'

'Honey now all I got is an unrequited hard on which has just genuflected in abject disappointment. And the correct time on my watch says it's three twenty a.m. and it's time for me to go home.'

Rabbi I stood there. She sat there. In this utterly gorgeous feminine room. The thought of novelty was really getting to me. Here I am in one of his Lordship's houses where he's conducting a fucking circus and totally under the control of his nanny. Correct that. Where he is totally out of control. And in the custody of his nanny. Who jesus even had the pleasant presence of mind in the mayhem to say to me 'I'm sorry Mr Schultz if you've been inconvenienced in any way. Basil does you know indulge in his high spirits. Please do avail of our hospitality for the night. It is quite a wretched fog out. One can hardly see one's lorgnette held in front of one's face.' Jesus what a sweet sweet old lady. That you could wish was your mother. And never again will I ever wonder what his Lordship does for fucking.

'You lousy Americans.'

'Hey baby I may be American but I'm also European acclimatized a little.'

'When guys see me coming in America they run a mile. Now you walk away. What about the investment you put in my film.'

'Look honey it's after three a.m. and you want to talk business. Come about five tomorrow or shit I mean today, to my office at Sperm Productions.'

'Fuck you, you joke some more.'

'Honey Sperm was a typist's error when we were forming the company. It was supposed to be a good healthy sounding word like sphinx or sparta. And so honey on that semantic note I shall leave you.'

'Fuck off then. You shit.'

'Boy. Goodbye. Miss Charm.'

'Hey why do you go.'

'What. Honey. Tell me. Are you giving me encouragement to stay.'

'Where you live.'

'Honey that's an international secret everybody knows. But I'm not telling you. Suffice to say I just cut diagonally across the park and hope I don't trip into the Serpentine. So long.'

Rabbi I closed the door. On what could have been the biggest opportunity for a new experience that never yet happened to me in my life. Relationships should be in sickness and in health, in sorrow and despair but shit never in racial hostility against Americans. Correct that. Hostility against Jewish Americans. Gloom goes with me walking down these magnificent stone curving stairs from the third floor. In America it would be the fourth floor. Past the portraits of his Lordship's ancestors. Listening to see if I could hear anything. And all was quiet on this Mayfair front. Rabbi I'm thinking of my whole life. My two lovely little twin daughters. That Priscilla, that fucking wife. Whose vituperousness is never ending. And keeps me away from two little creatures I adore and love. When she spat at me it burned a hole in my suit. Told me I was a penny pincher. When cheapness is a matter of honour and principle. The only time that so called helpmate and I ever got on was when she was sick in bed. And day and night I would nurse her. But when I was sick in bed she not only left me there to die but tried to hasten the exit starving me to death. And two insights. Louella is just like my wife. Rabbi, believe me, marriage is the grimmest fucking invention ever invented. Sigmund sometimes the worst wife is better than no wife, it at least, if you don't commit bigamy, stops other women marrying you. Holy shit Rabbi I admit that's one hell of a wonderful fucking advantage, but you don't expect me to put myself at the fucking mercy of that bitch ever again and be torn to emotional ribbons. Christ a few stones' throw away from here those guys at Speakers' Corner are carrying their big signs, Prepare To Meet Your Maker. The End Is Nigh. Sigmund you should not behave as if death is just around the corner, just in case it is. Rabbi, that's the kind of thing his Lordship would say. Locked up in his own dungeons in this traditional old fashioned kind of life he lives. Christ maybe I should just get the fuck out of here straight to the hustle of New York. Where the Broadway production is going to open. And where there's always action. And where there's always the smell of money. Even in those summers I walked down Seventh Avenue broke. Blast of heat up from the black asphalt. Waves of hot air from the engines of cars. Flashes of sunlight burning down reflected from the high buildings. Heated clouds of black exhaust hovering over the streets. Christ tonight has made me homesick. On the hot street corners vendors selling sunglasses in the sun, umbrellas in the rain. Scarves and ear muffs in winter to shield the ears from frost bite and noise pain. Here they should be selling fog horns to the pedestrians and they ain't.

Schultz pressing a button for the light in the entrance hall. Opening all the latches on this front door. Jesus I can't wake Jorricks this time of night to come get me in the car. But my god the fog is even denser. I can't even see the railings on the porch. Cold dreary. Christ dare I go out there and down the steps. Out into venereal safety. The door's open. The fog blowing in. Christ. Turn around Schultz. Take risks. Go voom. And hey Schultz what the fuck are you doing walking out of here like this in the first place. Jesus I need my head examined. Back up there on the bed upstairs is the biggest, if I can pardon my own pun, tall sensation of all time who if I can't fuck her could be a featured lead in the chorus line. Jesus let me get back up these stairs two at a time. Shit where's the door to the bedroom. I'm lost. Jesus that must be it. Christ no. I could be arrested by the hunchbacks who one of the whores said were out of one of his Lordship's forests on one of his estates. I'm on the wrong floor. One more up. And soon I'll be swinging from one of his Lordship's trees.

Schultz in the dark on the next landing. A shadow at his shoulder. Who the fuck is this. O jesus. It's a god damn bust of a statue on a pedestal which nearly gave me a heart attack. Maybe it's Kierkegaard. Who said something like mankind was haunted by an unconscious despair. Boy as I open this door I'm haunted by a conscious tingling in the gonads. Tiptoe quietly in. She's still stretched out. Face down on bed. Head sunk into the pillow crying. The candles still burning. What a scene this is for my autobiography one day. Never are my clothes in history ever coming off so fast. Holy shit, I didn't notice that before. Right there, big as life size on the wall. His Lordship's sister, Lady Lullabyebaby. Her picture. Her both eyes staring right fucking well at me as I stand here naked. And she was the hardest toughest woman of all time. I don't know if it was courage or just her ornery meanness but her honesty was like a scimitar lopping off your legs cutting you always down to size. There she is cream and peaches complexion. Hunts foxes. Owns half of Knightsbridge. And was another woman I briefly loved. O god and I'm still getting involved with people's sisters. And this big creature must have a brother or two who I'm going to avoid knowing. Rules I made long ago it seems but christ it was nearly only yesterday when I said rule six. Don't screw unstable women. Horror and sex don't mix. Now I'm mixing together insanity, prostitution and the risk of my prick being shortened by piranhas up the Amazon. Just creep over. Jesus she could think I'm a burglar after her gold sovereigns. Just lie down beside her so we can both be the same height. That's it kid, move over. While I rack my brain to make some kind of introductory conversation.

'Honey I'm back.'

'I know you were coming back.'

'You did.'

'Yeah.'

'What the hell I thought a cold night let's keep warm together.'

'I know what you thought. You thought you want to try the novelty.'

'Hey honey, you're an attractive kid. You know you don't dance half bad.'

'I ski better than I dance.'

'Well what do you say we give you a whirl. In the chorus. Dancing not skiing.'

'I could make more money in prostitution. I let you give it to me up the arse.'

'What.'

'The backside. For three hundred quid.'

'Jesus for three hundred quid honey I could get my prick cast in bronze and shove it up the front side of an angel in heaven. But let me take an option.'

'But first you whip me.'

'Honey, jesus, I'm no sadist.'

'I am no masochist but do you want to try whipping.'

'Honey, there are no whips in this room. And this time of night I wouldn't know where the fuck to start looking for lubricants either. Hey by the way how much does whipping cost.'

'Get your belt. I let you whip me free of charge. I have these pairs of stockings you use to tie my arms and legs to the four posts of the bed.'

Sigmund, remember you are a good Jewish boy. Don't whip ladies. Rabbi I have no intention. I had enough trouble with a zipper on my trousers and I'm not going to start pulling a fucking belt off me and end up choking myself or something. Plus the last thing I want to do is go fooling around looking everywhere all over this place for some kind of grease to go up somebody's corn hole even when I'm invited.

'Honey excuse me I'm getting out and am going to get dressed again.'

'Don't leave me alone. Don't leave me.'

'Honey, look let's just have some normal love.'

'Five lashes give me. Then I give something normal.'

'Why honey, do you want lashes.'

'Because I'm a bad girl.'

'Jesus honey that makes sense. Where's the stockings and just let me get my belt. My usual charge is fifty guineas but for you kid since you're in the trade, maybe I'll throw in a little discount.'

'I am not in the trade. I stop. I give back the sovereigns. I am me. Erica.'

'Jesus honey now you're getting a bad case of the romantics. Keep the fucking sovereigns. And I just hope I can give you pain.'

Anyway Rabbi, my family have never been invited to join the Rhode Island social register. But on top of everything I knew it wouldn't be polite if I didn't at least make some kind of stab at administering her five lashes of my belt in case she felt more rejected and humiliated than she already was. She rolled over on her face stretched out. A mile long. I tied the four ends of her to the bed. And there like two little soft hills, her ass. I wound up. Fantastic. Wham. Resounding right across the twin summits. Wow did it transform her. Like a miracle. She was whimpering and then purring. For good measure I gave her seven. You gave her eight Sigmund but who's counting. I am. I just gave her nine. And for each of the last six she said harder, harder. And she's looking back up at me with the most beautiful gorgeous soulful eyes. I untie her. Then she reaches up with her hand and takes mine. I couldn't believe what was happening. I sneezed. Then tears came into my eyes. This poor fucking big beautiful creature that I was beating. She was an impresario just like me. And after a few welts across the rear end she was like becoming the softest most pliable plaintive female human being. Like you dream women should be. Driven to prostitution to save her art. Even offering to be cornholed to get the extra investment. And the first fucking woman with whom I have something deep in common which is as profoundly life threatening as show business. Taken by her hand. I lie down on her. For the closest encounter of a venereal kind. Feeling not a particle of pain in my balls. Wiggling around on top of the pink welts laid across her white mounds. Still softly moaning. Putting her arms and legs around me. It was like being wrapped up for Christmas and Rosh Hashanah combined. No further trouble trying to get her to see the wisdom of using an already more than adequately lubricated canal. Learning for the first time in my life what a woman needed. Rabbi tomorrow I swear I got to find where to buy a cat o' nine tails. Sigmund, always when you know exactly what you want you never find a place selling it. Plus not everything with women is solved with a few lashes. Rabbi believe me, Priscilla is the perfect subject. Only in my enthusiasm I'd dislocate my shoulder like I did playing lacrosse. What you learn in the marvellous maturity of Europe they never teach you in American high school. And now this disciplining women stuff is only a recent most sudden insight in my life. Wow. Even as I took two steps towards her outstretched hand, my prick shuddered with an extra rigidity of excitement. Hey, your Lordship I really like your happy as a king laugh clinic. Even the couple of times Erica smiled with her beautiful teeth down in the ballroom was worth stumbling through the mud, bushes and fog. The sultry way her lips parted as she looked back down at me far below climbing behind her up the stairs. Fucking hell forty five thousand bucks I could siphon off from my percentage of the gross. Give the poor kid a chance to get out of prostitution. And then get into something worse. Like the abyss strewn terrain and blood thirsty cut throat treachery of show biz. Her tongue sticking in my mouth. We're eating each other's germs. An entrée this good who cares if I get a disease for dessert. Boy there sure are semantically sane and insane ways to use this language. Shit she asks about Kierkegaard. Who said you have to be God to know what God knows. Rabbi you lived twice as long as Kierkegaard. And knew what he knew three hundred and thirty years before he did. And hey honey do you know about Korzybski. Guess what he said. Mankind is by nature cooperative. And shit tonight the two of us couldn't be a better example. What could be more cooperative than using my belt as a fucking whip landing nine nice magenta stripes across your ass. Solving my problem with women for all time. The ruinous thing for my future is I've never had a fuck like this. My prick just dipping gently in, gently out. An orgasm starting at toe tip. Going up my legs and hanging around my knees before transcending through both my thighs and exploding my brain in a whirlpool of ecstasy with celestial choirs howling to high heaven. Correct that. It was me howling to high heaven.

'Honey for christ's sakes don't start crying again. I'm putting my clothes back on honey because I got to go. You're a good girl. Christ I'd even go as far as to say you're even a little bit wonderful. And never mind the novelty. But honey, just out of interest what were you doing coming out from behind the ballroom door downstairs.'

'I was making my début.'

'Your début. For what.'

'Into prostitution. Madame Dipompididor said Lord Nectarine has a preference for virgin whores who have never fucked for money before and who have him for their first customer.'

'Holy cow honey. Virgin whores. Will the wonders of his eccentric Grace's perversions never cease.'

'It was my formal introduction. Madame Dipompididor has the difficulty to find genuine new whores. They all tell lies and are clapped out old slags and scrubbers. And when she does find a girl who is not lying they fall in love with his rich handsome Lordship and they abandon the prostitution.'

'And jesus honey it's clear why.'

'Why.'

'Because, honey, of his Lordship's wonderful philosophy of happiness which all women I've ever met unanimously concur with. And jesus what a fucking generous host and entertainer he is.'

'I look his Lordship up in Debrett. And he is there.'

'Sure he is honey. With a lineage as long as your arm.'

'But why does he sing that song, the aristocracy is falling down, falling down.'

'Well honey, because maybe he sure ain't putting it back up, back up.'

'Hey you know what, you little squirt.'

'What honey.'

'I like you. And I like his Lordship.'

A smile at last out of Erica as she sees my arm go through the empty hole of my jacket. It really is a gorgeous four poster bed. I'm bending down tying my shoelaces. Wow. When she climbed up on top of me. Her nipples hardened like acorns hanging down from her breasts. And slowly slowly going up and down on my prick from its hilt to its tip. It was like being straddled by a giant spider. And my back feels broke. The crotch of my pants still wet. Lost the jacket sleeve downstairs. Now I'm out of my mind wondering what kind a secret life his Lordship leads giving débutante balls for virgin whores with hunchbacks kept down in his cellars. Who jump out of nowhere in tweed caps and knickerbockers to clean him up off the floor when he's pissed. Jesus and he once told me vanity had made me one of its greatest victims. He practises what he preaches. Him without a shirt, shoes and scratching himself up under the armpits like he had fleas. But christ this kid could have a real hot project. Upgrade it from a downmarket documentary into a major feature film with a team of scriptwriters. When I first suggested to his Lordship that we might go into the film business he said that I was perfectly suited to the philosophical rapture that Hollywood indulged in but such a move was sure to invite miscalculations of the most inordinately dangerous variety. Boy and now his Lordship, the Skyscraper and I could be balancing in a canoe as we paddle up the Amazon. And when it tips over and we fall out, if we get to the shore without the piranhas tearing us to bits we'll all then get spears up the ass.

Schultz crossing in the candlelight to the bedroom door. Opening it. Turning around to face Erica sitting up on the side of the bed. Her hands hanging between her open thighs, her head bent forward, her hair hanging down hiding her face.

'So long kid. See you at my office. Or see you another time maybe. Put some clothes on so you don't catch cold. And holy mackerel there's no reason for more tears.'

'There is. Madame Soignée say I have to get out of here. Madame Dipompididor say that Madame Soignée, with the big emerald pendant, take his Lordship away in her red Ferrari sports car.'

Honey
That's better than
The hunchbacks
Shoving him in a dungeon
At least together
They can go
Voom voom

 **21** The sun these days coming up earlier over the rooftop of the Ambassador's house across Arabesque street. The weather warming with gentle mists. And rains from the west tickling the window panes. At dusk each evening a gentleman with a black bag welcomed in the door by Jorricks. And led up to Schultz's bedroom. Stethoscope put to his chest. Temperature taken.

'Ah Mr Schultz judging from your last sample of blood you are coming along very nicely.'

'I'm glad doc, this bed gets pretty boring.'

'You must still take it easy. Plenty of fresh vegetables, garlic. Tomorrow begin a little mild exercise. Goodnight Mr Schultz.'

'So long doc.'

Jorricks entering Schultz's bedroom. Big Ben tolling nine. A stream of cars and taxis arriving at a reception at the Ambassador's across the street. Ladies in gowns and tiaras alighting and climbing the steps. Faint echo of names being announced within.

'The Ambassador sir really does keep this street busy doesn't he sir.'

'He sure does Jorricks.'

'A pity sir you were too poorly to attend. Ah let me fluff up sir's pillows a bit and is there anything I can get.'

'I'm fine just have a spoonful of honey and just lie here.'

'Goodnight sir. Sleep well.'

'Goodnight, thanks Jorricks.'

Schultz turning out the bedside light. A glow coming in the window from the street lamp. Take a deep breath. Stare up at the spider moving across the ceiling. Wriggle my toes to see if my motor reflexes are still improving. After the longest, saddest spell of loneliness I've ever endured in my life. All as a result of his Lordship's party. And jesus once inside all the time like a little kid I was waiting and dying to watch the candles on the birthday cake being blown out. In this bed four and a half fucking weeks and in delirium half the time. Triple pneumonia, and migraine nightmare visions of suffering from hepatitis, non bloody ruddy specific urethritis and athlete's foot. The only consolation being my testicles are fully recovered and haven't swollen up to the size of grapefruits with some kind of plague. But a gap left in my mouth where Deirdre the Dyke knocked out a tooth which never would have happened if, right at that crucial time when I was leaving and said voom voom to the Skyscraper, her smile hadn't been so endearing that it made me take off all my clothes again and get back into bed. Such memories of that night should even be excluded from

284

my unexpurgated autobiography. Deirdre the Dyke came stealing without a sound into the bedroom and tried to slam a cricket bat down on my ass that would have nearly broke both hip bones if it weren't for a foot thick duvet. Trying to get at Erica, the fucking weight lifting woman was like a tiger. Her clothes off and a huge two way dildo sticking out of her. Since the fight with my mother in law I never thought such a nightmarish event could ever come again. All I could think of was making my bar mitzvah and some obscene female intruder breaking into the synagogue. Not that I care that nobody has any god damn morals anymore. But shit this fucking naked apparition coming at you in the semi darkness. Looking for its own selfish indulgence. I was up the Skyscraper and it was a time for supreme civility, this dyke with a left hook that took Napoleon's jaw off. And fucking wham. Across the backside. It was all adrenalin without ecstasy from there on in. Jumping out of bed, already tired, shivering and nonplussed, I was fighting for my life back and forth across the bedroom. Feinting left hooks trying to land my right cross. Fucking dyke was a kung fu ju jitsu artist. Grunting and screaming. Going into paroxysms of hostile poses. Nothing worse than fighting a woman when you're stark naked. Especially when she's with a dildo hanging out of her. Rabbi a fucking unedifying sight let me tell you. And the Skyscraper did nothing. Just waiting there on her back for me to get killed. And then the dyke landed a blow. One tooth behind my canine knocked hanging loose. Then I'm spitting it out. Thought I could even hear his Lordship loose again, shouting out Schultz where are you. But it could at that stage of the battle been merely wishful thinking. Then everything suddenly went blank. Something hit me from somewhere which I didn't see coming. I woke up on my back in the middle of the floor. A cricket bat lying next to me. Erica and Deirdre the Dyke gone. And a pain across the back of my neck. I rang Jorricks. He came with Daniel. They had to support me back down the front steps. Which I had come up just to see if his Lordship's house was being robbed. Rabbi let me tell you. It's the last time I'll ever behave like a good citizen.

'Good morning sir. Breakfast.'

'Holy christ. Morning. I went out like a light Jorricks.'

'It's eleven sir.'

'Eleven. O my god. I was totally unconscious.'

'Lord Nectarine asked if he might call upon you sir and I took the liberty of saying yes.'

'Yeah that's OK Jorricks.'

'Indeed sir. I believe that may be him at the front door now.'

'Show him up Jorricks.'

The bridge of the breakfast tray placed over Schultz's knees. Curtains opened. Sunlight pouring in. Tall brimming glass of fresh orange juice. Look at this non kosher breakfast. Baked ham. Poached eggs. Swiss cereal. Wholewheat toast. Cream. Croissants. Normandy butter. Black cherry jam. Baxter's marmalade. Piping hot aromatically wonderful coffee. All the newspapers. Holy shit what a gem Jorricks is. Does all the shopping. Won't let Daniel even buy apples. If nothing else that's the one big signal thing that's good in my life is my household staff. It's like now I have a secretary, maid, bodyguard and nurse all combined. Jorricks with his little notepad. Wanting to know if I'm going to be feeling well enough to be leaving for New York next Wednesday or Thursday and listing what he has to pack. Each day keeping track of the temperatures and weather not only in New York but Chicago in case I might detour to go there. Has Daniel undergo inspection every morning for dirty fingernails. He even wastes time walking back half a mile all the way to Harrods to return two slightly overripe tomatoes. And I forgive him while Daniel who is usually looking across the back garden with my binoculars at that lady undressing, is polishing the car and taking care of the pigeons and I'm disturbed with phone calls and people getting the idea that I don't have a butler. Yesterday my first day out. Chauffeured around the park. Rug over my knees. Daniel sitting next to Jorricks while I played Ave Maria and watched the public getting their umbrellas blown inside out in a rain storm. I was like the Queen of Sheba. Hey no. Correct that. I was like the Ambassador's Emperor King Zumzimzamgazi. Then I had for the first time up, dinner. Watched the news on television. Rang the theatre to check the gross. It was up another miraculous thirteen pounds sixteen shillings from the record of the previous week. Then I thought fuck it, have something that's not good for me. And Rabbi I tell you what isn't good for you becomes good for you when you get your vintage Napoleon brandy and coffee the way Jorricks serves it. The glass warmed. The piping hot coffee. The molasses sugar. The silver spoon gleaming on the saucer. A chocolate mint sliver on a silver plate. Holy shit my toes tingle with excitement just as I hear his feet coming up the stairs. Guess all I lack in life is my own pair of hunchbacks. And he and Daniel have really kept me from being bothered by interviews and publicity. Plus the guy, like the best hotel concierge par excellence, is a walking encyclopaedia of information on share prices, companies, best airlines. Knows the layout and seating of every theatre in the West End. And in the middle of the long nightmare he even helped negotiate my loan to buy Binky out. With a banker who on top of the usurious interest, asks for a piece of the action out of the show. Jesus these money lending fuckers know when they think they can squeeze the last little bit of juice out of you. And today is only the second time his Lordship has dropped in.

'Lord Nectarine, if I may, sir.'

'Show him in Jorricks.'

'This way milord if you please.'

'Hey come in. Jesus Basil, you're all dressed up.'

'A wedding Schultz. To which I am on my way.'

'Hey sit down and have a cup of coffee first. Well as you see I'm still recovering. But no complaints.'

'I shouldn't think you would have Schultz by the manner in which this butler of yours appears to be ministering to you. One can hardly believe he magically materialized from an actor out of work.'

'He even does a bit of chiropody for me.'

'Good god Schultz you mean to say he actually puts his bare hands on your naked feet.'

'Holy shit, you don't have fucking well to use words like bare and naked.'

'I'm afraid one must Schultz, especially where butlers are concerned. There are certain obligatory restraints of which one must remain conscious.'

'Hey I was incapacitated. You make out like I'm compromising myself or something.'

'I hope I haven't in the least suggested such a thing.'

'He gives me the major city weather reports, and even if it's cloudy in Monte Carlo.'

'Awfully good coffee this, I must say. But why Monte Carlo Schultz.'

'Shit isn't it fucking obvious.'

'No Schultz it most certainly is not fucking obvious.'

'Well I might fucking suddenly wake up and suddenly want to go there and be a practising tax free Buddhist, that's what's obvious. And hey what about you and your butler.'

'Ah my poor old Noble, I fear I've had to send him off to Brighton to calm his nerves by the seaside. But then let us hope Schultz your butler may finally succeed in stopping you running in circles all over the globe.'

'Yeah well that's where I'm presently planning to go. All over the globe. Where no one is going to be sure where the fuck I am. With my god damn wife's lawyers licking their chops over my assets and now they got dates set down for hearings. They've even seized two of my London bank accounts. And lucky I just emptied them both. Some fucking thing they call the right of angary. I mean how the fuck does one ever have a few minutes peace of mind thinking you can trust anybody.'

'Peace of mind Schultz, is achieved by always assuming to be betrayed. And then one can await the pleasure of the contrary. Giving of course meanwhile no one the benefit of the doubt.'

'Jesus your Lordship sometimes you simply leave me speechless.'

'Well Schultz I hope this news doesn't leave you speechless. What on earth did you say to this tall Scandinavian lady. She says you are backing her and I'm the production manager on a bloody film up the Nile.'

'The Amazon it was.'

'Good god. I don't care if it's the bloody Mississippi Schultz.'

'Hey jesus I didn't say nothing.'

'You apparently said enough Schultz to have her appear arriving in my front hall with twelve cases of termite proof luggage, six safari pith helmets, mosquito netting, three large movie cameras, sound and lighting equipment and following parking the whole mass of stuff, she sat down on a bag and refused to move. Said you'd promised her forty five thousand dollars.'

'Holy shit.'

'Well you might say holy shit Schultz. That is only the tip of the iceberg. However meanwhile I should be most appreciative should you inform the young lady before I may have to rudely do, that my house is not the production office for her film.'

'Hey christ let her hang around in your fifty bedrooms a few seconds. She's built like a brick shit house not only could she be like an outstanding symbol for the feminist movement but also a lead in the chorus line of the show.'

'Well you put her in the chorus line Schultz but please get her out of my one kitchen and house where the lady also appears to have ideas of giving a dinner party for her friends.'

'Hey jesus why don't you trust me your Lordship, at least where women are concerned. The kid could have a hot property.'

'Well while trusting you Schultz and especially where women are concerned, there's also more than a rumour that you took advantage of Binky's rather eccentrically disturbed sister.'

'Hey where are you getting all these crazy stories from.'

'Never mind Schultz but adding to Binky's personal troubles at this moment, that profoundly beautiful not to say entrancing lady is with a small entourage indeed heading this way south.'

'She's not is she. Hey christ all this is going to ruin my appetite in the middle of a delicious breakfast.'

'Well Schultz my appetite for lunch has not been improved either, and if you've ever wondered why the Lord Chamberlain informs that the Queen regrets due to other commitments that she is unable to attend at our little show you have but to read this little note in this first edition of this evening's paper in Londoner's Diary.'

WRIT SEQUEL TO BACKSTAGE BEDLAM
WITH ROYALTY IN BOMB SCARE

As the result of a backstage imbroglio at 'Kiss It Don't Hold It It's Too Hot' some weeks ago, the firm of Sperm Productions is now being joined in an action for damages previously brought by the theatre's manager Mr Valentine against the well known impresario Sigmund Schultz, whose wife executed her brilliant dive from Tower Bridge which was watched internationally by millions of TV viewers. Lord Nectarine, the famed schoolboy cricketer and Master of Foxhounds and one of Britain's largest landowners, is a director of the firm along with Binky Sunningdale whose mother, the legendary society beauty, fell to her death recently.

'Holy shit your Lordship.'

'And well you might say holy shit again Schultz. Valentine is claiming that as a result of being socked on the nose by you he now wears a discouraged look which has permanently blighted his usually happy countenance essential to welcoming audiences into the theatre.'

'And that bow tied son of a creepy bitch I'll sock him again and obliterate his countenance. He threw a poor little kid out of the Royal retiring room. Here read this letter.'

Schultz taking a sheet of paper out of an envelope stuck in a book at his side table, and handing it across the bed to his Lordship who takes monocle from a waistcoat pocket and pops it in his left eye as he tilts his head towards the bedside lamp to read.

Dear Mr Schultz, sir,
I am nobody but please, I do want to thank you again so much. I apologize for all the nuisance I caused at the theatre.

I shall forever remain so grateful to you for the wonderful evening I spent at your very enjoyable show and for all the trouble you went to on my behalf. My parents and schoolmaster had warned against my going because of the nudity and vulgarity as they called it, and have confiscated my programme you so kindly had the stars autograph for me. I know the newspapers have said some not very nice things against you and depict you differently but you sir as far as I am concerned are a true gentleman and your show was a delight.

I shall sir remain your most obedient and faithful friend.

Hector Bartholomew

'Ah Schultz what a nice letter. You are sometimes a most surprising contradiction.'

'Hey your Lordship I fight my battles in this world and I might cheat and chisel occasionally some big fucking operations who themselves cheat and chisel but never am I going to stand around and let some big bully dish out unkindness to any poor little kid. And that's fucking gospel. By Schultz.'

'And most commendable Schultz. And I do hope you and Erica the Valkyrie have an agreeably pleasant safari together up the Nile.'

'The Amazon your Lordship. The Amazon.'

'O yes. Sorry. Of course, the Amazon.'

'And up that river is the last fucking place I'm planning to go I can tell you.'

'Dear me Schultz. She seemed absolutely certain you were joining her and her voluminous equipment to board a ship due in a few days to leave King George the Fifth Dock in North Woolwich on the Thames. And even purports reasons to support her certainty that you will be with her.'

'Holy shit my life with the way people are going in and out of it could suddenly be like a train station.'

'You may indeed then sympathize Schultz with my front hall being at this moment used as the main platform. And with my being designated her production manager and having not only to pay the three taxis which were necessary to transport her gear to Mayfair but also being presented with a bill for the shipment of her equipment all the way from Copenhagen to London.'

'No shit. Jesus. That's a good sign. Kid's a real hustler.'

'Well I have enough matters already severely hustling me Schultz

290

without having to now don a pith helmet to explore anaconda infested jungles.'

'Hey I only casually mentioned maybe that her Amazon picture had possibilities. Your name never came into it and was only mentioned as maybe taking a fraction of the action.'

'Well as to my taking a fraction of the action Schultz do let me also inform you that upon that particular past evening she also claims as her fraction of the action that she got raped.'

'Raped. Hey come on. I don't believe this. What is this blackmail. All I did was whip her.'

'O my god Schultz. So it is true. You whipped her. You mean you actually visited bodily harm upon her.'

'Hey jesus don't say it like that. Nothing is true. It was normal whipping I was invited by her to do. She was a willing fucking participant. There was fucking well no raping.'

'And Schultz I suppose you may have wondered how you got knocked out.'

'Yeah. Who the fuck did that.'

'A kung fu blow chopped you down from behind. Which Lilly from Lee's Place around the corner employed trying to save Erica.'

'Save Erica. Hey this is lies. Deirdre came storming in with a dildo.'

'Good god Schultz what ever kind of bloody disgraceful event were you involving in.'

'Hey jesus your Lordship. Involve. Don't look at me like that. I wasn't involving with anything. I just took my belt off and gave her a few whacks across her bare ass that's all.'

'You mean you slashed her naked buttocks with your leather belt. O my god, Schultz there could be scars used as evidence.'

'Hey come on. Cut out this word slash. They were just common ordinary everyday fucking red welts for christ's sake.'

'O my god. Welts Schultz are not just common ordinary everyday things. Especially when such word is intoned by leading counsel echoing it from the walls and ceiling in a court of law.'

'What do you mean, court of law. She was asking even for the lashes to be harder. Come on. I told you. She requested chastisement. I was asked. And I admit I fucking well for a change liked giving it too.'

'Lilly claims she was peeking through the door and witnessed you sadistically assaulting Erica who appeared helpless.'

'Hey look, that fucking pervert horny Skyscraper also asked me to tie her to the bed.'

'You tied her to the bed Schultz. O my god. It was menacing aggravated assault.'

'Hey. This is blackmail. I feel sick. My wife's lawyers are already trying to deny me custody of my children on the grounds of moral turpitude. And this is all that is fucking well needed to crucify me.'

'And did you while she was helpless in bondage introduce your organ into her.'

'Hey I fucked her. She was out of bondage. I undid the stockings. And let her loose.'

'Undid the stockings. O my god Schultz. First you must have ripped them off her to use as ligatures. This evidence is going to sound appalling when given under cross examination in court. Schultz you are had by the balls. You tied up the lady. Whipped her. And now you admit possessing her sexually. I suggest you have your forty five thousand dollars ready to invest. It's up the Amazon with you. O dear Schultz you really are you know a most dangerous guest.'

'Me dangerous. Holy shit your Lordship. You don't obviously remember that fucking night do you.'

'Of course Schultz I don't. One has such nights precisely not to remember them and to be obliviously extremely happy during the time one is having them.'

'O boy, this news has set my recovery back by two centuries.'

'Must rush Schultz. Thanks for the coffee.'

'And thank you your Lordship, for the sentence of death.'

'Ah not death Schultz. Indeed I think new life. Tonight I understand our little show opens on Broadway. And I trust that will be a happy event pouring yet more shekels into your secret coffers.'

'Jesus yeah. Tonight's the night. Amazing I nearly forgot.'

'And I nearly forgot Schultz, to tell you. Erica says you have made her pregnant.'

His Lordship smilingly nodding his head as he leaves. His footsteps going down the stairs. Front door closing. Rabbi I'm fated. Just when I'm regaining my physical confidence again with my testicles at last with the stitches out bouncing and swinging free and not dropping off like dried figs, they now go and get me into more catastrophe. And O my god. Pregnancy. No. No. It's a lie. His Lordship's joking. It can't be. Correct that. Holy shit it could be. The only consolation I got left now is the hope I got that with all these new problems all the diseases I could be still getting will run a mile. How could my nervous sperm travel all that way. Like three thousand miles up the Nile. They'd be exhausted. And what I discovered was his Lordship at previous of his little parties liked the household staff to gather round him in the bathroom while he takes a bath. Said it pleasantly reminded him of his childhood when his three nannies attended upon his ablutions in his grandfather's castle. And on that fatal night I heard his totally pissed Lordship who is as strong as a fucking ox, fighting like a ferocious tiger, with the whole household mobilizing to at all costs restrain him from going out to gamble and losing a fortune in a casino. And with the help of the hunchbacks Madame Soignée finally locking him in his bedroom. Then, threatening to jump, he broke out onto a rear balcony and was shouting socialist slogans out over the Mayfair back gardens. Imagine, he calls me dangerous. And then as the hunchbacks go in to quieten him, his Lordship is hanging off the balcony by his fingertips and drops fifteen feet down into a bed of roses and escapes. Which he did through the basement of Madame Soignée's house next door. And out on the early dawn quiet streets of Mayfair he was knocking on doors asking if they had any exotic whores inside, preferably of an Oriental variety with low slung asses, because the Oriental buttock had a distinctly delightful contour of which he was most enamoured. The Japanese Embassy being not that far away, he knocks there. The Vice Consul comes to the door in his pyjamas and nearly had him arrested. So jesus Rabbi here's the quiet guy who for years I wondered what he did for amusement. And it's simple. He just hires for a high price what is impossible to get at any price. And I know I keep bringing up the subject but is there anywhere I can go in this world to escape women of the past and to recommence the search looking for a trustworthy faithful woman of the future. Sigmund any second now like his Lordship you could have an unfaithful bunch of them sitting on your front door step, who maybe ain't going to let you escape. Jesus Rabbi what a little leisure has done to me. Sigmund you should get back fast to having to struggle to make money again.

'Ah sir, let me take away sir's breakfast.'

'O yeah Jorricks thanks.'

'Shall I draw sir's bath.'

'Yeah Jorricks draw it.'

Schultz slowly sliding out of bed. Putting his feet in his skin clinging kid skin slippers. Shuffling slowly to the bathroom. Pulling down sky blue silk pyjamas. Sitting on the toilet. Thumbing through a yachting magazine. O my god, look at this fucking beautiful one hundred and fifty two foot motor yacht. Transoceanic. Sleeps twelve in the owner's party plus crew. Twin cat engines. Two one hundred and twenty five kilowatt generators. Sophisticated electronics. Seven thousand mile range. To cruise the entire world. Quality, beauty and elegance afloat. Dining saloon seats twelve in luxurious comfort. Bow thruster. Underwater viewing ports. Boat deck for helicopter. Radar. Master suite with adjoining private study. Panelled teak main saloon. Jesus it could be just what the doctor ordered. Fucking anchors aweigh boy. Fucking anchors away. Ding dong go the dildos. Holy christ all kinds of crazy delirious notions are still going through my mind. Still feel weak. Lost weight. Wow in struggling to take a crap I don't even know if I'm constipated or not. And christ what's this I'm suddenly hearing. A mewing meow like from a cat out in the back garden. But shit, which is I think coming up at me out of the toilet bowl. Which if it is, and it must be and I can't believe it, is actually coming out of my rectum. O jesus Rabbi, shitting is the one thing I don't want to go wrong right now in my life. Sigmund then don't look for trouble, a yacht will give you more disaster than constipation. O K Rabbi, just let me now go for a little sail and get into my bath without breaking my ass. Which speaking of asses O my god. Maybe the whole fucking idea of pregnancy ain't so bad. Producing a whole bunch of skyscraping basketball players. The mere thought now of Erica's non Oriental but nevertheless beautiful mounds. O momma meo. Such cheeks so lofty slung. And my own custom made cat o' nine tails. Landing lashes on one of the tallest pieces of ass in the world. And feeling like a midget, no shit, it was wonderful. Forget the frisson you get from climbing Mount Everest. That belt smacking and her little marvellous twinge and squeal of pain. Jesus nearly just like the sound that just came mewing out of my ass. Then the sultry smile on her face looking up. Inviting me down. Her voice saying, hey big boy, even made me tremble. But Rabbi, before I fade into the middle of an erotic dream in this nice warm soothing bubble bath, let me tell you. In strict confidence. There is nothing like tangling with a rampantly raunchy lesbian which the Skyscraper turned out to part time be, with her arms and legs wrapped three times around you and growling and sucking everything in sight including swallowing all your toes. Sigmund no wonder you're complaining of athlete's foot. But could you blame me Rabbi, throwing all fucking caution to the wind. With the biggest hard on of my life. Followed by the biggest explosive orgasm that could have got even an elephant pregnant. Sigmund don't worry, you could by my calculations need to get an elephant to carry the big baby you're going to have.

'Ah feel better after your bath sir. And some fresh nice flowers. From the Ambassador as usual. I do think carnations in pink, white and red give a lift to the room. And his Lordship left you these sweets.'

'Gee thanks Jorricks.'

'And we don't want to gloom more than we have to, do we sir.'

'No we don't Jorricks.'

Schultz sitting up in bed through the afternoon. The pleasant outdoor sound of Belgravia going by till Sachertorte and lapsang souchong at tea time. A bird chirping. Put on choral evensong on the wireless as his Lordship does. Coming from a Catholic church in Wales. Jesus I'm going to go pray again in Farm Street Church. Maybe nothing Rabbi will ever bring Louella back to me. Well Sigmund let me give you some kosher advice, that looking for favours and praying to the opposition won't do it. Rabbi, no offence, but one thing I don't need in my life is a Jewish girl. Not tonight anyway with darkness falling. And Daniel bowing every step he takes in his white coat and clean fingernails delivering up supper. Salmon mousse, chicory salad. Wild rice and a pair of lamb chops not gobbled down by poodles. Watch the news on television. Have my wild strawberries and a glass of Château d'Yquem. While the world is in paroxysms as usual. What is it that's so fucking boring about other people's troubles. Even the Arab Israeli war. Turn off the turmoil. And I'm falling asleep. Going exploring up the Amazon. Hollering from a canoe. For the women for whom I've wept. And the women I must have loved. When your brave face comes off. When they don't love you anymore. His Lordship is hitting piranhas on the head with his polo mallet. The echo of my voice coming back from the jungle forests. Erica's head sticking out from the top of the trees. An anaconda around her neck. Before I fuck you fuck me big boy she said. Even bad publicity can be the best publicity for getting laid. And Sigmund for maybe getting indigestion of the soul, never mind three different kinds of clap. Hey Rabbi jesus be quiet a second here comes Binky down the Amazon in his own canoe. News spreading everywhere he's not got a pot to piss in anymore. And is pissing all over his own foot. He's got a placard up. I am poor but innocent. And now there he goes smilingly waving back as he paddles up shit's creek. Hysterical phone calls are coming in from natives way out in the jungle. Holy shit the fuckers are my wife's lawyers trying to put me boiling in a fucking vat to eat me. She let me die when I was dying. Forget, never, never, never. Remember always, always, always. That she was a fantastically beautiful fuck. And a treacherous traitorous bitch. Is this dreaming Rabbi or is this real. Who's ringing on my private line. Or my god am I awake. When I was asleep. An emergency. Holy shit where's the light and I can't even find the phone to pick it up. If it isn't my parents or my Uncle Werb who said Sigmund, go into diamonds, no girl gets engaged without one, it must then be the guy I had hired in New York to spy on preview performances. But then it couldn't be, he's in hospital after he gets mugged in the alley of the theatre when three guys jump him and beat the shit out of him. O jesus. I am. I'm awake again. And here I am bedridden when I should be there on the eve of Broadway opening night. A hit. It's got to be a hit. At least three thousand miles away gives me the peace of mind of not having to wait with bated breath for the raves of the critics. Jesus am I asleep again. Yes Sigmund. You are in the calm middle of your first good night's sleep. Hey no I'm not Rabbi. It's the phone. Just as I'm on the verge of a wet dream. At this god awful hour of four a.m. when I must have been sleeping like a log and ready to orgasm like a geyser in Yellowstone National Park. Hey Sigmund take it easy on the images. Or else all of North America could need an umbrella. Rabbi I've been a good son. Please don't let anything bad happen to my poor hard struggling mother and father. Holy christ I know something awful's happened. They went for a Sunday ride on the highway and hit something.

'Hello. Have I got the Schultz residence. A Mr Sigmund Schultz please. This is long distance New York calling. I have a party on the line for Mr Schultz.'

'Hello. This is Sigmund Schultz. Who is this.'

'It's Joe. Joe Jewels kid.'

'Holy shit Joe. Don't you know we're on a different time schedule. Do you know what time it is here in London in the fucking a.m. for christ's sake. Why can't you call me when I'm at my office.'

'Because you ain't been there kid because I heard you were home sick in bed. And I'm sorry you're sick in bed but I got a highly confidential offer to make.'

'Shit wait five seconds will you till I wake up. O K I'm awake.'

'That was two seconds.'

'Joe when I do business with you I don't waste a whole fucking five seconds to wake up. In case my shoelaces are already gone out of my shoes.'

'O K kid, I'll forget I heard that. And in case you don't know it you're hurting a genuine friend's feelings.'

'Yeah Joe I can hear your tears falling.'

'Never mind my tears, I got in front of me the opening night critic's reports. So now you can walk away with eighty five thousand dollars that can be salvaged. But I need yes or no right now.'

'Yes or no what. I don't even know what I'm walking away from.

All I know is a cheque for seventy seven thousand five hundred dollars is due me right now on opening night.'

'Kid you're going to be lucky to be able to walk away from sudden catastrophe. I never heard boos bigger or the hisses more prolonged. The show's a fucking flop. And you can forget the seventy seven thou.'

'You son of a bitch. You better believe I'm fucking forgetting nothing. Holy shit. I might have known.'

'Hey I don't mind what you say about me but watch kiddo what you say about my mother. I'm just telling you. The critics have torn the show to shreds kid. I won't bore you with the gruesomeness of the disastrous details. So I'm making you an offer.'

'An offer for what. I don't even know what the fuck I'm selling.'

'The film and ancillary rights kid. I hear you bought out Sunningdale so by my calculation that's you holding seventy percent of the film rights.'

'I got investors Joe who get nearly half.'

'So you walk away with slightly more than half. They could be the only thing to salvage down the line on the basis of a come back tour. The papers are all here in front of me in my deserted office this second and I have just come from a famous restaurant whose lousy name I won't ever mention again in my life where they practically refused to serve me food and the customers nearly stood up to boo me out of the place.'

'Hey come on Joe, who in New York would even waste that much emotional energy even to boo you producing a flop. Who you kidding.'

'Well I'm not kidding kiddo when I tell you that as soon as the first review anybody saw came out I was in two seconds flat left standing totally alone at the opening night party. On my stop watch it took thirty seconds to empty two hundred and fifty people out of the apartment with everybody trying to put on their coats and get out one door. Let me tell you they preferred broken shoulders and putting on the wrong fucking coat to staying there aside from two ladies scratching each other's eyes out over an imitation chinchilla. The hostess even grabbed the god damn drink I was drinking out of my hand, poured it into a flower pot, said it was better used to benefit the plant and told me the party was over. You want me to continue kid.'

'Jesus. Is every review bad.'

'Well a couple of suburban out of town rags thought it was crass and vulgar enough to recommend to their friends to see so that anybody who saw it could do their friends a favour and tell them to stay away.'

'Holy shit, I don't believe it. This could backlash and ruin business here in London. It could close us.'

'It sure could kid, it sure could, sad as that is true. But listen kid. No greater love hath a man than he lay down his life for a friend. And I'm kid doing better than that. I'm laying down my money. So keep your toupee on. Be philosophical about these things. Broadway is always a crap throw. We opened tonight, we let them see it. They saw it and so they all said phooey. Which we got to accept. But deep down kid I believe in this show. I'll keep some of the cast, give it a little artistic brushing up and start out fresh again somewhere that no one's heard of. And where no one's heard of us. Like Kalamazoo, or Chattanooga. And we slowly build up confidence again.'

'The fucking boondocks Joe, will give the cast confidence to quickly commit suicide.'

'Hey kid I got two shows already now out in the boondocks doing sold out business. In eighteen months or a couple of years I will build back this production's London prestige which it just lost tonight in New York.'

'Jesus Joe you got three other shows there running at capacity. I got one, only one, that my whole life hangs on.'

'Look kid it's a good show. But you know as well as I do that these smart wise guy stupid dumb critics out of habit say phooey to five out of six shows. And the public listens.'

'Jesus Joe, you're sounding just like Al Duke. Phooey was his favourite word. Wait I got to think. Jesus. This is really bad. Waking up to this like this. The fucking ultimate disaster.'

'It's the fucking penultimate kid. Tomorrow night it closes.'

'Jesus it's that bad and you mean you're keeping it open another night.'

'Yeah, my mother with her two nurses came all the way from St Louis in on the train, seventy six years old. She's right now in a very nice suite in the Waldorf. I said no mom to the poor sweet dear when she said she was for opening night. I said mom that's too much for your nerves and your bowel complaint. She said Joe I got better nerves than you which took me constipated through concentration camp. I said I believe you mom. But please let me keep you out of the crush and hysteria of first night. So I'm keeping the show open and giving one last special performance just for my mother to see. I already built her a mausoleum where both of us together are one day going to be.'

'Hey come on, you think I'm going to believe all this load of shit this hour of the fucking morning over here. No pun meant on your mother.'

'I love my mother. She's a dear person.'

'Fucking hell Joe. That's great your concern for your mother to see the show. A nice lady I'm sure.'

'That's right. She's all I got left in the world. Except for a brother who's a dentist mixed up in so many law suits from his patients that I'm having to help him pay some of his lawyers' bills.'

'Jesus don't bring dentists and lawyers into the conversation. It's just that I don't get it. No American mother even out of a god forsaken St Louis wants to see a bomb. And nobody especially you is going to lose one extra cent he doesn't have to on a flop. And no one is giving two cents for any fucking cinematographic ancillary rights. The only thing wrong here Joe is why you are.'

'What do you mean why.'

'You know fucking why. I want to know why you want suddenly a bigger piece of the film rights to a disaster. And nobody, and especially not you is ready to fork out eighty five thousand bucks which could earn interest at two and a half percent above the prime rate somewhere. And especially not fork it out to me in the vague hope to build back prestige for a big fucking expensive extravagance that has just laid an egg. And for which now the film rights are not even worth the dust that's going to collect on the contracts I got lying in my office for this show. That's why the why.'

'Kid, calm down. You're hysterical. And hey by the way my mother's Austrian, born in Vienna. And her Wiener schnitzel and apple strudel are wonderful. And holy shit kid this is a long expensive phone call but it's worth at least telling you you should take some kind of pill for your paranoia. They got beautiful recent chemical inventions.'

'My paranoia Joe has more than fucking once saved my fucking life and I ain't taking no pill for it made out of any recent chemical invention.'

'Do I have to say the numbers again. For one last time I will if I have to. Seventy five thousand United States dollars. New and crisp cash in a bundle. I want full cinematographic rights. Are you listening. I'll take the risk on a future tour.'

'I'm listening Joe. And ten thousand just fell off the price.'

'That's because of the cost of wear and tear on my nerves kid. You throw in your London share of the film rights.'

'Throw.'

'Yeah throw, kid.'

'I'll throw up my guts first, Joe.'

'So you don't want seventy five thou. Well don't say I didn't try, kid. The tour's dead as of now and I'll salvage what I can. Some amateur outfit wants to buy the sets.'

'Jesus fucking christ. I never should have sold you this show in the first place. When you even underpaid for it.'

'Don't be a bad loser kid. By the way, that friend of yours Freddie Joy. A fresh rose is on her grave each day. Why did a beautiful girl like that behave the stubborn way she did. I hope you weren't the influence kid.'

'Don't you fucking well bring up that girl's name to me Joe. As if I was the fucking cause of her death.'

'Nobody said anything kid. Nothing. She was just one of the most beautiful girls of all time. She was even fun to be with. That's all. And I'm glad you gave her my number.'

'I'm hanging up this fucking phone.'

'Hang up kid, it's your funeral. But any time you feel like detouring from the fast lane to the crematorium, ring me. The money is waiting for the next eighteen hours only. And by the way kid Al Duke was in the audience, a nice sweet young girl with him. He was so enthusiastic with his applause that he totally knocked his toupee off. So long kid.'

Schultz putting down the bedside phone. Clanking on its cradle. Black darkness. Again coming into my life. When I thought a dozen times these past weeks I was already from disease dead and fallen down into the abyss. To join Freddie Joy wherever that lovely creature's soul has gone. And now the very moment my health starts coming back and my balls are beginning to once more tingle with life, a new fucking abyss is yawning, the biggest yet. Holy cow, Rabbi here I am thinking of buying a motor yacht sitting a dozen people in the dining room and now I'll be lucky to sit two people in a leaky fucking row boat with busted oars stranded up shit's creek. Plus already a true reincarnation. Al. And it's got to be that no fucking Louella is with him. Because if she is I'll sue that overpriced detective I have following that god damn carpenter to watch him every night go up into tax dodgers' towers. And just like Al to blow his gaskets again killing himself trying to clap and cheer his head off so he can save his sinking investment in the show. And Louella was even ringing up only three weeks ago with me with a raging fever and she purring down the phone hinting again at how she would enjoy the sun on my yacht. Which from this moment can't even be a mythical dream anymore. And fuck a duck. She was at the same time cooking the carpenter my favourite pasta to eat with one

300

of Al's best wop wines. She even told me which wine. Go fuck your carpenter I said. Fucking women. Turn the charm on. Till they get something they want. Then they turn it off into sulking hostility till they next want something. Even at his Lordship's and it wasn't even during a recess, the whores were using his Lordship's laundry room to wash their own personal fucking clothes. And now. Can't bear the thought of it, jesus Freddie Joy. Why didn't the fuck I do something. We could have teamed up together. We understood each other. I never hassled her, she never hassled me. Even with guys propositioning her every five seconds, she could be straight as an arrow. All she had to do was let a little water wash over her face. Unlike every other fucking woman who thinks that after she uses a new cream on her skin or takes beauty lessons that the world is going to dawn in eternal bliss with dumb slobs buying diamonds and ready to drop to their hands and knees panting crawling in their direction. Freddie Joy wherever she went had to always in her friendly manner kick guys in the face away. And christ I don't know whether I'm crying for me or Freddie Joy but I can't stop my fucking tears. Her whole body, her whole whole body with all its soft gorgeous magic, will all be mouldered away to nothing by now. With the silhouette of Manhattan on the horizon. She's just one among all those thousands and thousands of gravestones. That you see there sticking up on the little hills just off the highway coming from the airport into New York. Makes me shiver in horror. Her legs, O christ her legs. How you could never figure out with all the hundreds you see how hers could be that so much more perfectly beautiful. Out of all the legs I've ever seen hers were like no legs that ever lived. Now they don't hold her up anymore. Or carry her dancing across the stage. Forget me not she said. And I keep remembering. She said please let me Sigmund sit beside you on Broadway opening night and hold your hand. Holy fuck I can't stop weeping. Why now Rabbi. Should my mouth go dry and a pain with the dull ache of doom go screaming up my rectum. That word used to be a joke growing up. Rectum, no it damn near killed him. And there's nothing funny now abandoned here a month in this bed half dead with not even the energy to prosecute those fucking tailors over my torn testicles. In debt nearly a quarter of a fucking million to the bank for Binky's piece of the show. The fucking guy's psychic. Knows how and when to get out. Now I could have no show. And instead have three legal actions in action. Correct that. Four. I'm suing a fucking Sunday rag for what they said. Plus now I'll lose if a paternity and rape suit combined is brought against me. I'm going to order breakfast. Wake up Jorricks.

But holy shit momma meo what if he and Dangerous Daniel are up to something together. Even though Jorricks is a fucking saint, even saints have sex lives. The other night I heard suspiciously disturbing noises going on downstairs. Just as well that when I got up to investigate and creeped half way there I nearly keeled over. And had to crawl the last steps back to bed.

'Jorricks.'

'Yes. Who's this. Who's this.'

'It's me. Sorry. At this time of the morning. But would you mind bringing up breakfast.'

'Very good sir. The usual sir.'

'Yeah Jorricks the usual.'

Holy cow. Five past four. And he's ready to go. There's got to be hope. When the Ambassador across the street sends me flowers every day. Grins at me when I wave back out the window. And no wonder. It must be fucking wonderful to be a Muslim, the lucky son of a bitch with a harem with masks on all their faces so you don't have to see any dirty looks. And they know who's boss. And just supply pleasure. While my wife in her twisted embittered revenge issues some new fucking writ. And Rabbi, jesus, such news as this I've got in the middle of the night. That I should now need developing a big hole in the head. Everything I held back for Broadway in order to make a killing of beautiful sweetness. And now ugly and sour I got killed. And have to go running for my life. Joe Jewels's mother loose out of her mausoleum he built for her and her two nurses sitting alone in the middle of an empty theatre. Correct that. No, not alone. The fucking unbelievable Al Duke alive and living is sitting right behind them in an orange sweater under an oxygen tent with probably electronic gadgets keeping his gaskets going while he's pulling his prick trying to get a hard on. In order to harass some innocent young girl he's snowballed with his big international celebrity act. And to her gasps in admiration, ready to beat his chest only he might put his electronic gadgets out of action. Holy shit Rabbi, please tell me all this is still the hysterical hallucination of fever. Because my life is nose diving into a tail spin out of control from high up when I was, even in bed here, carefree happy and nearly on the verge of contentment going bumpitibump over a bunch of clouds with brand new silver linings. Till long distance over my confidential telephone comes the announcement of the end of my life. Jesus they give prizes out to fool the fucking public into thinking something deserved to win. And I didn't win any prizes because I gave the public what it deserved to love. Spent my guts to make a hit. With everybody hindering, nobody helping. I could be a next to nobody now. And back in delirium with worry. A virgin whorer with her Dutch cap off fucks me free of charge and I eternally pay for paternity. Suddenly my life it's like it's inside an isolated log cabin with a grizzly bear trying to break in. O god. At four a.m. I got to do something with my brain. Sigmund listen, do something with your crown of thorns you think you're wearing on your head, take them off and put them somewhere for someone else to sit on. Fight Sigmund fight. Get up to battle, and don't let them do this to you. Holy shit Rabbi they've already done it. Ah but Sigmund still don't let them do it.

Touché
Rabbi
Touché

22

'Good morning sir, I have breakfast. You were asleep again earlier when I brought it and I didn't want to wake you. And did we have a nice sleep.'

'A nightmare Jorricks. A total and unbelievable nightmare. What time is it.'

'I'm sorry to hear that sir. It's twelve noon.'

'O my god. I got to go.'

'I thought I had better wait till I heard you were up. The papers sir. The post. And some rather new marvellous honey. I'd like to know what you think of this tiny bit of pâté de foie gras. It's sixty four Fahrenheit out. A record for this time of year. A nice sunny afternoon is anticipated. Rain towards evening from the west. Temperature is expected to fall.'

'Thanks Jorricks. For everything. Just pour me a cup of coffee and put the tray on the dressing table.'

'Daniel will collect the shopping sir and is polishing the car and changing the oil and doing a tune up.'

'O christ tell him not to. That car's for white gloved specialists who wear face masks when they're even changing a tyre.'

'He claims he's quite marvellous at mechanics sir.'

'Yeah, well I'll believe that when he hasn't got bloody screws left over or lost like he did last time he did something. And the stuff he took off and out of the car he couldn't put back again.'

'Well I thought seeing it's a nice day that you might like a drive. Daniel looks awfully smart in his grey chauffeur's uniform sir.'

'Holy christ Jorricks, he went up on the kerb and flattened a parking meter yesterday. And the two ladies' car he hit last week from behind. Their lawyer's letter is right there about the backlash dislocation they're claiming they got in their necks. Just let him take care of the pigeons and guard this place. Are the pigeons all right.'

'The pigeons are cooing sir. And Daniel will be awfully disappointed sir if he can't drive you sir.'

'Jesus Jorricks O K. But he only gets one last chance. Right now it's life and death battle stations. The show on Broadway has bombed. Critics tore it to shreds.'

'O dear me sir.'

'Holy shit Jorricks are you O K.'

'Just a little unsteady sir. That news has come as rather a shock.'

'I'm leaving for the office.'

'But sir, do you think you should.'

'No Jorricks, I don't think I should, but I got to. I'll just catch this quick cup of coffee and bite of croissant.'

'I'll lay out clothes for you sir. And do drink your grapefruit juice and let me at least put some breakfast down in the car for you. O dear that's the front door. Excuse me sir.'

Jorricks bowing and withdrawing from the presence. Schultz slowly dressing. Donning brand new silk underwear. Slipping on loafers. Black knit tie knotted on a nice broadcloth blue buttondown shirt. Look at the way everything is laundered, folded and smelling fresh. Jorricks is about the most marvellous thing now I got left in my life. And any second soon I ain't going to be able to pay his salary. Or anybody's salary. Or even buy a one way bus fare to somewhere like Hornchurch. Where I could go kick the living shit out of that bloody dyke Deirdre. Who did at least half of what was done to me. And this insistent long ring of the door bell could be more bloody writs being served by my wife. You'd think she'd run out of claims by now. But worse, if West End business plummets, could be bailiffs and debt collectors. Because man, this is a tidal wave coming to wash me right out of these fucking loafers Jorricks has gleamingly shined and here he is again, already back nervous as shit at the door.

'Sir. Excuse me. Daniel is ready and awaiting you at the car sir. But there's a young lady calling. Refuses to give a name. But says she is a personal friend.'

'Holy jeeze, I should need sudden personal friends now unbidden on my personal doorstep.'

'She has it appears accompanying luggage.'

'Is she beautiful with black hair.'

'No sir, she's tall, very tall, with blonde hair.'

'O my god no. I don't need this. Are there pith helmets.'

'Yes. As a matter of fact sir there are. Six I believe. Pith helmets. And much of what seems to be movie equipment. All stacked up out on the front porch sir. She did say something I didn't quite catch in reference to a projected film up the Amazon. Is there something wrong sir.'

'I got to get to the office Jorricks. Bring her into the hall. Keep the front door closed. I'll get out the basement. Then see if you can get rid of her. Like I'm gone on a plane to New York. No. Make that Moscow. Harmless but she's a little bit if not totally nuts. Got some weird fixation of exploration up the Nile.'

'She said the Amazon sir. But I quite understand sir. After you've safely left sir, I'll suggest she leave.'

'Do that. O boy. Today is going to be a day. Jesus I really do need

305

Ave Maria on the car sound system. If a Joe Jewels rings later tell him only ring me at the office.'

'Yes sir. O dear we still are a little bit poorly aren't we.'

'We sure are Jorricks. I'm rocky. But OK.'

'Here let me help you with your coat. Brush you up a mite. O dear I am sorry about New York sir.'

'Yeah Jorricks. I'm sorry too let me tell you.'

'I do believe there is noise and shouting at the front door sir. And sir I hope you're not going to stay in town and miss some nice consommé for supper sir, and salmon mousse. And duck à l'orange. For which I will decant a Bonnes Mares from the cellar.'

'Jesus Jorricks. Fuck a duck. Sorry I don't mean fuck a duck. I mean, holy shit I'm going to be back for the duck. Don't worry. That's wonderful, no kidding. But jesus it could be the last supper.'

'O no sir, O no.'

'O yes Jorricks, O yes. But what you do is, you don't let them do it to you. Voom. Voom. That's how you got to go. And I'm going. Right now. And I'm nearly gone.'

'O dear your private phone sir. Shall I answer.'

'No. I'll catch it. It will be that son of a bitch Jewels. Up at seven a.m. in New York in a panic trying to put me in a panic trying to pull some new wool over my eyes. Hello. Yeah it's the Schultz residence, Schultz speaking. Who's this. Hey come on who's this on my confidential number.'

'Who the fuck do you think it is you schlemiel.'

'Al.'

'Yeah, Al.'

'Al Duke.'

'Yeah. Al. Al Duke.'

'I don't believe this. Is this really you Al. Christ I heard from Joe Jewels that you were alive but I thought he was kidding. Because news was around you had passed on after your gaskets blew for the second time in LA. Hey sorry. Al. I don't mean that. It's just I can't help but put it in layman's language like that.'

'You would wouldn't you think that and use such expression wouldn't you, you schlemiel. And yeah I know, you were looking and waiting for my obit in Variety.'

'O christ. I'm sorry Al. But I mean jesus all this time I've been hearing you were a singed hair's breadth from the crematorium. And hey look I swear this is the best thing to hear from you. I really mean it. I'm up out of a sick bed this second. And let me repeat, it really is

306

great to hear from you. Al. After all this time. No kidding. I mean look we were, weren't we, close good friends. And we let something as silly as a woman come between us.'

'Cut out all the shit. I don't want to listen. This is no social call and this is what I got to tell you. I'll make it short and sweet. The show here is a shambles. Jewels is making an offer you stuck your tongue out at. Which is seventy five thousand dollars to help pay investors back.'

'Holy shit hold it Al. If this is business, call me again on this number in my car. I'm leaving my house Al this second in an emergency. No shit, please. I got a misunderstanding going on right now down on my front doorstep which could be coming closer my way any moment.'

'Like always, isn't it. And the fucking disgrace you're putting an innocent person like your wife through in the courts with two innocent children she's trying to protect from damaging publicity.'

'Al. What is this, a renewed vendetta. Come on. Innocent. She's suing me. She jumped off a fucking famed tourist bridge in front of the world. I got to go. If you want for old time's sake to say anything civilized to me call me in my car.'

Schultz hanging up. Creeping down the stairs. Jorricks motioning from the hall. Proceed. Past the door of the library. Jesus a good place to put her. I got it so happens not only Kierkegaard and Rilke in there but Korzybski. She'll think I'm a genius when I haven't read not one single book of philosophy since I've been in show biz. Because boy you don't need to. It's betray or be betrayed. O christ this stair squeaks. The back garden out there. O god it's weeks since I've been down in this kitchen. Hey hi ya there pigeons. Jesus they're fucking overfeeding you, you all got so fat. God Jorricks even got the paving stones of the floor waxed and polished. Go past the wine cellar. Les Bonnes Mares is next to that nice little vineyard Clos de Tart which also has an entirely seductive wine if I do say so myself. Which shit soon I could be having to auction off instead of groaning with pleasure as all those wonderful bottles go deliciously down my gullet. Open this door. Close it. O boy the outside world and fresh air at last. Just get up these steps. Slow one by one. A beautiful beautiful gorgeous day. The sunlight shining fabulous on the Ambassador's house. Holy shit there he is his Excellency, waving. His big black beaming face. Jesus look at the smile. Wonderful. He's really glad to see me. Up there in his window, welcoming me back out in the world again. Jesus my heart's pounding climbing up all the steps. His Excellency is shaking his hand up and down. He must have seen the Skyscraper. Boy I'll bet that randy black son of a bitch would like to try her for size. Fuck it. Why didn't I ever think of that.

Correct that. I just thought of it. His Excellency with his diplomatic immunity, could arrange for her to go up the Nile and if they ain't got no piranhas they may have crocodiles. And standing right now in front of my house are three ominous looking guys. O my god. Look at fucking Daniel, like he's a war decorated general in the Zumzimzamgazi army. What next, Rabbi. What next. Sigmund, hang medals on him, for valour he's going to need protecting you.

'Hey Gov. Excuse me. You live in there.'

'Who wants to know.'

'We do. We're waiting out here. The girl who went in and hasn't come out owes twenty seven quid to us.'

'Sorry can't help you.'

Daniel stepping between Schultz and the three taxi drivers. Putting out his chest full of medals and rearing up to his full six foot four.

'You heard the good gentleman now, fuck off before you get a beautiful kedgeree made of your ugly combined faces.'

Daniel with a sweep of his hand ushering Schultz in the open door of the limousine. Schultz sinking back into the soft upholstered perfumed interior. Door clicking shut. The long black vehicle pulling away past the three taxi drivers' faces glowering on the kerbstone.

'Holy christ Daniel I appreciate the interference you ran on that play, but strong words like that could make them call the police.'

'Sure the copper on our beat Mr Schultz is down having coffee and chocolate doughnuts with meself and Mr Jorricks every morning. No worry about that. And they'd be arrested for the disrespectful looks on their faces.'

'Well you give that strong arm of the law an extra doughnut then. First to the theatre Daniel where I just want you to drive slowly past. And then to the office.'

'Aye aye captain.'

Daniel frowning deeply, leaning intently over the steering wheel. Cruising past Hyde Park Corner and along Piccadilly. Swerving once, slowing twice, and stopping three times throwing me out of the seat but making a sincere effort to miss stationary and other moving objects. Population of London must have increased with all this traffic. Jesus I love this town. Fucking love it. And being on the top instead of on the bottom. And alas, to which latter I could be again returning soon. Look down there that beautiful vista between rows of these Binky and Basil attended exclusive clubs, with the clock tower of St James's Palace at the end, telling you what a wonderful time it is.

'Ah it's a great chariot this sir, purring its three hundred horse power plus.'

'Daniel just keep the three hundred horse power off the footpaths.'

'Aye aye captain and enough said sir. Now before I was a hospital porter I was a lamplighter up and down and around St James Palace itself. Ah god I loved that life. On me bike in the fresh air in the morning switching off and at evening tide switching on. But now in me latter occupation of hospital porter you'd soon get into the habit wheeling the deceased and that you never had to have a mind about running them into anything.'

'Well I'm not deceased. Yet. Daniel.'

'Understood sir. And you don't mind me making a personal remark.'

'No.'

'By god that's one big lump of an agricultural girl who was out there on the doorstep. You wouldn't mind me enquiring as to her business.'

'As a matter of fact I do mind, Daniel. But just to satisfy your curiosity this once, she's auditioning. I'm going into the circus business.'

'Is that a fact. Well sir I don't know what tricks she has up her sleeve but let me tell you you don't mind me saying she'd do to hold up the middle of any tent.'

'Yeah. A tent. Meanwhile she could hold up and fuck up my fucking life.'

'I didn't catch that Mr Schultz.'

'It was nothing Daniel.'

The limousine circling Leicester Square. Pigeons in great flocks in the park at the foot of the trees. But why Rabbi just when I was sitting pretty, before I even caught my breath, does the threat of financial unhappiness have to come so soon again. Ah Sigmund, always when you're purring on top of the pile of happiness, most of life's blows fall then. Rabbi I doubt I could ever go back to the face slaps. Like my poor father got selling his lingerie door to door. Or the struggle of those long agonized empty afternoons in a dusty office waiting for something to happen. No secretary to shoot the shit with. And always the desperate seconds before five o'clock came. Everyone in other offices gone home. Me still there waiting hoping the phone would ring. My fingers flexing to grab up the receiver off the cradle at the first tinkle. That it would be news to change all the downward trend upward again. The winds of loneliness howling around your ears. Binky and his Lordship long gone to invitations as long as your arm. And then me going out to a cheap Chinese restaurant up some alley. Ordering what was cheapest on the menu. And even then changing restaurants for the next course because it was cheaper up some other fucking dingy alley.

'Mr Schultz how slow now do you want me to go past the theatre.'

'Just slow, not too slow.'

'Ah then slow it is and not too slow.'

The limousine going past the streamer decorated marquee. Lights surrounding 'Kiss It Don't Hold It It's Too Hot', blinking on and off. A dim glow inside the lobby. And just as I thought. Not one damn customer anywhere waiting to buy tickets. Boy do I need two pennies to rub together now. With so many lawyers slathering at the mouth over what they imagine is my staggering wealth. Fuck I should take Jewels's money and run. Shit no. Schultz. Hold. Don't budge. Nobody but nobody like Joe Jewels buys what he can't sell for more. And a lot fucking more. Inveigling even Al to try to convince me he's doing me a favour. Al who with his gaskets fixed hasn't the nerve to call back. The cunt. Jesus his irritating voice is even sounding louder and more irritating than ever now that he's reincarnated again. As a big buffoon dragging little impressionable girls around his big celebrity orbit. And his phone call has left my nerves so bad, I've even forgot to soothe them playing Ave Maria.

'Now Mr Schultz, sure I hit nothing and here we are where you want to be. And shall I wait.'

'Yeah Daniel. Wait.'

Schultz slowly alighting out the car door. Daniel at an elbow shepherding across the pavement between pedestrians. Into the entrance of this old stone building. Smell of stale urine down here in the hall. Christ imagine on this site was forged my whole fucking future what's left of it. This is like nostalgia. Up in this elevator in which it's hardly big enough to get a hard on. And in which I may have also come down in ignominy and terror so many times and ready to dump my guts out on the sidewalk. Turn this old black knob, go through this door from this shabby landing. Which even when it was painted only made it look like it needed another paint job. Into the office after all these weeks. Ferret around in the clauses of god damn contracts. See what there is to salvage out of the fucking precious world I built of peace and prosperity which could now be ending.

'O Mr Schultz I'm so glad to see you.'

'Yeah Rebecca. How are you. Hey jesus kid, what's the matter what's wrong.'

'I'm afraid everything Mr Schultz.'

'Yeah that's what I thought. You heard the news from New York. Is Binky in.'

'Yes he is sir. Please. Please do go right in.'

Schultz moving down the hall. Looking in the waiting room door. No contortionists, ventriloquists, conmen, actors, actresses or mothers with their daughters in tow in sweaters with their big falsie conspicuous tits. No Magillacurdy pounding his chest and pouring champagne over his head. Hey jesus the whole place has a feel of a funeral parlour. Rebecca was like ushering me in to view the remains. Someone's moved my files out in the hall. What's this. The autographed photographs of the Hollywood stars parked stacked one against the other on the floor against the wall. Past all these familiar rooms. Christ where the fuck are the secretaries. Christ the pair of intellectuals are packing up. All their bullshit pamphlets and papers piled high on the desk. Jesus there's already like there's some kind of mouldering decay around this place. My god. An almighty jolt of pain is just gone up my ass.

'O Mr Schultz may I have a word with you later.'

'Sure Rebecca, sure.'

Schultz turning the crystal knob on the door. Silently pulling it ajar. Binky bent over a waste paper basket his foot crushing papers down. And two handedly dumping more in. A fire in the fireplace blazing.

'Good gracious me. I thought I heard a little click behind my back. Ah, my dear Schultz, this is a pleasant surprise. You are up and well again. And in your impenetrable mirrored spectacles no less. How nice. How superbly nice if I may join two such positive sounding words together. Now then, what's this you're at. I hear our good and dear Lord Nectarine Master of Foxhounds and your good and dear self had not that long ago a little greased wrestling with, ah was it mountain skiing girls. One lady topping the six foot six mark I understand. And all accompanied by furniture breaking. Or was it merely a little tête à tête with a very select topless group of the daughters of pleasure.'

'Holy shit Binky don't remind me of that night and of the breakage of such gorgeous antique stuff.'

'But one does remind. Nothing more energizing I think for the male spirit than ladies who smeared liberally in their exotic oils, squirm and squeal so deliciously about in his Lordship's nice ballroom doing their damndest to score a try in one of his Lordship's inimitable indoor rugby games. And especially exciting with his collection of effigies. I was most disappointed not to have been there. One it seems is never invited where one is wont to go. Among girls in their scanties tugging with hands upon the other various bosoms wagging in a downward manner in the scrum. I mean how wonderful you must have found all those naked rear ends bent over shoving and pushing which in turn provokes one to shove and push. Was Lord Nectarine belching all evening as he normally does on such occasions. And announcing loudly as he also does that it is down with small minded fuckers. And was my dear old pal Jill the goldfish swallower there. O and I nearly forgot. The immensely sportiff Madame Soignée.'

'O K Binky you finished. Obviously you heard. The show's a total flop in New York.'

'Ah yes, it must be all about town now. News does travel fast in show biz, doesn't it. Our dear old friend Al back from the dead, was only on the phone the moment before you walked in and he generously supplied one with the further and better particulars. A vulgar pathetic travesty is I believe how one critic put it. Indeed even those nincompoops at the box office here in London are alarmed and also have just tried to reach you. Forward booking is it appears slowing dramatically to a standstill.'

'Fucking hell Binky come on cut the aphorisms and prose, this is disaster I'm here about. I ain't got time for fucking goldfish going down some whore's throat. And you you son of a bitch knew we were going to bomb in New York didn't you. Leaving me with the grains of fucking sand falling between my fingers and minus a quarter of a million quid borrowed from a fucking bank.'

'Dear me, did I. Leave you with such grains of sand. O dear I am sorry. I fear I've got so many other troubles Schultz that that little transaction has totally slipped my mind. But I am always ready to watch carefully to see how acquaintances proceed in life and to be alert to those shoals they encounter, and by so seeing, avoid them oneself. But I do believe you already have the good news that Joe Jewels is trying to buy up the remnants.'

'Fucking Joe Jewels is waiting like he always is. Like a cobra to strike. And do a deal when he thinks he's got my back to the wall.'

'I like your image Schultz but surely a little compensation, however modest, is to be always seriously considered.'

'What the fuck why should you care anyway, you're out of it at a profit.'

'Indeed I shouldn't. And perhaps even don't. You see Schultz for me, it is all too late. Too late for me Schultz. Too late.'

'Hey what the fuck's going on in here anyway. And outside, my files in the hall. Why are you dismantling everything for.'

'Ah what a good and highly pertinent question Schultz. I thought you'd never notice. Or take off your impenetrable eyewear. You see I am inviting the most chic of designers over from Paris to revamp the place. Rid of all this Georgian brothel motif.'

'Hey wait a second. You're burning papers and files.'

'Ah and you spot there of course, that my coat and hat are neatly folded across the chair instead of being as they usually are housed in my little cloakroom which has of course the chairman's crapper and the chairman's basin and in which you unfortunately fractured your deputy chairman's balls.'

'Yeah I see your coat and hat.'

'Well I suggest you hold on tight to yours Schultz. And by the way that video I made of your testicles which got confused in your fly zipper may have to be disposed of to the highest bidder.'

'Come on stop. This conversation is wasting time. I want to know why my filing cabinets are shifted out of my office. And what the fuck you're doing destroying everything in here. And your intellectuals packing up.'

'I suggest you too Schultz go lay pronto claim to your files.'

'What for. You just make damn sure if you're redecorating this place that they go back in my office.'

'Well we wouldn't would we Schultz want the bailiff to cart them off. You know how they are grabbing everything in sight. And poor poor Mario. In the doorway not that long ago, weeping. No more are there to be any of his nourishing seven course slap up lunches. You see there, I have with me an apple and an orange bought off the stall just up the street, from a chap you would never believe, keeps racehorses. A stable of thorough-breds and from whom I've occasionally got a winning tip or two.'

'Hey jesus, wait a second, what is this. Are you abandoning ship. Or are you really redecorating this place.'

'Ah well put in your naval parlance Schultz. And these little stacks of cuttings you see here I shall take with me. Keep to read again on the train. But my word, your wife's bosoms centre spread in this newspaper. Forgive me my dear chap for referring, but they do leave many of the wondrous girls who've sought fame and fortune in these offices looking rather timidly inadequate in contour.'

'That fucking vicious Sunday rag. Only I was sick I would have sued.'

'You see dear chap, I have kept faithful track of your little difficulties in the marriage stakes. You must now indeed be very knowledgeable on that subject.'

'Yeah I fucking well am. Marriage is the first step in a man's ema-sculation. And then in his ultimate insolvency.'

'Dear me Schultz, dear fellow. I detect a distinct note of disillusionment if not outright pessimism in that remark. Join me. A little of my most excellent of excellent ports is left here in the decanter.'

'Jesus I will. And don't worry about the pessimism it's a fucking mountain of misery you detect. I don't know what the fuck is happening here but whatever it is your Paris designer is in for a shock. And I got to fucking well talk to New York in a second.'

'Of course you have Schultz. And please do so before the phones are cut off. Ah but I do believe there is even a rather important looking letter for you here.'

Castle Park
Stoat On The Wold

My dear Mr Schultz,
I do hope you'll remember our pleasant little meeting over a bottle of excellent champagne together in hospital which I now thankfully have done with. I can't tell you how much I enjoyed your wonderful stage presentation 'Kiss It Don't Hold It'. My convalescence was miraculous as a result. God's speed to you in future endeavours.

Yours
Leathers

P.S. By the way how are your pigeons. My tumblers are a treat.

'Look at this Binky. Look. Everyone they love the show.'

'My good gracious me. But this particular gentleman is not everyone Schultz. Dear me you are blasé, rubbing elbows over champagne no less, with one of our most famed and revered military commanders of all time. Marvellous opportunity Schultz for you to pop his endorsement on to a few placards in front of the theatre.'

'Come on Binky, fuck it I've got to get my office back into action.'

'Ah but might I first simply state that following a series of meetings with legal and banking gentlemen in various parts of the United Kingdom and in one or two places abroad over the last few weeks, days and indeed in the last desperate few hours, that my mother's wherewithal including her best castles and estates along with the entirety of their furnishings all of which were deeply mortgaged have had to be disposed of. I fear that my dear beautiful mother, much as were heaped riches upon her throughout her life, by various of her admirers,

314

was upon her death encumbered with debts so astronomical and numerous that in realizing her assets we succeeded in only dealing with the tip of the iceberg. And in my feeble attempts to make up the difference in paying such debts, I have Schultz, with my every investor backing out, been left holding the bag in which my extravagant new musical has just been shoved and now fully weighted down, such production has quietly sunk into the utter depths of insolvency, a word you've just so aptly used. And Equity that marvellous institution for the protection of mimes have declared me persona non grata.'

'First I don't believe this. And second, if I did believe it why the fuck didn't you just let your mother go bankrupt.'

'Dear me. Die in dishonour. And her name and her dear memory be stigmatized. Nae.'

'Holy shit. But why not. What the fuck do you care. It would be sad but she's dead.'

'Schultz you are, aren't you, insensitive to the ways in which some of us still insist to conduct ourselves in these isles.'

'Fuck you're not going to give me that shit that it's the way an English gentleman must behave. Most of whom have been the biggest bunch of chiselling dirty rats I've ever met. Jesus I'm beginning to believe this. The unbelievable. Pour me some more port and let me fucking well sit fucking well down a second if I can find somewhere. Well I guess for my part anyway, it will be a relief you're not riding on my fucking coat tails anymore.'

'Dear me. Your coat tails Schultz. If I do recall correctly your presence here has in these offices, long been one of gentle sufferance. Or perhaps I should rather be less euphemistic considering you did owe this company in the neighbourhood of eleven thousand pounds, and say to your face right now that you, you pathetic little cunt, are nothing more than a fucking jumped up little pipsqueak. O dear, temper. In these last few minutes together, recalling our previous board meetings, I do hope one won't have recourse to rudeness. I therefore as chairman vote to slap my own wrist. Slap, slap, you naughty chairman you.'

'Wow. The black abyss. Holy fuck. Here I am trying to shore up the production. And talk about board meetings. This, if it ever could be called one is one for the books.'

'Schultz just toss me over that photograph on that stack of Spotlights there from which casting volumes his Lordship and I were wont to populate our beds from time to time. Especially with those ladies who listed their Russian as fluent, which one always found was merely a form of fluent rubbish once they were under the covers and we were hoping to hear the exciting tones of an Eastern European tongue. Yes you cunt Schultz on your own coat tails take a seat. One doesn't want to dramatize one's life. But should it give you any satisfaction to hear, your quarter of a million was swallowed up in a trice. And so my dear shrewd Schultz. I am to put it mildly but again bluntly, simply skint.'

'Hey christ look a second someone is undressing in that window across the street. Hey but wait a second who the fuck is this here, with the mask on in this photograph. The utterly gorgeous body looks familiar.'

'She did try her hand at the stage. At singing and dancing as a matter of fact. Gave them all up. Eva. Do believe you must have met. Suffice to say that the world is these days, such a quickly changing place. In the face of all these young pop stars popping. And the young lady's voice trained for arias and other cultural niceties. Which these show biz phenomena on the horizon these days, so lack. But upon which one should have insisted when one chose to make her a star. I opened her up in Brighton. O dear, rather let me rephrase that. I produced her first solo engagement in that seaside town and had to close the next night.'

'O K I get the message, you're broke, your production's abandoned, but this beautiful broad is who you are now fucking.'

'Put somewhat crudely, yes Schultz. But alas I shall not be cohabiting with the dear lady for the foreseeable future. From now on, I shall distinctly lack that wondrous pleasure. Dear me such a barren road ahead. No Mario to cook lunch. No chauffeur to cart me to the station. But good port this, isn't it. Especially taken in the blaze of the fire. Here let me chuck this nice thick file on. However solicitors' letters appear not to burn that well.'

'Jesus Binky enough. Enough. I'm reeling. Let me get all this straight.'

'I have now Schultz no little cosy townhouse. Of course I've settled a spare trust fund producing some wherewithal upon my dear little wife, who has temporarily removed to her parents in the country. You didn't hear that I had a dear new little baby did you. Never having been one for adoring children, I was quite surprised to find the pretty little creature plucking at my heart strings. I do believe I have been dispossessed of rather a lot.'

'Yeah well if my troubles weren't facing me and an albatross hadn't landed on this show, I only wish I could ruin you even more. No jesus, sorry, that was a slip of the tongue. Boy this is becoming the most depressing afternoon of my entire fucking life. With you talking like this. And me having to sidestep the Broadway disaster like the most greatest matador of all time.'

'Ah I like that metaphor Schultz. But as must be obvious my selling out was not due to cleverness, and I can take no such credit.'

'Holy mackerel as if I need this happening to me across the other side of the fucking ocean. Hey come on Binky what would you do if you were in my shoes.'

'Well speaking as if I were in your shoes Schultz, which were I believe paid for out of the production account, I would do little but wait. See how old cobra Joe Jewels behaves. He always seems to have something up his sleeve. Rushing on stage, goosing the mimes. Or even attempting to piss as Magillacurdy does on the footlights and having every newspaper in town herald it across the front page. Indeed one strongly suggests you behave as some long accustomed lawyers do, following an acute skirmish in a litigation, and let the dust settle a little. But I dare say you, you cunning old codger, will manage. You must by now have a nice little bit of the best quality bullion stashed away at your various offshore addresses. And by the way did any of those charming ladies bring parsley from their gardens in the green belt to Lord Nectarine.'

'Holy shit, stop. Come on Binky. Nothing is making sense. I want to know what the fuck's really going on. No fucking vast fortune like you've got evaporates overnight.'

'Schultz you'd be surprised. And in finding out myself it required travelling to Liverpool, to Aberdeen, to Manchester, and even to such far away places as Norwich and Milton Keynes. Of course by the time I got to Milton Keynes, to say I was buggered, bewildered and baffled is a grave understatement. And to refer back to albatrosses, such birds did then seem indeed all over the town shitting from every perch. My how those big birds do shit. And as I quietly went to have soothing tea in a cosy little tea place, I could see such birds' deposit heaped high upon my own planned little musical extravaganza. Dear old Magillacurdy and Margot would have made quite a draw. Given it a wonderful long and prosperous run. Ah Schultz you sit there frowning and yawning. Very bad sign. Suffice now to say the entire premises is yours to rent if you like. Indeed you might also even like to consider the theatre I bought and which a bank has repossessed. Currently available on the market Schultz. The old Mercury as a matter of fact. I had planned to put my little extravagant musical in it.'

'Holy jesus christ. I still don't believe this. Binky is this really for fucking real.'

'I toast you on it with port Schultz. For real.'

'Hey come on there's got to be good news somewhere.'

'One does search in such detritus exculpatory empathic, moot and moonish climes. Such words Schultz being known as fluent rubbish. With which one can fuck up some legal cunt's jargon. Tends to steady the nerves when one is under pressure. Eases the panic. Can recommend it you know.'

'Detritus exculpatory empathic moot and moonish.'

'You've got it Schultz. By god you've got it. Especially beneficial when one is facing things which are considerably worse than bad. Creditors can be like howling hyenas. Whereas a single creditor can be quite pathetic and an object of sympathy. Dear me one such one was wailing so hard on the castle front steps, I dumped a bucket of ice water on him just to change his concern for a moment. But when they come in their many.'

'Christ let me change my seat and sit over here in your soft chair. Hey you got a bag here behind the desk. And holy fuck what's that now. Hey that sounds like someone's crying out there in the hall.'

'Ah. My. You do notice things Schultz after all. One or two members of the staff have taken matters rather hard. Distressing to say the least. Train time is approaching. I am proceeding in a very few moments to Victoria Station. And thence further afield. One does not want to be too sentimental and cuddlesome, but thinking back to moments here, when embattled in the cigar smoke we sat. Sometimes with as many as a dozen lawyers and accountants and meddlers at a time. And we were, with his usually absent Lordship, comrades in arms. You and I against the whole bunch of them. Each minute ticking away and costing at least a hundred quid. For which tidy amount they mouthed their usual inanities punctuated with their whys and wherefores and notwithstandings. And imagine. Not that long ago there could have been that moment when the two of us might have been bowing to receive Her Majesty the Queen. Seen close up a lady of great charm and beauty. Her skin like a peach and her smile welcoming like a mild spring dawn. And I was so looking forward to your meeting her. To watch as Her Majesty extended her hand to be taken. And then you Schultz extending your own to shake her hand and then to hear you in your inimitable way, exclaim.'

Holy fucking
Christ
My whole fucking arm
Is paralysed

A knock on the chairman's door of Sperm Productions. Rebecca's head peeking in. A dusty draught flowing into the room. Schultz seated behind Binky's desk as Binky snaps closed the top of a large leather worn valise.

23

'Ah what is it Rebecca.'

'May I interrupt a moment.'

'But of course. Mr Schultz and I are only just tying up a few last minute little loose ends in here before I depart.'

'I've just learned that the bailiff is soon to be on his way.'

'O dear. It always amazes how quickly gloomy one can get. How much time do you think it leaves me Rebecca. Would you say.'

'I wouldn't depend on any longer than half an hour at the most.'

'Ten minutes will do nicely. You see Schultz we have some kindly person warning us in the bailiff's office. But ah there you have it now. The actual crunch. About to befall. Designer's fees, estate agent's fees, seamstresses, the usual lot. Indeed even a few restaurant and hotel bills. From the less better restaurants and hotels you understand. And the outlandish rumour that I'm in possession of a few valuable baubles. Thank you Rebecca. And do call me a taxi. You see Schultz the offices are about to be besieged.'

'Jesus no.'

'Jesus, yes Schultz. But of course you'll stay to fight them off. Biff bam boom. And from these beleaguered confines maybe even get your call through to New York. But now then Schultz you clandestine dirty filthy fucker you have bedded my sister.'

'Come on Binky go catch your fucking train. I'm already beginning to feel sick to my stomach.'

'Dear me so many last minute emergencies aren't there. My dear beautiful sister. Possibly left in your clutches. And with her considerable trust funds. You know she is the one who alerted me to the use of fluent rubbish. Dear brilliant girl that she often can be despite her affliction of eccentricity.'

'Fuck Binky, I haven't seen or heard of your sister since I left the castle. And no woman is in my clutches. I'm trying to fucking well kick them out of my clutches.'

'Ah Schultz you shout. Do sit down, don't be so perturbed.'

'Perturbed. I'm trying to cope with disaster in New York. And you're accusing me about your sister. While someone's on the way here to raid this place with all my files in it.'

'O dear I suppose that I too am a little overwrought. In these past few days of desperately vulnerable and distressing moments which wax more than wane, I was trying to salvage as much as one can of one's faith in human nature. I had even, would you believe it Schultz, planned a feeble little dinner party at which you were to be guest of honour and to which you might come looking forward to being so honoured. But I am afraid that as the pain of my recent mother's death continues, and the attendant mostly financial circumstances obtain, that plan can only but be put into the future. It seems now I depart into the black abyss of bankruptcy, while you dear Schultz I daresay will go on to even bigger and better triumphs in the theatre.'

'Hey come on, hold it Binky. I'm going to be like I am, just never taking my mind off the round the clock battle. And that's how you should be.'

'Indeed that's how one has been, Schultz. Of course occasionally deluding oneself with the ameliorating unreality that one was merely a thespian taking the stage. Announcing such gems as what the actress said to the archbishop. That'll be a sovereign to shine your mace your Grace. But Schultz in our final moments left, I'd like upon this parting to convey one's most recently received perceptions. I won't deny I have been born to certain social and financial privileges. Which frankly haven't prepared me for some of the rude awakenings one has recently undergone. Even departing here our little cosy suite of offices produces a gnawing sorrow of sorts. And one does so try to avoid such pain, which frankly I don't think I can bear in the proper stalwart manner. Suffering as one does to say what might be a final goodbye to all of you.'

'Fuck nothing has me fully convinced yet that maybe you ain't just going off to the Riviera for a holiday.'

'Ah, what a wonderful idea of course. And on an equally reflective note, Schultz. Do you know it is every bit as much like leaving the dear lady to whom one was wed for many happy years. My own dear little wife. She actually had recently given me a couple of presents. Three pairs of pure cotton footwear made in Turkey with tags that said free size socks. Schultz I laughed when I saw them, having long time purchased a longer variety of sock in Jermyn Street. And then there was another present. The really thoughtfully nice one. Of lavender bath salts. Which suddenly at the last moment she took away, presumably to use for herself. Do you know, I broke down and wept. Ah and just so do the harsh realities of life come upon one. Those two presents were one of her few acts of affection she'd ever displayed towards me. But when I plaintively enquired after the disappearance of the bath salts, she told me that now I was broke I was to fuck off.

Not nice is it Schultz. In one's own front hall. In what was once one's own comfortable little townhouse.'

'Whew Binky come on. Have mercy. Have mercy. Don't try to convince me anymore. I'm convinced. Catch your train will you. I'll stay and beat the shit out of the bailiff.'

'But you see my dear chap, I'm afraid that it's had the most utterly gruesome effect on me. I shrink away now like a dog kicked in the face. And am even ashamed at my own dismay. But you see, there is even more to it than that. When she told me to fuck off, I actually packed my little things together on the spot. Minus the bath salts of course. And as I opened the front door latch to go she suddenly wanted me to stay. And I found myself not that many moments later, opposite her in bed. And doing such things are very unsuitable for parting, don't you think. Then suddenly I don't know what overcame me. I found myself having fucked her saying fuck you my dear, I am leaving. Most of the night however, had already passed. Her sobs there in the dark under cover of the counterpane were heartrending. I could hear her terrible agonized cries even as I descended the stairs with a guilt so agonizing it racked every micromorph of my being. Then down in the library with dawn breaking and my little bags about me I had an acute attack of sorrow. I too wept. And as I wept. Tears plopping on the paper, I composed these words. In a poem to her. Shall I read.'

'Binky I got to call New York I swear to christ. Before the fucking bailiff comes and rips the phones out.'

'O dear I keep forgetting no one wants to listen.'

'For fuck's sake, OK I'll listen. Holy jesus. And holy shit Binky I don't know what's hitting me here. Come on. Of course.'

'Ah I knew you'd understand Schultz, how one so smitten might behave. Poetry is always a damn good way to climb up out of one's emotions. And so ready, here goes.

'Where shall I ever look
To find thee now
As you were
When we were both only young years old
Suffering in your sorrow
When last as I left
You were
Turned on your side
With your body that had become
Such a familiar friend to me

Your brown pretty brown hair
Your back shaking in the shadows
Hands pressed at your tears
As you wept and I listened
So wishing with all my heart
That all was not finished between us
Even though it was.'

'Hey that's not bad. Jesus sorrow Binky is good for you. But now I got to really phone New York.'
'Schultz there's just this little tiny bit more.'
'O christ are you trying to kill me. OK go ahead. Read.'

'At least you still said you loved
Me as much as life itself
And would love me
Till the day you died
You reached out to touch me
As if just to touch me
And I took you once more close
And for the hours you slept
Quietly hugged in my arms
As I did so want you to be
For all our lives always there
And you will always be
And that's where
I shall always look to find you.'

'Holy shit you fucking bastard you've got me fucking crying. And you bloody hell never wrote that.'
'And why do you say that Schultz.'
'Because it's fucking beautiful that's why. And because how the fuck could anyone ever get to feel that about a wife.'
'Ah you are indeed an old clever codger Schultz. Your show biz savvy not having deserted you. You're quite right. I thought them so appropriate I stole such lines from a book. But I did, didn't I, for just the merest of moments, fool you and make those words sound as if they were mine. And then there are just these few more lines. Which better perhaps sum up matters at hand so nicely. But of course I believe these words are your very own written by you. And I mouth them merely as a reminder. If you don't mind listening just one more moment.'

'Holy fuck you know, you really are something for the books Binky. I never wrote nothing. But I'm listening, and so is my Rabbi let me tell you.'

'When
You find
A friend
Who is good and true
Fuck him
Before he fucks you.'

'Hey shit that was my motto used in the Coast Guard. Jesus Binky let me use this phone a second. Hello, hello. This you Daniel.'

'It is sir.'

'Look get out of the car. Go to the entrance, fuck up the elevator so it can't be used and stand by the staircase and block it to anyone looking like or admitting to being a bailiff.'

'Aye aye captain. Sure no problem. All identities will be checked, going and coming. And the pertinent parties told there's a recent murder upstairs and the body is on the way down. And the shooting isn't over yet as me combat medals will attest.'

'Jesus Daniel, you got it.'

Schultz hanging up the phone. Binky in his grey tweed herring bone suit and green tie. As he pulls on a black kid skin glove, brushing away a bit of fluff adhering to his pearl buttoned chamois leather waistcoat. A smile on his face.

'Ah Schultz ah. Dear me. I am quite speechless. Having heard your little speech. And you know I was just about to say you couldn't have appeared at a better time. Of course the bailiff will impound various of our little office equipment play things, and our brand new computer which jumps up and slaps you gently on the face to remind that you have just given it the wrong instructions. But imagine having to admit that I am actually glad that you are here. And dear me also having it appears, your own soldier at your side.'

'Binky I got action stations round the clock. Arson in my house. Writs on my doorstep. A wife gone bananas with hatred for me. Danger and betrayal on every fucking side. But boy your worries in the last ten minutes have driven all my worries out of my mind. The clock says five to two. Joe Jewels's office is open in a few minutes in New York. And I want to give that fucker a piece of my mind. But jesus you can't do this just to save the memory of your mother.'

'Schultz I've already done it. And come my dear chap, now that we've got your faithful guard on the building let me tempt you to just another spot more of port.'

'Jesus fuck, pour it. Pour it. That's it. To the top.'

'Ah this is nice isn't it. Little glow of the fire on the sides of the glass, always makes port taste better. And perhaps allows for a moment for me to be quite open and frank with you my dear old Schultz as I know I can be now that we're both going our separate ways and are both quietly sitting down. O dear one does wish one were made of sterner stuff. And could keep the emotions in better check. Schultz I know you do know what it means to be in love. And the condition of emotional exclusivity it seems to impose. Of course one soon finds it translated into the logistics of bathrooms, sitting rooms, cutlery, dishes, grocery bills and the like.'

'Jesus Binky, I didn't say I was going to guard this building all day.'

'Of course not. But you see I do have a last remaining matter. The saddest thing of all is that the wonderful lady in the photograph you've seen, and my isn't she nice.'

'She's nice Binky.'

'Well I have had the temerity to keep her as company. Not as a little bit of exotic fluff upon the side, but for companionship and walks. Which we have often taken together in the not altogether unacceptable area of Westminster. Vincent Square as a matter of fact, overlooking a rather nice cricket playground. Indeed one might think one was upon a pretty village green deep in the Buckinghamshire countryside. And there in a tiny rose bowered house, the little lady has her little flat.'

'I'm the last guy in the world Binky that you have to waste time adding adjectives to tell this story, so you don't have to elaborate. The picture is clear. You have or had a nice quiet piece of amenable ass going.'

'Nae Schultz. Nae. I have in fact rather more. Much more and someone of whom one has become deeply enamoured. Spending as I have many a leisure moment with her as she quietly embroidered her cushions or fussed in her little kitchen cooking up a splendid pasta dinner.'

'Jesus pasta. Don't mention pasta to me.'

'Well of course we did too occasionally take supper of casserole of lamb with parsley dumplings at one of your more staid and traditional hotel restaurants. Ah but more frequently we were seated at her cosy gas fire in her little quarters. Lights of other windows aglow across the square. It was admittedly without a dining room a bit of a squeeze with plates occasionally tipping over on our laps but we managed. One gets a little olive oil soaking into one's crotch. But following such little mishaps we were wont to go hand in hand, albeit sideways, into her small bedroom. Where there was just enough room to pleasantly exercise, if not flagrantly flaunt, one's perversions such as they are, without ridicule.'

'The clock's just ringing bells there and in New York Joe Jewels and Al Duke are just putting on their toupees to go to the office. And boy I'm sitting here wondering what the fuck you're leading up to next.'

'Ah these, Schultz these.'

Binky standing and putting aside his port on top of the stack of casting volumes of Spotlights, taking from both his bulging jacket side pockets necklaces, bracelets and rings. Placing each handful on top of the other in a pile on the desk in front of Schultz.

'Holy fucking christ Binky, jewels. What the fuck is this.'

'A few baubles. Indeed aside from the train ticket and bits of fruit the only valuables that I believe I have left. You know how people are when just before they die they get a wee bit sentimental. My mother had stuffed these where she knew I would find them between my undervests with a cryptic note. You will need these my dear. Signed Mummy.'

'Hey christ. Rock crystal, onyx and diamonds. This necklace and the earrings are Art Deco.'

'You don't say Schultz.'

'I fucking do say. And this is a fucking mid nineteenth century ruby and diamond necklace that would give my Uncle Werb kittens. Even the fucking quality of the mountings are incredible and beautiful. And this is an antique diamond bumble bee brooch. And this for fuck's sake is a nineteen thirties ruby and diamond dress clip. In an underwear drawer she left them, I don't believe this.'

'My my. Schultz I'm simply dumbfounded by your acute knowledge of jewellery you seem to be suddenly displaying. But they will look so nice on my little lady who is as it happens so fond of blue satin.'

'And look at this. Fucking black cultured pearl necklace. And another mid nineteenth century turquoise and diamond necklace.'

'Ah yes put those both aside. They are for Rebecca. And I think will suit her nicely.'

'Suit her nicely. What are you kidding. Hey jesus these ain't baubles Binky you can't give these to anybody.'

'Dear me why not.'

'Because these are valuable. In the trade they would be referred to as important jewellery. There's a fucking god damn fortune here, that's why not.'

'Do tell. Or rather how can you be so certain.'

'You mean you don't know that. What's here.'

'Well I do know some were my grandmother's. Some are presents to my mother from admirers.'

'Hey jesus I should be screwing you not helping you. Well let me tell you, I nearly fucking well was in the jewellery trade. With my Uncle Werb. And I regret plenty sometimes I didn't stay. These aren't paste. They're real.'

'But of course they are.'

'And for christ's sake, fantastically valuable.'

'But surely not extravagantly valuable.'

'Why, you just think by the dingy condition and just in a pile here they're not. I just hope you know what the fuck you're doing.'

'Well in any event Schultz I am pleased to hear your appraisal. But I would be grateful if you would please give those two baubles to Rebecca, and the remainder to deliver to my little lady. It may require your calling more than once. The dear girl is only really there when I'm there. But as the rent has not been paid and she will be chucked out, she I think will be there about the six thirty mark salvaging her few little bits and pieces. She will I'm sure be so glad to see you. She is on the first floor, of number three thousand three nine nine.'

'Jesus I don't understand. You fucking well tried to kill me in deal after deal. Now you're entrusting jewels that I could fucking well walk off with instead of giving them to some doll who can watch cricket balls go flying past her window. Why don't you give them to her yourself and be safe.'

'Because looking at my watch now dear Schultz and before I may be possibly arrested I have only twenty five minutes left to catch a special boat train to Newhaven for which I have the last remaining booked seat I believe.'

'Hold it. Hold it. Can I just say one thing before you do this disaster. This. This. I'm holding in my hand up to fucking light of the window. With it alone you could buy the fucking train. I'm sure. In fact I'm positive. This is D colour. With a D.I.F. clarity.'

'I haven't a clue Schultz as to what you're talking about.'

'I'm talking about a potentially flawless fucking diamond which could be worth approaching a quarter of a million quid. Look at it. A marquise cut diamond. It could nearly be fifteen carats. People kiss. Sorry another slip of the tongue. People kill for such things as this.'

326

'Or fuck Schultz.'

'Yeah but some expensive fucking fucking let me tell you.'

'Ah what a nice little morally impartial discussion we are having aren't we. Pity Schultz you can't join me on my little trip. Crossing the Channel to Dieppe is the longer journey and gives one a leisurely chance to enjoy the bracing sea air up and down the deck while beating one's fists upon one's chest. You know people do make light of it. But sea air does the general physiology considerable good. And I shall be with my considerable appetite late this evening in Paris.'

'And you mean to say Binky you'd actually trust me with this stuff.'

'Ah I must deliberate a second or two on that interesting postulation. O dear the lady in the window across the street has now fully divested herself of clothing. O my goodness. She's actually beckoning to us Schultz. To come over. Do you think she's just seen the diamond you held up.'

'Holy shit, she really is asking us over.'

'Dear me and I have a train to catch. Ah but coming back to you Schultz. No. As a matter of established fact, I wouldn't have trusted you. But then as I found myself joined as a defendant in an action for damages for your having busted Valentine one in the kisser, and amid all my other troubles, I enquired as to why this was so. Then I heard this little tale of the little boy at the theatre. And.'

'Yeah. And.'

'And I trust you Schultz. Sad I suppose. That so much time has gone by not trusting you. But there it is. I now must admit there is something sterling in you. Of course you may indeed rat on me yet you know. But only if ratting were your only way out of a life and death situation. O well. And that doesn't seem to surprise you one little bit that I should feel that way does it Schultz. O dear me perhaps it does, you've gone ashen faced Schultz.'

'You're fucking right I have. If I'm trusted you fucker. I'm trusted. And I'm trusted even when death is there facing to step into.'

'And O dear in a similar coup de grâce situation I suppose I might not trust myself. Ah but if I have any little qualm left it is not the jewellery Schultz I refer to. It is the lady. It is she I would not trust you with. Of course we have dear old Al's Louella as a perfect example. N'est-ce pas. Your unhesitating penchant for snatching another's lady when her usual gentleman appears to have departed.'

'Jesus Binky. Stop. I'm an hour out of my sick bed. What are you emotionally trying to do. Wrench the last fucking vestige of peace of mind out of me. Plus have you got something safe to put this jewellery in.'

'O yes. My apple bag here will do. O my. If I have a sou left I think I might have oysters tonight on Boulevard St Germain with one of those nice big glasses of beer referred to as a Sérieux.'

'Jesus shit that just sent a real pang of homesickness for Paris through me, Binky.'

'Welcome to join me Schultz sit on my knee on the train.'

'Boy for two cents, no shit, if I didn't have this crisis, I'd go.'

'Schultz, I read history at Oxford, managed to achieve a modestly good degree in fact. I disclose this not to thump my chest or crush laurels down upon one's head but only to reinforce my own faith in the observations I must now make upon my lot in life. It might be said I stand upon a precipice. But I rather prefer to see it as standing at the crossroads. A windy one at that. With four possible directions I might take except for the fact that three are already blocked. By the way, folk on the Isle of Man actually go and sweep the crossroads when the world seems against them. But I am without a broom. And for me my escape is not without romance. In the sense that the one road left points to a reentrenchment upon the Continent. And indeed in the direction a once famed poet took in not too dissimilar circumstances.'

'Yeah well your circumstances look to me like they are insane.'

'And Schultz you are, you know, an ever surprising surprise.'

'I'm a surprise. Holy fuck, each second I've been here in the last hour you've jumped something new at me, so that I'm not even thinking of the catastrophe in New York. Except that I can't forget it. Or what stepped up the steps of my house this morning.'

'Well I won't enquire as to what went up your steps this morning but pity Schultz we haven't the evening ahead together to have a moment to take a glass of champagne at Claridges. And to listen there sentimentally to their marvellous little Hungarian quartet.'

'Jesus Binky. Fuck Jewels. Fuck the New York production. Fuck Al. I'll tell Rebecca to cancel the taxi. I'll take you in my car to the station. What the fuck maybe it's appropriate that as you've tried to screw me in every deal we've ever done that maybe this is fitting I see you off to exile.'

'Ah beautifully put Schultz. You get more lyrical and romantic by the second. Dear me, dare I even think we might be described as friends. And gracious me. The lady in the window. Giving us a topless dance. Rather pendulously flapping aren't they Schultz. O dear she must be one of the desperately aspiring people we've had to turn away from auditions. Such can be the really sad moments. People still who as yet unaware of one's demise, approaching one, putting their best foot forward, hoping one will bestow upon them stardom.'

The shafts of afternoon sunlight beaming through the whorls of dust and Binky with the charred end of a ruler disturbing the embers of paper in the grate and ceremoniously dropping another paper into the flames. Phone ringing and Schultz with a lightning grab reaching across the pile of jewellery, to snap the handpiece off its cradle.

'Yeah. Who's this.'

'This is Daniel downstairs sir in the limo. The coast is completely clear as a whistle that would blow a tune for you to march from here the long way round back to Tipperary. Come down at your leisure.'

'O K Daniel, you're sure.'

'I'm as sure as a certainty is sure.'

'Thanks Daniel.'

'Ah Schultz Daniel is a rather unusual name, one does not hear that often. I do believe it stands for God is my judge.'

'Well in this case Daniel stands for danger is my speciality. And let me tell you he is distinctly dangerous.'

'Ah, do tell. What a comfort to know. As I've just this moment dropped my last writ served upon me into the fire.'

'O boy Binky, what do you say. It's time to go.'

'Dear me. Sadly yes, it is. Do take the jewellery Schultz and when I have departed out the outside door, give Rebecca those two baubles.'

'These two.'

'Yes. And do add that trinket you're examining.'

'This is by Fabergé. Jesus I don't know what the fuck you're doing but I'll do it. Fucking hell talk about crossroads this is more like the Tokyo stock exchange after news that Wall Street has just collapsed.'

'Ah yes Schultz one looks now for the calm sensible shafts of sunlight on one's life. Or as my sister might say in her fluent rubbish. My dilemma really nearly is really ordinary and not really extraordinary.'

In the dim light of the doorway to the landing, Binky kissing Rebecca on the cheek as she suddenly throws her arms up around his neck, squeezes, and her hands clutching at his jacket she suddenly lets go. Her grey eyes red. Binky patting her affectionately on the head as he moves away out on the landing. Schultz taking Rebecca by the elbow into her small office. She steps behind her desk, her chin and lips trembling and her hands up to the sides of her face.

'Mr Schultz O Mr Schultz this is so, so god bloody awful. So just god bloody awful. Sorry about the language.'

'Honey this might just all be temporary.'

'It's not. I could overhear on the telephone. At the last minute, everyone to whom he turned. People he had helped, done favours for, wined and dined, one after another, said no to him. No. They said no.'

'Honey, they got to do that. It's the first principle of show biz, is to swim away from the sinking ship or else you get pulled down with it. OK now. It's going to be OK. Just sit down here. Situations like this take a steady hand on the tiller. But right now these are yours. Find somewhere fast that's safe to keep them. They ain't paste.'

'O god he must keep these. Please. He has to. He hasn't a penny. All he's got is his ticket and a few French francs. And it will never take care of him. Who will take care of him now.'

'Jesus kid it's going to be all right, don't you worry. Binky's after all, a show biz battle hardened tough trooper. I'll see that he's OK. He'll be next to me in the car. I'll shove enough money in his pocket. Don't worry. I mean in two seconds he could be walking back in here with the whole town kissing his ass again. Now take these pieces of jewellery and fucking hide them till you go home. And excuse the language. I'll be back in an hour. You keep the home fires burning honey. If New York rings, I'm in my car. Don't let anybody, and I mean anybody, in. We'll fight them.'

'Thank you, Mr Schultz. Thank you.'

Schultz and Binky pausing at the last landing, tiptoeing to peek over the stair banister. Blocking out the daylight, Daniel standing splay-footed in the entrance way. His big gorilla long arms folded across his medals and massive chest. As Binky and Schultz step out and Daniel takes Binky's valise and bows them past. Following them across the pavement and rushing ahead to open the limousine door. Binky sniffing the perfumed interior and picking up the telephone to listen. Daniel slamming his door, turning back to look over his shoulder.

'And sir now in what destination would we direct the three hundred horsepower.'

'Daniel jesus, you did a good job. Now fast. Victoria Station please. This is Mr Sunningdale here.'

'Top of the middle of the afternoon to you Mr Sunningdale.'

'Daniel did the bailiff turn up.'

'He did indeed sir.'

'What happened.'

'Not a thing sir and he hardly had the time to tell me a thing either sir.'

'How come.'

'Well you know now he was in such a hurry that so he wouldn't lose his hat in the rush I stuffed it in his mouth, tied his hands behind his back with me tie missing now from me throat and popped him temporarily in the big dustbin, put the lid on it and before I had a chance to put it back in under the stairs there for the purpose, wasn't it collected and taken away while I was distracted in the midst of another loud altercation.'

'O my god.'

'You see, a woman out of the building across the street tried to gain entry. Made an indecent suggestion she did. Said she wanted to see sperm productions. And as I was on me guard duty I said not likely at the moment.'

'You did the right thing Daniel.'

'Thank you, sir.'

Schultz pressing a button and the glass division rising up across the limousine. Binky humming a tune and beating a rhythm on his knee with his fingers to the sound of pipes and drums.

'Dear me Whitehall this afternoon is looking so nice Schultz. The Admiralty. Horse Guards. My listen. And look. Rehearsing Trooping of the Colour. My what a glorious sight to take with me Schultz. Do hope all's well with the Prime Minister just up that unprepossessing little cul de sac. Always amazes persons from overseas that our empire is run from such a simple unpretentious habitation. And dear me. The Abbey. O memories. That day too when Lord Nectarine took his bride in there. And Schultz you did I believe come stumbling into the vestry your top hat crushed, your tie on backwards, fly open, your shirt front ripped, having broken through a police cordon without your invitation.'

'Come on Binky for christ's sakes. This is serious what's happening.'

'Ah well Schultz. It is along this Victoria Street and in and out the back and beyonds of these narrow laneways that my little lady and I do walk in our cherished and only too brief moments together. She's a great believer in the sensible shoe. And in the mackintosh. Indeed in that pub there we would sometimes stop to have some bitter ale with one of those hard boiled eggs they dip in something savoury.'

Daniel parking the car under the great canopy of Victoria Station. Pedestrians staring and a bobby making way for the vast limousine. Smell of exhaust. Queues of taxis. Roar of buses. Daniel handing Binky's valise to a porter. Inside the station Schultz shoving pennies in a machine for a platform ticket. Binky standing by, beaming a smile. The rhythm of his walk as if he were on a parade ground. And humming to himself Waltzing Matilda. Holy christ Rabbi, sorry so much has been happening that I haven't had a chance to talk to you. Cruising down Whitehall a sprinkle of rain was falling. Just as Jorricks predicted. Last time I was going somewhere on a train I was in purdah. Now I'm entrusted carrying a fucking fortune for the guy who was my worst enemy. Which jesus, he's handing out to women. Ah Sigmund, but they are loyal women to whom he gives such gifts. Jesus Rabbi, that means I know one and could even meet the other. That could make two loyal women in this world. Sigmund who knows keep looking you may find three. Or even four Rabbi, but who's counting.

Binky climbing up into car K. Mailbags being loaded on the adjoining platform. Whistles and chugs of trains leaving the station. Carriage doors slamming. Schultz talking up to Binky leaning out the open window.

'And Schultz as I head off in the direction I'm going, I'm sure I'm already wearing an expression of slight dismay. You are of course acquainted with that slightly apprehensive look the strictly upper aristocrat gets while far from his club and fireside and wondering what the fucking hell he is doing out among foreign woggish and common looking pedestrians.'

'Jesus Binky, please for christ's sake watch it will you.'

'Of course I shall Schultz. You know I did in fact try to ring you last week on urgent business. But at what appeared to be the most inopportune time of eleven o'clock in the a.m. Your deadly serious butler informing me that as you were retired to bed you would be asleep till three thirty o'clock in the p.m. And do, please do, give my dear lady a little peck upon her cheek for me when you see her.'

A woman behind Schultz on the platform tapping his shoulder to get by. Binky opening the train door. An announcement over the loudspeaker.

'The special boat train is about to leave from platform four. All aboard please.'

'Goodness. It's you Mr Schultz.'

'Yeah. Hey who. Holy mackerel. Matron. Jesus.'

'How are your balls, Mr Schultz. O dear forgive me, I am sorry. I mean your testicles.'

'Gee they're fine.'

'I saw your absolutely splendid show four times. And took my nephew and niece. And you've not forgotten have you. I believe we were to take a glass of champagne together.'

'Gee no I haven't forgotten. Hey let me give you a call. And hey let me introduce you. This is Binky Sunningdale. Matron is from at the hospital where my balls got sewn up. I mean testicles.'

'Delighted Matron. Delighted to meet you. And to know you may have attended upon Mr Schultz's very private and we hope, still procreative spheres. We were all so worried about them. Knowing they meant so much to him. Here let me help you on board.'

'Thank you. I'm on my way to see my parents who live in Newhaven. My father's had a fall and is also rather bronchial.'

'Well Matron I'm for that stop as well, which I do believe is the last. Might I have you for a drink while Mr Schultz's invitation is pending so to speak.'

'Yes. Please. Do. I am in seat thirty two. Mr Sunningdale.'

Whistle blowing. From the shadows of the station the light of the sky southerly out upon the tracks. The last carriage door slamming. Another whistle sounding. A green flag waving. Train slowly pulling away. Inside Binky waiting in the train corridor. A smile on his lips as he blows a kiss through the glass of the window. His blond locks forward over his brow. Eyes amused in their blue. And now he's bending over holding his stomach, laughing. But holy christ it just may be he's feeling sick. Boy Rabbi this is really one for the books. Saddest thing is, he could feel me slipping the money in his pocket. And I knew the last thing he wanted was to take it. Jesus and now there's Matron. God damn charming and even nice. But sad as hell in the eyes. Tragic ladies just litter the world. Sigmund, so do broken men. But Rabbi, even so. At the end of the day. And boy I've had some long days.

I'm sure
Still glad
I'm not
A
Woman

So
Am
I
Sigmund

24

Schultz reaching for the rug to put over his knees as the long black limousine pulls out from the roaring noise of Victoria Station. Into an afternoon pouring rain. Motoring around the sodden grass of the little park amid these busy streets and up past the terrace of enormous grey Victorian houses overlooking the greening tips of trees in the back gardens of Buckingham Palace. The rain drops streaking the car windows. A tear falling on the money and an apple left by Binky, hidden in the folds of blanket. Holy shit some guys' principles are hard to believe.

'Fortnum's Daniel.'

'Yes sir. Ah now that's a strange gentleman that Mr Sunningdale.'

'Yeah, Daniel. He's strange all right. Come back and get me in an hour.'

The tinkle of delft. The white tablecloths. A painted mural scene of the Côte d'Azur behind the soda fountain counter. Schultz seated on a grey banquette at a table in the corner of Fortnum's. A smiling waitress putting down a tray of tea and a piece of Sachertorte chocolate cake. The voices of ladies in from shopping, the art galleries, fashion shows, and jesus Rabbi probably some from talking to their solicitors. Rabbi if you weren't already listening on the radio telephone, then let me tell you in a nutshell this is getting to be another long day. The police looking for someone of the description of Daniel. Which means another tailoring bill for another uniform. At least I got him to put away all the medals. Jesus, the awful loneliness I feel. Walking out of Victoria Station to then find the money still there I'd shoved in Binky's pocket. I always believed the guy had no principles. Even on the way to the station as a last ditch try I asked him why didn't he for christ's sakes go to his Lordship who's rolling in money.

'My dear Schultz I would, as I probably will do soon, prefer to absolutely die before imposing my woe on his Royal Amazing Grace. One must leave that old dear, who is indeed as generous as he is amusing, in peace. So that he may remain the very lovable gentle old fool that he is.'

'Fool. Holy shit, he's going to be the only amazing one left solvent after all this.'

Schultz surveying the matrons. Each wrist with its jewels. The exquisite fabrics on every back. Not a care does one of them look to have. O boy. Crush down my lemon with the spoon. Maybe it'll give me vitamin C as I take a last sip of tea. And lick my lips clean of chocolate cake. Go on living a little longer, no matter what happens. Last night I had an unbelievable dream. Priscilla cooking me my favourite chicken with wild rice. Without a trace of strychnine in it. We lived in a pretty cottage in the country. My girls grown up in pretty dresses and I played croquet with them on the sunny lawn. Then I took a rest. I fell asleep in the balmy air, woke up and there my loving wife was putting a tray of tea beside me. The kids were singing a song together in a game with their nanny. And through a crack in my eyelids, I suddenly saw myself happy. In a blissful family setting of a contented marriage. Christ what a mirage. And holy fuck the jewels. How could I go forget what might be a half a million dollars in my pocket. Get up. Fast. Step backwards. And holy shit, what's this now. O my god, my fucking heel is crunching down on something which is a lady's handbag.

'Jesus excuse me.'

'O dear. O dear O dear. I heard something break.'

'It's me lady I did it.'

'Of course you did it. I just saw you. And O dear and it is. It's my mirror. Seven years bad luck.'

'Hey no kidding, I'm sorry madam.'

'Well it's your bad luck damn you, not mine. And it's a highly valuable irreplaceable mirror.'

'O K sure. Let me pay for the damage.'

'Certainly not. My lawyers will deal with it. What's your name and address.'

'Jesus madam it's nearly six o'clock, I got to go. Seven years is nothing and I'm feeling drained and exhausted please take some generous cash compensation and let me walk the fuck out of here feeling like a gentleman.'

'You dare use that language to me.'

'Madam I dare. No kidding. And whoever your fucking husband was. He's lucky to be rid of you. So long.'

A smiling bowing Daniel at the motorcar holding the door. The waiting limousine, drawn up on the kerbstone, blocking traffic behind. Horns honking. The woman with broken mirror following Schultz out through the tables and with a pad standing on the entrance step taking down the licence plate of the limousine.

'Why you rich bloody Jew, imagine.'

'That's right lady, I'm even richer, bloodier and more Jewish than you could ever dream. So go fuck yourself.'

Daniel closing the door. Saluting from the peak of his cap and giving a smiling bow to the lady. Schultz falling backwards on the upholstery and pulling the rug up over his head and face. The smell of wool and dust.

'Daniel take me to Farm Street Church.'

The limousine cutting in and out the narrow lanes through Mayfair and rolling to a stop down this familiar South Street. Past the children's school and their daily babble of voices I remember a couple of times walking by here. The red brick big block of flats. The pub. And the peeling boughs of the trees in front of this church.

'Daniel get me the evening papers, I'm just going in to pray awhile.'

'Right you are captain. And no harm should be befalling you in there with himself the biggest chest thumper of them all, up there looking down protecting you while I'm for the moment on other business.'

Schultz pushing through the doors. Entering this sombre darkness. Smell of incense. Dark figures, their backs and heads bend in prayer. I'm not the only one upon whom the trouble descends. Sitting here in a pew. Holy fuck. Binky. Gone. Busted. Finished. The office under siege. The whole world ended. But anti semitism still alive and kicking. Hey Rabbi they could, everybody, take me for everything. Sigmund, no they couldn't, first your foreskin is already gone. And second you would still have your good Jewish looks. O boy, fat lot of good they just did me in Fortnum's. And shit I was nearly on the verge of shouting out loud. That I am you cunts locked in the throes of a desperate depression on the fucking horns of a dilemma that's double pronged deep up my ass. O boy. I could be fucking next candidate for bankrupt exile. And here I am in the religious candlelight thinking of Louella. Looking for love is the wildest goose chase of all time. On her back opening her legs for the god damn carpenter to fuck her. Jesus that's where all this premature ejaculation has come from. A fucking hard up scruffy kid. That's who she was seeing or looking for the day once she said she walked by the theatre. That's who was there when every time she was pretending no one was there in Al's apartment. And other times she was gone somewhere else. Holy shit all these fucking progressive liberated women have all the god damn traits they despise in men. Like wanting to fuck anyone they want. And boy let me tell you Rabbi, that even includes these days the whole of the animal kingdom. And I hope I will never meet such a pervert. But jesus Louella. Also let me tell you Rabbi she has tits that when held sent a jolt of lightning down into my nerve cells. Sigmund, remember, your sensory palm fronds are above average in sensitivity. You betcha Rabbi. And it's time to light some candles. Read the little cards reminding of the deaths of the dead. Freddie Joy. O jesus. With you I could have been a masochist or a sadist. Now your memory is turning me into a necrophile. Because I just thought of fucking you. Even down in your grave. Holy shit Rabbi, like I saw a person do, I'm blessing myself with holy water. That's O K Sigmund, just don't drink it, or you'll be pissing like a Catholic.

Organ music playing and a choir singing. A bell ringing. A priest entering on the altar. This is beautiful. Smoke rising up from that golden thing they're swinging. Nearly as nice as the synagogue. Fuck. Why not. I could even get driven to begin to believe in a Catholic black magic God if things get any worse. Trouble pouring out of people everywhere you go. Now I'm on an errand of mercy. And got to get rid of these jewels. Before I'm tempted to fucking auction them off to one of those guys locked behind a dozen gates and doors trading in gems. Or even I could jump a plane to New York. Get Uncle Werb to get me a price on Forty Seventh Street. O christ why did someone have to rely their trust in me.

Schultz returning to the church entrance. Standing aside holding the door open for an old lady in a shawl. Wow. From the profile of her face, I nearly suddenly thought it was mom. My mom. With the scandal in my life making her premature old with worry. And having just learned one thing. The average age of people in prayer is not young. O jesus where's my car. Wait on the outside steps. It's got dark and chilly. When all this part of Mayfair was meadow, you could imagine this quiet little street, that ducks must have once gone down, going quack quack quack. Jesus I'm cold. And beginning not to feel safe out of vicinity of Daniel. O boy. Thank god, here he comes.

'Welcome back aboard sir.'

'Thanks Daniel.'

'And I trust the praying went well.'

'Yeah, I sure as hell hope so. Let's go the fastest way to Westminster, to three thousand three nine nine nine Vincent Square.'

'Ah I know the vicinity well sir. Not far from Pimlico. Didn't I work in the basement of a shop there by the military name of Army and Navy. And sure we will slip there in a jiffy. As now's the time to get back across town without too much traffic.'

The empty streets of Mayfair. Offices closed. The people gone home. The rich getting bathed and dressed in their flats, townhouses and hotels and ready to go to dinner. Or better with tickets booked to see the show. Champagne time. I could use a glass right now in the car. Switch on the reading lamp. Open the evening paper. Holy christ talk of where we're going and here is another page one headline scandal in Westminster. Another member of parliament caught consorting with

337

harlots. And holy jeeze. What's this on page three. Londoner's Diary are on to it already.

HAS OUR BINKY DONE A BUNK

The only son of the fabled society beauty the late Lady Ottoline and known to his intimates as the blond Adonis, this reporter not so long ago had the great pleasure to announce the impending extravagant musical to be staged by the elusively eccentric impresario Mr Binky Sunningdale. But we now understand from his lawyers that he has, due to an acute bronchial condition, left for the sunnier Continent and an unknown destination for an extended holiday. However, Mr Sunningdale has, it appears, left behind him considerable consternation concerning his now abandoned musical. According to stage-set builders, costumiers and other numerous prominent theatrical firms plus a prominent composer and playwright and others who have worked on the project, all seem at a loss to know when their bills and fees will be paid. And we hear as a result that Equity have declared Mr Sunningdale persona non grata.

Mrs Sunningdale, reached at her parents' country address, confirmed that she and her husband were estranged, but that she had nothing to do with her husband leaving a trail of unpaid bills. Pursued by creditors though he may be and Mr Sunningdale having taken his solemn step across the Channel, I for one still retain my faith in this gracious and graceful gentleman. And predict he will return, to amuse and entertain us once more. But meanwhile I suppose one says au revoir and bon voyage to his departed charm. And if one might indulge a mite more French, I shall reserve part of me, Binky dear, au plaisir de vous revoir.

Holy fuck look at the benign publicity he's getting while I get insultingly crucified and sexually ridiculed in the bloody rags. The bloody reporter is writing a public love letter to him. O boy Rabbi I get out of bed for my first few hours and look what happens. But Sigmund worse could be if you couldn't get out of bed.

The limousine passing soaring fluted shapes of the Houses of Parliament. Big Ben tolling six thirty. A hoot of a barge on the river. The car turning right, cruising through the Westminster streets. Into this square on this darkening eve. Daniel slowing reading the numbers of the houses. Stopping in front of number three thousand three nine nine. O christ it is just like the countryside. Look at this sweet sweet house.

'I'll only be a second Daniel.'

'Take as long as you want now. And I'll be reading the newspapers, and taking the long distance calls. No hurry.'

Schultz opening the little gate and walking along the narrow path between the flower beds. Entering a warm little hall and climbing the stairs. A white painted door at the end of a red carpeted corridor. Jesus amazing, that's a smell reminds me of something familiar. Flowers somewhere. No it's perfume. Boy what an idyllic cosy little place this is. Even a palm and plants in a flowerpot on the floor. This could be the answer to my life. A fucking girl already delivered and paid for. And if I know Binky this doll's got to be an exotic beauty. That I could team up with while he's all washed up and away. Jesus much as he may now be ruined, I still have to envy the son of a bitch. Plus the other flat he kept for his little seances. A stage, lighting and boy, what performers. And all this is hidden away here in this nice cut off peace and quiet smack in the centre of London. An area I never knew even existed. If only I didn't have such bad memories connected with pasta, I'd come here for pasta anytime. Christ if you're home, open up honey, will you, I really got the crock of gold they say waits at the bottom of the rainbow for you. Rap again. Jesus there's a key turning. Locking the bloody door. She obviously thinks with what's been going on that I'm the bailiff. And I better pretend in my best cockney to be a telegram announcing a lottery win.

'Who is it please.'

'Telegram madam. Urgent.'

The door unlocking. Opening a fraction. Lavender bath smells wafting out the crack. The sleeve of a white towel bathrobe. And just a sniff I catch of that rarefied musky perfume I know from somewhere. Holy shit this is giving me a fucking hard on already. Honey. Open wide will you. It's Santa Claus out here. He's got presents you're never going to forget, and wouldn't believe, that he's going to give you.

'Just hand it through the opening please.'

'I have something from Mr Sunningdale. Hey wait a second. Who is this behind the door. I don't believe it. Hey don't try and close this door. You've got, O my god, you fucking got my fingers. My fingers. Jesus open. Before I knock it open. And rip this fucking place apart. Let me in you fucking bitch Louella god damn it.'

Schultz a foot in the door pulling his fingers out. Leaning back. Shoving his shoulder slamming forward knocking the door open. A shadow retreating into the small sitting room and shrinking back into the darkness. The faint light through the bow window from a street lamp outside. Holy mackerel what's this, a motorcycle in the middle of the room and jeeze talk about cornered animals.

'Go ahead get back in there. Into the fucking room. No one is going to lay a hand on you don't worry. Do you fucking think I would even be bothered. Jesus I thought you were just a two timing bitch. Honey you're a triple timing bitch. Nowhere to go, huh. Except cross town. Sneaking out of the garage at Al's and over here to this nice and convenient little change of scene here in Westminster. I think they call this the area of the division bell or something for voting in Parliament.'

'I don't give a damn what you think. And it's none of your business.'

'Honey you'd be surprised how much of my business this suddenly is. Miss Nice. To all the guys. That's you isn't it. Hey and the menu. The carpenter's dinner. Pasta. Jesus you should change it honey. And what have you got cooking tonight honey. More pasta. Huh.'

'Get out please. Get out.'

'Honey. You think I've come here looking for you. I'm a messenger here. Nothing more and maybe plenty less. And nothing is more urgent on my mind than to get out of here as quick as I fucking can. Jesus. Here I am thinking for once the tables are turned. And it's me who's having the last laugh. But this is funny anyway. Ha. Ha. Ha.'

'Stop that bloody phoney laugh of yours.'

'Honey it's the first I've had for weeks I'm telling you and it's fucking genuine, no kidding. And I'm enjoying it.'

'Well I'm not.'

'So. After all this time. Comes the solution.'

'Get out and leave me alone please. Please.'

'Honey cry. Here's the towel you dropped. I recognized the perfume all the way out in the fucking hall. And I'm going to also leave you alone. For exactly the rest of my life. And maybe that old fart Al should too if he's smart.'

'O Sigmund. O Sigmund. It's you who I have truly always loved. I have. It was simply that Binky is so utterly beautiful as a person physically and spiritually. And he seduced me. And I couldn't help myself.'

'What. Hey hold it. I don't believe this. What are you an actress. Giving a performance. No one denies men are falling all over in love with you honey. But what am I supposed to be, physically and spiritually ugly.'

'Binky is my kind of person. You and Al are American. Not that you aren't beautiful too. You see I don't want to lose any of you.'

'Any of us. Hey what are you trying to conduct. A harem in reverse.'

'Don't you accuse me.'

'Well anyway I'm one less prick for you honey. And maybe there's two less since Binky left this afternoon on the train.'

'You don't know everything that's happened.'

'Yes I do honey. I sure do.'

'The caretaker has already been to say the locks are being changed. I have to get out of here. I've no money. This is just a furnished sublet flat. No job to go to. I can only go back to stay at Al's for a few days before I have to pack up. His wife smeared excrement all over the place. And until I find somewhere I have nowhere to go. Please and I beg you on my bended knees. Look I'm kneeling. I beg of you not to tell Al. He's now all I got left. And could you loan me some money.'

'Boy this conversation is getting ridiculous. Will wonders of the female imagination never cease. Ha ha. Lend you money.'

'O please. I'm not well. I'm not.'

'Jesus honey even standing there in this feeble light you look the picture of health. And I'd like to know what a fucking motorbike is doing here in the sitting room.'

'I've been so tired. I've been coughing and I've had headaches.'

'Well honey, my sympathy. I've just been nearly a month in bed and not once did you enquire or come to see me or give a fuck how I was.'

'Don't you see I was worried about Al. On his deathbed all these weeks.'

'Well get ready honey, he's off it. And with his toupee back on and according to recent reports from New York, you may not be all that Al's got left.'

'Why.'

'Well with Al's gaskets working again honey. As you know some poor little impressionable girl's getting her picture in the newspaper gossip columns having got a big snow job from Al that he's laying the carpet for her to stroll on into the big time. Need I say more about that trumpet tooting monster celebrity slob.'

'How dare you call him that.'

'That's what he is. And that's what I call him. But you've still got that fucking carpenter who can't drive a god damn nail straight and left one sticking out of the stage scenery which went an inch deep into the ass of Margot in the chorus line. While I was sick in bed with other worries. Now I have just one more action for damages pending. While I was wasting time mooning over you.'

'You're still married. What about me mooning.'

'I'm fucking well in the middle of a divorce pending. You know that. The whole nation knows it. If you read a certain Sunday rag, and if she has anything to do with it the whole fucking world is going to know it from New York to Vladivostok.'

'You're bitter.'

'That's right I'm bitter. And let me tell you being bitter is better than being bankrupt because that's what she thinks she's going to make me.'

'Well I know already how it feels to be bankrupt.'

'So honey this is the friend's house you stay in where I couldn't ring you a couple of times. And I guess the motorcycle is modern art in action or something. I'm tempted to say voom voom. Otherwise pretty fucking cosy honey. Pretty fucking cosy. Doesn't have Al's spacious dentist's modern atmosphere or aerial view but that's a nice night time rural looking scene out the window there.'

'Well why have you bloody well come here then. Who told you.'

'I was sent here, honey. On an urgent errand. And as it happens by the guy who presumably paid the rent and upkeep.'

'Well now that you've seen it why don't you just go and mind your own bloody business and leave me alone. I'm packing and dressing.'

'Because honey, at this fucking second, you are my business but I'm deliberating right now whether I do just walk out of here.'

'Well walk then. I've got to stay till people come to collect this motorbike. And you can enjoy the satisfaction that you leave me sick. And will soon leave me hungry. And leave me with nowhere to go. And I'll be relieved if you do.'

'You'll be relieved all right honey, let me tell you. O boy. Let a woman rat on you once. And jesus she won't stop till she's done it nine times like a cat has lives.'

'All right you've said your resentful piece. Get out. Get out. Leave me. Go get back into that big bloody pretentious car I can see parked down there. That your ego needs so badly.'

'Well I might just do that honey. I might just do that.'

'She's right your wife. You're nothing but a big show off embittered megalomaniac.'

'Honey do just one thing for me will you please. Before maybe you soon have to go out searching to get a cheap little flea pit hotel to stay in. Just stand back a little over there. And turn the shade on that lamp. And just put one of the sofa cushions there in the middle of the floor.'

'Why, why should I do what you tell me.'

'Well in the words of the lawyers honey, if you do like I say you may learn something to your advantage. I just want some room between us. So I can throw something on the floor.'

'I don't trust you.'

'Trust me honey. Go ahead. Do it. It could be you'll never have to worry about trusting anybody ever again.'

'Stop this. Stop. Get out. You're not going to set up some kind of criminal court to make a moral mockery out of me. I love Al. I love the carpenter. I love Binky. But I'm beginning to finally despise you.'

'Here. Let me then turn on this fucking light and put this pillow on the floor. Because I wouldn't do you the dignity of handing these to you. Yeah. That's right. Open your eyes in amazement honey. They're from Binky. Fucking jewels. That I'm fucking well throwing at your bare feet. Which you obviously all these months have earned. On top of what you extracted out of Al. And by the way when you're selling them get plenty of opinions. You don't deserve this good advice. But during appraisals don't let the jewels out of your sight even for a second. Someone could pull a switch and cheat you. And I won't ruin your evening with over optimism by telling you what I think they might be worth. But they sure are worth more than your moral value honey. That's right cry. Let the tears pour down. And just a thought. Maybe you ought to get a jeweller somewhere to make you a crown. Stick the gems in it. Then you'll have something nice to put on your head at your coronation as the queen of faithfulness and loyalty. And one consistent thing at least, could be that the guys, if you infect them, should all have the same diseases. And here's a little laugh. Right now honey, believe it or not you could buy and sell me. And here's an even bigger laugh. I still fucking well desperately love you.'

'O no. O god.'

'Those jewels haven't been polished or cleaned in years. And just one little parting thought honey, I just had. Was to take my prick out and piss on them to wash the dust off. But you know I wouldn't want to cleanse them with anything so pure. But one thing. I'll never figure out is why the hell you deserve all that that's lying there in that pile.'

'I'll tell you why. Because after I gave Binky his whippings there on his motorbike I also gave the best blow jobs any girl can ever give a guy.'

'Honey hooray. I knew that whatever it was Binky was getting, that it must have been something fucking priceless. And that's the first meaningful news I've heard in weeks. The world suddenly makes sense once more. Goodbye honey. Goodbye. Keep cool. See you on the

Riviera topless under your parasol, wearing those two natural gems
I've been so dying to touch again.'

But
I'm sure if
I did
They'd
Electrocute me

Schultz stepping back down these carpeted stairs. To the glass door at the bottom. Where the things I should notice now, like a tiled vestibule and a mud scraper for the feet are both what I could use in my own house. But let me first get the fuck out of this house. Where I might have known that that son of a bitch Binky had something again up his sleeve to trick me. And worse than any dirty deal he's ever pulled. Fucking god, imagine, all these weeks and months. And the bastard, at the time I saw him bending over on the train. Now I know what he was doing. I thought he was sick but boy he was well and holding his stomach laughing. Someday. Somewhere. Revenge. Somehow. I'll get even. And I only wish he wasn't already ruined so I could ruin him even more.

'Home Daniel.'

'Right you are captain.'

The limousine passing by the big gloomy mansion blocks of flats behind Westminster Cathedral. Another Catholic church. Wow don't remind me now of anything to do with that girl. Or Binky as we go by Victoria Station. All I want is to get back to the dignified peaceful surrounds of Belgravia. To the only nice memory I got now, is of what Jorricks is making for dinner. And then be as far away as I can from the quicksands of betrayal.

'Daniel, tell me, do you get sea sick.'

'Ah now that's a question straight out of the blue if you don't mind my saying so sir.'

'Daniel let me warn you, there's going to be stuff coming out of the blue every second now.'

'Well then the way I would answer your question is in the historical manner. While doing me brief stint in the Irish Guards I had occasion to get across turbulent rivers. And sure after they chucked me out of the Guards for insubordination wasn't I crossing the sea with arms for the Irish Republican Army in my poor nation's struggle for freedom. And long before that wasn't I in curraghs off the west of Ireland that would go up twenty five feet on a wave, do a somersault and come back down again thirty five feet and I'd be at the same time drinking a bottle of stout and chewing a potato. But enough said now. And I follow your train of thought exactly. There's the phone shall I take it.'

'I'll take it Daniel back here. Hello.'

'Mr Schultz it's me. Rebecca. Since the moment you and Binky left sir I've been trying to get you. But couldn't because of the radio interference. In the last hour the phone calls haven't stopped. There's even been one from Hollywood but they wouldn't say what it was about. Mr Jewels is now on the other line and is shouting and threatening legal action and demanding to be put through to you. I said you were not to be disturbed.'

'Put him through Rebecca.'

'Hi Joe. How's mom.'

'Look kid I'm going to have you in court rooms from Canarsie to Bondi Beach. One hundred and fifty thousand dollars I got here in a guaranteed cheque.'

'Joe take it easy I'm not selling.'

'Where's your fucking fiduciary responsibility to your investors. What are you crazy. You think I'm going to waste my time trying to save this show from this disaster so that you can go and clean up. Well kid you're fucking up and impeding the eventual movie sale.'

'What movie sale.'

'No movie sale. And maybe never a movie sale. But in this fucking contract you've got unreasonable artistic control and approvals. Which is why I am willing to pay this ransom to buy you out. And right now. As I even try a last desperate ditch stand to keep the fucking thing on one more night.'

'O K Joe listen carefully. You and Al both glue down your toupees. I know what I want for the movie rights when and if that day ever comes to sell. And then I want to make my personal artistic contribution to the standards I want maintained in any movie that's ever made.'

'You don't know what you're doing kid, believe me. You're standing in the way of progress. You're nothing in Hollywood except maybe a black fucking mark. They think you're crazy out there.'

'Joe I'm confused why Hollywood has such interest that I'm crazy. Joe by the way how's your mother. Did she enjoy the show.'

'You want a serious answer to that question or are you just being a pain in the ass.'

'I want a serious answer Joe. Come on. I got a mother too for christ's sake.'

'Look kid. Al. Me. Everybody. We're all over town on phones every second of the day, working to save the show. I'm pouring my own money in. I'm in no mood for kidding. Having just lost a bundle on your pal Sunningdale. And on top of it, that's the other big worry I got right now. My mother's indigestion and memory. Which both now have got suddenly worse.'

'Sorry to hear that Joe.'

'She don't eat even with the extra medical auxiliaries I got now round the clock taking care of her. She's gone a little bit vague but she knows me.'

'Well Joe, at least that's something.'

'The nurses try to feed her all day and she won't eat till I go over each night to the Waldorf. And when I get there I take the spoon from the nurse. And I say Mom this is Joe here. Eat. Please eat what's here on the spoon, this good purée of spinach. And you know what. She eats. She won't eat for anybody else. But let me tell you on room service the medical auxiliaries eat. Between taking baths and watching television, they eat like a thousand dollars a day.'

'Hey Joe, jesus maybe the show knocked your mother's last neurons out of action.'

'Look kid don't be a wise guy. My mother could die. Like it was just lucky the other day I bought two solid burial cases of pure carved marble for inside the mausoleum. One for her, one for me.'

'Shit Joe maybe that's what upset her.'

'No. She likes hers. It cost thirty two thousand five hundred dollars. And she loved the show. But now I've had to have a specialist fly in from Denver to see her. So I'm naturally concerned.'

'O K Joe, I've just come this minute from an emotional holocaust myself. But please. Don't hold guns to my head to do a deal.'

'Nobody's holding a gun kid. I'm just trying to proceed in the accepted tradition of intelligent business practice which seems accepted by everybody but you who wants to rock the boat.'

'Hey Joe, relax. Why don't you just come to London a day or two. Take a load off your ass and mind. I'll introduce you to a girl you'd die for. Maybe not with the looks and figure, but in other ways just as fantastic as Freddie Joy.'

'Hey look kid right now I got a father in law and brothers in law up from the mountains of Tennessee with guns and hatchets after me, plus their crazy lawyers. I need new girls like I need two way tunnels through my head.'

'Forget girls then Joe. I'll feed you fraises des bois, filet mignon, and the best fucking burgundy you ever had.'

'Hey that's an improvement over in law hillbillies and girls but what is this kid, you desperate for a social life or something. Maybe I don't have the fraises des bois at my local delicatessen but I have anything else I want right here. And when I'm in London I got a special reserved suite with those beautiful mirrors overlooking the river, where the Savoy Hotel staff treat me just fine. I'm going to make a final and last offer. Two hundred thousand.'

'Joe, from was it ninety you dropped to seventy five, from seventy five you go to more than ninety. Now you more than double. And I must admit I'm getting vaguely interested. But I'm not really interested until like in the pinball machine I see a sign blinking jackpot and ringing bells and in the words of dear old Al, I am zinging mit der dick dick.'

'I'm going to sue you kid for fiduciary obstruction and lack of coopera- tion.'

'Joe a lady I don't even know is suing from an hour ago over a ten cent mirror I stepped on. Join the crowd climbing my stoop. I got lawyers standing in line. Why don't you spill the real beans. You got something, like you always have, up your sleeve.'

'Forget my sleeve kid. And don't worry, already Al has filled me in on your previous past behaviour. That's what the word is going around here, that you are seriously suffering from the insanity of your self exaltation. You think the people staring at the obstacle clause you could implement in this contract want your artistic opinion to bring an eventual movie production to a fucking standstill. Two hundred and seventy five kid, plus two percent of the producer's profit.'

'Jesus, I'm just a few minutes more on the phone and I am a potential seventy five richer. While at the same time you're telling me I'm suffering from self exaltation. Joe you're wasting your time.'

'Look kid. I should be busy in a battle while I'm here wasting this time. Please whisper in my ear. You tell me in numbers what exactly it is you want.'

'Well for a start Joe a zero is missing off the end of the six digits. Plus if you didn't like my controls you shouldn't have signed the contract.'

'Well kid while your brains are stuck up your asshole, you just won the booby prize for all time stubbornness, stupidity and for being a jerk.'

'Hey, come on Joe, I'm tired listening to these accusations, I made this show in the first place. Out of my own tears, sweat, flesh and fucking blood. I put each gem together. Me. And then I was aban- doned alone to sink with it. In fact let me tell you. While I was surrounded by hatred and hostility loved by no one, I got the star, the choreographer, the composer. Picked out the best chorus line London's ever seen. I'm its original genius.'

'Your megalomania kid is at least dramatic. But let me remind. You got maybe some of the gems together. All of which are fucking nothing without the finance. And it was Al got you finance. And even found you Magillacurdy who was living in a cemetery.'

'Hey are you saying I can't claim credit for my show.'

'Nobody's saying anything kid.'

'You sound like you're saying.'

'I'm saying things like pick up some profit kid before it's too late. That's what I'm saying. Before I give the cast their notice which believe me I got right now in my pocket to pin to the backstage notice board. But O K kid. You're just too hysterical and nervous. But if you want to talk philosophically in some crazy notional way about extra digits on the number I can't stop you.'

'Joe. Please I'm going around Belgrave Square right now in my car. Please don't waste my time making me seem a dumb schmuck with words like notional philosophy.'

'You think kid I want to be forced to go talk to bankers who are going to think me nuts. But I'll go talk. I'll go talk to the banks this afternoon. I'll maybe be back to you and maybe not. Al by the way had a baby.'

'A baby. What kind of baby. An elephant, a dog. Or a new baby grand piano.'

'A baby girl. Human. He met a nice little kid from an old Kentucky family a year ago at his celebrity concert in New Orleans. I think it was around the time he flew back suddenly to London and caught you fucking his girlfriend.'

'What's this some sick joke. That son of a bitch couldn't get a hard on these past fifty years. So nobody is now telling me he could make a mother out of some teenaged fucking hillbilly.'

'Hey is it all you've got left in you is insults.'

'The insults have been coming from you Joe and my insults happen to be facts. Tell Al from me I hope he names the baby, Louella.'

'One half a million not a penny more. Take it or leave it.'

'Holy shit. Sorry, my voice just slipped Joe. Gee I'm just nearly reaching my house Joe. Joe look, I like the numerical sound. And for the first time some fiduciary reality, to coin a phrase, is beginning to creep into this situation. But let's leave it till you've had your deep philosophical discussion with your bankers. Right now I just stopped in front of my house in the car. After what I could say was euphemistically a long day. Because I'm the first day out of my sick bed. And I'm going this second to go into a nice quiet hot bath with bath salts and bubbles in the tub. Then with a roaring fire and the television to watch, I'm going to eat my nice dinner my butler's got ready waiting for me. And Joe. Don't you get nervous yet. I got news for you. Now in spite of the big black stupid mark that I am supposed to be, Hollywood has been through to the office here on the phone. My suspicions are aroused to say the least as to what is going on in New York. And to say the most, you better start philosophizing fast and start thinking of tagging on that zero. Because I know from past fangs you sank in me that something is up your sleeve. Ready to come down. And I'm waiting. Say hello to your mother for me. Goodbye. And thanks for the conversation.'

In the wind and rain, the air chillier. Daniel with the car umbrella held over Schultz as he mounts the steps to number four Arabesque street. Daniel looking back over his shoulder and up and down the thoroughfare. The door opening. The warm light flooding out, as Schultz steps in.

'Hi Jorricks.'

'Good evening sir.'

'Gee I just got to go take a pee fast. Gee what's wrong, Jorricks. Something's happened.'

'Well sir. If I may just whisper. After I paid the taxi drivers, I did my very utmost to persuade her to leave. Short of calling the police. And as it began to rain her equipment had to be taken in and is now down in the boxroom.'

'Persuade who. What equipment.'

'Sir this morning. The lady explorer. I said you'd left for Moscow. And then she wouldn't stop speaking what I believe is Russian sir.'

'Jesus I'm losing my memory. That lady. You mean the Skyscraper.'

'Indeed sir. She said that you had said this was to be the expedition headquarters. She's been all afternoon in the library using the telephone and now she's in the drawing room. And has simply refused to budge. I did so try sir.'

'OK Jorricks, don't worry. I may faint and die in the effort but I'll tackle it. O boy Jorricks. Christ what a wonderful aroma.'

'The duck à l'orange sir. And sir there's been another lady. Quite a humorous young lady. She's left this number. She asked if there were to be another pigeon party. Although I did not quite know what she was referring to I took the liberty of saying yes.'

'When did she phone.'

'She didn't sir, she came to the door. And left a message in this envelope.'

Schultz taking the envelope to the hall water closet. Opening it as he pissed into the bowl. O god what's this now. Something to make my day. Jesus Rabbi. I have a feeling things are going to get to be awful. And I'm not going to be able to stand it.

Dear old Ziggy Pops,
No kidding I was just passing your big house. Don't get
scared I really am not working for my father tracking down
tax dodgers. Your address I got out of the hospital files
where I was reading in more detail about your balls. You
really are a celebrity. I like celebrities. I like you. Please call.
I like your butler too. And pops, one more pigeon party
please. And telephone me.

Your old cocksucking friend

Cynth

The scrawled writing blotted and the words bunched tightly together
on the torn piece of paper. Holy shit. And after reading this and taking
a pee, I now got such a hard on I can't fucking get my prick back into
my pants. Or the buttons closed. Whew. Look at this. Fantastic. Jesus
by the size of it it's got to be a sign of returning health. Maybe Rabbi I
could go on living for years to come yet. And maybe busted and beaten
I am not going to be. In show biz when things are looking bad at least
that's good, because when you think things are looking good, they
could be really bad and that's fucking worse. While the universal
search continues by girls for guys to support them and nobody, but
nobody is going to fool me by telling me any different. And I got to
remind myself again. That the exact moment you think everything is
going all right with a woman, be sure of one thing, it ain't. But be sure
of another thing. Women love jewels.

Schultz buttoning the last fly button coming out of the water closet.
Turning to look close up at his eyeballs in the hall mirror. Leaning
over the fresh bouquet of flowers, sticking out his tongue. And taking a
deep breath. And catching it as Jorricks comes up to his shoulder.

'Sorry sir I didn't mean to startle you. But there was another call, I
meant to mention from a lady called Catherine who wants you to call
her back, she's at the Savoy. I trust Daniel drove safely sir.'

'Yeah, as a matter of fact. He was excellent in every department.'

'And sir what would you desire for pudding this evening. With the
other cheeses I have some very nice farmhouse cheddar and blue stilton.'

'Gee. Pudding. Christ.'

'There's poached peaches in rum, French glacé fruit, mint biscuits,
strawberry tarts or fruit salad.'

'Let's go for the poached peaches, Jorricks. And maybe a few mint
biscuits.'

'Very good sir. I found the most delicious and wonderful apricot chutney at Harrods today. And got some Wiltshire cured bacon for breakfast tomorrow and some wood smoked pork pie for lunch. Is there anything wrong sir.'

'No. I'm just blessing myself like the Catholics do in church, Jorricks. I think I'm at a sudden crossroads in my life.'

'Of course sir. I quite understand.'

Schultz pushing open the door entering the drawing room. A fire blazing. A champagne bucket and bottle of champagne. Erica seated back in a chair. A green skiing suit, running shoes on her feet. Her long legs stretched out resting up on a footstool. A magazine open across her lap. A stack of books at her elbow, a tulip champagne glass in her hand.

'Hey, what the fuck is this.'

'Dobry vecher. Mozhno. O I am sorry. Maybe you don't speak Russian. They say you were gone to Moscow.'

'I'm back from Moscow, spasibo.'

'Ah you have Russian. Please. Do sit down.'

'Hey thanks in English honey, a whole bunch.'

'No problem. I pour you a drink. Hey I ring here. The button I push. Yes. For your Jorricks to bring another glass and another bottle of champagne.'

'You just do that. Make yourself at home.'

'O it is so nice. What a very beautiful house. It is not what I would expect you have. I like it more than that far too big house of Lord Nectarine. Cold and draughty. How come you so rich too. Big car. Servants.'

'Honey please don't let appearances fool you. But it's nice to know his Lordship's house is too big for you, considering all the space you seem to need.'

'Hey big boy, are you a recluse.'

'I'm probably as much of a recluse as you are a socialist honey. And you don't mind during this discussion in my house if I just sit down a second, do you.'

'O no. But I am a socialist. Sit down.'

'Thanks.'

'Hey you're not all big talk, you're a big deal. Your name everywhere. On the posters. In the newspapers.'

Erica draining her glass of champagne. Smiling and leaning back in her chair and recrossing her long legs. Her fingers flicking her long hair. A clipboard and pencils at her elbow on the side table. A knock at the door as it opens. Jorricks peeking in.

'You rang sir.'

'I didn't ring but it makes no difference. Looks like another glass and bottle of champagne are required Jorricks.'

'Very good sir.'

Schultz staring across the carpet at this apparition rotating a huge foot on the end of an ankle. The zipper of her jacket open. And the swellings of her tits. But christ not only has she got my god damn clipboard, but is using my telephone, pencils and erasers. Holy shit shoving midgets or normal sized people out of a house you can do on the end of your foot. This doll, Rabbi is going to take a bulldozer. Sigmund, don't be optimistic too soon. Maybe to get her out of the house and back up the Nile, excuse me, I mean the Amazon, could take an earthquake act of God.

'Hey big boy. I come for the forty five thousand dollars you promise. The ship I go on is ready to sail. I call your office they all the time tell me you are not there. I read this Korzybski you got in your library. What about cooperation. Ah but I apologize to come in here like this. But Lord Nectarine say he does not want visitors because his mother just die and he had to have a funeral. He said you are in this nice house lonely all by yourself. He said you were needing friends.'

'Well honey. Some facts I can give you. I ain't got no forty five thousand dollars at this exact minute to go up a river. And I may be lonely, needing friends, but let me tell you, this is where you can't stay.'

'I stay.'

'You don't, honey. Sorry.'

'Hey you think you throw me out. But maybe we wait, huh. After we fuck. Come on. You whip me. I give you a good fuck.'

'I don't want to whip, fight or fuck honey. I've been practically in bed since the last time I whipped and fucked you.'

'Hey you already rape me too. When you whip me. And now I have nowhere else to go with so much expedition equipment. You scared because I maybe am pregnant. Relax big boy. I am not pregnant. Ah now you feel better. Without any fear. See I make men happy.'

'Honey truth be known you scare me shitless. And in two seconds I'm going to have no appetite for dinner. And jesus now what's that. Fucking barking.'

A knock. A flushed faced Jorricks, in his rolled up shirt sleeves and an apron, peeking in the door.

'Excuse me sir, but there is a van at the door. And a gentleman with a dog. Who it appears is requesting payment of fifteen pounds.'

'Ah it is my dog. My snookie. My snookie nookie. Out of the quarantine. O my dog.'

'Your dog.'

'Yes. I visit him all this time and now he is at last free. He is called Azorr.'

'Hey jesus honey you're not going to bring a dog into my house.'

'You will love him. He is wonderful. He go up the Amazon with us.'

'Honey you go up the Amazon, right now will you. My chauffeur will take you, the fucking equipment, the dog, right now to the boat for fucking loading. And fucking well leave me here to have the dinner I've been all day dreaming of having.'

'Azorr, he no mess. He obedient. He behave. He obey. You cannot turn my dog away. He would be offended. Crushed. He love me.'

'Honey, I don't give a fuck who he loves, you just can't do this to me.'

'I am an artist. I need freedom.'

'Well I'm a fucking dog hater. And I need peace and quiet at this fucking point of time in my life.'

Jorricks jumping away from the door. Azorr bounding into the room. Schultz jumping up from his chair. Grabbing on to the mantelpiece. Erica falling to her knees throwing her arms around the neck of the monster. Rubbing its head and running her hands through its dirty blond hairs and kissing the canine between its wide set eyes. Azorr wagging its tail. And sticking its nose nuzzling in under Erica's hair.

'Jesus christ. The fucking thing's huge.'

'O he is so very very gentle with those he loves.'

Erica standing and bending her head under the chandelier as she pets and cavorts with Azorr leaping around the room. Azorr suddenly stopping and looking at Schultz who steps back over the fireguard in front of the fire. Azorr advancing and sniffing at Schultz's crotch, and baring its teeth and growling.

'Get this big vicious fucking thing away from me. I can smell my pants, they're burning getting scorched by the fire.'

'Stop Azorr. Stop. Back. Back. Lie down. Good dog. You see why I call him Azorr. In Hungarian it means nose. He like to sniff and smell with the nose.'

'Not my private fucking parts just back to health he ain't honey.'

Schultz sidling away from the fire. Standing by his chair. O my god, Rabbi. This is it. Convene all rabbis. Tell me what to do. I got a whole fucking string of ethical and could be even suicidal questions. Which I am too emotionally weak to even figure out suddenly tonight after what I've been already through today. Here I am. I lose by a final betrayal the woman I love. And now I get left three possible pieces of ass. Not enough for every direction of a crossroads. But two of which came marching right up on my stoop. And the third. O my god. She could be with her nurses and is not that far to get to. Straight down Constitution Hill, and along the Mall and into the Strand. I could even stop off to check the box office. If I wasn't here as I am under canine siege fucking cornered now and shit scared in my own house.

Sigmund
Don't give complaint
Get the whip
Give
Discipline

26

Dinner served by Daniel in his white coat. Jorricks pouring the wine. Daniel bringing in plates could be heard outside the dining room door attempting to control and stifle his laughter. Azorr as he sat in the corner of the dining room, catching duck bones on the fly in his mouth. Crushing and crunching them in his lightning snapping jaws. Erica choosing from her plate and throwing the best savoury bits while she polished off two bowls of consommé, three helpings of salmon mousse, two platefuls of wild rice and both legs of the duck à l'orange. And hard to know who had the bigger appetite, Erica or the dog.

'Madam do try our local water biscuits and our Normandy butter.'

'Ah Jorricks, it is all very good.'

The sound of the splintered duck's bones going down Azorr's throat in big gulps. Daniel reeling out of the room convulsed. Spilling the remainder of the salmon mousse off the plate and then stepping in it. But nothing stopping Erica. Boy Rabbi did she hit those poached peaches and then slam into the blue stilton. Then wolfed down the glacé fruit and mint biscuits. Plus the champagne on the table, she gurgled back three quarters of the two bottles of Bonnes Mares. If only my emotional nerves weren't so shot by what was already the day's events and by what was now going on, it would have been the best most enjoyable fucking meal and burgundy I have ever had in my entire life.

'Shall I serve the Château d'Yquem with the poached peaches sir.'

'You do that Jorricks.'

Erica smiling down the other end of the table. On her second bowlful of peaches. The candlelight flickering across the pink rose petals floating in the finger bowls. The back garden out beyond the darkness of the window panes. Erica pushing back her chair. Getting up. And coming to put her long arm around Schultz's shoulder and to plant a kiss on his brow. Her chiffon evening gown falling forward from her two delicious pear shaped breasts. A musky perfume from her hair. And boy she has charm when she wants to. But jesus I am so starved for affection Rabbi I was grateful. Just fucking plain grateful to feel her lips nibbling on my ear and one of those great long arms wrapped round my back and her hand going through my hair. And here I am. Discarding my dictum I just made two seconds ago of keeping away from any woman. Because. No matter what. She's going to make you pay, pay, pay. And in innumerable fucking ways. And in other ways not yet invented.

'Ah now I must go kiss Azorr. He sit all alone so patient in the corner. And he be jealous. After he see me go kiss Mr Schultz. But Azorr I love you but I love too Mr Schultz's black so black rich hair. The big curls. So soft.'

'Hey honey I hope it's a little bit more than just my hair you like better than the dog's hair.'

'But of course. A little better. Ah but Azorr and I are so happy together again. Like tonight it is a celebration. Come. We go. Upstairs. Yes.'

'Hey honey who you asking. Me or the dog.'

'But I ask you both of course.'

'Thanks a bunch.'

Schultz puffing his cigar following Erica and a tail wagging Azorr out of the room. Daniel in his white coat just on the kitchen stairs beyond the swing door, having another attack of laughter. Holy jeeze Rabbi I've never felt so safe and unsafe in my whole life. But what the fuck must my staff talk about down there with what's now going on up here. And who gives a fuck. My head is swimming in semi bliss. After, no kidding, the most delicious meal in my life. God the size of her, when she's a step ahead up the stairs. Somewhere I remember out of a previous scientific conversation we were having that she said she weighed one hundred and sixty eight pounds. And I weigh one hundred and sixty six. Jesus here I am. And the dog I'm sure is not far behind. Or shit did he run ahead. Desperate like me. On the verge of sexual suicide again. Wanting to grab her sashaying ass in its mouth watering delectability up the stairs. O god Rabbi. Self control. Here I am slavering at the chops like the dog. When I should hit the sack with my head deep in the pillow, to wake fresh for the raging battle of deals ahead. But I just don't have the energy and fight left to deprive myself of what appears to be women on all sides offering ass and blow jobs. Jesus it's pathetic. All any woman has to do, is to be kind and loving for two seconds. The way she just suddenly got up, came right down the table and put her arms around me. And after that big black cloud of a wife hanging over my life, I'm just putty in their hands. She's pulling me now by the arm upstairs even before I can finish my cigar. And jesus she's got the whole pink bedroom suite all set up for herself. And for this god damn huge mutt. Foaming just like I am at the mouth. Fuck it. After such a good dinner, who am I to object this late at night to what suspiciously looks like bestiality. Could be the distraction I need with juggling Joe Jewels's last numbers around in my mind. Especially with that son of a bitch's deeply entrenched habit of always offering to buy at ten percent of what should be the real purchase price. So that he keeps not only the remaining ninety percent but the original seventy seven thou he owes me. The way I figure it there could be exactly four and a half million at stake. Jesus. Could it be. Dare I feel in my bones a special situation is brewing. Requiring the masterstroke of all time. Behave like my cousin Saul, and never give in to pressure and hang on to every shekel. Keep my portable radio telephone right in my pocket. Hold tight to the gunwales, don't rock the boat. Rabbi, from being storm tossed on the sea, I could sail back into the safe harbour of contented solvency. Well Sigmund at least your quarter of a million borrowed from the bank at two and a half percent interest above the prime rate, could be covered. And also Rabbi, I'd be feeling less vulnerable standing in front of this big mutt. And she's not kidding. She's planning to stay. Three of her trunks up here already in the bedroom. And wow. What do we have here. Not only the pith helmets. But a black leather cat o' nine tails.

'Hey you're not letting the dog stay in here honey.'

'He stay. He be good.'

'He no stay honey.'

'Why. What is wrong. He stay always with me.'

'Honey, how the fuck do I know he's going to be good. Look at the way he keeps looking at me. He could be bad. In addition he has me nervously embarrassed. Why don't you just keep him somewhere in a kennel ready for the expedition when he can then go chew up the anacondas.'

'Ha. Ha. He is trained to kill snakes. But the anaconda could kill us all.'

'Yeah I guess it could honey. Well let's thank god a bunch we're right now in Belgravia.'

Schultz taking a puff of his cigar. Erica lighting a candle on the dressing table and switching off the lamp. The faint gong of Big Ben. And there she is. In the grey chiffon. Christ she looks good. For style her gown's not half bad. Maybe her belly's out a little after the good dinner. Nice orange sash round her waist. That she's undoing. And undressing and smiling so nice at me. O boy, talk about bedroom eyes. She's got them. Right up there in the sky. If only that fucking dog would close his. Jesus how many real brain cells are in a dog's brain. Because this fucker looks like he's got this whole deal figured out. He's even licking his chops watching her like a hawk as she takes off her string of imitation pearls. That would give Uncle Werb a fit. Who hated anything imitation. But who gives a fuck so long as the pair of tits they are hanging down between are real. Uncle Werb had his own words of wisdom, never he said let enemies sit down with you, eating and drinking what you're paying for. Holy jeeze as we take our clothes off, this fucking mutt who has already gobbled down half a duck, and is now curled up on the bed putting his head resting on his paws, is like he's in a ringside seat and staring out at me with a pair of fucking suspicious eyes. In my own private house. Where I'm privately trying to live and he's publicly like a lion making himself at home, lying on the private property of my bed. This monster mutt. Holy shit, a pair of skis against the cupboard. Snow shoes too. And there surrounded by a pile of pith helmets and mosquito netting, is a stack of thick big sweaters, and snow goggles. What is this. Where's she going. To the Equator or the North Pole.

'Honey come on. Tell the fucking dog to go outside in the hall at least.'

'He watch. He like watching.'

'I don't want that fucking mutt staring at me like that as I stand here like this stark naked.'

'He friendly wag his tail while he watch. You see.'

'Look. My tail I want to wag. I don't want to fucking well watch him friendly wag his tail honey.'

'Look, he see your nice big prick. He smile.'

'He was already growling at me and snarling at me downstairs for christ's sakes. Look right now. I step towards you. He's growling.'

'Stop Azorr. Stop. Be quiet. Ah now big boy. Come look at me. You forget Azorr. See I give you a modern dance display. Look.'

'Jesus honey. You are unbelievable. Everything's in proportion. You have the most gorgeous pair of tits on that amazing body.'

'Ah now. You watch. See. Azorr. He like my tits too. You see. Watch, he kiss and lick them. Ah, it is good. It is good. See he kiss the nipple.'

'Christ almighty. Hey who is it honey. Me or him. Who is good. Take a fucking choice will you. That's unsanitary.'

'Azorr, he is not unsanitary. He like. I like. His big cold nose. So delicious. He have such nice moist cold nose. He is gentle. He obeys. He like my earlobes too.'

'Hey what the fuck am I supposed to be doing honey standing here. With my earlobes.'

'Ah you watch. You see. He like you. Watch now how big his big prick is. Lift leg Azorr. Lift leg.'

'Honey, I got the emergency life saving of my life to attend to. I'm getting the fuck out of here. You go sleep with your dog. This is too much after a long day and a big dinner. Plus I'm only just regaining my fucking health.'

'No, no, no. Don't go. Please. You should not be jealous. I am only being friendly. He has all this long time in the quarantine been alone without me. Now. You see his prick.'

'I don't want to see his prick.'

'See. You see.'

'Holy shit honey, boy I see what you mean. But I still want to take mine small as it is the hell out of here.'

'Wait. Here now. Your turn. Some nice red cords I have. You tie me to bed. You take the cat o' nine tails.'

'Tie you. Like hell I will. Not while that monster's loose, let's tie him up first.'

'See, big boy. Special nice silk cords I have.'

'Well you see big girl. I just reach to touch you on the tit and you look and listen. How the fucking mutt's growling and showing those fucking killer teeth at me.'

Rabbi I thought holy shit, since this is already like a fucking jungle. Instead of my crown of thorns I took one of the pith helmets and put it on. We both laughed. And she put a pith helmet on Azorr. And I swear, as you are my judge Rabbi, the fucking dog laughed. Something I thought I'd never see. He went ha ha ha. I swear it. Which shit, throwing all my principles to the wind I thought was an open invitation to us all to have a good time. And she was ready for anything. Sigmund, Sigmund listen, if you have any intention of getting these individuals out of your house, you should not be doing what you're doing. Touché Rabbi, touché. But I can't stop. I tied her face down to the bed, her arms and legs hanging over the edges. Using my best naval knots tightening the cords to the bed legs. Was it a bowline, Sigmund. Yeah Rabbi, the mutt was intrigued and looked now like he was smiling. It was amazing. The fucking event was getting exciting. And there's no doubt anymore. How I deeply enjoy laying welts across a nice smooth delicately female curved soft ass. But on the first swat, the mutt reared half up off the bed and growled and bared his teeth. So O K Azorr that was too hard. Next swat I make softer. And I swear Rabbi the next lash I made softer and the mutt shook his head up and down in approval. But Erica is saying harder. So I increase. Each time a little harder. With the mutt Azorr getting up higher and higher on his hind legs on the bed. Shit it was I swear, touch and go Rabbi. And never was delicacy of touch so crucial. Satisfying two individuals at once. But everything still proceeding fine. In fact it was going wonderful. Her ass glowing crimson with criss crossed welts in every direction like a dozen crossroads any one of which I could take a departure on towards a golden sunset. Boy like you said, don't give complaint, give discipline. Then just as a little tennis elbow was setting in, she in that wonderful mewing plaintive way of hers asked to be untied.

'Big boy, now we fuck. But first I suck.'

Rabbi god what a preliminary blow job she started giving. While all the time I was pleasantly nervous keeping my eyes glued on the fucking mutt. But he was just simmering there grunting and keeping his jealousy in check. Boy he may have been a dog. But this was purely a human situation for both of us.

'Fuck me from behind big boy. I go on my hands and knees.'

Rabbi I know I am sometimes a foolhardy risk taker. Fucking hell. But everything was going swell. There it was. All bent over at a high altitude, waiting. The inevitable heading for the irresistible. She just about left room at the bottom of the bed for me to kneel. I paused looking. Hesitating. The mutt growling deeper and deeper. But what a glowingly pink ass. With the welts looking like crimson ski tracks. Like a sinking sun was shining on one of those pristine snow shiny peaks in the Himalayas that the mountain climbers climb because it was there and you see in full colour in magazines. Which talking about heights I had to instead of kneeling, stand.

'Come on big boy. Let's go. Give it to me dog style.'

Rabbi. It was halfway in into her silken gorgeous chamber when the fucking mutt jumped off the bed straight at my throat. I grabbed up a pillow in front of me and could hear the jaws crunch as the teeth met through the feathers of swans' down. And locked together, Erica and I fell forward. My prick plunging all the way in. History nearly repeating itself. Right in the same room where I was once attacked by my behemoth bald mother in law. But instead of screaming for help at the top of my lungs I was screaming in the greatest of all great orgasms of my life.

Sigmund listen
I don't know
About modern satisfaction
But they heard you
Even here
In
Prague

27

Rabbi even you must have seen those teeth flashing when Azorr ripped the whole centre out of the pillow which saved my life and gave him a choking mouthful of swans' down and gave me a chance to throw the eiderdown over his head and tie one of the red silk cords around it. While Erica was lying somnolent on the bed, not moving a single one of her mile long muscles. Leaving me in the most embarrassing situation. As Jorricks and Daniel in raincoats and slippers got as far as outside the door. Me inside shouting come in. And then shouting don't come in. And then my fucking portable radio telephone goes off near him on the floor which sends Azorr again lunging back and forth and twisting in a circle not knowing what to bite next. So I didn't lose an arm or my testicles, I let it ring. Leaving Erica and I covered in more feathers. But even lying there exhausted in mind and spirit I had such a glow in the gonads I couldn't care about anything.

'Hey honey that was an event and a half.'

'Yeah big boy.'

'Did you take any precautions.'

'What.'

'You know, honey. Pregnancy.'

'No.'

'What. Holy jesus. You can't just not take precautions you got to do something.'

'It is too late. It is the middle of the month. I feel it go up me.'

'Hey you deliberately did this. Didn't you.'

'Why should it be your business if I have a baby.'

'Vacate honey, this is blackmail. Jesus go up the fucking Nile.'

'The Amazon.'

'I don't care if it's the fucking Mississippi. See my lawyer. He'll draw up the production investment. Only don't you or your mutt ever cross my doorstep again.'

'Ah you would like me to name the baby Sigmund if it's a boy. Or Sylvia if it's a girl.'

'Don't you think you're going to get some paternity suit going against me honey. You sign a fucking release paper before you get one penny of investment. Jesus honey. Don't start crying. Why the fuck did you do this.'

'Why did you do it. You did it.'

'Because I'm fucking crazy honey out of my mind. That's why. But I'm not crazy fucking well out of my mind to let an innocent child come into this world of death disease and disaster who could have for a father someone running hysterically away from the responsibilities of his paternity. Holy shit. Don't let this happen. I'm getting the fuck out of here and you be out of here in the morning. Call the dog away from the door.'

'No.'

'O jesus there goes the fucking phone now again.'

'Hello. Who's this.'

'Hi ya kid, me.'

'Jesus Joe. It's two in the morning. How many times do I have to tell you of the time gap.'

'Yeah kid, I know about the time gap. So how you doing.'

'I'm doing, shit I don't know.'

'Well our little philosophical discussion you remember.'

'Yeah. Jesus Joe can't you leave this situation just another ten hours or so.'

'Kid believe me, it's now or never. My wife who's divorced me has got hungry lawyers howling for my blood, trying to have me arrested to put me into alimony jail. After which a deal like this is dead. You should be thankful you don't have to deal with that kind of inhuman greed.'

'Wait Joe I got feathers in my mouth.'

'Feathers.'

'Yeah feathers.'

'Well I got something serious to put in your ear, so listen good. This conversation is now switched to a conference, Al's on the other line and we got a final proposition.'

'Look before you say another word Joe, I know that my answer is going to be no. And hello Al.'

'Now wait a minute kid, Hollywood is mildly interested.'

'So you wait till now to tell me, Joe, of the mild interest.'

'I've been making a full disclosure of the situation all along the line. All I ever said was you and your megalomaniac vanity approvals were an unacceptable contractual obstacle. We want to come to you now for the final and last time to make progress.'

'I know what's got to be happening Joe.'

'What's got to be happening.'

'Hollywood's interested because there must be a line around the block buying tickets. Or else you wouldn't be on this fucking phone running up a long distance bill.'

'Hey come on kid. Maybe there are a few desperate people out waiting who want to see the show like my mother did before it closes.

But there isn't a scalper around for miles. Just a few inquisitive people who think because your show's been running to packed houses they now wonder why the Broadway edition is shutting down.'

'Joe there's something in the sound of your voice.'

'Hey look I'm putting on Al to talk to you. Al.'

'Listen Sigmund, this is Al. I've been listening. For the sake of avoiding financial ruin we got to take you, the fly, out of the ointment, so that future ongoing deals don't get stalled on your demands.'

'I'm no fucking fly in any ointment Al.'

'Well let's say, if we were using a classical simile, this is like Hercules and Diomedes. One of us has got the other by the balls. Hey Sigmund what's that noise, barking.'

'It's a dog Al.'

'A dog.'

'Yeah a dog.'

'I thought you hated dogs.'

'Al I hate dogs. That's right.'

'So now you have a dog. Just like you.'

'Al I'm glad for your gaskets working again but you're a fucking spy now in my life.'

'And you're paranoid sick in the head. Two million dollars.'

'What. Say that again. I didn't hear you.'

'Two million dollars, you heard me the first time. Two followed by six zeros. Two zero, zero, zero. Zero. Zero. Zero.'

'O K enough Al. Six zeros. Like eight hours ago, it was a five and five zeros.'

'Look, in the room here with us are four legal representatives all amazed listening in to this conversation on the conference loud speaker. But they are ready to draw the contract terms. Which let me tell you loud and clear is an outright buy, a straight clean purchase of all your cinematographic and allied movie rights. That's why I ask about the barking in the background. This is an important discussion. And just by the way, in case you ain't heard or read the big story in Variety, Joe has set up the Freddie Joy Scholarship for deserving young actresses.'

'Al wait, jesus another feather is in my mouth.'

'I'm waiting.'

'O K it's gone. Wait now the dog's barking. Shut up you fucking mutt.'

'Hey change phones Sigmund we'll call you back.'

'I can't the dog is at the door blocking it. It already took a miracle to tie him up under an eiderdown from trying to tear my throat out.'

'Sigmund what the fuck are you in a zoo there.'

'That's nearly right Al.'

'OK now look. No one could have predicted this situation. We would love to dream about what could have happened here overnight in New York. With the lines around the block.'

'So now you at last admit Al. Lines around the block.'

'And OK we are richly pleased that a few discerning people are waiting.'

'Yeah, well something's fishy Al. Let me remind I was being offered seventy five thousand dollars for my movie rights, minus the seventy seven thousand Joe owed to pay on the theatrical performing rights. Leaving me, if I took the seventy five, minus exactly two thousand dollars.'

'Sigmund. Please stop making muddy water that's already gone under the bridge. This is an entirely new situation. Tell me do you want sincerely for the real first time in your life to zing mit der dick dick. You heard me already say two million dollars. What's the matter, do you hate money that much. Do you.'

'Al, holy shit hold it. I just barefoot I think stepped in some dog shit.'

'Hey what's going on. I got legal gentlemen here. Feathers. Now dog shit. I'm talking about money, Sigmund.'

'And so am I Al.'

'Well then what have you got against being rich. And standing in a shower of shekels for the rest of your life. To keep you clean. Tell me. I want to understand the philosophy. Why should you go on resisting.'

'I'm resisting Al because you and Joe in cahoots with your philosophy are offering me two million which means there's an offer at least more than twice or three times that somewhere.'

'Sigmund the deal's dead and worthless unless we buy out completely your unrealistic and unreasonable artistic controls. Don't you understand. People fear you. Two and a half.'

'Absolutely not interested. But keep going Al. Keep going. The other factor is. That payment is by confidential cable transfer to a sudden confidential designation.'

'No problem. Carrier pigeon. Anything you want. And look no one's going to broadcast this deal. Two and three quarters.'

'Not interested.'

'OK Sigmund. The magic of show biz maybe has you hypnotized into thinking the sky's the limit. But let me tell you there are limits. I am empowered to notch up to three, as a final definite last position.'

'Goodbye.'

'You fucking imbecile Sigmund. You fucking imbecile.'

'Who you calling an imbecile.'

'You, that's what you are. O K wait. O K I am empowered to go to three and a half. Or I am instructed now to say goodbye and a definite final phooey on you.'

'A definite final phooey on you too Al. And I'm glad Al you haven't lost your ability to con people with your charm. Goodbye. And don't call me again. I'll sell these rights. And get you and Joe, the flies out of the ointment.'

'Boy Sigmund you're a comedy cliché. We have a motorcycle messenger ready to put papers straight on the plane. Instead of walking away from three million dollars, you should have stayed in lingerie. Maybe that's where you learned to try to wholesale at retail prices. You're going to regret this.'

'Maybe Al. But I don't think so. And as for lingerie maybe you should try it as a trade. Or even better, maybe as underwear.'

'O K so you make with insults. But for the sake of all the investors that there is a fiduciary responsibility to and those here patiently listening I'll ask a reasonable question. O K what is it you want. Tell us. In sincere words from your own lips. We just want to fascinated hear it here for the record.'

'I want at least three quarters of what I think Hollywood is offering you right now. And I don't know why they're offering but I might just wait to find out. You see Al. I don't hate money. I don't despise it. I don't even mildly dislike it. In fact I like it. No I'll go even further, let me say I am deeply and seriously fond of it. In fact Al. I love money. I worship money. I adore it with my body and soul.'

'Sigmund such sincerity could win you a Hollywood Oscar. Look I already explained to the gentlemen here what to expect in this conversation. But never mind three five followed by five zeros. There's this number. Take it down. Nine nine nine four three eight seven.'

'Now Al, at last for the first time at least we're talking reality.'

'That's right, reality. I just gave you the telephone number of the best psychiatrist in London. You ring it. He'll help you. We can all hear the barking and growling here over the loud speaker. It's too bad. We're all sorry that you are in need of custodial care. Are you listening.'

'Yeah Al I'm listening. And for your information there is Al a real live and breathing dog here.'

'Well we're glad to hear you're not alone in life. But we're not going to let you amputate our balls. Or put our financial necks on the chopping block. Joe went talking to the banks all afternoon. Sure we admit we did everything to produce a nibble out of Hollywood. But the line around the block and people fighting over who's in front of who is hired from out of work actors and actresses who are giving the performances of their lives. The pictures of the fights over tickets in the newspapers were staged. We admit all that. But while you're there in London. We were here on twenty telephones all over this city and right to the back and beyond to the boondocks of Connecticut. Full page adverts went in all the papers yesterday. Blazing your phoney London quotes with fictitious critics and other frauds which could send Joe sitting here to Sing Sing prison to serve a stretch for fraudulent misrepresentation.'

'O K Al. Calm please. Congratulations first on getting a raincheck from the crematorium and second on your baby.'

'I'll forget I heard that first remark. But that's right. The most wonderful, the most beautiful the most gorgeous little creature you ever saw.'

'I am glad Al. I'm glad. That in such a fucked up world wonders never cease.'

'Hey Sigmund. Wait a second. We're sending signals here. Someone's holding up a hand. With fingers. We want everybody to have a decent situation out of this. Are you listening.'

'I'm listening Al. So's my Rabbi.'

'O K I'm counting again the fingers.'

'I'm still listening Al. How many fingers are we counting.'

'Five.'

'With six zeros Al.'

'With six zeros, Sigmund.'

'Al it's a deal.'

And
You have just lifted
This big fly
Out of the ointment
And maybe sent him
To the Riviera

28

Schultz waking to a knock on his bedroom door. Jorricks with breakfast and the morning papers and weather report. Plus a staff request.

'Daniel would like a reduction in wages sir.'

'A reduction, what for.'

'He says he is enjoying the job too much and he could get into a rut.'

'Holy shit. Excuse the language Jorricks but he could be soon paying me, and get into an even bigger rut because he's going to enjoy it even more.'

Action stations. Fly out of the house. Daniel warming up the engine of the limousine. Crossing London. At the office, having taken the whole place over with polo mallets, cricket bats and shotguns, his Lordship, witnessed my next to last act at Sperm Productions. The Joe Jewels papers signed. And far far away in Switzerland, like the greatest angel of mercy of all time, the money fluttering gently down to land in the bank, and the vault clanking closed over my secret numbered account. Rabbi no three days ever happened faster in all my life. Saw the production three times. Each time better. The whole chorus cast were fantastic. I even gave a little drinks and buffet supper party after the show in a suite at Claridges. Where we all sang songs at the D'Oyly Carte piano. And Louella must have sold Binky's jewels. Because behind Magillacurdy's car hogging the stage door entrance was parked the carpenter's car. A red Ferrari just like Madame Soignée's.

You know Rabbi the only thing that's better than being big is being smart. Plus being calm cool and collected. Just let me tell you, I only this minute ago got reminded. And everything's going to be OK. I'm on my way to where I may in five minutes flat do the second biggest transaction of my life. Because you heard them on my front stoop this morning. Priscilla, her mother and two lawyers. The four of them with a process server with about five injunctions. Like I always do when I'm trying to be calm cool and collected, I got hysterical. Opened up the window. They shouted up. And I shouted down.

'Our lawyers are with us. You're not going to deprive us of our just rights.'

'I see your fucking lawyers. I'll fight you him and him and any other dozen fuckers you want to get together in any and every fucking court in every land anywhere in the world. Now it's my turn to cause you pair of conniving black cows fucking anguish and horror.'

Rabbi all I know is I need just to live a little while longer. If not cheaper. Keep warm keep cosy and mobile. Go on holding out against the mob. And I knew I had to do what I was doing, hurrying through this glass door into a lobby and then pushing through another. Jeeze, two such good looking girls seated behind their desks, making me wonder if they were for sale.

'Hi.'

'Hello.'

'I'm Mr Schultz.'

'O yes indeed, how nice to meet you Mr Schultz. Your butler rang us this morning. What a most helpful gentleman he is. Do come this way sir.'

Schultz bowing his own headful of black curls to the lady remaining behind the desk with her long blonde tresses curling along her cheek. Over this moss green deep pile carpet. And into an office with a carpet you could drown in.

'How do you do Mr Schultz so good to meet you. I'm Mr Starboard Jones. Everyone of us here in the office has seen your show. And now what can we do for you.'

'Can I speak strictly confidentially.'

'But of course Mr Schultz, all our business is conducted on that understanding.'

'Well I want one of these.'

'Purchase or charter, business or pleasure sir.'

'To buy. For escape. With buoyancy, privacy, secrecy and unsinkability the first priorities.'

'Ah no problem. And how many guests do you think you might want to accommodate.'

'So far just myself, my butler, my bodyguard. But I still want plenty of room and space.'

'I quite understand sir. Now here's a nice little item. Accommodation for up to twenty four guests. With crew's quarters and officers' quarters.'

'Holy cow how big is that thing.'

'Length overall two hundred and sixty five feet. Eight hundred and ninety six gross tons. A yacht offering quite superb comfort and luxury. In fact everything you might expect to find in a transatlantic liner.'

'Jesus christ pardon my language but that could take eighty to ninety gallons of fuel an hour to run.'

'Ninety four, cruising at fourteen knots. I see Mr Schultz you're familiar with nautical matters.'

'Yeah I am. Maybe too much so. Have you got anything a little smaller.'

'No problem. Now let me see. Ah here. I think we have rather something you might like.'

'Hey that's utterly gorgeous.'

'And very much a gentleman's yacht. Indeed Mr Schultz we've just recently sea trialled on this vessel. Fully furnished with a fully experienced crew aboard. Length overall two hundred and seven feet, and at the water line one hundred and eighty two feet. Beam thirty three feet. Displacement seven hundred and twelve tons.'

'That's still a floating hotel. But I like it. And excuse me if I just get up and pace the floor. Let's get the fuel on that one.'

'Sorry Mr Schultz that appears not to be specified. But the machinery is two one thousand four hundred horsepower diesels giving a cruising speed of fourteen to fifteen knots.'

'O christ.'

'Anything wrong.'

'I'm going to need at least another three to four knots. I got people after me. Sorry, I mean you know how it is. I just don't want to be bothered at sea with a bunch of nosey sightseers around. When a lot of the time I got international stars aboard. And with the paparazzi annoying us.'

'I quite understand. A most regrettable but I fear unavoidable species that every serious sailor abhors. But in the case of this vessel when pushed there is a maximum speed capability of seventeen knots, and indeed the engineers presently aboard are regarded as the best in the Mediterranean. There are of course these days undesirables in their speed boats. But do remember Mr Schultz you can quite quickly take most speed boats out of their fuel range.'

'Christ the god damn thing is a dream. It's beautiful. A marine masterpiece. Fucking gorgeous. Sorry that's a slip of the tongue. It's got, like a woman, the most beautiful lines I've ever seen.'

'Ah I thought you might like her sir. She is in fact one of the world's most sumptuous motor yachts. And your slip of the tongue if I may say so perfectly confirms it. She is sir called the Catherine Ahoy.'

'What, I don't believe it.'

'I take it the name is a welcome coincidence sir.'

'Yeah well maybe. It sure is giving me premonitions.'

'Ah well, I see we are at least opening doors or rather bulkheads in the right direction. Now here's her little layout. On the bridge deck abaft of the wheelhouse are the exercise and recreation areas. Convenient in heavy weather. The owner's stateroom suite and apartments are.'

'Look hold it. I didn't really come in here to do this you understand. It's still like an option I'm examining in my life.'

'I assure you Mr Schultz we always understand this in a commitment so large.'

'Holy christ. What really I need is someone here to stop me doing this. Stop me.'

'Ha ha sir. That is rather putting the pressure on us but Mr Schultz I still understand.'

'OK let's just on that understanding peek some more at the pictures.'

'The entire large aft deck of the recreation area is teak sheathed. From the owner's stateroom, the circular stair leads below to the owner's panelled private saloon, and adjoining is the owner's library and also adjoining is an office directly under the radio room above with full international phone, radio and television access.'

'O my god.'

'Is there something wrong sir.'

'No. There's just one more fantastic thing right. That's what's wrong.'

'The dining room is ideal for today's international type of guest. Stabilizers of course keeping everyone's digestion calm. And sir an additional plus here, the crew, all the furnishings, and provisions aboard can be included. With its unusual seven thousand mile range this vessel sir will provide nine weeks survivability in the North Atlantic in mid winter. You need only to step aboard. Of course as a naval man you'll be familiar with all these other matters. Radar and navigation with its every modern system in place. Crew of twenty.'

'Gee, that's less than I already got employed in my production.'

'Well if I may put it in that way sir, this is in every way a production. Conveying to the world in one launch as it were, your status. And we do act as charterers, you know. You might even find yourself making a profit.'

'Nobody but nobody goes aboard and gives orders on Schultz's ship but Schultz. And if I was crazy enough to buy this thing that's the first rule the captain would enter in the log book. Boy, I like the rake of the bow and the stern. Somehow they're just perfect.'

'Which of course Mr Schultz in no small way has, to her credit, allowed ten Atlantic crossings. Panamanian registered, lying in the South of France, we would be very happy to show you over the vessel sir.'

'No. There's no time. Christ I got to pace back and forth on this.'

371

'I quite understand sir.'

'OK I'm back. I've paced.'

'As you can see here from our colour brochure there is Mr Schultz, adjoining the owner's stateroom, and next to the sauna, this rather marvellous innovation, a water swirl bath. And very much liked by the ladies. Hot and cold air conditioning throughout. Walk in refrigerators, freezers, vegetable rooms. And a gyroscopically self stabilizing wine cellar. And never being a stationary target and having a mind to quick shore access, there are two speed boats aboard, each capable of sixty miles per hour and which, along with the automatic security system, your bodyguard I'm sure will find useful. Dear me Mr Schultz is there something wrong.'

'Yeah. One thing.'

'I'm sure sir, it can be put right whatever it is.'

'It ain't got no pigeon loft.'

'Ah ha ha ha. Or are we being serious sir.'

'Serious. Absolutely.'

'Abaft the main mast, a loft sheltered from rough weather could be put right there Mr Schultz.'

'OK. Got it.'

'And as you see here, for your VIP guests, their stateroom has double doors opening directly onto the sundeck. And of course there is the unique Queen suite with its appropriate murals and to which there is a secret and private access from the owner's cabin.'

'Jeeze stop. Stop. I got to sit down. Sorry about this. Little battle fatigue from being too long at action stations. Hey could somebody get me a glass of water please.'

'No problem, Mr Schultz. None whatever. Which if I may mention as you bring up the subject, this vessel is capable of providing a total of twelve thousand litres of fresh water daily.'

'O boy. Jesus. Should I do it, Rabbi.'

'What's that Mr Schultz.'

'Nothing. I'm sort of having a little conversation with myself.'

'Steel hull, and main deck superstructure. Lloyds one hundred A one. And I'm sure you will believe me Mr Schultz when I say there is nothing left to be desired in the soundness of this vessel.'

'Jesus Mr Jones you don't have to convince. I believe. Just from this picture I can tell just looking at that white majestic palace gliding through the blue water there, that it is the most perfect god damn thing afloat since they first sailed a dug out canoe. Wow. I'm perspiring.'

372

'Well Mr Schultz you have in a manner of speaking taken the words right out of my mouth and put it in terms that are colourful to say the least. The present owner I may add, due to sudden financial economy, is most keen to sell. And she is at this moment lying at her own mooring in Monaco ready to board.'

'If fifteen percent comes off that price listed there. You got a deal.'

'If you'll excuse me Mr Schultz and in just a moment I'll be back to you.'

Smiling blonde girl putting down the glass of water in front of Schultz. Downing a mouthful. Rabbi it's going to be water water everywhere, and beautiful wine to drink. But Rabbi. Stop me. If you think it is too extravagant. Sigmund living's no bargain but there is nothing extravagant about staying alive and afloat. Shit then maybe don't stop me. O my god. Hey Catherine Ahoy. I'm already in love with you. Anchors aweigh. And all it took was staying hysterically calm through a few middle of the night phone calls. I could be aboard in that steel inner sanctum, cutting bow waves. Ave Maria playing. The pigeons in their coop cooing up on top of the bridge. The radar scope sweeping the sea ahead. The helmsman avoiding the blips. Jorricks masterminding the kitchens. Daniel sergeant at arms, ready to break legs or clap any crew troublemaker below in irons.

'May I suggest Mr Schultz twelve and a half percent off.'

'Thirteen.'

'Done. And the owner, Mr Schultz does have one small request, he asks if in taking the crew, you keep on Joseppi, his barber.'

'No problem. I haven't had time for weeks to have a haircut.'

'O splendid. And may I congratulate you Mr Schultz. And may you have many happy hours aboard the Catherine Ahoy.'

'Hours.'

You mean
Lifetime

29

Daniel in his false beard and sunglasses opening the car door. Schultz alighting in front of Sperm Productions. Taking a puff of his cigar and stepping up over the grey stone step. Into this dingy hall. Up on the creaking elevator, out on the landing. This could be the last time I ever go through this familiar door. Jesus I have to admit as much as I have nothing to thank that fucker for, with Binky gone the place is like a morgue. Rebecca's got to come aboard. Be the ship's secretary. Holy christ. In the waiting room. Sitting. Waiting. The fucking pair of hunchbacks. Sending a shiver up and down my spine. O christ. Rebecca's office empty. Go down the hall. Jesus is there nobody else here. Try the chairman's door.

'O hey hi your Lordship.'

'Good god Schultz you gave me a fright. My word what a very attractive outfit you're wearing. I thought you might be loaded up and ready to sail.'

'Hey how did you know.'

'Of course there really are anacondas and piranhas up the Amazon.'

'I'm not going up the fucking Amazon. I bought a dinghy with a pair of oars. And I'm going to row around the Serpentine.'

'Schultz you're sounding awfully cheerful.'

'Am I. I hadn't noticed I thought I was always like this.'

'But pray tell Schultz, you do also seem rather all in a dither. And your face flushed far too pink for this early in the afternoon.'

'It's the decisions in my life.'

'Ah perhaps you've been reading the theatrical trade journals.'

'I'm taking a long holiday from all that shit.'

'Now that you are a multimillionaire.'

'Yeah and I've probably notched you over into being a billionaire.'

'Well Schultz according to this Variety just off the presses here. I could have been considerably richer. Hollywood bought the movie rights from Joe Jewels for ten million.'

'Where. Let me see that. I don't believe it.'

'Right here. In headlines.'

KISS IT, IT'S SOLD
JEWELS SEALS CELLULOID DEAL
FOR RECORD SUM

'Why those charlatan cunts. Give me that phone. I'll get that son of a bitch Al.'

'Don't Schultz trip over the carpet.'

The cradle in one hand receiver pressed between ear and shoulder, Schultz pacing back and forth, and chewing off the end of the cigar in his mouth and spitting it on the floor.

'I want to speak to Al Duke.'

'One moment, please, who's calling.'

'You just tell him honey it's London and he ought to know and get him on this phone fast.'

'Yes sir.'

'Al. This you.'

'Yeah.'

'Why you fucking chiselling schlemiel Al. I'm going to get you for this if it's the last thing I do.'

'Hey Sigmund. We're on our way to a funeral here. Joe Jewels's mother died. But I want meanwhile to give you some good advice. Why don't you just go and make a big and lasting impression on the world. And in the contortion of a pretzel, go fuck yourself. Goodbye.'

'Hey your Lordship where's Rebecca. I'm going to sue these fuckers Jewels and Duke for fraudulent misrepresentation.'

'Dear me. Haven't you heard.'

'Heard what.'

'About Binky.'

'Don't mention that fucker's name ever again to me.'

'Well Schultz I'm afraid I must as it explains what you want to know.'

'Well tell me then. Reluctantly I'll listen.'

'Rumour has it that in Paris he'd met up with some nurse from a London hospital. And spent all his money in a nightclub. And was last heard of in the Rue Pigalle, where he was found believed to be starving in a heap halfway down the steps of the metro. Rebecca has gone to Paris to find him.'

'Holy shit thank god for all the precautions I take in my life. So that I don't become a situation I don't want to happen. And even if it does mean I cannot get what I want.'

'Dear me Schultz that leaves one open to imagining the awful prospect of your desiring to view the spectacle of naked virgins being executed.'

'Hey what kind of a remark is that when I'm upset hearing this. Binky deserves what he's getting. But I don't deserve to have Rebecca gone. And by the way before she takes off for the Amazon I'm unloading off Erica, her dog, her whips, pith helmets, batteries, snow shoes, skis and cameras back at your house.'

'You can't do that Schultz.'

'Why not. I got to.'

'My mother has just died.'

'Jesus twice I hear this in five minutes. Your mother did that over a week ago.'

'Well she's suddenly doing it again this week. Would you like to know what that lady did in my house.'

'Jesus your Lordship I'd love to. But listen I don't have time. But you could just tell me if I can depend now upon Binky's life becoming a permanent tragedy.'

'Well Schultz I suppose all lives do ere long as they quietly proceed. But in Binky's case I daresay he will one day make a comeback. But the burden he carries is bigger than most.'

'What burden.'

'Guilt.'

'Boy that's one thing you can never make me believe.'

'Ah perhaps you recall his exquisite sister Catherine.'

'As a matter of pleasant fact I do.'

'Well Schultz she was as a young girl up in the Highlands, betrothed to a handsome, kindly, rich, young laird she'd loved since childhood. And on the grouse moor in her sight he was killed.'

'Jeeze.'

'Accidentally shot by Binky.'

In the setting sun of the afternoon, Schultz alighting from the limousine outside Farm Street Church. Entering and standing in the back. Voices in vespers. A chain clinking and the smoke and smell of incense. In the dim light the few figures seated and kneeling in the rows of pews. Rabbi don't for christ's sake kill me for being here. There's going to be, believe me, a synagogue where we can talk aboard the yacht. Love first brought me to this church and I guess betrayal has kept me coming back. But I got to go light all these little candles in memory. Jesus and even one for Binky. Although I still can't forgive the son of a bitch. And jesus going back all those years now. To when my cousin Saul was short changing the customers. And that lady who came down the basement to our lingerie store. This candle is for you, honey. For the vestige of hope you instilled in me which is still there in my heart, a tiny tiny ember still flickering. And for Cynthia. Jesus kid I'm sorry. I forgot to put you in the chorus line, anyway it's better for curing people to remain a nurse. And I can remain dreaming of the blow job you unselfishly gave me.

And back that night Rabbi, I was standing naked again in the middle of the pink bedroom. With Azorr tied up lying under the blanket quietly snuffling through his new muzzle Jorricks got him from Harrods' pet shop. I really took the cat o' nine tails and let Erica have it as hard as she wanted over the ass. Because one cheek was Joe and the other Al. Who as Binky predicted did fucking well pull the wool over my eyes. The cunts with mounted police as an escort had a band go marching up and down the street outside the theatre with half the chorus line nude, kicking up their heels and with religious leaders protesting. A sky writer in an aeroplane writing 'Kiss It Don't Hold It It's Too Hot' all over the sky. And had that very night I did the deal, every seat in the theatre sold. Christ, then I find even the thrill of sadism palls and I'm sad and looking absent minded between strokes out the window. Like when you know you're going to leave somewhere and this place I'd come to feel was home. The backs of houses just like they always were. Again Erica soon as she got fucked, this time normal and not dog style, forgot me and fell asleep. Her snores reaching a crescendo like every seventh wave on the ocean. At least it was an interruption in the sobbing and crying. Her arms wrapped over the top of the bed, the feet sticking out the bottom. Rabbi I was trying to place her face I knew I saw somewhere before. And it wasn't as a whorer. But who said anything about prostitution. It was when Al mentioned Hercules and Diomedes, the statue in Florence, where one of these fuckers has the other fucker by the balls and by the way it's something I want to know, who's got the fateful fistful. And then suddenly I remember where I first saw Erica's face. Also in Florence. In a picture. The Birth of Venus. By Botticelli. One of the most beautiful but saddest faces in the world. Jesus they could be nearly identical twins. And if I could just stand once more the thought of Al. Who once said to me, when are you ever going to learn women are like nice toys you play with and if you break the toy you have nothing to play with. Like a pet you take good care of them. Treat them nice. They like it. Such knowledge coming from Al, Mr Bigamy. With wives he still got clawing around tax dodgers' towers. Because he says, they still love him. And holy shit, maybe they do. And maybe with all I've been through, even I still love women. He should have seen me tonight. With wham, this cat o' nine tails. And even in all the down to earth reality of these moans out of Erica and breathing noises out of Azorr. I still can't believe it. And still don't believe or trust it. But I have to believe it. A few insults on the phone. Papers coming all the way across the ocean. And in two seconds, losing two million, I signed them. In the full knowledge that without my beautiful taste the show would make a total disaster and flop as a film. And leave my artistic reputation for previous theatrical aesthetic excellence in tatters. And also with money in the bank. And with that kind of gold who needs a reputation. Then Rabbi, standing in the candlelight, and looking at my profile in the mirror and brushing back my big black tumbling curls, I put back on a pith helmet. I guess you'd really have to say that this safari image makes me look romantic. I'm really good looking with the most fantastic set of perfect teeth. I should smile more often, it suits me. I'm really a fucking nice guy. I am even tempted to go down to the kitchen and get a snack for the dog. And stop him suffocating as he seems to be doing right now. The fucking mutt. Boy if I can just keep my cool. Nothing must slip up in the next twenty four hours. Confidentiality is the supreme priority. With Al in constant contact with my wife and her lawyers. Everything has got to stay hunky dory. Christ maybe I'm going nuts, and thinking about the money is giving me a hard on. Rabbi it's been some life up till now. And hey Rabbi can't you hear me shouting for joy that I've come this far. From three flops to one hit. To a townhouse. To a floating palace on the Riviera. With a faithful butler and bodyguard. Jesus Rabbi where are you, I'm waiting, will you please return my call. Sigmund let's call a moratorium and when you're on your ship with the very latest in international communications I'll listen. Because from the last time you were screaming.

I had
To put
Ear plugs
In

'Sir wake up wake up, the captain wants you to take over on the bridge, we're in a hurricane.'

Schultz waking in the pink bedroom. Azorr with his muzzle on, asleep against the door. Erica snoring. And awaking me out of a dream. I was aboard my old ship back in the Coast Guard, being awakened by a sailor. Then Erica woke speaking a language I'd never heard before. Because it was fluent Hungarian. Then in the morning. Trying to get them out of the house. The wailing, the sobbing, from Erica. And even from her dog who howled. You'd think the two of them would be instead laughing since courtesy my investment, they were both at last heading for up the Amazon. While I'm just still like a snail in a hurry cautiously going onwards.

30

Rabbi, please what do you say to the present situation. There's no sense to it that I should not be at this mature golden time of my life having peace and contentment. Especially when I can afford the cost. Sigmund it would be wise if I told you at this time, for the sake of your health, sanity and continued solvency, to cut down on the number of women. Jesus Rabbi you don't understand. In order to keep one woman, you got to have two. And jesus I'm learning fast that if you want to go on keeping two, you've got to have three. Well Sigmund go on like that and you may need five nurses at an autopsy to put your pieces back together and bury you, but if you want three, go ahead, who's counting.

Four taxis this time to take her away. I nearly got a last second rupture lifting a camera. Then talk about guilt, christ the Skyscraper Erica wasn't such a bad skin after all and I even nearly got to like the dog. And I even anteed up with an extra five thousand for up the Amazon. For which I thought I could at least keep her cat o' nine tails. What the hell Uncle Werb said always be a good Jewish boy Sigmund and give and get value for money.

'O K Erica, you take care of yourself, honey.'

'I don't want to go. And leave you all alone.'

'Honey that's O K, no kidding believe me. Bye bye Azorr. Don't stick your nose in the river and get bit by a piranha.'

O jeeze Rabbi I was at the very last moment sentimental. I was about to say, O K, kiddo stay. What did I really want. Bodies or souls. And my own soul up for grabs. For the talons to sink in from the three possible women now left available in my life. Added up briefly, a choice between whipping and bestiality, blow jobs, strip tease dancing or just teaming up to go sailing with a nut who could spout her marvellous fluent rubbish. Who somehow Rabbi I swear I couldn't get the thought of this gorgeously eccentrically insane girl with her honesty dropping bricks on my foot, out of my mind. A shotgun blast going off and sending her dreams to hell. If she is what I select to make permanent in my life I promise you it will be the last piece of ass I am ever going to attempt to come to civilized decent terms with. Like shit why don't women just go peel onions in the kitchen and let their eyes water that way. And Rabbi I sincerely ask, how do they keep finding new devious ways to get a guy up the aisle. Sigmund the tricks women will play to land a man no fisherman in history could ever invent.

'So long Erica, send me news from rain forest when you get there.'

Rabbi that's one down and two to go. And I nearly told Cynthia to go apply for the Freddie Joy Scholarship. And get all the practice she could ever need to become a singer by blowing that fucker Joe Jewels's brains out. But I'm finished doing favours for all women. What the fuck plenty of new ass on the horizon and it's not that bad to be alone. The iron shutters put up over the ground floor windows of Arabesque Street locked from the inside. And with bags, books and files plus the pigeons all packed up, I waved goodbye to the Ambassador. Tears in both our eyes. As usual he was having a big reception that night. And just as I was putting my head down to get into the car, he held up a sign to me in his window.

ISLAM WILL ALWAYS
COME TO YOUR AID

But Rabbi I was just lounging back in the upholstery and jesus Catherine, I still couldn't get her off my mind. I hadn't called her for two days. Still nearly in a dilemma. But the limousine loaded and already facing down the street to the airport. The heavy luggage already sent on. And I picked up the phone. And she sounded so glad to hear from me. I got instantly carried away.

'Jesus honey, let me take care of you, forever.'

'Is forever never. Or is it now. Or when. You see. I wouldn't want you to want me just for my trust funds.'

'Holy shit, honey. I'm taking you to a ship. Which if, once you see it, could lead you to believe I don't need your trust funds, because it is not exactly paupersville afloat.'

'Ha. But you may have only chartered it to impress me.'

'O K honey. You win. Let's do this your way. Try it for a day or two. And every time I try to stick my hand in your trust funds you just slap it away.'

Down a long Savoy Hotel hallway, right past the gents. Where I vomited the day Al got me my first investment money and blackmailed me into marrying the black cloud. I go up to the fifth floor on an elevator in this strangest part of the hotel. I knock. Catherine answering and her nurse looking out the door of an adjoining room. And jesus there standing in front of me. I'd forgotten what such a total knockout she is. Unbelievably beautiful at the door. In a funny purple and crimson jockey's cap and a corduroy pair of jodhpurs, black cashmere sweater, and a long string of real pearls. Her eyeballs so white like her mother's. Who I always loved from first sight anyway. And it took me nearly all my nerve to say.

'Honey here I am with my raincheck.'

'I guess I'm so glad.'

'Gee, don't guess honey. And it's good to see you.'

'Yes, isn't it good. I see you. And so nice to see you too.'

'Like I told you on the phone, get your hat, we're going to the Riviera.'

'Here, already ready, I've got my hat. I am rather looking forward. You know how one does when one does not want to look backward, over one's shoulder. Nurse is so thrilled. So thrilled. This is the sunny day, you spoke about. But I am. I am nervous. Not extraordinarily nervous.'

'I know honey just ordinary nervous. But this is, no kidding, the sunny day honey I spoke about.'

'And you know speaking of skies, you do have the most blazing blue eyes.'

'Come on honey. Let's go. There's no time for flattery. Bring those dimples on your cheeks. We're in a hurry.'

'Nurse has all the packing done, not to worry. Porter's on the way. You know I was so certain you would never come. I was many of these past days going to go and knock on your door. I'm so glad I didn't. I wanted so much to see you. See you. And now like a dream come true. You're here. You're here. But are you sure you really want me. I've had an abortion. Been nearly raped twice I think. And at this moment I believe I may be coming down with a head cold.'

'Honey, just like they do in the song, pack up your troubles in your old kit bag.'

'I shall. I shall. And you know I do like smoked salmon in my morning scrambled egg. Can I have that on your little boat. This morning instead I had poached peaches for breakfast. Have some for you left over in the bowl. I am a shareholder in this hotel and I hate to see them wasted. Wasted. But O dear it's such an expensive hotel, one is glad to have an account and not have to see the bill.'

'Honey, thanks. I adore poached peaches. And please bring the peaches along. My car's waiting in front downstairs.'

'Ah, we're going.'

'We are honey, we are.'

'Then I shall fling my big black gangster's coat over my shoulders. And you know Sigmund, and may I call you Sigmund mayn't I. And apropos of nothing at all, except it is apropos, we do need heroes don't we, in the world, and not persons of moral despicability.'

'Honey you took the words right out of my mouth.'

'O dear, that's the phone. I'll answer it. See you, see you downstairs.'

Under the silver shiny canopy of the Savoy Hotel tucked in its little cul de sac in from the Strand. The smiling deputy manager, the doorman, concierge, three porters, Daniel and Jorricks all in attendance. Loading on luggage. With not a fraction of an inch to spare. For once the limousine is full up. The doorman brushing off seats with a whisk. The concierge putting a rug over Catherine. And also nurse's knees, who is as Scots as they can come. From the Outer Hebrides. Daniel already giving her the eye.

'We do so hope Mr Schultz we will see you back here soon again.'

The deputy manager smilingly closing the limousine door. Boy Rabbi do I really rate. Or is it Catherine. Or maybe both of us together. And here we go. Me and my entire entourage. Slowly pulling away. And I couldn't believe it. There parked nearly beside us, a reminder of all my past fucking misery. The carpenter's red Ferrari. And Louella inside. Looking at me.

Rabbi I swear there seemed like to be tears in her eyes. Sigmund you should know better than to get romantic. The light from the jewels she is wearing is reflected upwards. Rabbi she ditched me. And maybe even now ditched Al. So that a fucker who can't drive a nail, but can drive a Ferrari, is hammering her. Just give me a basic reason why women behave that way. Sigmund you should already know that there are ladies who if they can go out dancing with a guy who is living.

They will
Gladly leave
A guy who is
Dying
For dead

The aeroplane gliding across the blue water on this blazing
sunny afternoon to land on the Côte d'Azur. Catherine
clutching her lizard skin jewellery box on her knee. Sun
tanned folk on the airport terrace waving to the arriving
passengers. Two ancient Daimler limousines motoring
Schultz and entourage under the palm trees along the bay of
Nice. And up past the red roofed houses stacked back into the dark
green hills. Yellow awnings. Flowers pink, lilac, rose and violet on the
garden slopes. Concrete gutters for torrents of rain. The little town of
Eze perched on its mountain top.

'O Sigmund, doesn't it for you as it does for me, set little cheerful
flags flying, flying in your heart.'

'It does honey it does.'

The cars passing the customs barriers and down into the principality
of Monaco. Past the markets and stacks of vegetables. Out along the
harbour sea wall and along by the smooth gleaming sterns of all these
big yachts. The cars stopping at the next to last and biggest. A massive
radiant white sight, dressed overall. Catherine turning to kiss Schultz
on the cheek.

'O Sigmund. The name. It's mine. It's mine. It's me. Me. Me.'

'Yes honey yes. You.'

On the aft deck, in their whites and gold braid, captain and officers
assembled. Introductions and welcoming owner and party aboard.
The valet showing the nurse to her stateroom and Catherine to the
Queen suite. Schultz reviewing the crew on the foredeck as the captain
held inspection. Everything shipshape. Right from the radio room
down to the bilge. And Rabbi the brass winches polished gleaming like
they were gold. You could eat fraises des bois off the engine room floor.
Forget the price. If now I just blind myself to the cost of just swabbing
all these teak decks, and to the overheads of six tons of fuel for a day's
steaming. And instead just keep reminding myself. Is this really me.
With a gorgeous lovely girl. Here in the sunshine. Here in this glory.
The pale brown and green dome of the casino across the harbour. Out
of which I've got to keep Catherine. But the pea green colour of the
Hôtel de Paris, where both of us can go. And sit free of charge in the
lobby.

'Tea sir.'

'Gee Jorricks why not.'

'Very good sir. And may I congratulate you.'

'Thanks Jorricks. Not a bad little old tub is it.'

Jorricks announcing the water temperature in the harbour as he served tea on the aft deck at a round mahogany table set with flowers. Catherine in a purple jersey and white slacks, an orange chiffon scarf tied round her waist. Daniel again in his general's uniform and medals and sweating profusely but grinning as he did a little skip and dance of joy ferrying the hot water, strawberry jam and fresh scones. And nearly tripped flat faced over the bulkhead. Coming up to whisper to me when I was going for a pee to the powder room off the saloon.

'Ah confidentially Mr Schultz, take it from me, you've pulled a fast one on us all this time. Taking us to paradise, long before we ever get to heaven.'

'Well I guess Daniel you can take it from me that everybody in this world wants to step as far away from the shit as they can and swim in the cream and bump against the fraises des bois floating in season.'

'Well sir I don't know about them phrase day whatever they are. But I wouldn't mind any bumping into nurse Macphearson.'

And nurse wearing a big straw hat and a flowered long sleeved dress said she was from an island so small in the Hebrides that it rocked in the waves. I put her up on the bridge deck aft of the captain's day room to keep her out of Daniel's way. And by an amidship's stair, she could get to Catherine installed in the Queen suite. To which from the King suite I had access through the secret door. And the first thing Catherine did while I went to see Joseppi for a haircut, was take a water swirl bath and use up extra fuel spinning the generators by having a sauna. As she came out on deck in a bikini, a fucking guy went climbing the mast to spy and the crew everywhere were apoplectically trying to sneak looks at her. But even with the ship's company's uncontrollable erections it would still take a lot to stop this from being a fucking floating palace of bliss. Letting life wait for me instead of me waiting for life. The barber Joseppi was the funniest little Italian guy with too much garlic on his breath but a lot of good jokes up his sleeve. Only, in the styling, the fucker really made a mess of my hair. He even had eyelash curlers for the former owner's girlfriend. After a shower, I went on another tour. Every bit of the boat more gorgeous than in the photographs. The sculptural decorations on the wood panelling, tasteful antiques like you never saw. Beautiful pornography in the library. Ebony door knobs. The poor fucking bastard who had to sell this, Carl the captain told me, had a bank overnight squeezing him by the balls. Even some of his silk socks and two silk shirts left behind in a drawer. Plus a truss and corset I didn't need yet. But his socks, and the shirts fit. So since they were silk, why not, I wore

384

them. And holy shit it was dawning on me, this fucking thing I got, is such a bargain I should now sell for a profit.

'Excuse me sir, the chef would like to know at what time you would like dinner served. And would you like it in the dining room.'

'O gee Jorricks. Let's see. Maybe at twenty hundred hours we'll have it outdoors aft on the main deck.'

'Tête à tête sir.'

'You got it Jorricks.'

'Very good sir. The evening is expected to be balmy. And the pigeons sir, are cooing.'

Night settling over the harbour. Moon rising over Monaco. And the starboard green and port red lights on the passing boats. The gold lit windows ashore. Table set. Sparkling glass. And gleaming cutlery. A bottle of champagne popping just as Catherine in a black dress of Chantilly lace, stepped over the bulkhead out of the saloon doors. Looking so gorgeous and speaking beautiful French to the valet who was doing pirouettes of admiration behind her. Her black sandals clicking on the deck. Rabbi I nearly fainted. You'd never seen anything like it. Style to knock your eye out. Her slender pale arms look gorgeous. An antique emerald and diamond bracelet on her wrist. A jade bead necklace at her throat. A gem of a female in my possession waking up suddenly in my life. So what if she's a tiny little bit off her rocker. The utter sanity of the soft waves of her black gleaming hair and her patrician profile more than make up for it. Just dining there a hand's touch away in the candlelight. A long long way from Woonsocket and the lingerie store.

'He is, isn't he, such a gay valet.'

'He sure is honey.'

'And you know they are wearing their wristwatch bands over their shirt cuffs this season. Très snob. Très chic.'

'Yeah honey, so I see, très ridiculous.'

'And you know Sigmund, I do of course try to get by without thinking but it's entirely possible I may be well one day. And you may say well, well, well. She's well. And I will be. I will be. If you help me. Help me. Help.'

'Honey jesus eat that little piece of parsley there the chef put on top of your lamb chop, there's vitamin C in it. You'll be fine. Fine.'

In the dimmed light of the saloon, coffee, chocolate mints, and Armagnac after dinner. Sunk down deep in this soft primrose coloured couch, the two of us holding hands. Fauré's Requiem over the sound system. Jesus I swear, Rabbi, I know it seems like I'm going a little strange in the brain box. But a couple of seconds ago I was thinking of maybe buying a few racehorses. And then tears came into my eyes as I thought about the poor guy's corset and truss in the drawer who had to sell all this. And then leave the shirts, and the socks I'm wearing, behind. Which were lying folded on top of a photograph of another gorgeous girl whose name was obvious from a hundred magazine covers I'd seen her on. Then I thought of Freddie Joy. Who in one of her low moments said if there are too many men running after one woman it never gives the woman a chance to concentrate on trapping just one guy. That should have right there put the caution light on to slow down to stop. Just me now after this girl. Beware. Women have been my downfall. And jesus I couldn't believe it. But I believe it. I was willing to be in this gorgeous girl's arms, trapped all over again. And maybe for even all time. And while she slipped back into her Queen suite I went a stroll up around the bridge deck looking at the lights of Monte Carlo. Taking in lungfuls of the ambrosial Mediterranean air. Wondering what tonight's Broadway and West End gross was. And nearly for a second erasing the memory of Al Duke and Joe Jewels. Back in my stateroom I looked again at the framed photograph of the model and even put it back up on my dressing table. At least she had a nice smile like she could be from a small Rhode Island town and work in the dead letter department of the post office. At eight bells in my pyjamas I go tiptoeing into the Queen suite. Catherine reading with a pair of thick lensed eyeglasses. Tolstoy. War and Peace. Jesus something somehow with this vulnerable girl made me feel cruel as I tried to look pleasant unfurling the cat o' nine tails.

'Please O please Sigmund don't beat me. I know that it does give some people pleasure but I've had, had already, enough pain.'

'Sorry honey.'

'I just prefer, prefer soothing caresses. And if they be delicious, soft and delicious I prefer them even more.'

'Honey. No problem. I just only started recently doing this anyway. And I thought, why stop.'

'O dear. Crestfallen. Poor poor you. You do want to play, don't you. O K just let me turn over and lift up my negligee. And expose my contrite bottom. Now there. Not too hard. Because, because. I do. Do prefer the gentle, the soft, and the delicious.'

Rabbi I swear. I got to admit. At long last. And I can't stop myself from saying it. Women, for all their faults, some of them are still fucking wonderful. Especially when they lay down and welcome you to lie down with them.

Touché
Sigmund
Touché

32

Rabbi the captain was really impressed by my sea duty in the Coast Guard. And working out our trip to the Aegean, it was nice to shoot the shit and scuttlebutt and get back over a nautical chart once more. Radio room reporting sea calm and weather fair all the way to Cyprus. While at the same time I could be becoming a storm tossed victim in love.

'What I suggest Mr Schultz is that we make south for the Strait of Bonifacio and into the Tyrrhenian Sea past Ischia, Capri and through the Stretto di Messina.'

'Sounds like just what the doctor ordered, Captain.'

Nurse Macphearson sitting in the corner of the saloon knitting and smiling. Daniel making eyes at her when he wasn't glowering at and terrorizing the crew. He had already knocked the chef's cap off into last night's celery soup and threatened to stuff him through a porthole for making a remark about Jorricks. Otherwise Daniel kept dancing around like he was in a musical. Rabbi, the only thing wrong was the dining room. Chairs covered in leopard skin. Catherine wouldn't sit on them. But the thing wrong with dining on deck in port was, I see some son of a bitch come along the quayside walking his dog who he then lets go lift a leg up to piss on my nice white painted gangway.

'Hey get that god damn mutt out of here.'

'Fuck you monsieur.'

Rabbi I was really shocked at the rudeness shown by these Monégasques to big yacht owners. I nearly rushed up to the palace to give them a piece of my mind, if not a bust on the nose. But last night lulled by the ship's movement and enveloped in Catherine's arms, it was so pleasant that I was able to stare right at my own moment of death. One woman can cure you of everything done to you by all the others. And give you the best sleep of your life. It was like music just lying back and listening to her.

'Sigmund. Can you hear me whispering. Clinging on to you here in this suite fit for a queen. Clinging to conversation. The Riviera nights are still. The vipers awake up in the piney scrublands. Where the cork and olive trees are. And men wade through the needle sharp thickets to get the bark to make their champagne corks.'

'Honey, you really know this place.'

'Yes. Yes. I do. I do. And above on higher land. In day, up a pine scented lane. There are sounds strange in the blinding sunlight. The noises are haunted in the silence behind your walking feet. Under the singing birds. And tonight. I'm waiting for tomorrow. Till the morning blue sea goes waving past on the cerulean blue of my cabin walls. As the engines throb and the foam crashes by over the portholes. Goodnight my sweet. I won't cry again for help till dawn.'

'Jesus honey. You're a poet. Cry for help anytime. Goodnight. Sleep tight.'

Deckhands loading the provisions arriving all morning long, along the quayside. Lugged aboard on the crew's shoulders up the gangway. Celery, oranges, tea, coffee, figs, butter, plums, steaks, non kosher roasts of pork and beef, tomatoes, peaches, cheese, bananas, lettuce, fraises des bois. And the last. A gleaming grey Mercedes Benz squeals to a halt to unload the brandy and boxes of chocolates.

At seven bells on the forenoon watch, a bank of clouds accumulating high up over the land. But the sun beaming down on Monte Carlo. Making lighter all the dark green up over the hills and brightening the white specks of villas on the hillsides. Daniel feeding the pigeons happy in their coop on top the bridge. Sailing flags hoisted. All shipshade ready for sea. The gangway lifted from the pier at eight bells. The gleaming brass capstans winching dripping hawsers aboard. Puffs of diesel smoke rising from the funnel. The sixteen cylinder twin cats throbbing and the twin screws of the Catherine Ahoy churning the water. In the main saloon, the other Catherine all wrapped up in a great pink towel robe. Her black gleaming hair brushed back loose over her shoulders. Having her smoked salmon omelette for late late breakfast. Plus figs in whipped cream to help move her bowels. And engrossed in a volume of erotica from the library. Join her for a cup of coffee. Hand her a rose and kiss her on the nose.

'Honey I'm going up on the bridge. The captain wants me to help him take this tub out to sea.'

'Gosh Sigmund do forgive me if one uses such a common word but this is all so really uncommonly nice. And you know, your charming little boat is so full of wonderful toys.'

'I thought you might like it honey. I thought so.'

Schultz on the bridge in an orange and blue barrel striped jersey and Bermuda shorts. Cigar in his mouth. Taking off sunglasses to watch the radar. Whistle blowing blasts. The Catherine Ahoy slowly pulling out clear of her mooring into the open water of the harbour. Coxswain at the helm. Carl the captain looking ahead from the wheelhouse windows. A sailor signalling on the bow. Christ we're underway. My god Rabbi the magic of it. I must have been living for this moment all my life if I only knew it. Carl a really sweet guy. Who I guess ought to be, at his salary. The boat's whistle sounding again.

And listen to the blast echoing back from the hills around Monaco. They sure know we're coming. Or in this case going.

'Mr Schultz, Mr Schultz.'

'Yes captain.'

'That vessel coming ahead over there, is not obeying the rules of the road. I may have to hove to a bit till he's proceeded out of the harbour.'

'What's his tonnage, captain.'

'Maybe a hundred net sir.'

'Well we're more than three times his size. We got the right of way. Proceed ahead. Cut the little fucker off, captain.'

'Aye aye sir.'

'Jesus will you look at that. In a hurry the son of a bitch. Doesn't know what he's doing. He needs a spinnaker pole shoved up the ass. Thinks he owns the fucking place. Christ he's going to cut across our bow to get out the harbour entrance ahead of us. Some upstart in a fucking glorified gondola.'

'Shouldn't I take avoiding action sir.'

'Like hell. I didn't spend millions of dollars to buy this boat to get pushed around.'

'Aye aye, Mr Schultz. Coxswain, ring down full ahead.'

'Aye aye captain.'

'Yeah. That's it. Voom. Let's go. Imagine. Jesus everywhere you look these guys in their damn little runabouts thinking they're master mariners. And look at that. The nerve. Showing off to his friends. Honking his fucking hooter. Give him a fucking blast or two from our hooter. Knock him on his ass. No even better, where's the loud hailer.'

Schultz stepping out on deck from the wheelhouse. Balancing his cigar on the ship's rail, and leaning over the bridge wing and raising the loud hailer to his lips.

'Hey ship ahoy. Vous êtes stupides. Out of the fucking way will you.'

Heads turning. Holy jeeze, wait a second. I swear I know that fucking face. The fat guy on the bridge amid the girls, with the cap and binoculars, white shirt and bow tie. My god I don't believe this. In a deck chair under a straw hat, like he's in a coma, that's fucking Ezekiel, the tailor, Saul's old father. And that. Trying to think he's a sailor. That's my fucking cousin Saul.

'Captain dead slow.'

'Aye aye sir.'

'Stand by.'

'Aye aye sir.'

'Hey Saul. Saul.'

'Hey who you shouting to, me.'

'Yeah you. This is Sigmund Schultz shouting to you.'

'Hey Sigmund. Not Sigmund Siggy Schultz from Woonsocket.'

'Yeah, the very same.'

'Hey Sigmund. Forgive me. But is that really you. Sigmund Franz Isadore. Formerly of exotic lingerie.'

'It's me Saul. Up here. Who else have you seen recently with my distinctive big black curls, blue eyes and shiny teeth.'

'How you doing up there, kiddo. Hey who's your host with that ocean liner.'

'I'm the host, Saul.'

'Hey, ha, ha, quit the kidding. That boat's not yours is it.'

'It ain't my rabbi's.'

'Hey Sigmund, let me back this thing up a little, and please, don't rush away. I'd like to talk to you and like you to meet my friends.'

'Saul if your yacht down there can do seventeen knots to the Aegean, we'll see you there.'

'Jesus hey Sigmund, you must have made a bundle. Who did you wipe out.'

'Lots of people. But before I wiped them out at least I always had the good conscience to sit down and cry copiously first.'

'Hey ha ha, kid. Well I got some special mid town Manhattan real estate development situations might interest you. And I'd like to go aboard that boat.'

'Sure Saul. And you can give me a cheque to compensate for all our lingerie customers you short changed back in my father's store. And maybe next time when you return my calls we'll talk. Only I won't be calling.'

Schultz taking a long puff on his cigar and blowing out the smoke. And tapping the ash off over the side, dropping it on Saul and his guests below. A gleaming speedboat zooming by, a flash bulb going off as Schultz steps back over the bulkhead into the wheelhouse.

'OK captain, quick, a little dangerous navigation. I'll take the responsibility. Full ahead. Hard left rudder. That speed boat plus us will rock the bastard on his beam ends in our wake.'

'Aye aye sir.'

'Here, let me take over.'

Schultz grabbing and spinning the wheel in a hard right rudder and the water foaming up astern. The Catherine Ahoy gaining speed. Heading for the harbour exit flanked by its twin little white lighthouses.

Sweeping her two hundred and seven foot gleaming bright hull length past Saul and his guests grabbing to hold on pitching and rolling in the waves. O my god Rabbi. When I'm just beginning to live, get ready for death. We're too close starboard, we're going to hit the rocks below the lighthouse at the end of the fucking sea wall. Jesus hard to port, hard fucking left. Stop engines. No. Full ahead. The bow is only, if it does, just going to miss. It's got to. Christ we're scraping by. Just. With what I hope is only a superficial scratch out of sight below the water line. Which if it goes deep could sink us. Jesus Rabbi is revenge the strongest of all emotions.

No
Sorrow and shame is
After appalling
Seamanship

The Catherine Ahoy steaming south south east into the Mediterranean. A fortune in paint scraped off a still seaworthy hull bottom. Saul's yacht left colliding with another vessel in the middle of the harbour and the two, with anchor chains entwined, churning in a circle. Rabbi I guess we've come a long way from Belgravia. Well, Sigmund not only that but let me tell you, after all these years in show biz, you sure have lost your touch at the helm.

33

Hove to, three miles off shore, the Catherine Ahoy's Boston Whaler Outrage tender with twin hundred and fifty horsepower outboard motors, lowered and Catherine in her bikini skimming over the waves at forty knots, waterskiing. Paparazzi in a flotilla of speedboats arriving and taking photographs through telescopic lenses. Rumour having spread through Monaco that the gorgeous curvaceous raven haired Catherine was an overnight just discovered new radiant international star. Being groomed by the previous bankrupt owner, a movie mogul, no longer aboard.

'Captain we got to shake those fucking parasites off.'

'Aye aye, sir, full ahead.'

The Catherine Ahoy diesels reverberating at a steady seventeen and a half knots, now nearly in the middle of the Mediterranean. In her wake fins of following sharks cutting through the water. Snapping down scraps thrown overboard from the galley. And Rabbi they told me there were no sharks in the Mediterranean. Catherine who is taking a sauna and swirl pool bath and sunning topless and bottomless aft on the bridge deck, could have got gobbled down. Instead of, as she now is, creating a sensation aboard the boat. The crew falling over themselves to be at her beck and call, just to get a glimpse of her, preferably unclothed. A star she is. No doubt about that. As now I go apoplectic with jealousy struggling to keep her in my own private orbit. Which was getting more elliptical by the day. As I started feeling seasick going through the Strait of Bonifacio. Meeting Jorricks in the companionway as I was heading for the bridge deck to privately vomit behind a lifeboat.

'Well sir, I do believe we are having some plain sailing and it is rather nice isn't it. But O dear. We seem sir, to be in some not entirely untroubled waters.'

'We sure are Jorricks.'

'O dear sir. Head up. Shoulders back. Breathe through the nose. Can I suggest tea in the saloon as usual might help. And to alert madam.'

'Yeah, christ tea. Yeah alert madam. Do that Jorricks.'

'I was just going sir to catch up on the weather news from the radio room to put in your study.'

Schultz spattering the contents of his stomach on the breeze and returning to the main deck down the circular stair. One hand on the polished mahogany banister and the other across his midsection. Heading along the companionway, entering his study. Lowering slowly into a soft leather chair. Reading the teleprinter news sheet from the radio room. Stocks on the New York exchange closing narrowly mixed in light trading. British share prices rocketing to their highest level in three years. Finland devalues by three percent. Soviet trade gap narrows. And just faintly do I hear the sound of laughter which I thought I heard behind me coming down the companionway. Keep remembering his Lordship once said you should never phone a woman, without realizing that she may have a guy next to her listening in bed. Jesus hearing laughter now could be a symptom of paranoia. And christ it's getting louder. Or is it coming from the library. Jeeze, even supposedly safe out here in the middle of the Mediterranean and distracted with being sick, it doesn't take long to imagine things. Especially the worst.

Schultz stepping out of the study, walking past twin guest cabins. And a photograph of the Statue of Liberty on the wall. Hilarity inside the library. Shit. That couldn't be Binky's voice. The son of a bitch. Who has in my present emotional escapism, come back to haunt me again. And sending an electric current of about ten thousand jolts just slammed through me curing my seasickness on the spot.

Schultz pushing open the library door. Catherine her feet up, drinking a glass of orange juice. A TV screen secreted behind little doors adorned with the exotic leather bindings of the world's great books without their pages. The sound of Binky's voice giving a commentary. And O my god. There I am. On the television screen. That's me. In extremis. My balls zapped in the zipper. And me supine getting loaded into the ambulance head first. And shaking my fist back at the camera. At the lowest most painful moment of my life.

'O Sigmund. It is droll. So droll. Isn't it. Not ordinarily droll. But extraordinarily droll. I do hope you don't mind my watching.'

Jesus and how many times these past few months did I think I'd have to conserve my strength just so that I'd have enough left to commit suicide. All it would take right now is just a short climb back up a deck and then lean over the side and let gravity do the rest right into the Mediterranean. Just be a blood red spot left on the water by the sharks.

'Hey honey I do fucking mind. What the hell is this all about. What is this sadism.'

'But it's your expression. Your expression is so wonderfully so exasperatedly pained.'

'Hey listen to me honey, you may not know it but in the peace and serenity aboard this boat you're presently dealing with an exasperatedly dangerous man. Who's just accumulated about as much situation comedy as he can take in his life.'

'O my darling. Darling. Don't you see. You really are so funny. So funny. That I love you. Love you. But you're not, are you, going to be uncharitable to me. Or mean. I am so happy, happy. I'm just a little waif. A waif. And wouldn't you so hate for me to lose my sense of humour. But O dear, my sweet, my sweet, let me give you a kiss, a kiss. You are hurt, aren't you.'

'Look, all I ask is you don't use me for some kind of emotional punching bag.'

'O darling I do promise I won't. But you see, I am a confirmed devotee of sumo. Those great massive wrestlers with their big bellies who go bump bump, bumping one against the other. And you remind me so much of how a sumo wrestler looks when he loses.'

Rabbi it is positively amazing how the fuck in two seconds when I should give somebody a kick up the ass, I get a hard on I could plunge in there instead. To say I am helplessly falling in love is the understatement of this century. The nervous shock of hearing Binky's voice permanently curing my seasickness and giving me an appetite. And no shit I started to laugh. Then to laugh my head off. Till the two of us were holding our stomachs. Catherine throwing herself back on the blue velvet sofa, her black stockinged legs the calves of which made my mouth water, kicking up, sending a pair of grey high heeled shoes flying across the library. I locked the door and right on the mattress deep rug, her sweet skin tasting of salt, we knocked off the most gorgeously fast bumping piece of ass in the history of sumo or of fucking. Then she grabbed the phone. And rang the galley. Rabbi in all my life I never came across anyone who knew how to enjoy luxury so much. And whose sanity was so fucking sane. A crimson ribbon tying back her hair. Her so white smooth skin turning tan. Her hands so young and childlike.

'Is that you chef. Good. Last night's dinner was very good. But tonight. It must be superb. Tonight, Mr Schultz and I shall have. Let me see. I have it all written down here in front of me. OK. Now chef. Listen. Here we go. We're trusting you. Get your pencil and pad poised. Everything has got to be absolutely perfect. And I mean absolutely deliciously perfect. You wouldn't would you, want me to come down there and tweak your nose if our fillet steak is even the teeniest weeniest bit over or under done. It should be rare. Not blood rare. But rare. No not blue rare. Just exactly rare. And hot. It must come perfectly to our awaiting lips hot off the grill. And the mushrooms. Now you know don't you, how exactly they should be in the sauce. Like little white firm tips of knees sticking up out of a pond where a little girl is pretending to drown. And the spinach. That must, absolutely must be really perfect. Just a hint of paprika. And just a shade darker than moss green. Not pea green you understand but moss moss green. And creamy but not too creamy. And since I am ordering for Mr Schultz as well, you realize, everything had better be double good. Now if you make a mistake I shall come to your galley and it won't do you any good dodging behind the pots and pans for I shall bang one of them right over your head. And of course chef we want some fantastic burgundy and not any old Algerian piss the crew's been drinking. Now if you get all that correct I won't have to send Daniel after you, or for good measure, come down there later and shoot you.'

Rabbi I just sat there watching her. Transformed. And she was transformed. A wonderful laughing smile on her face. No hesitations in her voice. Just a few of those marvellously lilting repetitions. To the humming of generators, and twirling of the twin screws. And then I was wondering after what I had already been through how the fucking hell could I now be mad enough again to fall in love.

'Honey you know I'd like to have some kind of understanding with you.'

'O dear. Is this going to be the greatest truth ever told, you're telling. Till doom do us part. Do you think that's wise. When I'm so nuts. Of course you know, I'll betray you. Betray you. As all women must. To keep you on your toes. But you can. You can. Have an understanding. Any you like. But you know don't you, that I'm always on the edge of the whirlpool. That goes swirling, swirling down to death. And you'll always have to snatch me back from there. You'll have to say don't sink with your limbs all akimbo. Don't die. Just yet. Just yet. Just yet. But when life looks awfully good you can, you can hold me back. And then maybe we shall still be together. Even when our faithfulness and fidelity wane, wane, wane. Into our old age. Or are you trying to say. That when the time comes. Like the grey gauze of a ghostly morn. How then are we going to get rid of each other. You of me. Me of you. And tell me. I know you love my breasts. You seem so enraptured kissing nuzzling and fondling there. Did you have a mother who gave you milk. Her milk. Enough milk. So that you didn't have to go waaa waaa crying for more. And what's so funny, so funny.'

'Honey I'm just thinking. And maybe I think I did have a mother. Who maybe didn't have enough milk. And maybe that's right. I cried for more. And if her tits were anything like yours, I'd go sobbing forever all over the universe.'

'Well such flattery will get you another nipple. A nipple. But you know my mother hardly nursed me. She did not want to ruin her beautiful breasts which were so admired by men. And you see, that's why I've ordered us both such a very good dinner. So that I won't lack for energy. When I give you your lashes with your cat o' nine tails tonight.'

And
Instead of
Softly
Waaa waaa
You can cry
Loudly
Ouch
Ouch

34

A balmy breeze. The temperature perfect. At twelve and a half knots the Catherine Ahoy making for the Isle of Stromboli. Over the mile deep Tyrrhenian sea. The sun high and sparkling on the water. The twin screws turning at eight hundred and forty five revolutions per minute, boiling up a foamy wake. The bow wave spreading its wings of whiteness out across the blue.

Schultz skipping rope on the bridge deck. And punching a speed bag in the gym. Repairing to the sauna and lying back in the heat. The red glow of light tinting the wood panelling. Salt stinging sweat seeping into the eyes. And holy christ Rabbi. This is idyllic. This ship is like an empire where I am the emperor. Soon to die unless I blind my mind to what it is really costing. The stack of cheques in three cheque books has gone down like water flushing away in a toilet. Which could use the leak alarm invented by his Lordship's wife's boyfriend. The insurance of the superstructure. The insurance of the hull. The salaries. Never mind mooring fees and the burning of sixty five imperial gallons of fuel an hour and seventy five meals served a day. But at least till we hit an iceberg I am safe from the world. The way I thought really wealthy people were secluded in houses lighted up for Christmas back in America. Where once Uncle Werb went delivering a diamond ring one Christmas eve, and brought me along. All my ambition to be where I am now came from that moment. Standing in that room on the deep soft carpet. Seeing this rich man in his dark suit in this library with real books. The windows of the house glowing their light out through surrounding trees. The warmth inside. Emerald velvet sofas and a leopard skin rug with the animal's canine teeth showing snarling in front of a real wood fire. The guy had cuffs and cufflinks and held the ring up to the lamp and then handed Uncle Werb five hundred brand new one hundred dollar bills two inches thick. While I stood in my short pants hiding my hands still dirty from handling marked down lingerie. And that night seeing my own poor hard working mother in a torn and worn apron and my father with his sleeves rolled up sitting over a bowl of noodle soup in the kitchen, and a cockroach sailing along the edge of the table, jesus I knew there were things and places better than that. And Rabbi needless to say the guy's wife was in a mental institution and the ring was for his girlfriend. Well one thing's for sure, money makes a difference, and on a ship leaves nothing to do except enjoy yourself. Back in Monaco moored in the next yacht along the pier, there were those grey haired couple of rich Americans. Husband and wife playing cards together. Catherine from our deck waved and they waved back. Carl the captain said the game had been going on all afternoon and every evening solidly for the last six months, and they never left port. The wife with blue rinsed hair in a flowered sun suit, and her husband in a baseball cap. Maybe that's what the struggle is all about. You battle and bust your balls to make enough money to go sit on a boat costing a fortune just to play a game of cards. Like Catherine sits the afternoons away over backgammon with nurse. If masochism is not her cup of tea, boy, sadism sure is. Last night in her Queen suite I had to jump off the bed and run for my life. She nearly belted the shit out of me. Lashing the cat o' nine tails down across my ass with all her might. And did it twice before I even had a chance to scream ouch and get out of the way to protect myself. I had to jump up into the fucking closet. Then as I closed the door she was convulsed rolling in a paroxysm of laughing on the floor. At least it was a revelation to her of something she really liked to do. Like waterskiing, sunbathing and taking a sauna. And Rabbi, I've found there's nothing you can do to make women love you. But if you don't do anything at all they'll forget you. And Sigmund remember, you were for a long time supporting and paying for a woman to get sick of you. Which is worse scars than lashes.

Under the white awning on the aft deck Jorricks and the valet serving tea. The table set with a silver tray of fruit, cakes and pies. Crystal pots of strawberry, gooseberry and apricot jams. Jorricks perspiring in his black butler's coat, ferrying the freshly baked scones in a hot napkin. The valet bowing his head to Catherine and smilingly retreating from the presence as he spooned out her favourite black cherry jam. Inside the saloon's open gleaming mahogany doors the phone ringing. Jorricks returning to the table. Schultz chomping on a scone slathered in clotted cream and strawberry jam.

'Sir there appears to be an urgent call from London which the radio operator is having difficulty with. And asks if you might perhaps take it up in the radio room.'

Schultz jumping up. Tripping headlong over the bulkhead and crashing face down on the saloon floor. Holy christ what's wrong. Why can't I the fuck stay calm. Instead of breaking the furniture over the first phone call in two days and thinking it's going to be his Lordship telling me the theatre's finally been bombed. And I'm running up this ladder as if my mother has just died. Or worse, my wife's lawyers have found out which banks my money's in and how I am now spending it like sand in the desert.

'Hello.'

'Hello.'

'Hello for christ's sakes, will you speak up. I can't hear you. Hello.'

'Sigmund, it's Louella.'

'Who.'

'Louella. I had to talk to you.'

'Hey christ's sake how'd you get this number and know where I am.'

'This evening's Standard interviewed your wife and has a big picture of your yacht. It's so beautiful. Sigmund I love you. In spite of all the vicious things your wife says.'

'Hey gee that's swell honey. But this is an awful connection.'

'The carpenter ran off with a necklace and the Ferrari. Al's getting married. To a seventeen year old hillbilly.'

'Holy shit kiddo. Guess you sort of backed a couple of wrong horses. Honey for christ's sakes don't cry.'

'And Binky. He was starving to death. And now no one knows where he's disappeared. Please. Can I come there.'

'Honey I'm this second just a few miles from the Isle of Stromboli in the Mediterranean.'

'Please, O please can I come there.'

'Honey I'm sort of trying to get away from it all and want to be alone awhile. And I wish you didn't connect my yacht and your declaration of love in the same breath. But believe me I'm sorry for your troubles. Hey honey this is a terrible connection. I'll call you back when the static is less. Goodbye for now.'

'I beg of you Sigmund, don't please, hang up on me. Please. Please. I'm at Al's. I'm packing. Nobody wants me. And I'm going to do it.'

'Do what honey I can hardly hear you.'

'It doesn't matter. I'm going to. Cross the room now.'

'What are you talking about honey.'

'I'm going to the window.'

'Hey come on honey. Come on.'

'And I'm opening the window. Now. And nothing, nothing is going to matter anymore. Nothing. Goodbye.'

'Honey, hey honey. Jesus stop. Stop her somebody. Stop her. Holy shit.'

Rabbi
It's a long way down
Into concrete
And Sigmund listen

400

She ain't no
High diving
Champion
Like your wife

35

The air still. The pale moonlight like liquid gold rippling across the water. The salt sea into which the mouths of the Nile empty. The shadows of islands and the bobbing lights of fishing boats. A massive oil tanker slowly passing, silhouetted against the shore. Lighted decks and portholes. South over the horizon, the tip of the foot of Italy. That my geography teacher in high school said could kick you in the ass.

The radio operator left on the radio telephone trying to get back to London. Schultz sitting and waiting. And finally going below to dress for dinner. Under a musky pink dark sky. The coxswain reducing speed from full to half to dead slow, to stop. The clank and clatter of chain, as the anchor splashes into the water. The Catherine Ahoy sitting like a sleek white duck on the gentle swells of a glass smooth sea.

Rabbi when will the dust of disaster ever settle and leave it that I don't have to run like wildfire and crouch in shame. All the hours, phone calls and spying I wasted on that girl. And all the months needlessly terrified I'd lose her, uselessly spent. And more than a thousand miles away, she still has me cliff hanging by the fingertips. I should have long ago given her a knife as a present so she could stab me in the heart. Women are like playing with a yo yo, they go up and down. And you go in and out on top of them if you can. And if they let you. So Sigmund maybe now at long last a nutty raven haired girl you found up on a mountain side in a fairy tale castle, is something you have to be grateful for. She could help let the dust settle. So long as you don't let it settle on your life.

Under a white awning, candles flickering, the table set for dinner on the aft deck. Pigeons cooing up in their coop. And the sound of feet pounding from the pantry to ferry hot plates and paraphernalia in preparation for the chef's cooking perfections from the galley. Out of the open saloon door piano music tinkling. Schultz freshly shaved and showered in his white dinner jacket, silk shirt and maroon bow tie, lighting up a cigar. Stepping out over the bulkhead of the Catherine Ahoy. Eight bells. Sounding the end of the second dogwatch.

A shooting star plunging down over the southern horizon. Moonlight reflected golden on this water. The busiest sea lanes of the world. Rabbi I struggled to get rich for this. For this right here. This washed white paintwork. These beautiful teak decks scrubbed smooth. And the fucking tears are blurring my eyes. Louella. Just like Freddie Joy. Could have jumped. What a waste. Of two gorgeous women less in the world. Maybe this for me is the exact time to die too. On my day of atonement. Just sinking away down out there fathoms deep in the

402

dark. Into this Mediterranean's nice million square miles of freedom. Don't worry Rabbi, with all the good food and wine already paid for, I'm not climbing over the rails and diving in just yet. Plus, after Binky, I've got other scores left to settle. I'm going to get those two other fuckers Joe Jewels and Al Duke. Even if it takes me years. And I'm going to make sure all the while that I got life preservers under each armpit and one encircling my balls. And grow old gracefully. Like someone who didn't have to work in a lingerie store starting at six years old.

Catherine in a long white embroidered voile dress, crossing the saloon and tiptoeing out on deck. Toenails bright crimson on her bare feet. A long strand of pearls around her neck. And one white kid skin glove pulled up past her elbow. Her head looming up over Schultz's shoulder her lips whispering gently touching the edge of his ear.

'A farthing for your thoughts.'

'Hey jeeze.'

'O dear did I frighten you. I frightened you.'

'Honey I didn't hear you coming. And my mind was miles away.'

'What's the matter. What's the matter.'

'Nothing honey, nothing. That maybe you won't cure.'

'Then let me stay by you. Close close. Be near, be near when you need me. And darling Sigmund. Did you know. Did you know. That from the Strait of Gibraltar to the shores of the Gulf of Iskenderun, the winds called sirocco, bora and mistral blow. Blow. Blow. And all over these seas the Saracen pirates plundered. See there, the headlands looming in the dark. Isn't that the Isle of Stromboli.'

'Yeah honey it must be some beautiful place.'

'You've got tears in your eyes.'

'Just the breeze.'

'There is no breeze.'

'Yeah. I guess that's right.'

'Then what's wrong. Wrong. Bad or sad news I hope did not come on that naughty old telephone today. My old nanny used to say, to stir up animosities, is to stir up strife.'

'Well honey, your nanny was right.'

'Do you, I do, like Italy. Where in their gardens one can walk under the eucalyptus trees, even when the flowers are not in bloom. The wintersweet, the lavender. I was once a whole summer there. In Italy. And did then have boyfriends who did so swarm about me. While always trusting and hoping it was for me, me, and not my trust funds. I was I suppose having a rather rum time. Dear me, men do get an awful sameness about them after a while. But of course, I was but a girl child. Thinking it so excruciatingly romantic if one held a flower in one's hand. And yet so impatient. Ready to sweep back to London to visit other galleries to look at beautiful things. And where, when pleasantly fatigued, one could repair for tea. Seems long ago now, that for such a long time, I'd turned my back upon the world. My mind not able to tackle great problems. Hoping to leave them till much later in life. And I suppose then hoping to postpone them even further still. Till one is no longer living. But now is now, isn't it. Even though one rather lives on the verge of dying. And you see, selfish to say, but for the most part, my interest in you is your interest in me. And I must confess I do like this motor yacht and the way people do look upon us with such awe as we go floating by. Nurse says she waves to everybody and makes believe it's hers. But what shall we do when a larger boat comes along and they look upon us with pity. Must we then, look upon them with awe. With awe.'

'Yeah honey, yeah. Because they're going to have to be god damn fucking awesomely rich.'

'O dear, is all this, and all this selfish selfish pleasure, costing too much, too much.'

'Honey you're gorgeous. And christ, tonight I'm not going to start counting, counting. Hey what do you say we go have a little god damn champagne.'

'I'd love to. And it does, doesn't it, even before one's lips touch it, sound so delicious. But can I say something first.'

'Sure, honey. Shoot.'

'When natural causes, cause my removal. I won't mind being used and then discarded. Provided I am pleasantly used and then gently discarded. Although I should so hate to be just told. Go away. Go away. Be gone. Be gone. Rudely kicked out of your life. Crashing back again upon my arse. My old wonderful wonderful faithful arse. Always there to land on. But when your spirit has left me. And when you must say goodbye. As mourners do at the edge of the grave. I shall then in my illegible scrawl, leave a little note behind on my dressing table in the Queen suite. And say thank you so very much for having me and for your kindness.'

'Hey come on honey. Who the fuck is leaving who. And you don't have to thank me for anything.'

'But I shall want to. Want to. And shall also want to tell you. Betray me not. And I will die with you when you die. Betray me not. And I will live with you while you live.'

'Excuse me sir. Dinner is served.'

'Thanks Jorricks. Thanks.'

'And Daniel, sir, who is feeding the pigeons would request you to watch them fly overhead later in the ship's searchlights.'

'No problem, Jorricks. No problem.'

Schultz moving aft along the deck behind the smooth tanned skin of Catherine's back. An oval opening down her dress. The black soft curls of her hair gently shaking and touching her shoulder blades as she walks. Towards the round mahogany glass topped table. Adorned with red roses. The pop of the champagne cork. Candle flames glimmering in their glass holders. Jesus Rabbi. Although my heart is bleeding in tears and ready to break. And I don't want to ask questions. But can this be now like it could everlastingly be.

Sigmund
Life is a changing situation
Where always
You look for bargains
And if you find none
Don't stop
Looking